GIRL GONE MAD

GIRL GONE MAD

AVERY BISHOP

This is a work of fiction. Names, characters, organizations, places, events, and incidents are either products of the author's imagination or are used fictitiously. Any resemblance to actual persons, living or dead, or actual events is purely coincidental.

Published by Lake Union Publishing, Seattle

www.apub.com

ISBN-13: 9781542018715
ISBN-10: 1542018714

Cover design by Damon Freeman

Printed in the United States of America

For anybody who's ever been bullied, and to anybody who's ever stood up to bullies, this book is for you.

Sticks and stones may break my bones,
but words will never hurt me.

—*Children's rhyme*

She kept screaming long after they'd left her—putting all her strength into it, everything she had—but it did no good, not with the towel they'd stuck in her mouth and tied around her head. The towel tasted musty, like it had been sitting in a drawer for a year. She imagined Mackenzie or Elise or one of the other girls finding it in the cabin and storing it away in the bright-pink backpack. Along with the ropes that now held her in place against the tree.

She struggled against her bindings, but the girls had knotted them well, making sure she couldn't move. The one rope crossing over her chest, right beneath her breasts; the other rope crossing over her bare thighs, digging into her soft pale skin.

The tears had stopped, but her face was still wet with them, cooling in the spring night air. The back of her head hurt where she'd slammed it against the tree, and she knew she'd drawn blood, that it was already matting her hair.

No matter how many times she'd slammed her head against the tree, no matter how much she'd cried, the girls hadn't let up. Peppering her with insults. Laughing at her. Even spitting on her.

She fell quiet for a moment and listened to her surroundings. Besides the sounds of the woods—insects and a distant owl—there was silence. Even the girls' hushed footsteps on the path leading back to the cabin had faded.

It was another hour until midnight, and she had no idea how long they intended to keep her here. Mackenzie certainly hadn't said, and neither had any of the other girls. And because she couldn't do anything else—and because her throat hadn't yet gone raw—she did the only thing left for her to do.

She screamed.

PART I:

The Ghost

1

The girl cut herself.

With a knife, most likely—a paring knife or steak knife pilfered from the kitchen when her parents weren't around—or maybe she used a pair of scissors already in her bedroom, opening them up and then pressing the tip of one of the blades against her skin.

It was one of the things I would eventually get to, but not today. Today was the girl's first appointment. An intake, really. All I had was the referral that had been sent from the psychiatric inpatient facility where she'd been for eight days. It didn't include much information. Her name: Chloe Kitterman. Her age: thirteen. The reason she'd been admitted: cut her wrists with suicidal ideations. The aftercare recommendation: continue med management and start outpatient therapy. Which was what had brought Chloe and her mother to my office today.

Still, even without the discharge summary, I might have guessed Chloe was a cutter. She had that look to her. Thin and petite. Long red hair. A splash of freckles on her face. Her fingernails painted black. But none of that keyed me in to her penchant for cutting.

It was her clothes. She sat on the black pleather couch beside her mother, staring down at her phone. She wore faded low-rise jeans, sneakers, and a gray Hollister hoodie.

It was late April, and the temperature outside had just tipped over eighty degrees. Way too hot for a hoodie. She was trying to hide the cuts on her arms.

Her mother, Mrs. Kitterman, seemed to have perfected her role as a trophy wife. She was in her late forties but looked much younger, her face smooth and bright without the hint of a wrinkle. Her sandy-brown hair perfectly coiffed. Either she ate next to nothing or exercised every day, probably with an extra session of yoga. The diamond on her finger was so big I was surprised she managed to lift her hand without assistance. Her husband probably brought in a hefty six-figure salary; she dressed like she bought all her clothes from Neiman Marcus. Her cotton chinos, block-heel dress sandals, cotton Henley shirt—her wardrobe today alone had to cost more than I made in a week, and that didn't count the leather Hermès bag she had propped between herself and her daughter.

The woman had been droning on ever since they'd entered my office. Saying how all this was very new to them. Saying how nobody in her family had ever needed therapy before. Was her daughter supposed to lie on the couch and tell me about her feelings like they do on TV? On and on she went, lamenting how terrible life was now because of her daughter's depression, while Chloe sat quietly beside her, her gaze glued to the screen of her phone.

At one point, Mrs. Kitterman stopped midsentence, as if suddenly realizing where she was and to whom she was offering up such private information. She glanced around the cramped room—the walls mostly bare, only spotted with the occasional framed motivational poster—and then glanced at her daughter. She spotted the phone and gave a heavy sigh.

"Chloe, I thought I told you to put that away."

Chloe didn't answer, kept staring down at the phone. Her thumbs moved across the screen in the strange choreography known only to teenagers.

"Chloe, don't make me tell you again."

A second ticked by with no response, and then Chloe issued a heavy sigh of her own and slammed the phone down on the arm of the couch before hugging her arms across her chest.

Mrs. Kitterman stared at her daughter, then shook her head and rolled her eyes at me.

"I mean it, I have *no* idea what's going on with this girl. She's just . . . *different*. She used to be happy. I used to be able to have conversations with her. Now all she ever gives me is attitude."

My cell phone vibrated on my desk, two quick buzzes, signaling a text message.

Ignoring it, I nodded at Mrs. Kitterman to continue.

She frowned at me. "You're younger than I expected."

"I'm twenty-eight."

"So you haven't been doing this very long."

Her tone suggested that I lacked the necessary experience to work with her daughter. Which in a way was true. I'd been working full-time as a therapist for only four years. Some of the other therapists at Safe Haven Behavioral Health had been working full-time for decades.

"If you'd like Chloe to see another therapist, I can certainly make that referral. From what I understand, though, you requested me specifically."

The woman's perfectly shaped nose wrinkled at this suggestion.

"Well, not *you* specifically, but yes, you were recommended by the therapist at the inpatient facility. She was young, too, and she thought Chloe might be able to open up to somebody who's not so much . . . older."

She said it dismissively, like she couldn't begin to fathom why her daughter wouldn't be able to connect with someone three times her age.

I forced a smile. "Again, if you'd like Chloe to see someone else, I can make that referral."

"No, you don't have to do that. But it's just—" She paused, spotting the ring on my finger. "Are you married?"

"Engaged."

I looked down when I said it. My diamond was much smaller than Mrs. Kitterman's.

"So you don't have any children."

She said this almost judgmentally, like I was expected to have at least two kids at home right now being taken care of by an au pair.

I told her I did not.

"Then how—" She waved her hands around as if hoping to pluck the right word from the air. "How are you supposed to help my daughter?"

"Mrs. Kitterman, I've worked with many girls Chloe's age since I graduated from college."

"And you've helped them all?"

"No."

She seemed to flinch at the bluntness of my response.

"No? Then why should my daughter waste her time seeing you?"

She was being combative, which was to be expected. This was new to her. She was scared, uncertain what would come next. I didn't blame her.

"Mrs. Kitterman, you have to understand: therapy is not an exact science. There are many factors involved besides me and your daughter. There's you and your husband and all the students at Chloe's school and any friends she might have outside of school. I can't promise we'll establish a connection immediately, and any therapist who will promise you that is not a therapist I would recommend your daughter see."

The woman stared at me, clearly flummoxed by my answer. Maybe she'd expected me to be more servile, since I was the one being paid.

On the desk, my phone vibrated with another text message. Again, I ignored it and kept my focus on Chloe's mom.

"Mrs. Kitterman, I think I should make it clear that my role here is not to work *for* you or your daughter. My role is to work *with* your daughter. Does that make sense?"

She nodded. It was slight, almost imperceptible, but she nodded.

"This is our first session," I said. "In fact, it's not even a session—it's an intake. I'm listening and gathering information. Assuming you would like Chloe to see me, I would typically only meet with her one-on-one."

Mrs. Kitterman looked stricken by this idea, but then she shook her head.

"This is all new to us. I've never even *known* someone who needs therapy, let alone my own daughter."

And then she started up again, going on and on about how she couldn't believe this was happening to her family.

"She's on medication now too. My own *daughter* is on medication. They say she has depression. I don't get it. What can she *possibly* be depressed about?"

There are three sets of parents I typically deal with.

The ones who understand there is something wrong and want to do whatever it takes to help their child.

The ones who just don't give a shit that something is wrong and aren't about to put in any effort to help their child.

Then the ones who are in denial that anything can possibly be wrong. Their child has now become an inconvenience. And, nine times out of ten, it's something at home that has caused the problem. Something that the parents don't want to talk about, which causes treatment to last much longer than it needs to.

Mrs. Kitterman fit in this last group. Chloe was the one who'd had a crisis—she'd cut her wrists, for Christ's sake—but it was her mother who felt like her entire life had been upended.

My phone vibrated once again. This time, instead of ignoring it, I reached over and held the "Power" button down long enough to shut it off.

I forced another smile at Mrs. Kitterman.

"Would you mind giving Chloe and me some time to talk alone?"

A guarded look entered the woman's eyes, which confirmed my suspicions.

"But I thought you said this was the intake."

She said it coolly, calmly, but just beneath the surface there was an edge to her voice.

"It is. At least, it's the first part. We will still need to create her treatment plan, which are the goals we want to work toward, such as learning appropriate coping skills to deal with her depression. But for now I'd like to speak to Chloe alone."

Mrs. Kitterman clearly didn't like the idea, but she nodded anyway and rose from the couch. She clutched the Hermès bag to her shoulder like she feared I might try to snatch it away and started toward the door, but then turned back to her daughter and held out her hand.

Chloe sat, unmoving, staring down at her lap.

Mrs. Kitterman cleared her throat.

Chloe sighed, grabbed her phone, and nearly flung it at her mother. Mrs. Kitterman dropped the phone in her bag, gave me one last look as if to say *Good luck*, and left.

I closed the door behind her. Turned around. Smiled at Chloe, who kept staring down at her lap.

Then I crossed over to my desk. I sat, leaned back in my chair, and stared up at the ceiling.

A full minute of silence passed.

"Your mom seems fun."

This caused Chloe to laugh, a soft little snort. If anything, my comment had caught her by surprise.

I leaned forward in my chair and stared at Chloe.

She stared back at me.

I said, "You're scared, aren't you?"

Without her mother's presence, the girl no longer had to keep up her guard, and she allowed a small nod.

"Do you want help?"

Another small nod.

"Good. The fact that you can acknowledge that now, especially at your age, is incredible. But I'll be honest with you—whatever you're going through, it will take time to figure it all out. I'm here to listen, and whatever you say to me is between the two of us. But please do understand, I am what's called a state-mandated reporter. If you tell me something that causes me to suspect you're being abused, or if you admit to thoughts of harming yourself or others, I have to report it. Do you understand?"

Another nod.

"Good. Now, as long as you are willing to be honest with me, I'll be here to help you. Deal?"

This time the nod was almost nonexistent.

"You're going to have to do better than that, Chloe. I'm going to need to hear either a yes or a no."

Her gaze shifted back to her lap. She didn't move for a long time, just sat there, but then she finally looked up.

"Yes," she whispered.

Twenty minutes later, after sending Chloe and her mother away with an appointment scheduled for the following week, I turned my phone back on. It took a minute to power up and find a signal, and then the text messages that had come through popped up on the screen. For some reason, I'd expected them to be from Daniel, but all three were from my mother.

Call me.

Do you remember Olivia Campbell?

She KILLED herself!

2

My mother's new obsession was tea.

Not the box teas found in grocery stores—your Lipton and Celestial Seasonings and Bigelow and Stash—but loose specialty teas. The kind in the large glass jars that sit on racks in their own section of the store and need to be scooped into paper bags and weighed. The more expensive the tea, my mother reasoned, the better it tasted.

"What would you like?"

She asked me this as she glided around the kitchen, opening and closing cabinets, pulling down two cups and two small china plates while the teakettle warmed on the stove.

I sat on a stool at the kitchen island, watching her. Twenty years ago, I'd sat at this same island while my mother moved from one end of the kitchen to the other with a frantic grace, making my father and me breakfast before I went to school and they went to work. At the time I'd thought she had too much energy. Now I realized she had ADHD.

"I'm fine, thanks."

This stopped Mom in her tracks. She paused as if stunned, turning toward me with a crestfallen expression.

"Are you sure? I bought a quarter pound of loose white tea the other day. It's called Jasmine Silver Needle. It cost ninety-nine dollars and ninety-nine cents a *pound*."

I opened my mouth, not sure what to say, but it didn't matter anyway, because my mother turned back to the counter, put down the cups and plates, and started shuffling through the basket of loose tea bags.

"I have Sakura Sencha, which is a green tea from Japan. And chrysanthemum, which is a loose herbal infusion from China. I also have some chamomile from Egypt."

"Sure, that's fine."

She jerked her face around to give me a quick look. "What's fine?"

"The chamomile."

She wrinkled her nose. "I'm not sure you'll like it."

I sighed. It had been a long day, and this wasn't helping relieve my normal daily stress.

"You asked me to stop by on my way home from work—which is out of the way, as you know—and so here I am. I don't want any tea."

"What about coffee?"

"Mom."

"Water?"

Because I knew she'd keep asking until she broke me down, I said, "Yes, fine, water sounds great."

She turned back to the counter, grabbed one of the cups and plates, returned them to their proper places in the cabinets, and then turned back to me.

"Bottled or from the tap?"

"Do you have any water from Japan?"

My mother paused as if to think about it.

"Mom, I'm kidding. Bottled is fine."

She got me a bottle of spring water from the fridge. The teakettle started to whistle. Mom made her tea and, at last, drifted over to the island and sat down.

I let out a breath.

"How's Daniel?" she asked.

"He's fine."

"I haven't seen him in a while."

"He's been working a lot. So have I."

"I'm not getting any younger, Emily. Grandchildren would be nice at some point."

"Yes, well, Daniel and I should probably get married first."

My mother shook her head, absently pushing a strand of graying hair behind her ear.

"I don't know what you're waiting on. You've been engaged for four years."

Technically it had been three and a half, but I didn't blame her for rounding up. It was a sore subject. My father had passed away three months before Daniel and I were supposed to get married. Because of his death, because we'd suddenly needed to plan a funeral on top of a wedding, I had convinced Daniel that we should wait a bit, and he of course agreed. And then . . . we just never settled on another wedding date.

Daniel had never known his birth parents, having grown up in the system, moving from foster home to foster home, so it wasn't as if he had anyone breathing down his neck. There was only my mother, and truth be told, she had laid off the guilt trips after about a year, only bringing it up every once in a while to test my patience.

To change the subject, I said, "So what exactly happened to Olivia Campbell?"

My mother closed her eyes, all at once somber. "Yes, it's terrible, isn't it? She was your age."

If I remembered correctly, Olivia was five months older. In the seventh grade, the year before everything changed, she'd had her birthday party at the local roller-skating rink. During couples' skate, Jimmy Klay had asked her to skate, and his hand had been so clammy, she later told us, that he kept wiping it on his jeans as they circled the rink to "I Want It That Way" by the Backstreet Boys.

"How do you know she died?"

"I read about it on Facebook."

"But how did you come across it?"

"Beth Norris sent me a message. She remembered you'd gone to school with Olivia. She said her daughter Leslie graduated with you. Do you remember her?"

My graduating class had 119 students. The name *Leslie Norris* didn't ring a bell.

"Beth's friends with Olivia's mother on Facebook. Speaking of which, I really wish you'd sign up for an account. I want to tag you in the old photos I upload."

"Mom, we've been over this. Because of my job—"

"Yes, yes. You need to be private because you work with a bunch of kids who will try to friend you or learn about your outside life. I understand."

That was the reason I gave everybody when they asked, and while that certainly had something to do with it, the real reason was that I didn't want to have a social media presence. Once you did, people tried to connect with you. Not just coworkers and family, but friends. Old friends. Friends you might not have seen or talked to in years. Friends who would remind you of all the terrible things you'd done, once upon a time.

"Mom, tell me about Olivia. When did this happen?"

She picked up her iPad, swiped and tapped at the screen.

"Do you know what happened to your yearbooks? I thought they were in the basement. I looked for them earlier but can't seem to find them anywhere."

"Last I saw them, they were down there in some box."

Actually, the last I saw my yearbooks was when I'd sneaked them out of my bedroom right before college and tossed them in the trash cans out on the street, just before the garbagemen came rattling by in their truck. But my mother didn't need to know this.

Mom nodded as if to herself and then handed me the tablet. I wasn't sure what I'd expected to see, but I most certainly wasn't expecting Olivia Campbell's mother's Facebook page.

My mother had centered on a rather succinct status update written five days ago. Olivia's mother had said that God had called her baby girl home, and that, oh Lord, she'd had no idea Olivia was in so much pain, but she hoped her daughter was in a better place now.

The post had over three hundred reactions, mostly hearts and sad-face emojis, as well as more than one hundred comments offering condolences.

My mother took a sip of her tea and gently set the cup back down on the china plate.

"I sent Olivia's mother a friend request and message this morning, telling her how sorry I was to hear what happened. I wasn't sure I would get a reply—I haven't spoken to her since you and Olivia had your falling-out and they moved away to Harrisburg—but she wrote back two hours later thanking me for my condolences. She told me the viewing and the funeral are this Saturday. I told her I would talk to you about going."

"What?" My tone shocked my mother almost as much as it did me. "Why would you tell her that?"

"Despite what may have happened in middle school, you were once best friends with Olivia."

I shook my head, at a complete loss for words. Then something occurred to me.

"Wait—I thought you said Olivia killed herself."

"She did."

"But there's no mention of it on the Facebook post."

"No, of course not. Olivia's mother wouldn't want to make that widely known."

Patience, I had to remind myself, was a virtue.

"Then how exactly do you know about it?"

"I told you: Beth Norris. She told me Olivia had taken her own life. It's just so"—my mother paused, shook her head again—"it's just so awful."

"I wish you wouldn't have told Mrs. Campbell I might go. Daniel might already have something planned for this Saturday."

Daniel didn't have anything planned for this Saturday, at least as far as I knew, but using him as an excuse felt like the best course of action.

"I'm sure he'll understand if those plans need to be changed."

"Honestly, Mom, I don't want to go."

"If the tables were turned, wouldn't you want Olivia to come to your funeral?"

"You know, if I was dead, I don't think I would give a shit."

My mother gave me another glare. She could stop rush-hour traffic with that glare.

"It would mean a lot to Olivia's mother if you went."

My elbows on the countertop, I dropped my head into my hands and tried not to scream.

My mother's voice dipped to a soft whisper.

"I know all I went through with your father's passing, God bless his soul, but at least he was in his late fifties. Olivia? She was just a young woman. I can't even—"

She paused again, and I glanced up in time to see her wipe a tear from her eye.

"But it doesn't matter. If you don't want to go, Emily, you don't have to go. I certainly can't make you."

Great. The guilt-trip angle.

My mother, maybe sensing my hesitation, said, "If you *do* decide to go, Olivia's mother gave me the address of the funeral parlor. It's maybe a forty-minute drive, depending on traffic."

"I don't think Daniel will want to go."

"Then don't take him. I already have plans that day, unfortunately. Otherwise I would be happy to go with you. In fact, if you'd like, I'll change my plans . . ."

"You don't have to do that."

"What about some of your other friends from school? When was the last time you spoke to Courtney? Maybe she'd want to go."

"Maybe."

I didn't want to get into it with my mother. She didn't have to know I'd fallen out of contact with most of the people I went to middle and high school with. The few friends I'd kept were from college. Because in college, I was able to reinvent myself. I was able to act as if the girl I'd been in middle school didn't exist. It made things easier.

Courtney, well, Courtney was one of the only friends from the original middle school clique I'd stayed friends with into high school. Even when she'd gotten pregnant and dropped out, we'd kept in touch. Until the summer after graduation, right before I'd flown out to California. I hadn't spoken to her since.

My mother shook her head, wiping at another tear. She picked up her cup and sipped her tea.

"This is so good. Are you sure you don't want some?"

And because I didn't want to disappoint her any more than I already had, I forced a smile.

"I'd love some."

3

The town house Daniel and I shared was always meant to be temporary. Maybe it still was, but we'd been living in it for three years already, and it didn't seem like we were ever going to move.

Senior year of high school, I'd applied to colleges as far from home as possible. I'd been accepted by most of the schools but had ended up deciding on one in California, which had put a decent three thousand miles between me and my past. I would come home on break, visit my family, and fly back. I'd known early on what career I wanted, so I didn't waste any time. I took the right classes, shored up the appropriate number of credits, and applied for the best internships.

I loved California. Having grown up with the unpredictable seasons on the East Coast, I welcomed the steadiness of the weather. I had planned to stay. Go to grad school. Get a job. Settle down. I'd dated throughout college, but nothing serious ever came of it. When things did start to become serious, I pushed whoever it was away.

Then my father got sick with cancer.

I started making more trips home, but the cost got to be too much. I vowed to transfer to a closer school, but my parents told me no. They wanted me to finish where I started. They wanted me to be happy.

I transferred back home my last year anyway and managed to get into the state college a half hour away. I lived at home and commuted. Part of me was afraid I'd run into old high school classmates, but while

I saw a few, none of them were close enough to have been considered friends.

For my internship, I worked as a crisis worker at the local emergency room. When somebody came into the ER with thoughts of harming themselves or others, it was my job to assess them and determine whether they were okay to return home or if they needed psychiatric hospitalization.

That's where I met Daniel. He'd just graduated from nursing school and was working as an ER nurse. To say he was handsome would be an understatement. Dark blue eyes, an even tan, slightly mussed-up hair, and a perpetual five-o'clock shadow—the first time I saw him, I was immediately attracted to him.

And there was more. Daniel was patient with the people who came into the ER, even the combative ones, and he was sweet, especially to the kids. I learned that on his days off he volunteered at the Boys & Girls Club. We would see each other often in passing, and sometimes we would talk. Then one day Daniel asked me out for coffee, and I said yes. A year later, we were engaged.

By that point, my father was in remission, and it looked like he was going to pull through. He was thrilled about our engagement. He really liked Daniel. So did my mom. Everybody liked Daniel.

I started spending more and more time at Daniel's apartment, but it was cramped, so six months after he proposed, we decided to lease a town house together. It would be for only a year or two, we told each other, until we got married and started looking at houses. Assuming we even wanted to stay in the area. Part of me wanted to head back out to California, though I didn't want to leave my family behind, especially with my father being sick. Daniel, who had no family to anchor him to one location, said he would be happy wherever we ended up, just as long as we were together.

We set a date and started planning the wedding, a small outdoor ceremony. Only a few family members and friends. Nothing over the top. But then my father had passed away. Almost two years had gone by since then, and we were still living in the town house.

Daniel wasn't home. For the past couple of months, he'd been working doubles. The money was good, and Daniel loved what he did, though it seemed like we rarely saw each other.

I'd become accustomed to the empty town house. Our neighbors on both sides were quiet. Jim and Tom, the couple on our left, always grabbed packages left out on the stoop so that nobody driving past could steal them. Andrew and Barb, the older neighbors on our right, had a Jack Russell terrier that sometimes yapped too loudly, but mostly they kept to themselves.

I changed into some sweats and a T-shirt and headed downstairs to the kitchen. A few dirty dishes cluttered the sink; I loaded them in the dishwasher, wiped down the counters, checked to see if the trash can needed to be emptied.

In the living room, I settled onto the couch, remote in hand. A yawn hit me hard. Fighting it back, I tapped the button for Netflix, scrolled through the movies and TV shows Daniel and I had each added to our queue. Nothing looked appealing.

I kept thinking about Olivia. About how she'd taken her own life.

I hadn't thought about her in years. Hadn't thought about any of my friends from middle school. Our special clique. The popular crowd. Harpies, we called ourselves, after Courtney overheard Mrs. Cochrane, our seventh-grade English-lit teacher, use the term to describe us to another teacher. Courtney, unfamiliar with the word, had immediately consulted a dictionary to learn that *harpy* meant "a bird of prey with a woman's face."

We all thought the name made us seem tougher than we really were, but Mackenzie took the term most personally, as her last name was Harper. Mrs. Cochrane, Mackenzie reasoned, was clearly targeting her, because *she* was our leader.

The rest of us knew Mackenzie was just being her typical egotistical self, but we did like the name. It was cool, we decided, and so the Harpies we became.

I remembered their names, of course—Elise and Mackenzie; Olivia and Courtney and Destiny—but I'd successfully blocked them from my mind. Or at the very least I'd opened up a box, shoved the memories inside, locked it, and thrown away the key.

I turned over my left hand. Looked at the scar along the palm. It was so thin that you could barely see it if you didn't know it was there. Daniel once commented on the scar, asked what had happened, and I had given him some line about accidentally cutting myself when I was young. Which wasn't technically a lie.

Another yawn hit me, this one too strong to ignore.

Settling on an HGTV home-improvement show, I lowered the volume and got comfortable on the couch. I closed my eyes, thinking a small nap wouldn't hurt. Just a few minutes to clear my head of the ghosts.

The bell rings, an obnoxious blatting sound, and the kids in the hall disperse into classrooms.

I stand in the middle of the hallway, unable to move. My backpack hangs off my shoulder. A textbook is clutched to my chest; the mold-scented pages key me in that it's for eighth-grade science.

The hallway goes silent. All the doors have closed.

I'm going to be late for class, but I still can't move.

Something hits the floor loudly, like fireworks. Whatever it is, it's coming from behind me. I want to turn around, but I can't.

Boom!

A beat of silence.

Boom!

I spin around.

A girl stands at the end of the hallway with her back to me. Her arms are down at her sides.

Blood courses down her wrists to the tips of her fingers. The drops hang suspended for a moment, and then fall to the linoleum floor.

The sound of fireworks—*boom!*—each time a drop of blood hits the floor.

Now that I can move again, I hurry to class. Mr. Barrett's earth science, three doors down to the left. My seat will be empty. I'm afraid I'll be marked tardy. Three tardies and I get detention. Detention means I'll be grounded on the weekend and won't be able to hang out with my friends. Which means that they'll probably spend much of that time talking about me behind my back.

Despite all this, I walk past Mr. Barrett's door.

Toward the girl with her back to me.

Olivia?

No, it's not Olivia. Of course it's not. Why would it be Olivia?

When I'm just yards away, the blood starts pouring faster from the girl's wrists. The drops of blood fall now like raindrops. *Boom boom boom boom!* The two pools of blood at her feet start spreading.

The girl doesn't move.

I'm feet away. I don't want to be here. I want to be in earth science, listening to Mr. Barrett enthusiastically discuss continental drift and seafloor spreading and the theory of plate tectonics.

But I can't control my body in this dream—and I know now this is a dream, a nightmare—so I lift my hand to reach out toward the girl.

The tips of my fingers are inches away.

All I need to do is take one more step.

Just one more step . . .

I jerked out of sleep so quickly it felt like I'd punched the girl in the dream. Not only had I punched her, but I could hear her too.

Only it didn't sound like a girl crying out from being hit. It sounded like a man, and his voice was somehow familiar.

"Jesus Christ."

A second later, I'd gained better consciousness and become aware of my surroundings. I was in the living room. The TV was on. And Daniel was stumbling back, holding his face.

I sat up straight, jumped to my feet. "Oh my God. Are you okay?"

He raised his other hand, holding me off. "Yeah, I'm fine. Just wasn't expecting it. That must have been one crazy dream."

I opened my mouth to respond, but nothing came out. I looked around the living room, as if an appropriate response might be hiding somewhere.

Daniel still had on his brown scrubs. He must have just gotten home from the hospital and found me in the throes of a nightmare on the living room couch.

"Emily, are you okay?"

I swallowed, forced myself to nod. "Yeah, I'm okay. Like you said, one crazy dream."

"It sounded like a nightmare."

I ignored this and took a step forward. "Let me see your face."

I went to gently push his hand aside, but he shook his head, stepping away.

"I'm fine."

"Daniel."

"I said I'm fine. I'm going to take a shower."

He turned away and started toward the stairs. I watched him, helpless, not sure what to say or do.

He was halfway up the stairs when I spoke.

"What do you want to do for dinner?"

He paused, shrugged. "I don't care."

"You want to do takeout?"

"Takeout's fine."

Before I could ask him what kind, he started up the stairs again, his hand touching his cheek.

Daniel came back downstairs just as I'd closed the door on the courier. He'd brought Chinese. Daniel and I had gone to the restaurant often during our first year together. Now all we did was open an app, tap a few buttons, and voilà: food. Sesame chicken for me, moo goo gai pan for Daniel, along with two egg rolls.

Daniel checked his container, grabbed a bottle of water from the fridge, and sat down at the table, his focus on the phone in his hand. I sat across from him and absently probed the sesame chicken with my fork.

Daniel must have sensed me watching him, because he looked at me, forced a smile, and then shifted his focus back to his phone.

"Your face looks okay," I said.

He glanced at me again with a frown. "Um, thanks?"

"I mean, on your cheek. Where I hit you. It doesn't look bad from where I'm sitting."

He shrugged, taking another bite of food. Next door, Andrew and Barb's Jack Russell terrier started its nightly yapping.

I glanced back down at my dinner. Because of Daniel's schedule, we rarely ate together anymore. I usually nuked a Smart Ones meal in the microwave or made a sandwich, sometimes just a bowl of cereal.

A few years ago, Daniel and I had made the decision that when we were home together for dinner, we would sit at the kitchen table like grown-ups, and while that tradition had continued, I'd begun to wonder what the point was. Daniel rarely asked me how my day went, as he knew I couldn't really talk about my clients. We both worked in the medical field. We knew how HIPAA worked.

Years ago, Daniel would sometimes tell me about his day and the people he dealt with in the ER, maybe some gossip from his coworkers, but eventually that had tapered off. Now we talked to each other when we needed to, simple communication, but never much outside the basics.

I didn't put all the blame on Daniel. He'd been open before, warm and loving. Sometimes I wondered what our relationship would be like if my father hadn't died. If we'd gotten married and moved out of the town house. If maybe then things would have been different, and Daniel and I wouldn't spend so much of the time we shared together in silence.

"My friend Olivia killed herself."

I said the words without really thinking why. I just wanted to break the silence between us.

Daniel glanced up, pausing midchew, and stared back at me.

"It happened a couple days ago. I found out today. My mom told me."

Daniel swallowed, set his phone down on the table, and used a napkin to wipe his mouth.

"Who's Olivia?"

"She was an old friend. From middle school. We were close then, but I haven't talked to her in years."

"I'm sorry."

Why I kept talking, I had no idea. "The funeral is Saturday."

"Are you going?"

"I'm not sure yet."

Daniel watched me for another moment, waiting for me to say something else, and when I didn't, he said, "Well, shit, I'm sorry to hear about that. That's awful."

On an alternate timeline, I imagined a completely different reaction. That timeline is the one where my father is still alive. Daniel and I have been married now for two years. We've left this town house and moved into our own home. Maybe we have a dog. We still go hiking when the weather is nice. We drive north during the winter to go skiing.

We go to the bars with Daniel's friends, to their cookouts and parties; sometimes I even accompany Daniel to the Boys & Girls Club, where he still volunteers.

Yes—even on this alternate timeline, we don't have children of our own. It's a sore subject between us, something that causes arguments. But those arguments never last long. We always make up. We hug and kiss and end the night in the same bed, our bodies touching under the sheets, feeling safe and loved.

On that alternate timeline, if Daniel had just learned that one of my old friends had passed away—had killed herself, no less—he would immediately get up to give me a hug. Tell me that everything would be okay, that he'd go to the funeral with me. Even if he had to take off work or skip volunteering, he'd be there to support me.

But that was an alternate timeline, and this was real life. Here in real life, Daniel picked up his fork and phone, and again entered that bubble where he was content, off in his own little world.

And me? I had my bubble too. I picked up my fork and probed again at the sesame chicken, while Daniel sat across from me staring at his phone, and next door Andrew and Barb's dog kept yapping and yapping and yapping.

4

"Did you ever see her face?"

"No."

"Did you ever get close enough to touch her?"

"No."

"Who do you think it was?"

I didn't have an immediate response. I sat on the leather couch—an actual leather couch, not some cheap pleather thing like in my office—and stared down at the hairline scar on my left palm.

When the silence stretched, I glanced up at Lisa. She sat on the mesh ergonomic chair beside her desk, her thin legs crossed, watching me. She was in her late forties. Had a slender frame, a strong jaw. She had never been a hippie, as far as I knew, but she always dressed like it—colorful bohemian dresses and tops, beads wrapped around her wrists that clinked and clacked when she moved her hands.

Lisa was the second therapist I'd seen since high school, and I'd been seeing her for the past two years. Like all good therapists, she never told me what I wanted to hear, and always pushed me further than I typically wanted to go.

She tilted her head, raising a flawlessly trimmed eyebrow.

"Well?"

I said nothing.

Lisa took the notepad off her lap, tossed it on her desk, and crossed her arms.

"Why are you being difficult today?"

"I'm not being difficult."

"You're not answering my question."

"Maybe I don't know the answer."

"Yes, you do."

Lisa was what you'd call a private-practice therapist. Her office didn't accept government medical assistance, so clients either needed to use their private insurance or pay cash. Because of that, Lisa's office was much nicer than most therapists' offices. She had a large oak desk with an iMac sitting on top. An expensive throw rug protected the hardwood floor. A leather couch, plus a leather chair. An artisanal wall clock hung near the door, its circle of numbers roman numerals to add a sophisticated touch.

When I didn't answer, Lisa swiveled in her seat to check the time, swiveled back to me.

"We have twenty minutes left. You want to call it a day now, or do you just want to continue sitting there being difficult?"

"I'm not being difficult."

"Sure you're not."

"I know what you're doing."

Her eyebrow lifted again. "Do you?"

"You're purposely making me defensive. You think it's going to help me work through my dream."

"Now why would you think that?"

"Because I sometimes do the same thing. And I learned it from you."

She smiled at this but didn't laugh. I'd heard her laugh maybe a handful of times since I'd started seeing her, and I had made it a goal to try to make her laugh at every session. It was difficult to crack that professional veneer of hers—all I could ever seem to do was make her smile—but it felt good to have a conversation with somebody who had no ulterior motives, somebody who didn't judge you when you said or did something stupid.

My eyes went to the framed photograph of Lisa and her husband on the desk, and not for the first time I wondered what their relationship was like. Whether they shared meaningful conversation during their dinners or if they let the silence build up into a wall between them.

I liked to think they had a good relationship—a good, strong relationship, the kind that never faltered—and there were times when I thought that what Daniel and I needed was an older couple to befriend, a couple who clearly had their shit together and who could help us see what was attainable.

But that, of course, was never going to happen, at least as long as I was a patient of Lisa's, and besides, even if I broached the idea with Daniel, I felt certain he'd knock it down.

Lisa glanced at the clock again.

"Fifteen minutes."

My purse started buzzing. I pulled out my phone.

Lisa said, "Don't you love it when your clients' phones go off during a session?"

Ignoring her, I checked to see who was calling. It was a local number I didn't recognize. I hit the "Dismiss" button, then pressed the button on the side to power it off. Once the screen went dark, I held up the phone.

"There, I turned it off. Happy?"

"I would be happier if you answered my original question."

"And what was your original question?"

"Don't be coy, Emily."

I sighed and looked away. "I don't know."

"You don't know what?"

"I don't know who the girl was."

Lisa's expression turned skeptical, but she said nothing.

I leaned forward on the couch.

"I can't remember the last time I had a nightmare."

"And last night you had the same one twice."

"At least that I can remember. The first during my nap, then later . . . I could hardly sleep. It didn't help that Daniel kept snoring."

"I didn't want to say anything, but you do look rough." Lisa said it with a straight face but grinned when she saw my expression. "That was a joke, Emily. How are things between you and Daniel?"

I didn't want to talk about Daniel today—just like I didn't want to talk about him most other days—but I knew if I didn't answer her, Lisa would keep digging.

"The same."

"And what does 'the same' mean?"

"Just . . . the same."

"Distant?"

"Yes."

"When was the last time the two of you were intimate?"

"Pass."

Lisa smiled. "Okay, fair enough. Has your daily routine changed much recently?"

"No, it's pretty much the same. I go to the gym, have some yogurt and a granola bar, and then head into the office. Same thing this morning. Except today is Friday, the one day a week I get to grace you with my presence, so I hurried over here on my lunch break so that you could give me a hard time."

Lisa smiled again but didn't speak. A moment of silence passed, and I issued another heavy sigh.

"I think . . . maybe it was Olivia."

Lisa watched me, waiting me out.

I said, "But you don't think it was Olivia."

"I wasn't there in the dream. I didn't see what you saw. But your mother just told you about Olivia's death yesterday. The fact that you would have a dream so vivid so quickly . . . maybe your friend's suicide triggered something you'd been keeping hidden for a long time."

I shook my head, ran my fingers through my hair.

"No, this isn't about Grace. We've been through all of that. I told you everything. There's nothing I would have kept hidden."

"Maybe. Or maybe there's something that you didn't tell me unconsciously. Maybe in your mind you told me everything, but there's still something there."

"Like what?"

"You tell me, Emily. You became a therapist because of that girl. Your entire life was redirected because of your guilt. That's not small."

"I know it's not."

"You never did track her down."

"I tried."

"Maybe you didn't try hard enough."

"Are you kidding me? I hired a private investigator. I wasted three hundred dollars. When she and her mom moved away, she essentially disappeared."

I inwardly cringed at the desperation in my voice.

"Nobody disappears," Lisa said. "Have you tried looking her up online? Maybe she's on Facebook."

"I don't use Facebook."

"Good for you. But maybe Grace does."

"I don't think Grace is the reason I had the nightmare."

Lisa glanced back at the clock.

"We're running out of time, so let's make this quick. Emily, be honest with me. How frustrating is it for you when you know exactly what your client needs to do to help herself, but she refuses to see it?"

I didn't answer.

"I think that's what's happening here. As therapists, we can see what's going on with other people, but when it comes to ourselves, we can be very obtuse."

"So what do you think I need to do?"

"You know exactly what you need to do."

I let that sink in, then shook my head. "It would be awkward. I haven't seen or talked to Olivia in years. Showing up out of nowhere . . ."

"Let me be blunt." Lisa leveled her ocean-gray eyes straight at me. "This isn't about Olivia. This isn't about Olivia's family, though I'm sure they'd appreciate it if you showed up. This is about you getting closure."

"What kind of closure would I possibly gain from going to Olivia's funeral?"

"You tell me. You're the one dreaming about a girl whose wrists keep bleeding."

I sat up straight on the couch again, so suddenly that it startled Lisa.

"Shit, I can't believe I didn't connect the dots."

"What dots?"

"A new client of mine. Her name's Chloe. I saw her just yesterday, right before I met with my mom and she told me about Olivia. She's a thirteen-year-old cutter."

Lisa said nothing.

"Don't you see? Chloe cut her wrists. Maybe . . . maybe having met with her right before I learned about Olivia's suicide caused me to have that dream."

Lisa didn't speak, just uncrossed her legs and stood up from the chair. She smoothed out the creases in her skirt, then started toward the door.

"Don't you think I'm right?"

Lisa paused, turned back to me. "I guess that depends. Have you ever had a nightmare about any of your clients before?"

I didn't even have to think about it. I shook my head.

Lisa made a knowing smile.

"I'll see you next week, Emily."

5

Whoever had called from the unknown number had left a voice mail. I played it as I crossed the parking lot toward my car, the phone against my ear.

"Hey, Emily, it's Courtney. Been a while. Your mom reached out and told me about Olivia. So crazy, right? She said the funeral is tomorrow up in Harrisburg, and I wondered if you planned to go? I thought maybe we could ride together. Call me when you get a chance."

I slid behind the steering wheel and stared at my phone. I almost wanted to listen to the voice mail again—Courtney's voice, so familiar yet so strange—because surely I'd misheard the part about *my mom* contacting her.

Ignore it. That's what I decided to do. And have a word with my mother the next time I saw her about giving my number out to people I hadn't talked to in years.

It was five miles from Lisa's office to Safe Haven Behavioral Health. The drive typically took ten minutes, fifteen if traffic was heavy. I always made sure to keep my schedule open the first hour after my lunch break on the days I saw Lisa. Which meant when I did arrive back at work, I had time to kill. I usually finished up paperwork, but today I couldn't concentrate.

When I got to the office, a woman was already in the lobby with her son, who played with the block toys in the corner. I didn't know them—the boy wasn't one of my clients—but I smiled at the woman and continued on to the door, which led back to the offices and was locked by a panel code.

Claire, the receptionist / office assistant, sat behind a glass partition. When I opened the door and stepped inside, she hit me with her bright smile.

"Have a good lunch?"

I nodded, smiled back, and was about to start down the hallway toward my office when Claire called, "I posted a new picture of Teddy on Facebook in case you missed it."

Teddy, from what I could remember, was Claire's grandson. Or grandnephew. Grandsomething. She'd shown me a picture on her phone, and she'd mentioned Facebook then, but I'd stopped reminding my coworkers that I wasn't on social media. They'd either frown at me or ask if I was kidding. So I'd just nod and smile and say I'd check it out.

Which I did now—"Thanks, Claire!"—and continued down the hallway.

Cocooned in the quiet safety of my office, I slipped my phone from my bag and placed it on the desk. I knew what I needed to do, but I refused to do it. I'd worked too hard to block out my early life. In less than twenty-four hours, a lot of that hard work had started to come undone.

First the news of Olivia's death; now a voice mail from Courtney. Two of my very best friends in middle school. Two people who shared the same burden as me.

I turned over my left hand. Stared down at the scar on my palm.

"Shit."

I picked up the phone and hit "Redial." It rang three times, and with each ring I thought I should disconnect, turn the phone off, and never turn it back on. I could buy a new phone with a new number. A new number that I wouldn't even share with my mother, because apparently she couldn't be trusted.

After the fourth ring, it went to voice mail. Courtney's voice saying she wasn't available right now but please leave a name and number and she'd get back to me.

Before the beep sounded, I disconnected the call and cradled my head in my hands.

What the hell was I doing? Olivia was dead, yes, and that was terrible, but what did it matter to me? I hadn't seen or talked to her in years. We used to be best friends, but that was a completely different life. I was sorry about what had happened, but I didn't have to go to her funeral. Doing that wouldn't change anything.

My cell phone vibrated on the desk.

I opened my eyes. Stared down at the screen.

Courtney.

I could simply not answer it. Let it go to voice mail again. Turn off the phone for the rest of the day. But what Lisa had said kept niggling at the back of my brain. Her telling me I could use some kind of closure.

I answered the phone.

"Hello?"

"Emily, it's great to hear your voice!"

"Hi, Courtney, how are you?"

"I'm okay. But holy shit—the news about Olivia? It blew my mind. I searched Facebook for hours trying to figure out how it happened. I mean, I immediately thought about—"

I cut her off.

"So what's up?"

"Did you listen to my voice mail?"

"I did."

"And?"

"And . . . what?"

"Are you going to the funeral? From what I can tell, it's like a forty-, forty-five-minute drive. If you want to carpool, I'm up for it."

"I honestly don't remember the last time I spoke to Olivia."

"Me neither. But so what? She was our friend."

The way Courtney said it—so simply, so matter-of-factly—made me realize I should be ashamed. But stubbornness won out.

"Did you say my mother contacted you?"

"Yeah, she sent me a message on Facebook."

"You're *Facebook* friends with my mother?"

"She sent me a friend request. I accepted it. That's what you're supposed to do on Facebook. Are you even *on* Facebook? I couldn't find you."

I checked the time on my computer. My next client would be arriving in ten minutes.

"My break is almost over. I need to get back to work."

"Oh yeah? What are you doing nowadays, anyway?"

"I'm a therapist."

"That's cool. So, do you get to prescribe medication and stuff?"

"No, that's a psychiatrist. Listen, Courtney, I need to go."

"Sure. But what about tomorrow?"

I hesitated. "I'm not sure yet what my plans are."

"Okay, cool, but can you let me know as soon as you can? I shot Elise a message on Facebook to see if she was going, but she hasn't gotten back to me yet."

I jolted at the sound of Elise's name. I remembered seeing her less than a year ago, only for a moment, and how I'd been so embarrassed that I'd tilted my face down so she wouldn't see me.

"What about Mackenzie?"

Courtney gave a disdainful snort.

"Remember how Mackenzie was in middle school? She's worse now. She lives in a McMansion near Philly. Married a brain surgeon, if you can believe it."

"If Elise and I can't go, are you still going?"

"I'm going to try."

"Can I ask why?"

A beat of silence on Courtney's end.

"Because Olivia was my friend," she said.

My desk phone rang. I asked Courtney to hold on a second, then I grabbed the desk phone and placed it to my other ear. Claire told me my one o'clock had arrived early and was waiting in the lobby.

"Courtney, I have to go," I said, hanging up the desk phone.

Her voice took on a defeated tone.

"I understand. Let me know if you change your mind."

"I will."

"Thanks. Call or text when you know for sure."

"No, I mean I will go to the funeral."

Her tone became all at once more hopeful. "Really?"

"Yes."

Excited, Courtney told me she would text me her address and see me tomorrow. Then she disconnected, and I just sat there with the phone against my ear.

I closed my eyes again. Saw Olivia as she had been when we were in middle school. Her dimpled chin. Her perfect smile.

The hairline scar on my palm seemed to throb. I remembered the morning: all of us in Mackenzie's bedroom. The flash of the paring knife Mackenzie had sneaked upstairs. How we all gasped when she cut her palm and asked who was next.

6

In the beginning, there were two of us.

Elise Martin was the perky girl with hazel eyes and bright-red hair in pigtails who could talk to anyone, including the adults. I was the shy girl in OshKosh denim overalls and ponytailed brown hair who cried when her parents dropped her off at school.

It was kindergarten, and our teacher was Mrs. Miranda, and there were nearly twenty other kids I'd never met but with whom I was now supposed to be friends.

It wasn't until recess—everyone taking turns on the swings and slide and monkey bars—that Elise approached the corner of the playground where I was hiding and told me we should be best friends.

"Best friends?"

For some reason, the concept was foreign to me.

"Best friends," she repeated with a smile. "Your name is Emily. My name is Elise. Our names start with the same letter."

This reasoning was utterly ridiculous, of course, but we were kindergartners, and I needed a friend, somebody I could trust. Besides, it was true: we were the only girls in our class whose names started with *E*.

There was another kindergarten class at our school, taught by Miss Greenham (who championed Dr. Seuss's *Green Eggs and Ham* as the classroom book), and it was in that classroom that Mackenzie Harper was a student. A spunky honey-blonde-haired girl with bright-blue eyes, she would have won all the beauty pageants in the state if her mother cared about such trivial things, which was something Mackenzie actually said once and which caused me later that night to ask my mom what *trivial* meant.

Over the next week or so, Elise brought Mackenzie into the fold. Then I had *two* best friends.

Courtney Sullivan was in Miss Greenham's class too. She had green eyes and strawberry-blonde hair and had a slight gap in her front teeth that would eventually be corrected with braces in middle school. She had become friends with Mackenzie, and pretty soon I had *three* best friends.

Olivia Campbell showed up in the fourth grade, her parents having moved to Lanton from Harrisburg, and Elise and Mackenzie immediately decided she would be a perfect fit for our group. Same for Destiny, when she arrived at the beginning of eighth grade. We were already dubbed the Harpies then, and once she was adopted into the fold, our clique was complete.

Was there any rhyme or reason to our friendship? In retrospect, it's difficult to say. Mackenzie's parents had a lot of money (like, *a lot*). By all rights she should have gone to private school from day one, but her father had gone to public school and managed to make something of himself, and he didn't want Mackenzie to be spoiled—or more spoiled than she already was—so her parents kept her in Lincoln Elementary and Franklin Middle School. It wasn't until the end of eighth grade that Mackenzie's parents pulled her out and made her promise never to speak to any of us ever again.

Elise's parents also had money, what with her father being a Lanton County judge. Courtney's parents were well off, as were Olivia's and Destiny's. Looking back, it was the common denominator among them, the one thing that made them stand out from the other students in school.

Only my family was what you'd call middle class—our two-story home in a so-so suburb, my parents only ever buying preowned cars that already had over a hundred thousand miles on the odometer, my mother clipping coupons from the Sunday paper.

Eventually I started getting an allowance—ten dollars a week—and half of that was immediately put into a savings account. "You'll thank us later," my mother told me when I complained.

For me, the tangibility was everything. The feel of the five-dollar bill always gave me a burst of satisfaction, this knowledge that there was money and that I had it. But it was short lived. I always ended up thinking about how it was nothing compared to the other girls' allowances. One time at the mall, Mackenzie flashed us the crisp one-hundred-dollar bill her father had given her, and we all stared at it, our mouths agape, like it was buried treasure.

It was almost disgusting how easily the girls flaunted their money, though in retrospect they hadn't really shoved it in my face, even if that was how it sometimes felt. Mackenzie or Elise would just buy whatever they wanted at the shops or the food court, slipping cash out of their purses as if it were pocket lint, while I needed to conserve the little money I had.

And it was because of this that a sliver of resentment started to build toward my parents. Didn't they realize how embarrassing it was? The other girls always had the nicest clothes and top-of-the-line makeup, while I had to settle for stuff my mom bought me from Walmart.

Part of me feared that my being poor—because that was how it sometimes felt, like we were destitute, just waiting for the bank to take away our house and force us to live on the street—would one day force me out of the group. In elementary school, being popular was never really a concern, at least not for those of us who were already there, but once we reached middle school, it became imperative for me to stay in the group.

Because if I was forced out, where would I go? I had no interest in sports—none of us did—so I couldn't be friends with the girls who played field hockey or basketball or soccer. My parents didn't have the extra money to sign me up for gymnastics even if I wanted to join. My grades were decent but not spectacular, so I couldn't be friends with the nerds. The thought of ending up with the losers was unbearable. I'd probably become a nomad, one of those random kids who doesn't fit in with anyone and grows up alone and dies without any family or friends.

Melodramatic, sure, but that was my thought process at the time.

It wasn't until middle school that I realized I held no influence over my friends. When deciding what to do or where to go—to the mall, the movies, somebody's house—it would always be Elise or Mackenzie who made the call. Sometimes Courtney. Even Olivia once in a while. But never once me.

Oh, I would offer suggestions, but it soon became clear that my opinion didn't matter. I might get a smile, a nod, but that was the extent of it. Pretty soon I stopped offering my opinion at all.

This was compounded when Destiny arrived in eighth grade. I'd been friends with Elise and Mackenzie since kindergarten, so you'd think I would have more sway. But no. Maybe because Destiny's parents had more money than mine did, maybe because she was prettier than me, she ended up having more say. More power. More influence.

Which made me realize I needed to do whatever it took to remain a Harpy.

Even if it meant breaking the law.

Looking back, it's difficult to pinpoint when our delinquent behaviors began. And to call them delinquent is a stretch, at least when viewed against real crimes. The worst we'd ever done was some light shoplifting;

I guess calling it light doesn't quite make sense, but that's how it felt. When we stole, it wasn't for any nefarious reason. It was just something to do.

Before that, though, we'd started competing. At least, Mackenzie and Elise and Courtney had started competing.

Some things were beyond our control, like whose father made the most money (Mackenzie), while others were up to nature, like who had gotten her period first (Courtney, toward the end of fifth grade, though Mackenzie refused to believe it, and so Courtney marched us into the bathroom to prove it; the sight of the blood was enough to almost make me throw up and dread the day I finally got my period).

Then, of course, there were the things we had full control over, more or less. Like who got the first boyfriend (Mackenzie), who got her ears pierced first (Elise), who got kissed first (Mackenzie), who gave the first hand job (Elise), who gave the first blow job (Courtney), and who had sex first (Mackenzie, with her then-boyfriend Billy Maddox during Christmas break in eighth grade).

Sometime during middle school, our evolution from little girls to maturing teenagers had begun to take shape.

Mackenzie, who had been petite for years, grew several inches. She was always beautiful, but now her beauty had become much more pronounced, more palpable, but it was an artificial beauty, the kind that reminded you of a Barbie doll. Everything was just so perfect—her nose, her cheeks, her chin, her ears, not to mention her silky-smooth blonde hair—that it made you think she spent several hours in front of the mirror every morning, brushing and plucking and tweezing and searching her pores for any treacherous trace of acne.

Come to think of it, in all of middle school, I don't think I ever once saw Mackenzie have a single zit.

Elise was different; she was just as beautiful as Mackenzie, but her beauty was more natural, more wholesome. I swear, there were days when she didn't even wear a dollop of makeup and still looked pristine.

Plus, it helped that everybody liked Elise—the boys especially but also most of the girls, even the teachers—and she had a slow, adorable smile that always made you smile too.

Unlike Mackenzie—who was popular because of her money and her looks and because she exuded a presence that demanded popularity—Elise got along with everybody. Walking through the hallways between classes, it felt like everybody wanted to say hi to her. And Elise said hi right back, that easy smile lighting her face.

Olivia, on the other hand, lacked the cool confidence that came with beauty. Starting in seventh grade, Olivia had begun to struggle with her weight. She had a sweet tooth, as my mother would say. Oreos were her true vice—eating them was a nervous habit—and Olivia would often keep a pack in her locker to snack on between classes.

She wasn't overweight, but Mackenzie constantly gave her a hard time, sometimes reaching out and pinching her belly in the locker room after gym, more than once calling her Double Stuf while Olivia was in earshot, and despite myself I would giggle along with the rest of the girls, happy that I was able to maintain more self-control when it came to treats and that for once Mackenzie's ire was focused on somebody else.

Still, the harassment drove Olivia crazy, and there were periods of time where she would try to starve herself or would force herself to throw up after lunch, yearning to reach some predetermined weight in her head.

Courtney had always had a willowy body, but it became more lithe in middle school, especially once she started gymnastics (her parents, of course, had the money to sign her up). Even before she learned how to vault and master the balance beam and uneven bars, she moved with a gymnast's grace, seamlessly weaving between students in the hallways, performing handstands outside after school, and more than once she'd mentioned about one day trying out for the Olympics.

Despite being part of the popular crowd, I was still shy. I had a series of boyfriends in middle school (Matt Callow and Peter Lyons and Adrian Fitzsimmons), but those relationships didn't last long, not after the guys realized I wasn't going to put out or even jerk them off. I'd make out with them and I'd let them rub themselves up against me, ignoring the heat between my own legs, but that was the extent of it. It wasn't because I was prudish, though my mother, who'd been raised a devout Catholic, lectured me more than once that I should save myself for marriage because "that's what good girls do." I just didn't feel comfortable and always worried I would somehow mess something up if I let things get too far.

One day, Elise found me in the bathroom crying because Jake Reynolds had told me he didn't like me anymore.

"I heard what happened," she said, softly placing her hand on my back. "Jake is such a jerk."

I'd wiped my eyes, hating for Elise to see me crying. It made me feel weak. Vulnerable.

"He wanted me to—"

I cut myself off, embarrassed by what Jake wanted me to do and worried about what Elise thought of me because I had refused.

She shook her head, waving my words away.

"Like I said, he's a jerk. You shouldn't let Jake or any of those boys make you do something you don't want to do. That's what my mom told me."

This shocked me, the idea that Elise's mom knew what her daughter was doing. I'd die if my mom knew half the things I got into.

"Does your mom . . . does she know about—"

Elise shook her head again, her heart-shaped stud earrings flashing in the restroom's fluorescents.

"She told me she used to be my age once, so she knows the type of stuff that goes on. She just told me to be careful. Especially at the Farmhouse."

The Farmhouse was what we called the small two-story house near the edge of the country club golf course. It was an old house, part stone, part wood. It smelled of damp earth no matter the season. From what I'd heard, it was at least one hundred years old and had been labeled a historic structure, so the country club left it as it was. They knew that local kids went there late at night to drink and do drugs and have sex, but those local kids' parents were country club members who paid expensive dues, so the security staff didn't bother keeping the kids out unless the partying got out of hand.

The Farmhouse was where we all first drank—a bottle of Smirnoff vodka Courtney had swiped from her dad's wet bar—and where we first smoked the cigarettes Olivia had stolen from her dad's stash.

And it was where something terrible happened to Grace Farmer.

I wasn't there that night, but I heard about it later. Afterward, the idea of spending time in the Farmhouse disgusted me. I never wanted to go back, though it wasn't like I had much say in where we hung out. It didn't matter anyway, because soon after, some tenth graders got in trouble for setting the place on fire.

But the stealing? I don't know when that started. I just remember being at the mall one weekend with the girls. We were at Forever 21, and there was a silver rhinestone wrap bracelet I thought looked cute, but it was ten dollars and I only had seven dollars in my pocket.

"I'll pay the rest," Elise said, stepping up behind me to check out what had caught my attention.

I'd almost given in. I really wanted that bracelet, but it felt like charity, like Elise—and by proxy the rest of the girls—was looking down on me.

"No, I don't need it."

And I didn't. It was a cute bracelet, but it wasn't like it would change my life. I put it out of my mind, browsing the rest of the store and following the girls through the mall.

Later, we ended up in Mrs. Sullivan's van—the thing was always spotless, because she took it to the car wash every weekend and had it washed and waxed and vacuumed—and on the ride home Elise pulled the bracelet from her pocket and put it in my hand.

I'd stared down at it, at first not sure what I was looking at. Then I glanced up at Elise, who was smirking at me.

I whispered, "I told you I didn't need it."

She'd shrugged. "Yeah, but you wanted it."

"Thank you. I'll pay you back."

"Why? I didn't pay for it."

It took me an extra second to understand what she was saying. My eyes must have widened, because Elise smirked again.

"Don't worry about it," she whispered. "We do it all the time."

"You do?"

"Yeah, where have you been?"

And that was when Mackenzie leaned forward from the back row, inserting herself between us, her bubblegum-scented breath hot in my ear.

"Little Emily, you better not squeal."

Little Emily. That was what Mackenzie called me when she wanted to make me feel insignificant, just like she still sometimes called Olivia Double Stuf even though Olivia claimed to have sworn off Oreos. As middle school wore on, Little Emily changed to just my last name.

"I won't."

"You know what she needs to do," Mackenzie said, now directing her bubblegum-scented breath toward Elise. "She needs to prove she's a real Harpy."

Elise smirked at me again, and gave me a quick wink. I saw a flash of the Elise that was my first friend, my best friend.

"Next weekend, then. Emily is definitely one of us. Aren't you, Emily?"

What else was I going to do? I'd nodded, stuffing the bracelet into my pocket, and whispered what had become our motto.

"Once a Harpy, always a Harpy."

After the incident with Grace, we all went our separate ways.

Some of us were pulled out of school—Mackenzie to attend private school, Destiny because her dad started a new job down south, Olivia because her family moved back to Harrisburg—but a few others stayed. Like Elise and Courtney. But Elise started hanging out with another crowd, and despite calling her my best friend for years, I almost never saw her.

Courtney and I didn't talk much freshman year, but we started hanging out again in tenth grade, and she became my best (maybe only true) friend.

Junior year, she got pregnant with some guy in vo-tech. She hadn't been dating anybody, was just talking and hanging out with random guys, and then one day she pulled me aside in the bathroom and told me that she'd been throwing up the past two mornings and that—she paused, swallowing, her face an uncharacteristic pallor—she thought she might be pregnant.

She'd picked up a pregnancy test the night before but was too nervous to go through with it on her own, so we sneaked out after lunch and went back to my house.

When she checked the results—both of us in my bedroom, the house quiet because my parents were at work—she started crying, though I wasn't sure if the tears were because she was happy or sad. She just sat on the carpet, leaning against my bed with her knees pulled up to her chest, and bawled.

I knelt beside her, placed an arm around her, held her close.

Courtney kept whispering the same thing again and again—"It's over, it's over, it's over"—but it wasn't clear what she meant by it.

The unspoken question was whether Courtney wanted to get an abortion. There was a clinic one county over. It would be an easy drive. I offered to take her. I told her we could skip classes for the day. Courtney said she would think about it. She hugged me, told me that I was a good friend.

"Everything will be okay," I'd said.

She'd shaken her head, her body trembling against my embrace, her voice a tremulous whisper.

"No, it won't."

"How do you know?"

And she'd looked at me, tears in her eyes, and asked, "Remember Tyler Marshall?"

Tyler was Destiny's older brother. He had been a year ahead of us, athletic and cute, nice whenever he saw us. Especially to Courtney. Tyler had asked her to go to the winter formal, which was a big deal because Tyler was a freshman, and so this was a *high school* dance. Courtney was thrilled, but also troubled, which didn't make sense to me until the day she told us she had no choice but to tell her parents.

She'd had Elise and me come over. She'd told her mother first, and her mother looked so excited, clapping her hands together in joy, and she asked about this Tyler because she hadn't heard of him before, and pretty soon it became clear something was wrong.

Elise and I sat close together on the couch, watching the drama play out, and at one point Elise whispered, "Oh shit."

I hadn't realized it until that day, but never once had Destiny been invited over to Courtney's house. Never once, as far as I could tell, did Courtney's parents learn that Destiny was one of Courtney's friends. But now Courtney's mom rushed to grab the most recent school newspaper—Courtney had let it slip that Tyler was on the high school JV basketball team—and after paging through to find Tyler, the smile on her face started to fade.

Courtney's father was home, but in another room at the time, and Courtney's mother dropped her voice when she said, "You can't do this to your father."

Courtney, I realized, was already on the verge of tears, and her mom's comment didn't help.

"Mom," she whispered urgently.

"He needs to know."

"But, *Mom*."

Courtney's mother turned to Elise and me.

"I'm sorry, girls, but I think it's best if you head home. Would you like me to give you a ride, or do you think you can walk back to Elise's house?"

Elise didn't live far away. Maybe a half mile. We could cut through a field and make it in no time. But the request was unusual, the kind of thing you'd never expect somebody's mother to make, and Courtney immediately started crying.

Elise stood up from the couch. "We'll walk."

We left the house but didn't go far.

Elise led me around the back, to just outside the living room. We could hear Courtney's father. His voice was loud and full of menace.

"Absolutely not. No goddamned way my daughter will ever go out with a nigger."

I'd heard that word before, but never spoken by an adult I knew, especially by one of my closest friend's parents. Along with the menace in his tone was a malice I'd never thought existed, and from that day forward I could never look at Courtney's parents without thinking about her father's words.

All this was obviously on Courtney's mind that day in my bedroom, the positive pregnancy test on the carpet beside us. Tyler Marshall had moved away three years ago, along with Destiny and their family, but the episode where Courtney's father railed at her because she'd agreed to go to a dance with Tyler still haunted her, and she was afraid of what her father might do now once he learned the baby's father was black.

In the end, Courtney decided against the abortion. She eventually told her parents. Her mother, from what Courtney said, was understanding, willing to do whatever needed to be done, but her father wouldn't hear of it. He'd screamed and hollered even louder than that day in eighth grade. Courtney later admitted to me that she'd often been intimidated by her father, but never once scared for her life like she felt in that moment.

Her father kicked her out of the house, and her mother, who Courtney said was always a bit afraid of her husband, didn't do anything to stop him.

Courtney eventually dropped out of school. Her maternal grandmother, who detested her son-in-law's racism, took in Courtney and the baby and helped raise them.

The baby was a beautiful little girl named Terri. Her eyes were hazel, just like her father's, Courtney told me once. After that, she never spoke of the father again. He had decided not to be part of his daughter's life, and Courtney was okay with that. His name wasn't even added to the birth certificate.

Her grandmother didn't have much money, so Courtney was forced to work. She got her GED, though, and during senior year, I visited her often. I was her only lifeline from her old life to her new. She asked me about school, about the friends she used to talk to every day. Some of them still saw her, but most had gone on with their lives.

I think it was then I realized it was true—a lot of the friends you have in high school will be friends you'll never see again. The only thing keeping you together is a giant building. Once you're out of that building, the invisible binds snap, and you're set free.

The last time I saw Courtney was the summer after graduation, right before I flew out to California. Her grandmother had called me late at night because Courtney was drunk. I'd gone straight to the house and stayed there for several hours until I was able to get Courtney to bed—though not before words were spoken, words that could never be unsaid.

After that, I stopped returning her calls and emails. She even called my mother, asking if I was all right and if she'd done anything wrong, and I had promised my mom that I'd reach out and tell Courtney I was fine, that everything was great between us.

But it wasn't. And as far as I was concerned, it never would be.

7

Highland Estates was the type of apartment complex that tried to fool you with its name. Ritzy moniker, subpar housing, right beside the highway.

Courtney and her daughter lived in building E. I parked in an open space in front and kept the car idling as I texted her that I was here.

A couple seconds ticked by, and then her reply came through.

Coming now!

Something about the exclamation point irritated me. I knew Courtney probably meant nothing by it, but the enthusiasm in that simple symbol this early on a Saturday morning didn't seem right, especially considering where we were going.

When Courtney emerged from building E, I didn't recognize her. I thought she was another tenant. She took several steps forward, her hand propped on her forehead to shield her eyes from the sun. When she spotted me, our eyes met, and in that second, when I realized it was in fact Courtney, I was shocked.

In high school, Courtney had been thin, but it was a fit thinness, even though she'd stopped gymnastics. After the baby, she'd managed to maintain that fitness. Now . . . she looked skinny. And not fit skinny either.

Even though we hadn't coordinated it, I saw Courtney was wearing an outfit similar to my own: dark skirt, gray top, and flats.

As Courtney neared—moving gracefully as she always did, like she was gliding across the pavement—she bent down, her drawn face filling the open side window.

"Emily?"

"Hey, Courtney."

Courtney nearly tore open the door in her excitement. She hopped into the passenger seat and leaned across the center console for a hug, enveloping me in the scent of her shampoo and perfume.

"It's been so long. I can't remember the last time I saw you."

The hug caught me by surprise. I'd never been a big social hugger. At least not after high school. That was the kind of thing we girls did in middle school, hugging each other in the hallways, pecking each other's cheeks, but after everything that had happened, the idea of embracing somebody so closely left a bad taste in the back of my mouth. I had no trouble hugging my mother or Daniel (on the rare occasions Daniel and I hugged these days), but friends, especially those I hadn't seen in years, were another story.

As Courtney leaned back, she spotted the diamond on my finger and snatched my hand to get a closer look.

"Oh my God, that's huge! I didn't know you were engaged. Congratulations!"

Part of me thought she was going to hug me again, but Courtney kept staring down at the diamond, which was large but not huge, not by a long shot. Back when we were dating and began discussing the possibility of marriage, I'd told Daniel I didn't care about the size of the ring, and it hadn't just been something to say either. I would have been just as happy if there hadn't been any diamond at all. I'm not sure the Emily from middle school would have approved, but maybe that was the point.

I took my hand back and placed it on the steering wheel.

"Thanks. And before you ask, his name is Daniel, and he's an emergency-room RN."

"That's great. Do you have a picture?"

Before I could answer, Courtney had her phone out and was showing me the screen.

The phone's wallpaper was a picture of a young girl. Clearly it was Terri, and she was maybe ten years old. Black hair pulled up in a bun. Dimpled cheeks. Hazel eyes, just like she had when she was a baby. The resemblance to Courtney was in the face.

"She's beautiful," I said.

Courtney tilted the phone to look at the screen, her smile beaming even brighter. I noted the tattoo on the inside of her left wrist: *Terri* in cursive.

"She is. She's smart too. And I'm not just saying that because she's my daughter. She's, like, *super*smart. Gets all As in school. Reads a couple of books a week. She's amazing."

"Sounds like it. Where is she now?"

"She's with a sitter. You should come by sometime. She'd love to see her aunt Emily."

Aunt Emily. I hadn't heard those words in years. Courtney had started calling me that after she'd had Terri. She would always say her baby didn't have her grandparents, but she had her mother and she had her great-grandmother and she had her aunt Emily. It had been cute then, but not so much now.

Courtney slid her phone into her purse, still smiling at me. This close, I was able to appraise her. She had her blonde hair tied back in a ponytail, but I noted the pink highlights and the fact that she wore hardly any makeup.

"What?" I said.

Her green eyes widened.

"Well? Aren't you going to show me?"

Realizing that we weren't going to leave until I gave in, I dug out my own phone and scrolled to find a picture of Daniel. I needed to scroll longer than I should have, though I didn't have many pictures, period. In the past year or so, I hadn't felt the need to document our time together. Neither had Daniel.

Finally, I came to one from when we'd gone hiking maybe a year ago. Daniel wore shorts and a T-shirt and had a backpack slung over his shoulder. He had on sunglasses, but he was smiling, and it was a cute picture, I had to admit—even as I wondered what pictures Daniel might still have of me on his phone.

Courtney offered up a high whistle.

"He's hot."

I stuffed the phone back in my purse, happy to get this charade behind us.

"Thanks. We should get going. We don't want to be late."

8

Grayson Funeral Home's viewing area was a large room decorated with calming, dark-hued wallpaper. Flower arrangements, most of them displayed on small tables, added a much-needed touch of vibrancy. Folding chairs had been set up, maybe four dozen of them, and most were already filled.

There was a short line of people up front by the casket. I could see Olivia's head from where we stood. Her eyes closed, looking peaceful.

Olivia's parents were on the receiving line. So was Olivia's sister, whose name suddenly escaped me. She had been two years younger than us, and I hadn't had much interaction with her besides sometimes seeing her at Olivia's house. Olivia's father worked at a bank—something to do with loans—while Olivia's mother was an accountant. Or at least they had been back when we were in middle school.

Courtney took the lead. She grasped her program in one hand and leaned forward to give Mrs. Campbell a quick hug. Mrs. Campbell looked taken aback at first, unsure who this young woman was, and then recognition filled her face.

She forced a sad smile. "Courtney Sullivan, right?"

Courtney nodded, her expression all at once solemn, and gestured at me.

"We drove up together. I was so shocked when I heard what happened. Please accept our deepest condolences."

Mrs. Campbell's gaze focused on me. "Hello, Emily."

She said it quietly, almost with a flat affect, and I felt something wither deep inside me.

I offered up a quick, somber smile. "Hello, Mrs. Campbell."

She held out her hand, making it clear she didn't want to be surprised by another hug. Her hand felt thin in my own, her skin like paper.

Mrs. Campbell said, "It was very thoughtful of you to come. When your mother told me you might, I wasn't sure what to expect."

I didn't know how to respond to this, so I just nodded, shook Mr. Campbell's hand, and moved down the line to Olivia's sister.

Courtney said to her, "Do you remember Emily Bennett? Emily, do you remember Karen?"

Karen shared the same full face as Olivia. She wore a black sheath dress, her long brown hair spilling over her shoulders. She clutched a ball of tissues in her left hand, and sniffed as she smiled at us.

"Thank you both for coming. I'm not sure anybody else from school made it."

A quick glance around the room showed that most of the people were older—Olivia's parents' ages—and many looked like professionals. Most, I figured, were Olivia's coworkers, or people who worked with Mr. and Mrs. Campbell.

Karen pointed toward the front row, at a man and young boy in gray suits. She said that was her husband, Jerry, and their son, Dallas. Jerry wore horn-rimmed glasses and held Dallas on his lap, a cell phone propped up to distract the boy.

Karen wiped at her eyes. "I think Olivia would really appreciate that you two came. It would mean the world to her."

Courtney placed a hand on Karen's arm, gave it an encouraging squeeze, and stepped toward the casket.

My stomach tightened as I followed her. It wasn't that I got nervous around the dead. It was that Olivia was a friend—or had been, once upon a time. We'd gossiped about boys. Shared secrets. Painted each other's fingernails.

And now she was dead.

At least she looked peaceful. At least there was that. I remembered what her mother's Facebook post had said, about how she had been in so much pain. How Olivia had killed herself remained a mystery, as did the reason why, but she looked like she was at rest now, and in the end that seemed like the most anybody could ask for.

Secrets.

One of the most valuable currencies to a girl in middle school. The kind of thing that could make or break friendships. The kind of thing we obsessed over. We liked to gossip, but we made sure to keep our secrets within our group. Which made it especially strange when Mackenzie wanted us to take the blood oath and swear we'd never tell anybody what we'd done to Grace Farmer.

Secrets were the lifeblood of being a Harpy. The thing that kept us going. The thing that made us strong.

I remember one day in eighth grade—early in the school year, months before Grace showed up, when it felt like I was on the verge of being stripped of my status—I found Olivia in the bathroom outside the gym. She was in one of the stalls, sobbing so quietly it sounded like a cat's mewling.

I'd knocked on the stall door. "Is everything okay?"

The quiet sobbing halted, and there was a beat of silence before she answered.

"I'm fine."

"Olivia?"

Another beat, and then a *click* as the door was unlocked and pulled open, and Olivia stood there, wiping her eyes.

"Emily?"

"What's wrong?"

"Nothing."

"Tell me."

"I said it's nothing."

I'd crossed my arms, trying to give her the look Elise had perfected when she wanted someone to cut the bullshit. Elise got that look from her father, who dealt with criminals and lawyers in court, peddling their nonsense.

Olivia wiped at her eyes again, sniffed back tears.

"Just leave me alone, okay?"

Normally I'd listen to her, nod my head, apologize, scurry out of the bathroom, and act like the whole thing had never happened. But something was clearly bothering Olivia, and so I felt the need to step in, as Elise or Mackenzie typically would.

At first, I thought maybe it was snack related—I'd seen Olivia sneaking Oreos from her backpack just the day before—but the distress in her face was different, so I asked the first question that came to mind.

"Did somebody hurt you?"

Her eyes widened. "No! It's not like that."

"Then what is it?"

Maybe Olivia realized I wasn't going to give in, or maybe she really did want to tell somebody, because she sighed.

"It's just," she said, sniffing back more tears. Her gaze darted all over the bathroom so she wouldn't have to look at me. "My parents . . ."

"What about your parents?"

"I overheard them last night. They were arguing. They—" Her voice broke, and she started to tear up again. "I think they're going to get *divorced*."

I wasn't sure what to say. There were other girls at our school whose parents had gotten divorced, but so far none of our parents had done so. It didn't hit me until that moment that I'd never once imagined my own parents separating. While they sometimes argued, sometimes went through an entire family dinner without speaking to each other, their love was so pure that the thought of them being apart was devastating. I imagined if I'd learned my parents were talking about divorce, I'd have locked myself in a bathroom stall to cry about it too.

"You can't tell anybody," Olivia said, her eyes intense. "Karen doesn't know, and I don't *want* her to know. Promise me you won't tell the other girls. Please, *promise* me."

A secret. A secret between the two of us.

"I promise."

And I kept that promise, proud and true, until two weeks passed and we were all over at Mackenzie's house. Olivia hadn't gotten there yet, and Mackenzie had looked around like there was a crowd in her bedroom before leaning forward and lowering her voice.

"She made me promise not to tell anybody, but guess what's happening with Olivia's parents."

Destiny asked, "What?"

"They're getting divorced!"

Mackenzie nearly squealed it, like she couldn't contain her excitement, and the rest of the girls gasped, even me, because I knew that was expected.

As it turned out, it wasn't really true. While Olivia's parents had discussed separating, they'd ultimately decided to stay together. But that day, I acted surprised, like I hadn't already known. Like it wasn't already a secret Olivia and I had shared, just the two of us and nobody else.

Because, of course, it wasn't.

The commotion started halfway through the ceremony. Karen was telling a story about her wedding and how Olivia, her maid of honor, had been so nervous to make her speech but had done an amazing job, had everybody laughing and crying.

Right when Karen got to the part where Olivia read a poem she'd written for the newly wedded couple, voices sounded out in the hallway, tense and angry. The door at the back of the room opened, and a big man in his early thirties stepped inside. He was bald, had a thick beard, and was dressed in dark slacks and a shirt and tie. The moment he appeared, Mr. Campbell was on his feet, a steady finger pointed at the man.

"You are not welcome here."

He didn't yell it, but the intensity in the words caused everybody to shift their attention to the back of the room.

The man took a few steps forward, his hands held up in surrender. "I want to see her one last time."

The young man who'd been handing out the funeral programs hurried through the door. He placed himself between the man and the front of the room.

"Sir, I told you: you can't be here. My father is calling the police."

Mr. Campbell was already striding up the aisle toward the intruder. He didn't rush, walking at a measured pace, his face impassive.

"Philip, you need to leave."

Philip shook his head, his eyes starting to water. "But—"

"Don't!" Mr. Campbell held up his finger again, pointed right at him. "Don't do this here. Not today. Don't disrespect her memory like this."

Karen's husband, Jerry, had passed off Dallas to Mrs. Campbell and was on his feet, hurrying up the aisle to give his father-in-law backup.

The door opened again, and a new man stepped past Philip and turned so he was standing right next to his son. He was older and wore a dark suit, and I pegged him as the funeral director.

"The police are on their way," he said.

Philip stood, frozen, staring toward the front of the room at Olivia in the casket. More tears fell down his face. Several seconds ticked by, and then his shoulders dropped. He bent his head, turned, and exited.

It took a few minutes for everything to settle down—for Mr. Campbell and Jerry to return to their seats, for the funeral director to apologize for the inconvenience—and all that time Karen didn't move from her place at the front of the room. She stood there, still clutching a ball of tissues, until it became clear that everything had been reset and she should continue with her story.

"I . . . I don't remember where I stopped. So let me"—she paused, wet her lips—"let me start from the beginning."

The cemetery was ten minutes away. A white tent had been set up with several chairs underneath. That was where Mrs. Campbell and Karen sat, Karen holding her son while Mr. Campbell and Jerry and a few other men helped carry the casket from the hearse.

Courtney and I stood with the rest of the crowd. The sky was bright, and almost everybody wore sunglasses. I was glad I'd worn flats; otherwise, my heels would have kept sinking into the ground.

Once everything was set, the casket positioned and the family members seated, a pastor began the burial service.

Halfway through, Courtney nudged my arm.

I looked at her. She had her face tilted toward me, and because of her sunglasses, I wasn't sure what she meant at first. Then she lifted her chin, just slightly, and I glanced in the opposite direction.

Across the cemetery, maybe fifty yards away, Philip stood leaning against a pickup truck.

The pastor had just finished a prayer. Mr. Campbell rose from his seat. He stared off across the cemetery, past all the grave markers, toward

Philip. Without a word he walked forward until he reached the edge of the crowd and stood, hands at his sides.

Philip didn't move for the longest time. He stayed where he was, leaning against his truck. Finally, he shook his head and climbed inside. Seconds later, the pickup truck was coasting down the hill toward the cemetery's exit.

Mr. Campbell didn't move until the truck was out of sight. Then he turned and walked back to his seat.

"Sorry about that, Pastor Henry. Please continue."

When it was all over—when the casket had been lowered into the ground and it was clear that everybody was free to leave—I immediately turned toward the car. Courtney could stay and chat as long as she liked. I would be waiting when she was done.

But before I could even take two full steps, Karen found us.

"We're having a get-together back at the house. Would you two like to come?"

I turned, an excuse already forming on my lips, but Courtney beat me to it.

"Of course, Karen. We would *love* to."

9

The platters of cold cuts and veggies looked as bland and unappealing as you'd expect post-funeral platters to look, but that didn't stop Courtney from digging in. She loaded her small plastic plate with carrots and celery, took one of the rolls, stuffed it with sliced turkey, and added a slice of cheese. She only paused when she noticed me watching her.

"Aren't you hungry?"

"No."

"I'm *starving*. Haven't eaten all day."

She turned back to her plate, stuffed another roll with deli meat—this time, ham—and then nodded at me that she was finished.

I stepped back, turned to the rest of the house, but didn't know where to go.

Strangers were everywhere. Older strangers and younger strangers and strangers our age. Nobody spoke above a whisper, as if a normal tone would be somehow disrespectful to Olivia's memory.

Gently nudging me, Courtney whispered, "Come on."

I followed her through the crowd, glad we were moving. I had spotted Mrs. Campbell a few minutes ago—she was making her way through the house, thanking each person for coming—and I was hoping to avoid that interaction, if possible. Despite her flat tone when she'd spoken to me, she had been congenial at the viewing, but maybe that was because her dead daughter lay only yards away, and decorum didn't call for her to lose her shit.

Maybe she wouldn't lose her shit here, either—not today, at her own home, in front of all these guests. But the last time I had seen her, fourteen years ago, her displeasure had been clear. As far as Mrs. Campbell was concerned, her daughter would never have done the things she'd done if a few bad apples hadn't talked her into it. Olivia, Mrs. Campbell reasoned, was a nice girl who had fallen in with the wrong crowd.

Forget the fact that Mrs. Campbell had loved us in middle school, encouraging us to come over for sleepovers, always volunteering to drive us to the mall or the movies. She had wanted to be the cool mom, the one we could rely on, whom we might even be bold enough to share our secrets with, but once everything had fallen apart, she'd excommunicated us.

Courtney and I ended up on the back patio, interspersed with a few others who kept their conversations to whispers despite being outside. Several brand-new lawn chairs had been set up, a few still sporting price tags from Target. Courtney took one, I took the other, and we sat in silence, me watching the crowd, Courtney chowing down on her first sandwich.

To distract myself, I pulled out my phone. On that other timeline, I might have found a message from Daniel asking how things were going, a quick note saying that he missed me, maybe a kiss emoji, but in this reality, there was no message.

As I slipped the phone back into my purse, I felt Courtney's eyes on me.

"Checking in with the fiancé?"

For some reason I didn't want to acknowledge that I hadn't received any messages, either from Daniel or anybody else, so I nodded and said yes.

"What's his name again?"

"Daniel."

"And you said he's a doctor?"

"Emergency-room nurse."

Courtney started on her second sandwich, speaking between bites. "That sounds like a pretty intense job. When's the wedding date?"

"We haven't set it yet. Courtney, what are we doing here?"

Maybe she sensed the impatience in my voice. She watched me for several seconds, chewing the last bite of her sandwich, and swallowed. "We're celebrating Olivia's life."

I kept my gaze steady with hers. "We did that earlier. First at the viewing, then at the cemetery."

Courtney shrugged, taking a bite of celery. "What else do you have to do today?"

I opened my mouth to respond, my frustration having snowballed, but then suddenly everything became crystal clear.

Gossip. That's what this was about. Courtney had always loved gossip, probably more than any of the other girls. What was it she had said yesterday—how she had searched Facebook for hours trying to figure out how Olivia had passed away? She wanted that burning question answered, despite the fact it had nothing to do with her.

Based on her expression, she knew I had figured it out. She looked hesitant, unsure how I might react. But then her eyes shifted away from me; she smiled and set her plate aside as she rose from the lawn chair.

Karen stepped into view, wrapping her arms around Courtney. When they broke the embrace, Karen turned, leaning down to give me a quick hug too.

"Thank you both again for coming. My parents might not say it, but it means a lot."

"Of course," Courtney said. "We're happy to."

Karen had freshened up her makeup, the mascara no longer running. She surveyed the backyard, the few people milling about, and sighed.

"God, I could use a drink. I told my parents we should have something here, some wine at least, but they nixed the idea."

As both women were still standing, I rose to my feet as well.

Courtney said, "Can I ask you something?"

"Let me guess," Karen said. "You want to know about the guy at the funeral."

"Was he somehow responsible for Olivia's death?"

I didn't know why, but Courtney's bluntness shocked me. I shot her a warning look, but she ignored me, keeping her focus on Karen.

Karen released another breath, and shook her head.

"You don't know what happened, do you? Of course not. My parents have been reluctant to talk about it. It was actually on the news, but they asked that the media not release Liv's name."

Courtney asked, as innocent as could be, "What happened?"

Karen glanced around the patio once more, making sure nobody was listening.

"Liv took her own life," she whispered. "She jumped off a bridge, ended up in the Susquehanna River."

Courtney's hand went to her mouth, her eyes going wide. "Oh my God. That's awful."

Karen nodded, her bottom lip trembling. "The whole thing is horrific. And as far as my family is concerned, Philip is to blame."

I asked, "How so?"

"He was her fiancé. They'd been together a year and a half. The first two months they were together, he cheated on her. You ask me, he always had that look, like a guy who would cheat. You know what I mean, right?"

She waited for us to nod, to give her the satisfaction that we understood just what kind of a creep this guy was, and then said, "I never trusted him. He seemed nice, and he was always polite to my parents, even to me, but there was something . . . shady about him."

Karen glanced around the patio again to ensure nobody was listening, then grabbed one of the lawn chairs, dragged it over to ours, and sat down.

She leaned forward, her voice conspiratorial, and told us about how one night Philip had gone out drinking with his buddies. He'd gotten wasted and hooked up with an old girlfriend, then had waited a couple of days to tell Olivia.

When he finally did, he said he was too racked with guilt to tell her sooner and begged her to forgive him.

"And you know what?" Karen shook her head. "She did. I told her she was crazy, that she needed to drop his sorry ass, but she liked him a lot. She said she understood he was drunk and that stupid shit happens. I told Liv she was crazy. She said she didn't care, that she loved him."

After that, Karen went on, nothing happened for a year. Philip was on his best behavior. He proposed, and they set a wedding date for the fall. Olivia was happier than Karen had ever seen her. She was clearly in love with Philip, posting pictures of him on Facebook, tagging all the places Philip took her on dates, and sprinkling her status updates about Philip with emoji hearts. Olivia had told Karen she couldn't wait to have a baby of her own.

Everything was going great, and then—here Karen paused, shaking her head—Philip went and did it again.

Courtney's eyes went wide. "He cheated on her *again*?"

"Yep. And this time the asshole didn't even have the decency to confess."

Part of me wanted nothing to do with this conversation. It was just gossip, and I felt it disrespected Olivia's memory. But this last part made me curious.

"Then how did she find out?"

"The fucking cunt sent her pictures."

Karen's voice had risen higher than she had intended, catching the notice of the others on the patio. She glanced at them, stared until they looked away, and then swung her attention back to us.

Courtney said, "The girl Philip cheated with sent *pictures*?"

"Yeah. Can you believe it? Who the fuck does something like that?"

Something wasn't adding up, and I shook my head.

"Wait a minute. Are you saying Olivia killed herself because Philip cheated on her a second time?"

Karen looked incensed, like the whole thing was happening again. I imagined that if Philip decided to crash this party, she would go after him with a baseball bat.

"That's exactly what I'm saying. I mean, Liv has always suffered from depression. She was able to regulate it with her meds, but when that bitch sent those pictures, it broke my sister. She called me, crying, saying he had done it again, and I just"—Karen paused, looking all at once ashamed—"I told her, what did she expect? Once a cheater, always a cheater. I mean, I wish I hadn't said it. After Liv was found, I immediately thought maybe if I hadn't—"

She broke off, her eyes tearing, her mascara running again.

Courtney handed her a napkin and said softly, "You know you had nothing to do with it."

Karen wiped at her eyes, sniffed back the tears. "I know. But I just—I was so mean to her. I should have been nicer. I should have been more understanding."

I asked, "Why would this girl have sent Olivia pictures?"

"God knows. Like I said, she's a fucking cunt."

"But I don't understand. How would she even know who Olivia was?"

Karen shrugged. She admitted that she hadn't seen the pictures herself. Olivia had told her they were sent via Facebook, and nobody had managed to figure out Olivia's password yet. The family had even contacted Facebook about deleting her account, but so far they hadn't had much luck.

"And people keep posting stuff on her wall, telling her how much she's missed, like she'll ever read it. The whole thing drives me nuts."

Courtney asked, "Did Philip finally confess?"

"I don't think so. She may have reached out to him, I don't know. I refuse to talk to him. He's tried contacting me a few times. I had to block him on all my social media."

Karen paused again, staring down at the crumpled napkin in her hand.

"You see, Liv jumped off the bridge later that night. She'd called me, all upset, and I was such a bitch about it. Like I was rubbing it in her face. I . . . I should have been more understanding. Maybe then she wouldn't have jumped."

I traded glances with Courtney. I could see the regret in her eyes. She had wanted some gossip, and she'd certainly gotten it, but in the process she'd caused Olivia's sister to relive that terrible night. It hurt my heart to see Karen like this. I wanted to reach out, give her a hug, tell her that of course it wasn't her fault, but then Karen wiped at her eyes again and shook her head.

"I don't know who the girl was, but Liv did. I mean, she never said a name or anything, but she talked about the girl like she knew her. She didn't call her a bitch or a cunt or a whore, none of the stuff I sure as hell would've called her."

Courtney gave me another look, then leaned forward, placed a comforting hand on Karen's arm.

"What did Olivia call her?"

Karen's eyes shifted back and forth between us.

"See, that's the weird part. She called her a ghost."

10

We'd barely been in the car thirty seconds, the Campbells' home still visible in the rearview mirror as we drove through the quiet suburb, but Courtney couldn't contain herself any longer.

"Holy shit. Holy *shit.*"

My fingers tightened around the steering wheel, but I said nothing.

Courtney shifted in her seat to look at me. "Do you think it was her?"

I tried my best to focus on the oncoming traffic, the stop sign looming ahead—but her gaze burned into me like a solar flare. Still, I said nothing.

That didn't stop Courtney from trying the question again.

"Emily, do you think it was her?"

I glanced at Courtney, annoyed, wanting to tell her to be quiet, to stop being ridiculous, that *of course* it wasn't. Instead, I shook my head, kept my attention on the street.

Courtney was watching me. I could see her out of the corner of my eye. After a minute, the staring became too unnerving, and I glanced at her again.

"What?"

Courtney said nothing. I turned my face away, squeezing the steering wheel even tighter.

"Do you ever think about her?" Courtney asked.

I knew exactly who she meant, but still I played dumb.

"Who?"

"You know who."

I paused at a traffic light, watched the passing cars.

"It's been a while. What about you?"

Courtney shifted in her seat, leaning back to stare out her window.

"I actually thought about her the other day when I heard about Olivia . . . you know, taking her own life. God, we were so mean to that girl."

A full minute passed in silence, the only sound the radio on low volume and the hum of tires on the street as we neared the highway. It was late afternoon, and dark clouds had started to cluster on the horizon.

Finally I said, "It wasn't her."

Courtney shifted in her seat again. "But Karen said Olivia told her it was a ghost. A *ghost*, Emily. Why would she say that if she didn't mean Grace?"

"I don't know. Maybe Karen misheard her. Or maybe Olivia meant somebody else from her past."

Courtney snorted. "I can't tell whether you're being naive or just in denial."

"Why would Grace send Olivia pictures like that?"

"Why *not*? We practically destroyed that girl's life. Maybe she's looking for revenge."

"Don't be ridiculous."

"Why is it ridiculous? Grace did what she did because of us. Because of what we did to her. To be honest, I wouldn't blame her for wanting revenge."

I twisted my head to the side so fast it almost gave me whiplash.

"That's a fucked-up thing to say."

Courtney raised an eyebrow.

"Is it? Put yourself in her shoes. The new girl in school. All she wanted was to fit in with the popular girls. And we treated her like shit. Like our slave. Wouldn't you hold a grudge?"

I said nothing. Not because I had nothing to say, but because I didn't want to hear myself agreeing with Courtney. Of course I'd hold a grudge if I'd been treated the way we'd treated Grace. I had been treated badly by the group, but never to that extent. For me, it was mostly feeling powerless. Like the girls were always talking about me behind my back. Sometimes they'd volunteer me for menial tasks—to throw away their trash or get their drinks—but it had never gotten to the point where I felt like a slave.

Sometimes I wondered just how far I would have let them push things. Maybe if Grace hadn't come along, it would have gotten as bad for me as it had for her.

Courtney asked, "Who came up with the name, anyway?"

"I don't remember."

"The Ghost," Courtney whispered. She shook her head. "Grace the Ghost. Jesus Christ, we were fucking awful, weren't we?"

It wasn't that we had decided from the start that Grace was unworthy to be our friend. We tried to be nice to her. Or at least I did. But Mackenzie had realized immediately just how malleable Grace was. How easily she could be molded into whatever Mackenzie wanted. And Grace, maybe sensing she had no choice, did whatever Mackenzie—and later, the rest of us—told her to do.

But it hadn't stopped there. We'd needed to take away the one thing she owned, the one thing that made her who she was—her name. She had very pale skin, almost as if she had never been outside for more than five minutes, and long dark hair.

The Ghost, we'd called her when she wasn't around.

Did you see what the Ghost was wearing today?

Did you see the Ghost's hair? So greasy!

Did you get a whiff of the Ghost? Eww!

Courtney shifted again in her seat, pulling out her phone.

"You know what we need to do to confirm this? Find those pictures. I mean, I know it's been fourteen years, but we should be able to recognize her, right?"

We were on the highway now, about a half hour from Lanton. Those clustered clouds on the horizon were even darker in that direction.

Staring off at them, I said, "No."

Courtney frowned at me. "No what?"

"Just no. We're done with this. Olivia is dead. We went to the funeral, and now we're going home. That's it."

"But Karen said Olivia told her—"

"I don't care. It has nothing to do with us."

"Are you *kidding*? If Grace is out there seeking revenge, it has everything to do with us."

"Stop it, Courtney. She's not. She's just out there . . . living her life. We need to let her be."

"If she came back to screw with Olivia, what's to stop her from coming for one of us? Or *both* of us?"

I shot her a quick glance. "Don't be a bitch, Courtney."

"A *bitch*?"

"I'm done with this conversation."

"What the fuck—"

"I said I'm done."

I leaned forward and increased the volume on the radio, ignoring the daggers Courtney was glaring at me.

We drove the rest of the way back in silence, heading into the oncoming storm.

11

Grace Farmer had always haunted me, in one way or another.

In college, it was usually during class when we'd discuss the effects of bullying, or I'd sit in on sessions where kids talked to their therapists about the trauma of being bullied and abused by either their peers or their own family members. And I would wonder about the fallout from those three months in middle school, whether or not Grace ever had a chance to address what had happened to her.

Mostly, though, when I thought of Grace Farmer, I would not think of her as we had known her—the quiet girl with the button nose and shy smile—but rather Grace *before* she had ever walked into our lives.

This was a Grace Farmer I found myself coming back to again and again. A Grace who hadn't yet been tainted by our touch. Who hadn't yet stepped onto the stage of our middle school melodrama that would lead to so much pain.

Instead, this Grace Farmer was happy. Still curious about life. Excited about all the possibilities that awaited her.

Even now I can picture her and her mother as they drive south from wherever they once called home—we'd never gotten much out of Grace, though in truth that was probably because none of us cared.

I can't picture her mom well, because I never saw her except for one brief moment, and that was when she'd dropped off Grace at the start of that fateful Memorial Day weekend.

She had driven a beat-up red hatchback. She had frizzy hair. That was it.

Grace's features, however, are much more vivid in my mind. Her pale skin. Her sharp, dark eyes. Her long dark hair. A smattering of phantom freckles on her face.

I picture her sitting in the passenger seat, her window partway down, enough to allow the wind to come slicing in and cause her hair to dance wildly.

They're headed south, away from wherever they once called home, the red hatchback packed with all their things, or at the very least just the essentials, the stuff that will help them start a new life.

Was Lanton always their final destination, or were they just driving until something felt right, a place that called to them as home?

No matter the case, Lanton is where they ended up. They didn't keep going to one or two towns farther south. If they had, maybe things would have turned out differently for Grace. Maybe their lives wouldn't have been ruined.

I imagine Grace, like any fourteen-year-old girl, is excited for that first morning at Benjamin Franklin Middle School, but she's nervous, too, anxious about being the new kid.

She dresses in the new clothes. They're not very nice, not the most fashionable, but that's okay, because she's never really cared about such things. Her mom already has breakfast waiting; Grace scarfs it down, not wanting to be late, but even so they arrive at school a couple of minutes after the homeroom bell.

Her mom doesn't walk her inside. She was once Grace's age, and she knows how teenagers think. She places the hatchback in park, waits for Grace to lean over to give her a quick hug and kiss on the cheek, and then watches her daughter hurry toward the school entrance, her purple JanSport backpack hanging off her shoulder.

I picture the smile Mrs. Harrington, the front-office secretary, beams when Grace enters.

"Hello, dear. Are you Grace Farmer?"

Grace bites her lip, suddenly nervous, and nods.

"Perfect," Mrs. Harrington says. "Let me get your schedule. We'll have somebody walk you down to your classroom. In fact . . . Principal Ackerman?"

A man in a suit breezes through the school office but instantly pauses, smiles at the secretary before directing his smile at Grace.

Mrs. Harrington says, "This is our new student, Grace Farmer."

Principal Ackerman turns on the charm he does for all new students. He makes a fuss about how excited he is to have Grace in his school and that he's positive she'll love it, and would he be happy to walk Grace to her very first class on her very first day? Absolutely!

And so Grace follows Principal Ackerman, maybe a step or two behind, listening to him as he tells her about the different extracurricular activities Ben Franklin has to offer. By then, classes have started and the hallway is empty, Principal Ackerman's loafers squeaking off the freshly waxed linoleum, Grace starting to really feel the butterflies in her stomach. There aren't one or two or even a dozen; there are hundreds in there, fluttering about, and she takes a slow, steady breath, trying to steel her nerves because she can tell by Principal Ackerman's slowing pace that they're almost there.

"Ah, here we are," he says, gesturing toward one of a dozen doors in the hallway. **Mrs. Galloway's Class**, reads a laminated sign taped to the wall just beside the door.

It's one door out of a dozen, just one classroom out of several, and oh, how I wish Grace had somehow been assigned to another class. That she'd been enrolled in another school. That she and her mom had ended up in another town.

But those are all different realities, and in the true reality—one that would soon become darker for all of us—Principal Ackerman smiles at Grace one last time before he knocks on the door and reaches for the handle.

"Ready?" he asks.

12

A light rain pattered the car as we pulled into Highland Estates. I drove through the complex to building E and pulled up close outside the entrance.

Courtney was already rummaging through her purse. At first, I thought she was looking for her keys, but then she pulled out a crumpled ten-dollar bill.

"I hope this is enough for gas. It's all I have right now."

"Don't worry about it."

She held the crumpled bill out to me, her eyes downcast. She'd gone quiet after my outburst and hadn't spoken since, just shifted in her seat to stare out the window. I hadn't bothered to break the silence either.

"Take it, Emily."

"Keep it."

She dropped the money on the center console, and turned to unbuckle her seat belt.

I picked the bill up, stared at it for a moment, then frowned.

"If this is all you have right now, what are you going to use to pay the babysitter?"

Courtney froze, staring down at her lap for a beat before opening her door. She spoke without looking at me, her voice close but distant.

"I paid the sitter before I left. Thanks again for the ride."

"Wait."

I put more force into the word than I'd intended, the tone shocking even myself. But it did the trick. Courtney paused, her back to me, both feet planted on the pavement.

"There is no babysitter, is there."

I didn't bother making it a question, so maybe that's why Courtney didn't feel the need to answer it.

"Goodbye, Emily."

She started to lean out of the car, to stand, but I reached over and grabbed her arm.

"Courtney, don't tell me you left your eleven-year-old daughter alone this entire time."

Courtney didn't answer, only glared back at me.

"Do you know what it is I do?"

She wet her lips, her voice hoarse. "You're a therapist."

"That's right. And do you know what else I am? A state-mandated reporter. Which means that if I even *suspect* any child abuse or neglect, I have to call it in."

She'd looked uncertain, but now her face closed up. Her green eyes went flat.

"Do what you need to do, Emily. It won't be the first time Child Services shows up, and it probably won't be the last. Now if you don't mind, it's fucking raining, and I don't want to get any wetter than I already am."

She pulled her arm free, and slammed the door shut.

Drive away. That's what I thought at first. Just drive away, go to the town house, and take a shower. I felt dirty after what Karen had told us, as if the truth about Olivia's death was a stain that had soaked into my soul and would never fade.

I shut off the car, opened my door, and stepped out into the rain.

"Let me check on her."

In the entranceway, Courtney half turned to look back at me.

"What?"

"Let me check on Terri. Make sure she's safe. Then I won't have to call it in."

Her face tightened again, her eyes going narrow.

"I'm not a bad mother."

"I'm not saying you are. But like I said, I'm a state-mandated reporter. I have no choice. Unless I can check on her. Besides, I haven't seen her in years."

I forced a smile, hoping it would do the trick and erase whatever offense I'd shown, but I felt ridiculous standing in the rain, my hair getting soaked, and the smile quickly faded.

Her face still tight, Courtney sighed.

"Whatever. We're on the second floor, apartment three. I'll leave the door open."

◆ ◆ ◆

I'm not a bad mother.

It wasn't the first time I'd heard Courtney say that, though I had never expected to hear her say those words again.

That night before I'd left for college, a Friday or Saturday in late July, I'd gotten the call from Courtney's grandmother well past midnight. Jane—she always wanted me to call her that—had my cell phone number in case of emergencies.

She must have been watching for my car, because she opened the door before I was even halfway up the porch steps.

"I'm sorry to have called you. Thank you for coming."

Her voice was a raspy whisper, and she looked frazzled. I had known her for two years now, and I had never seen her like this.

I stepped inside, smelling the scented candles Jane kept around the house, and let her shut the door behind me.

"What's wrong?"

"She's drunk again. Worse than before. I don't know what to do with her when she gets like this."

"Did she drive home?"

"Some boy dropped her off. I never saw him before. He looked drunk too. God, she's eighteen years old. She should know better."

"Where's Terri?"

"Asleep in her crib."

"Courtney?"

"She's downstairs in the basement, still drinking."

This surprised me.

I glanced toward the basement door, and took a deep breath.

"I'll see what I can do."

Even before I opened the door, I heard the TV. The volume was loud—MTV, a music video roaring from the speakers. Courtney was slouched on the sofa, a bottle of vodka gripped between her legs. Her head bounced with the beat; she was trying to sing along to the music, but her inebriation caused her to fumble the words.

She didn't notice me until I was standing a few feet away, and even then she barely glanced my way, maybe thinking I was a figment of her imagination. Her eyes were heavy lidded as she lifted the bottle to her lips and took a swallow.

"I think you've had enough."

My voice startled her; she cried out and nearly jumped up from the couch. But when she realized it was me, she grinned and held out the bottle.

"Emily! Have a drink with me!"

I'd seen Courtney drunk before, but never this bad. Her words slurred together so much they were barely comprehensible.

I took the bottle and set it on a table. "You've had enough."

"Shut up."

"Courtney."

"You're not the boss of me."

"You've had too much to drink."

She snorted. "Like you fucking know. You could've come out with me, but you wanted to stay home and *pack*."

She put extra emphasis on this last word, and I realized that somehow she was making this about me. That the reason she'd gone out tonight was because I was leaving. I didn't want to believe it, but it didn't surprise me.

"You can't keep doing this, Courtney. It's dangerous."

"You don't know what you're talking about."

"What if something happened to you, something bad? Who would look after Terri? Jane isn't going to be around forever."

She shot to her feet, unsteady, swaying back and forth like she was on the deck of a ship.

"I'm not a bad mother."

For the first time her words had lost their slur, had taken on an edge. She stood there, glaring back at me, and then all at once her face crumpled.

"Yes, I am. I'm a terrible mother, aren't I?"

I reached out, meaning to comfort her, but she shook me off.

"I made a mistake. I shouldn't have . . . I shouldn't have had Terri. I can't be a mother. I can't do this. Maybe . . . maybe Terri would be better off if I was dead. Maybe I should do her a favor and just kill myself already."

She was rambling now, her eyes going wide, and without thinking, I slapped her across the face. It surprised both of us. Courtney's eyes were wide again, in shock now.

"Stop it," I said. "You don't mean that."

"I'm not cut out to be a mother. I can't do this."

"Yes, you can. You're stronger than you think."

"No, I—"

Her expression changed. I scanned the basement, spotted a plastic trash can in the corner, and managed to retrieve it just in time.

It took nearly two hours to make sure it was all out of her system, to help clean her up and get her into bed. I checked in on Terri, asleep in her crib, and then I was back at the front door ready to leave when Jane, now wearing her bathrobe, gave me a hug.

"Thank you again for coming. You're a very good friend to Courtney. I don't know what she would do without you."

I said nothing. I was feeling shaken. Had already decided that this was the last time I would see Courtney. But how was I supposed to explain that to Jane? I couldn't. She wouldn't understand. Part of me didn't understand it myself.

Courtney's words were ringing in my ears. I could see her, bent over the trash can, waiting for another bout of vomit, asking about Grace.

Asking, "Do you ever think about her?"

Asking, "Do you ever feel guilty about what we did?"

Saying, "If anybody should feel guilty, it's you."

Saying, "If it wasn't for you, none of it ever would have happened."

13

Despite Courtney's promise, the door was closed, and I didn't feel right opening it on my own. I knocked and waited maybe ten seconds before I heard movement. Then the handle turned and Courtney stood there, no expression on her face.

"I said the door would be open."

It was like we were no longer the good friends we'd been on the drive up to Harrisburg. Which made sense. That's usually what happened when you called somebody a bitch and threatened to call Child Services on them.

Courtney motioned for me to enter. I hesitated. Not because I didn't want to see Terri—I'd always loved the girl—but because I was afraid of what I'd find inside. A pigsty. An unsafe environment. Terri in dirty clothes, not having bathed in over a week. No food in the cabinets. It may have sounded extreme, but I'd heard of homes like that. And if that was the case, I'd have no choice but to notify Child Protective Services. Which probably meant Terri would be taken from the home.

"There's no light in the stairwell."

I said it just to say something, to break the uneasy silence, and felt awkward.

Courtney's gaze didn't leave mine.

"I know. Been that way for weeks. I've complained to the landlord about it, but nothing's ever done. That's what happens when you've got Section 8. Now, are you coming in or what?"

I stepped inside, and Courtney closed the door and headed deeper into the apartment. The place had a distinct odor, a sort of ubiquitous mildew scent. It wasn't clean, but it wasn't necessarily dirty either. *Cluttered* was a better word.

I turned the corner into the small living room to find Terri lying on the carpet, her knees bent, her socked feet in the air. She was using colored pencils to draw on a large piece of paper.

Courtney said, "Terri, this is Miss Emily."

I was Miss Emily now, not Aunt Emily.

Terri looked up from her drawing. Her dark hair was in braids, framing her pretty face. The TV was on, some Disney Channel show, and the light from the screen flickered off her pink rectangular-framed glasses.

"Hi."

"I bet you don't remember me. The last time I saw you, you were barely a year old. I went to school with your mother."

Courtney said, "Terri, would you like to show Miss Emily what you're drawing?"

Terri set her colored pencils aside, climbed to her feet, and brought over the piece of paper, holding it up so I could see what she'd been working on.

I was stunned. The picture was good. Really good. It looked almost as if Terri had traced it, but I didn't see any pencil marks.

It was a turtle, standing on two legs, a backpack on its shell. The turtle wore rectangular-framed glasses just like Terri's, only its glasses were black.

"This looks amazing, Terri."

"Thank you. That's Jefferson. He's the main character in my book." Terri looked down at the picture as if she were seeing it for the first time. She wrinkled her nose. "It's still a rough draft. I have a couple more pages to do. But in this story, Jefferson has his first day of school."

"What's the book called?"

Terri offered up a nervous smile. "*Jefferson's First Day of School.*"

I gave an impressed nod and glanced at Courtney, who stood in the doorway, her arms crossed. I remembered her talking, only hours ago, about how smart and talented her daughter was, how she read a couple of books a week. It hadn't really registered with me at the time.

"I can't wait to read it when it's done."

Terri shifted her eyes away, embarrassed by the attention.

"Thank you. Mom is going to help me try to get it published."

I glanced a question at Courtney, who uncrossed her arms and cleared her throat.

"Earlier this year, some of the students in Terri's class volunteered to read to the kindergartners. One of the kindergartners Terri read to didn't like any of the books, so Terri said she would come up with one of her own. She started working on it and asked me how she could get it published. I told her she should finish it first."

I smiled again at Terri. "That's amazing."

She looked away, smiling herself. "Thank you."

Courtney said, "Keep working on your picture, baby. I'm going to show Miss Emily around real quick, okay?"

Terri nodded and then offered her free hand to me. "It was nice to meet you."

I shook her small, delicate hand. "It was nice to see you again, Terri."

As Terri returned to her spot on the carpet, I stepped out into the hallway with Courtney.

I whispered, "She's incredible."

Courtney nodded. "She is one of a kind."

There was only one bedroom. When Courtney flicked on the lights, I expected to see a large bed, but a twin sat on the floor. Two bookcases leaned against the wall, each of them stacked high with middle grade and YA books.

"This is Terri's bedroom?"

Courtney nodded but said nothing.

"Where do you sleep?"

"You saw the couch in the living room? It's a pullout."

"Why don't you get a larger apartment?"

The instant the question left my mouth, I regretted it.

Courtney's face tightened again, her eyes once more going flat. "If I could afford it, I would."

Leave. That's what I told myself right then, just as I had told myself to drive away back in the parking lot. But I couldn't leave, not yet.

"So it's just you and her."

"Yes."

"What about Jane?"

"She passed away."

Even though I hadn't seen or talked to Courtney's grandmother in years, the news staggered me.

"I'm so sorry. When?"

"Three years ago."

"What about your parents?"

"My dad's gone, too, and until the day he died, he wanted nothing to do with me or his 'half-breed' grandchild."

The term made me wince, which seemed to fill Courtney with additional power.

"*Half-breed*. He actually said that. He called Terri that. And when he did, I promised myself I would never speak to my parents ever again."

"You work, though, right?"

"I work as a cashier at Walmart, Emily. It barely pays minimum wage, but I make just enough that I don't qualify for food stamps. You have to understand, everything I do, I do for Terri. The food we can afford goes to her. I saw your face when I was loading my plate back at Olivia's parents' house. You were judging me."

"No, I wasn't."

"Yes, you were. I know you were. Do you think I would ever tell Mackenzie or Elise where I live or work? Of course not. Part of me is always going to worry about what they think of me, even after all these years. But I thought you were different."

"I am different."

"No, you're not. You may have gotten older, but you're the same mean girl you were back then. You're still just a Harpy."

Her eyes were narrowed, her gaze steady on my face. She took a step forward, and I found myself taking a step back.

"Why didn't you want to go to Olivia's funeral? Because you think you're better than everybody else. That you can write off old friends like they don't exist. To be honest, Emily, I feel sorry for you. You have a nice life, got the handsome fiancé, the big ring on your finger, but you still can't be happy. It's kind of pathetic."

Courtney led me back out into the hallway.

"I can give you the rest of the tour, but there isn't much else to see. We don't have much food in the kitchen, and most of what we've got is what I can pick up from the food bank. I try to make sure Terri eats as healthy as she can, but sometimes it's just not possible."

"How do you get to work?"

"I take the bus. I can't afford a car, let alone insurance. Now, you've seen Terri's living situation. If you feel she's not safe, then do what you need to do and call Child Services. Otherwise, I think it's time for you to leave."

Courtney stared at me, waiting for me to say something else. I didn't. I stepped out into the hallway and started back toward the front door. As I passed the living room, I paused briefly to say goodbye to Terri.

"Great seeing you again, Terri. I can't wait to read your book when it's done."

Terri beamed up at me. "Thank you! I can't wait until I'm finished!"

I kept moving, my hand slipping into my purse.

Courtney stepped up behind me, her voice a harsh whisper.

"Don't."

My fingers pinching the crumpled ten-dollar bill in my purse, I slowly turned.

"I told you," she whispered. "It's gas money."

I stared at Courtney, and she stared straight back. I realized I wasn't going to win this. That whatever else I might try, I would only make things worse.

As if reading my thoughts, Courtney's eyes hardened.

"We don't need your pity. We don't need anything from you."

I watched her for another moment. Searching her face for any vulnerability, anything that might help lighten the moment. But there was nothing.

I kept the crumpled bill in my purse, stepped out into the hallway, and started toward the stairs.

The moment they entered the apartment, her mother got on the phone. She'd been agitated in the car—her fingers practically strangling the steering wheel, her angry voice cracking as she railed on and on about those little bitches—and she became even more heated once the person on the other end answered.

"Sheila, you're never gonna believe it. Those little bitches went too far. What's that? No, I don't know, exactly—Grace won't tell me—but there's a nasty bruise on the back of her head. That one rich girl's parents, the one who took them to the lake, they acted like they had no idea what happened. I should sue them. Do you think I should sue them? Maybe I should get a lawyer."

She left her mother in the living room, the phone cord wrapped tight around her hand, which was one of those things her mother did when she was anxious.

The apartment was small, only two tiny bedrooms and one bathroom.

"Grace, honey," her mother called after her, "where are you going?"

She heard the worry in her mother's voice. Her gaze shifted away from her bedroom to the door on her right.

"The bathroom."

Her mother said nothing else, just waited a beat before restarting her phone conversation, her tone becoming even more frenzied.

"I'm telling you, Sheila, this place ain't any better than home. Maybe we never shoulda left. I thought the kids would be nicer down here. But they're animals."

She went into the bathroom and turned on the light. One of the bulbs above the mirror flickered a few times before going out. But that was okay; there were two other bulbs, and their light was bright enough.

She stared at herself in the mirror, at her small pale face, her long dark hair. The spot on the back of her head pulsed with pain.

She'd taken a shower once the girls had returned and untied her and led her back to the cabin. She had gotten most of the blood out of her hair, but not all of it, because her mother had noticed it almost immediately when she'd picked her up. The other girls had looked so scared, like Grace would tattle on them. The fear had been palpable, though it hadn't lasted long, at least for Mackenzie and Elise. They'd known that Grace wouldn't tell.

And she hadn't. She hadn't said a word, though she remembered what they'd said. That she was worthless. A waste of space. That the world would be better off if she'd never been born.

The metal rings screeched on the rod when she pulled the shower curtain back, and she leaned forward, put the stopper in the drain, turned both taps on full.

Back in the living room, her mother was sitting on the couch, the phone still to her ear, the cord wrapped even tighter around her hand.

"I don't know what's wrong with her. She's been strange the last month or two. So quiet. She won't tell me anything."

Her voice was a hushed whisper, and when she realized her daughter had returned to the room, she stopped at once, looked at Grace, and forced an awkward smile.

Ignoring her, Grace continued into the kitchen. Sunlight slanted through the window, pooling on the cheap linoleum floor. She opened the drawer by the microwave.

They didn't have many utensils. It was just the two of them. A few forks. A few spoons. A few butter knives. Only one steak knife.

Grace pulled it out, felt the sharp edge.

"Grace, honey," her mother called again, "are you sure you're okay?"

She paused briefly, not sure what to say. In the end, she decided not to speak, and returned to the bathroom, closing the door behind her. Twisting the knob to lock it.

She placed the knife on the edge of the tub and started to undress. First her shoes. Then her socks, T-shirt, shorts. She stripped off her bra and her underwear last and stood in front of the mirror.

The Ghost. That was what the girls called her. They thought she didn't know, but she knew. She knew more than they thought she did.

The tub was almost full, a tiny tumultuous ocean contained by porcelain. Grace placed her hand in the water to test the temperature, adjusted one of the taps, and waited another minute before she shut both off.

She heard her mother's distant voice. She heard the blood thumping in her ears. She heard the taunts and laughter of the girls from last night, echoing in her head.

Grace ignored them all and stepped into the water.

PART II:

Vesper

14

"So no nightmares?"

"None."

"That's positive, right?"

"I guess."

"Emily, last week you told me you'd had the same nightmare twice. Now a whole week's gone by and you haven't had any nightmares at all. I'd call that positive."

It was Friday afternoon, which meant we made up the same tableau we did every week: Lisa draped in another bright bohemian dress, sitting with her back straight on the mesh ergonomic chair in front of her desk, legs crossed, notepad on her lap; me on the right-hand side of the leather couch, my purse beside me, trying not to feel as small and inconsequential as I typically did during therapy sessions.

Staring at the artisanal clock on the wall, I asked, "Have you ever had a client kill herself?"

Lisa was silent.

I shifted my focus away from the clock, back to Lisa. She was still watching me, but there was something different about her face, a tightness I hadn't seen before.

"Sorry. That's none of my business. But it's just . . . Olivia's sister said Olivia had depression. That she was taking medication for it. She didn't mention therapy, but I've been wondering all week whether or not that would have helped. Maybe she did see a therapist, and maybe that person tried to help her work through her depression. Maybe . . . maybe they didn't do enough. Or maybe the therapist did everything that could be done. Maybe she pushed Olivia as hard as she could, but none of it made any difference in the end."

I paused, shook my head, glanced back at the clock on the wall.

"I wondered how I would have dealt with Olivia as a patient. I mean, obviously I couldn't have seen her because we share a history, but like somebody in Olivia's position. Especially knowing then what I know now. I wonder how hard I would have pushed her to try to get to the root of her depression. I wonder . . . I wonder a lot of things, because that's my greatest fear: a client of mine killing herself, and the knowledge that I could have prevented it."

Lisa shifted in her chair, and softly cleared her throat.

"Every therapist I know has the same fear, Emily. But there's only so much we're able to do. Your friend could have had the greatest therapist in the world, seen the best psychiatrist prescribing the best medication, and in the end maybe none of it would have mattered. Our job is to help people, but ultimately those people are the ones that need to want to help themselves."

"You don't think Olivia wanted to help herself?"

"I didn't know her. All I know is what you've told me."

I stared again at the clock, not sure what more to say. I usually enjoyed these sessions—Lisa's mere presence oftentimes put me at ease—but today I didn't want to be here.

All week I'd been thinking about how Karen most certainly must have heard Olivia wrong when Olivia called the woman who'd slept with her fiancé a ghost, and typically I could share that with Lisa—she would listen and give me advice—but already I had soured things.

Because I'd lied to her. I was still having the nightmare. Seeing myself in that school hallway. Approaching the girl, her wrists raining blood. Every time I closed my eyes, she was there.

Lisa did that thing where she kept watching me, waiting for me to speak. When I didn't, she quietly cleared her throat.

"Everything good with your clients? Last time you mentioned a new patient. The cutter."

"Chloe. I saw her yesterday. Half the session was dealing with her mom, trying to wrap up the intake so I could get some one-on-one time with the girl."

"What are your initial thoughts so far?"

"I got the sense during our session yesterday that she might be gay. Or at the very least is questioning. And it's causing a lot of stress at home. Her mother mentioned they went to church every week. I think maybe Chloe's scared to come out to her parents and cuts herself as a means of escape."

I didn't mention how I'd spent the entire time thinking about Grace. Seeing a shadow of Grace in Chloe, in the way she sat on the couch, her shoulders slouched forward. Hearing an echo of Grace's voice every time Chloe spoke.

"How has your sleep been?"

"Fine."

"And your relationship with Daniel?"

"I don't want to talk about Daniel."

Lisa continued to watch me. A good minute passed in silence with the two of us staring at one another. Then Lisa, never one to back down, smiled.

"Remind me, how long have the two of you been engaged?"

"I said I don't want to talk about Daniel."

"It's been, what, five years now?"

She knew she was overestimating the time frame. She was doing it on purpose. To provoke me.

"If you were to go home later today and tell Daniel you wanted to get married next month—or, hell, next week—what do you think he'd say? After all, you told me he was always pressing you to set the wedding date, always bringing up how much he wanted children. But I realized recently that you barely mention him anymore. It's been at least a year. Are you two even still together?"

I didn't want to play her mind games. Not today. Not with everything else going on. So I sat in my place on the couch, kept my mouth shut, and just stared back at her. Letting her know that I wasn't going to let her win.

Lisa shifted in her chair and recrossed her legs.

"Are you familiar with the boiling frog parable? You know, that if you put a frog in boiling water—"

"Yes, I am, and it's a stupid example. It's not even based in reality. I read somewhere about how a scientist actually tried it, and the frog jumped out before it was cooked to death."

I said this with some snark in my tone, hoping to put Lisa on the defensive, but she continued without missing a beat.

"The point is, Emily, you've been with Daniel for several years now. You were going to get married, but then your father passed away. Believe me, I know that can be traumatic. I lost my mother when I was a teenager, and I still think about her."

"Where are you going with this?"

"You used to talk about Daniel all the time. Even after you'd postponed the wedding, you would still talk about him, and when you did, you were happy. Now I bring up Daniel, and look how you get."

"So are you saying I'm the frog or the boiling water? Or am I the pot on the stove?"

I was purposely being difficult, trying to provoke Lisa, but she wasn't having any of it.

"You and Daniel might have the best relationship in the world. I certainly hope that's the case. But from where I'm sitting, it seems like you both have been in that metaphorical pot for some time now. The water is getting hotter and hotter, and it seems like both of you are waiting for the other one to jump out first."

Silent, I stared at Lisa. She stared back at me. I thought she was going to try to wait me out again, but she cleared her throat and said, "Obviously you're irritated with me right now, so I might as well dive straight in. There's something I've been wondering for a while."

I wet my lips, held her stare. "What's that?"

"The thing that's truly holding you back with Daniel. It's my impression you don't want to marry him anymore, but you do still care for him; otherwise, you would have broken up with him long ago. And Daniel, from what I remember, seems like the kind of guy who isn't going to break up with you first. He's a good guy, but emotionally he isn't strong enough to stand up for himself. So you're stuck. And maybe that's what you want. I've always thought part of you feels like you aren't allowed to be happy, not after what you did to Grace. Like it's some type of perpetual penance. It's why you never had any serious relationships before Daniel."

"That's not true. I had a serious boyfriend in high school."

"Oh yes. Ben something? If I remember correctly, he started talking about marriage, children, and suddenly you two broke up. Would you say that was a coincidence?"

I didn't answer.

"Maybe you decided it was okay to be happy, and you were ready to marry Daniel, start your life with him. But when your father passed away, you saw how much the loss affected your mother. Part of you became scared of being alone. You like being in a relationship—you like the safety of always knowing somebody is there for you—but at the same time, that other part has decided you still aren't allowed to be happy, so both parts keep pulling back and forth in a never-ending tug-of-war."

Beside me on the couch, my purse vibrated: a text message. I took it as a welcome opportunity to focus my attention elsewhere. To get Lisa to stop picking at a wound that kept scabbing over but never properly healed.

I pulled out my phone and glanced at the screen.

"What's wrong?" Lisa asked.

Something in my face must have given it away, but I shook my head and rose to my feet.

"I have to go."

Lisa leaned forward in her chair. "Is everything okay?"

My phone vibrated again. I dropped it back in my purse, pulled the strap over my shoulder, and headed for the door.

"Everything's fine. I'll see you next week."

As I stepped into the parking lot—the midday sun warm and bright—I pulled the phone back out of my purse.

It was my mother. She'd sent only two texts this time.

Do you remember Destiny Marshall?

I just learned she died ☹

15

Put a frog in boiling water and it'll jump out right away.

Put a frog in tepid water, slowly turn up the heat, and eventually the frog will cook to death.

I gave Lisa a hard time, but I knew exactly what she meant. I'd thought about the same thing many times. Not regarding my relationship with Daniel, but my friendship with the girls in elementary and middle school. Especially middle school, when things had started to escalate. When the sweet, pretty girls had started to become more manipulative. Started to figure out what they could get away with, what power they could wield.

Had Emily Bennett been a new girl in middle school, would she have sensed the toxicity oozing from the clique and stayed far away? I like to think so. To think that, because she hadn't grown up with Elise Martin and Mackenzie Harper as friends, she'd have established a healthy sense of worth. That she would have been happy with her life, content with who she was and friendly with everybody she encountered.

At the same time, she would have known to steer clear of the popular girls. She would have sensed that there was something off about them. They weren't *bad*, so to speak, but they weren't good either.

Unfortunately, that version of Emily Bennett never existed. Instead, she'd met Elise Martin on the very first day of kindergarten and they became best friends. That was when little Emily, just six years old, was placed in the tepid water. And from that day forward, the heat had started to increase, bit by bit.

Ben Franklin Middle School was located in the affluent suburbs of Lanton, so the majority of its students were white. Which meant when Destiny Marshall came to our school in the fall of eighth grade, everybody noticed more so than usual.

One of our math teachers—Mrs. Galloway, a frail, dark-haired woman who dressed like it was still the 1970s—had this annoying habit of making new transfer students stand up in front of the class on their first day to tell everybody about themselves. The way classes were structured, our group was oftentimes split up, so it was Mackenzie and Olivia who had been in math that morning when Mrs. Galloway noticed a new name on her attendance sheet for first period.

The elderly woman surveyed the room, her chin tilted down so she could gaze over her tortoiseshell eyeglasses, until she spotted the new arrival. Then she smiled—"She looked like a shark," Olivia would later say—and asked Destiny to come up.

Destiny didn't seem at all nervous as she strode to the front of the classroom. In fact, the way Mackenzie described it, the new girl looked thrilled to get to speak. She had long black hair and dark skin, and wore the same kind of trendy clothes as Mackenzie and Elise. Calvin Klein jeans, ribbed-hem Ralph Lauren sweatshirt. Mackenzie would later admit that she felt jealous at first, that Destiny had automatically become an enemy to her—and thus to the rest of us—but that quickly changed when Destiny smiled at the class.

"Hi, my name is Destiny, and I think it's pretty mean of Mrs. Galloway to make me come up here like this, but whatever."

A few audible gasps sounded around the room. Mrs. Galloway's severe expression somehow darkened, but Destiny kept on going without missing a beat.

"My dad works as a district manager for Macy's, and he was recently transferred to this area, so that's why we moved. My mom used to be an actress in Broadway musicals, but she never played any major roles; she was just always in the chorus. Then one day she met my dad, and they got married and had my older brother, and she decided to stop acting. A year later she had me. Because of my mom, I love to act. I've been in every school play since elementary, and I hope to try out for the play here. I also love animals, especially horses. I've taken riding lessons and hope to continue once my parents find a decent riding school around this area."

Without another word, Destiny started toward her seat, the sound from the soles of her white Michael Kors slip-on sneakers echoing in the sudden silence.

Mrs. Galloway watched her the entire way. Mackenzie would later tell us she had her doubts about Destiny's story—"A district manager for Macy's?" she'd say with a mixture of excitement and skepticism—but there was something about how easily Destiny had spoken, how directly, that made it clear the new girl was telling the truth.

Mackenzie waited for Olivia, who was sitting two rows in front of her, to glance back her way. Then she allowed a slight nod.

Without input from anybody else, Mackenzie had made the decision.

Destiny would be a Harpy.

◆ ◆ ◆

Destiny instantly gelled as part of our group. She was the missing piece that made the puzzle complete.

By that point, I'd already begun to feel like my time as a Harpy was coming to an end. I'd started to overanalyze conversations, even quick back-and-forths in the hallways, trying to decipher some hidden meaning to somebody's joke or tone. When I saw a folded note pass between two girls during class, I would immediately assume it was about me, that they were making fun of my worn Keds or my faded Jordache jeans or a pimple I hadn't managed to properly conceal with makeup.

Maybe that's why, at first, I avoided Destiny as much as possible. I was nice to her when she was around, but it was fake niceness, the kind perfected by Mackenzie. Maybe Destiny sensed it; maybe she didn't. I didn't care. It wasn't that everything was perfect before she came, but I felt that her presence somehow made me weaker in the eyes of the group. And because of that, I resented her.

My opinion changed the week before Christmas. We were all at the mall food court, holiday music drifting down from the speakers in the high ceiling, a distant bell ringing nonstop from the guy standing by the red Salvation Army bucket.

A rival clique—this one led by Denise Brown, whom we had known for years, a counterpart to Mackenzie in a way—was sitting off on the other side of the food court, and they kept glancing over at us, giving us dirty looks, because the boy Denise had been dating—Billy Maddox—had broken up with her and was currently dating Mackenzie (in part because we'd started a rumor that a pimple on the side of Denise's mouth was really an STD), though the way Mackenzie said it, she didn't even like the boy, just agreed to go out with him because she knew it pissed off D.B.

We called Denise D.B. to her face all the time. To teachers or anybody else who didn't know better, it stood for her initials. The way we meant it was for Diving Board, because we liked to say Denise's chest was so flat it was like she was smuggling a diving board in her training bra. Denise knew this, of course, but there was nothing she or the rest of her group could do about it.

Back when we were in sixth grade, one of the eighth-grade cliques had a falling-out, and one of the girls, to get back at the others, had stolen their burn book—a journal where they wrote down all the mean shit about other kids in the school—and made copies and distributed it to everybody in the cafeteria during lunch one day. It had become a huge deal; several of the students didn't come to school for a week, and Principal Ackerman had eventually made us all sit through an assembly about the dangers of bullying.

Because of this, Mackenzie and Elise had realized that moving forward we needed to be smart about whom we made fun of and whom we targeted, that we never left any evidence that might later be used against us. This had especially worked to our advantage when, just for the hell of it, we'd started an awful rumor about Elise—the perfect target, in our opinion, because everybody in the school liked Elise—and made it so the evidence all pointed back at D.B. and her crew, who of course had adamantly denied starting such an awful rumor. But the more they'd denied it, the guiltier they'd looked, and in the end, all of them had gotten detention and been forced to write apology letters to Elise.

Anyway, D.B. and the rest of her gang were sitting off on the other side of the food court, and they kept giving us these dirty looks. We gave them dirty looks right back, though ours were dirtier. Occasionally a middle finger would get flashed, and I started to worry that we might get into a fight, especially when Mackenzie made a blow job gesture at D.B.

I pictured the melee that would ensue—chairs tipping back as everybody shot to their feet, plastic food trays flying through the air, painted fingernails scratching and digging at faces—but then D.B. dramatically huffed and got up and stormed off, and the rest of us laughed as her friends scurried after her.

Then, all of a sudden, Mackenzie looked at me, and the smile slid off her face.

"You know, I just realized something," she said. "I don't think Bennett's ever borrowed anything yet."

Borrowed. Elise once told me they used that word because they didn't *steal* stuff. Stealing was what bad people did, and the Harpies weren't bad. If we wanted to pay for whatever we took, we could do so—all except me, of course. Borrowing was all about the fun. Pushing the limits. Once Elise had "borrowed" a tube of lipstick from Sephora and tossed it in the trash on her way out of the mall like it was no big deal. For her and the other girls, it really wasn't. It was just a rush. A way to kill time. To see how far they could take things and get away with it.

But me, well, I had managed to get by so far without having to borrow anything. Until today. Just six days before Christmas. The mall was packed. Parents and children, young and old couples everywhere. Also, mall security guards, with their gray uniforms and walkie-talkies and badges. Because of the holiday season, there were more of them than usual.

"Of course Emily has," Elise said, taking a sip from her Diet Coke. "Remember, I told you about the time I was with her in Sears. She borrowed a rose-gold pendant necklace."

While Elise and I may have been together at Sears in the past, I'd never stolen anything, and Mackenzie knew it.

"Well," she said, still watching me, "I wasn't there. Double Stuf, were you there?"

"No," Olivia said quietly.

"What about you, Courtney?"

Before Courtney could answer, I looked Mackenzie right in the eye and said, "What if I don't want to borrow anything?"

She said, "Who says it's your decision?"

And just like that, it became clear I had no choice. Elise had tried to cover for me, but it was no use. Even if I *had* borrowed something, Mackenzie would refuse to believe it unless she saw it with her own eyes.

I imagined Mackenzie making the other girls swear to never talk to me again. She had that kind of power. The only one who would ignore her would be Elise, and while I still thought of Elise as my best friend, I didn't want to be kicked out of the group. That was the last thing I wanted.

"Fine. What do you want me to borrow?"

Mackenzie shrugged and started to examine her bright-red nails, like I was wasting her time.

"Whatever. I don't care."

Courtney said, "How about Hot Topic?"

Olivia grinned. "Or the Disney Store."

"Not the Disney Store," Elise said. "What is she going to borrow, a stuffed Mickey Mouse?"

Mackenzie looked at me now, a smile in her eyes.

"No, I like the idea of Hot Topic. Borrow something edgy. Something punk rock."

I knew there was no arguing with her. As I stood up from my seat, I felt more nervous than I'd ever felt in my life.

To my surprise, Destiny also stood.

"I'll go in with her," she said.

Mackenzie made a face. "Why?"

"I'll be a black girl in their store." She smirked. "All the employees will be watching me."

And so we went, Destiny and I, weaving through the crowd, past the families and couples and security guards. Blood was pounding in my ears. My breathing had started to increase.

Destiny leaned forward to whisper in my ear.

"Relax. It'll be fine."

But it wasn't fine. I wandered around Hot Topic like I had no idea where I was going. I felt all the employees watching me, even though they weren't. I kept looking around for hidden cameras, which would be used to prove to my parents what a criminal their daughter had become.

I scanned the store for items that could be slipped into a pocket—a key ring, some jewelry—but every time I picked something up, I looked over my shoulder to make sure I wasn't being watched, which made me all the more conspicuous.

Finally, Destiny sidled up beside me. Because of the loud rock music pouring from the speakers, she had to nearly shout in my ear to be heard.

"Let's go."

I felt even more panicked then, realizing my time was up. The girls would be waiting for us outside the store. Mackenzie would expect me to have nothing, and she wouldn't be disappointed.

"Not yet."

Destiny grabbed my hand and started to pull me toward the front of the store.

"Let's *go*."

Who was I kidding? I wasn't going to borrow anything. I knew stealing was wrong, and I just couldn't do it. And so I let Destiny lead me, pulling me forward, leaning in to give me a hug to let me know that everything was going to be okay.

The hug surprised me; it didn't make sense, not until we'd left the store and spotted the girls lingering outside Victoria's Secret. That was when Destiny whispered, "Your left-hand jacket pocket."

Frowning at her, I touched the outside and felt something there.

Mackenzie stood with one UGG boot in front of the other, arms crossed.

"Well?"

I nodded, feeling a pride I'd never felt before.

Mackenzie's blue eyes narrowed. "Show me."

"Not here," Elise said. "Let's head back to the food court."

Halfway back, with Mackenzie swaggering ahead of me, I slipped the item from my pocket. Even I was surprised when I saw what it was:

a black cord bracelet with five white beads. Each bead sported a letter, and those letters together spelled a word that nearly made me laugh out loud. But I kept my face straight when I passed off the bracelet to Mackenzie.

The beads spelled out BITCH.

Elise and Olivia sniggered. Courtney held a hand to her mouth to hide her grin.

Mackenzie didn't look all that amused.

"Funny," she said.

She took the bracelet, ran her thumb over the beads, and tossed it in the nearest trash can.

I never did thank Destiny. There wasn't a moment when we were alone in the next week, and after more time passed, it felt weird bringing the whole thing up. But she didn't seem to mind. It was like our own little secret.

Still, I felt like I needed to prove myself, especially after Grace Farmer showed up. Like Destiny, Grace had no problem stealing. When she'd passed off her stolen item to Mackenzie at the mall, Mackenzie had given me a knowing smile. Like she knew I'd cheated and was just waiting for the right time to use that bit of knowledge against me. I didn't think Destiny had told her. Still, I figured it wouldn't be the last time Mackenzie tried to embarrass me in front of the group. So I decided to practice. To see something and just take it. To figure out how far I could push things without getting caught.

It was the first week of March, and I was at Walmart with my mom. We were clothes shopping. Mom pushed the cart. When she wasn't looking—when nobody was looking—I snatched a pair of pearl earrings off a spinner rack and slipped them in my jacket pocket. They cost less than ten dollars. They weren't real pearls. Just knockoffs. As far as I could tell, they were junk, and nobody would care if junk got stolen.

But somebody did care. An undercover security guard named Gregg. He waited until my mom and I had reached the glass exit doors before stepping forward.

"Young lady"—his deep voice haunted me for years—"I'm going to need you to come with me."

16

My mother had bought more tea on her weekly trek to Whole Foods. She rattled off the exotic names with a strange sort of pride. None of them sounded appealing, but I knew the sooner I gave in, the sooner I could get some answers.

"How much were those?" I asked, looking at the selection. Immediately I shook my head. "You know what, never mind. I don't want to know how fast you're blowing through my inheritance."

My mother set the burner and turned to lean against the counter, a slow smile spreading across her face.

"Who says you're even in the will?"

"I'm your only child."

A shrug.

"No grandchildren, no inheritance."

My mother thought she was a riot.

I shifted on the stool and set my elbows on the kitchen island.

"So, how do you know about Destiny?"

The smile flickered out.

"When was the last time you spoke to her? Did you ever see her after middle school?"

No, I hadn't. Her parents had pulled her out right after the incident with Grace. Destiny's father had been transferred a month earlier; he had moved to South Carolina while Destiny, Tyler, and their mother stayed in Lanton. The kids were so close to finishing out the school year, they reasoned, and it wasn't like they were hurting for money. They could afford two houses. I remembered Destiny saying it had given her mother more time to pack, though I later learned they'd hired professional movers to box things up and load everything onto a truck.

Realizing that I was in a daze, my mother said, "Emily?"

I blinked, shifted my eyes to meet hers.

"After she left school, I never saw her again."

My mother pursed her lips as she nodded, clearly troubled by the memory. The shame her only child had brought to her family. Not just once, but twice.

And the second time—the last time—was so much worse than the first.

When we'd finally left Walmart—after an hour in a stuffy, windowless office with just a table and four plastic chairs, Gregg the security guard having lectured me for most of that time about why stealing was wrong while my mother sat silently fuming—the sky had darkened to early evening.

I didn't say a word as I followed Mom through the parking lot. I was silent as I slid into the car and pulled on my seat belt.

My mother inserted the key into the ignition but didn't turn it. She just sat there, hunched forward, staring at the steering wheel. She didn't even look at me when I whispered, "Mom?"

I'd cried most of the time in that stuffy, windowless office, saying again and again how sorry I was. Gregg had pointed out several times that he should call the police, press charges, make me go in front of a judge, but in the end he didn't. Instead, he'd taken my picture with a Polaroid camera and told us it would go up on a corkboard in the manager's office.

Why? Well, that's simple, young lady: you're now banned from this store.

The entire time, my mother hadn't once looked at me.

I tried again, this time louder.

"Mom?"

"Don't."

The word slipped out through her clenched teeth.

"Mom, I'm sorry. I didn't mean to—"

She moved faster than I'd ever seen her move, twisting in her seat and slapping me across the face. My mother had never hit me before—my father was the disciplinarian, the one who spanked me when I was younger, though that had always been half-hearted, more for show than anything else—and I saw the same shock in her eyes that was no doubt in my own.

But hers was short lived. Her eyes hardened.

"Don't you dare try to explain. I don't want your excuses. I don't want your apologies. Do you know how *embarrassing* that was? I've shopped there most of my life, and now I can never show my face again. If you ask me, you got off easy. I would have been perfectly happy for him to call the police."

Without another word, she started the car and headed for the highway. We didn't speak for the rest of the car ride. She didn't tell me what to expect once we arrived home. How she would tell my father what happened. How I would be grounded for two weeks, which meant I wouldn't be allowed to go to the mall on the weekends. Or to any of the girls' houses. Or to even use the phone.

I would cry again at the mixture of anger and disappointment in my father's face when he heard what had happened. He didn't yell, just shook his head and told me to go to my room.

Two hours would pass before my mother came to get me for a late dinner. She opened the door to find me lying on my bed, clutching a ball of tissues. She sat on the edge of my bed and touched my arm.

"I'm sorry for slapping you. I shouldn't have done that. But you shouldn't have done what you did either. Do you understand?"

I nodded but said nothing.

"I don't know what's happened to you, Emily. You . . . you aren't the girl you used to be."

I wanted to ask her what this meant, but I never did. If I had, maybe it would have changed things. Maybe her answer would have helped redirect me.

But I always knew better. In the end, I was who I was, and there would be no changing that.

That evening in my room, Mom leaned forward to hug me.

"I love you, Emily."

I hugged her back. Held her close. Didn't want to let go.

But I had to. You always have to let go. Even when you don't want to. It was one of the things I'd learned early in life.

Later, after news got out about Grace's suicide attempt and everybody learned what we'd done, my mother's response wasn't nearly as emotional as it had been in the Walmart parking lot. Neither was my father's. When they looked at me that time, it wasn't with disappointment and anger, but disgust.

Still leaning against the kitchen counter while she waited for the teakettle to warm, my mother nodded solemnly.

"Yes, well, it seems Destiny passed away too. Six months ago, according to the obituary."

"How did you find out about it?"

"Anne Wolff."

"Who?"

"Jennifer Wolff's mother. Do you remember Jennifer? She was a year behind you, I think. Her mother sent me a friend request months ago. If those yearbooks of yours hadn't gone missing, I could find her, point her out. Don't you remember Jennifer?"

I didn't remember most of the people in my graduating class, let alone those in lower grades, but I didn't want to get into it with my mother.

"The name rings a bell."

"Anyway, Anne said she had come across Destiny's obituary the other day and wanted to pass it along. She said she knew you had been friends with Destiny in middle school."

I wanted to feel some sort of violation. The mother of a girl I couldn't remember communicating with my own mother, talking about me like she somehow knew me. But that was how parents were back when I was in school. They constantly wanted to know what was going on. That was why they signed up for the PTA and volunteered to go on field trips and chaperone dances. Like Courtney, some of them were simply gossips, and apparently that itch didn't disappear once their children graduated.

"Do you have the obituary?"

My mother nodded and gestured at the iPad lying on the kitchen island. Before she could take a step toward it, though, the kettle started whistling.

"Take a look. I left it open in the browser."

The iPad showed a local Maryland newspaper called the *Lighthouse*, dated October 12. Destiny's obituary was the first one listed on the page. The picture showed a woman about my age. Dark skin. Long black hair. A pert smile. It had been fourteen years since I'd last seen her, but I recognized Destiny at once.

I scanned the obituary. Destiny was a graduate of the Virginia–Maryland College of Veterinary Medicine, and she had worked at a vet clinic in Berlin, Maryland. Of course. She'd loved animals, horses especially.

In terms of her death, the obituary was vague. There was no cause given, but the words *passed away suddenly* raised a red flag in the back of my mind.

My mother brought over one of the cups and set it down beside the iPad. She shook her head as she perched on the stool next to me.

"Terrible, isn't it? I mean, what are the odds? Two of your old friends passing away within six months of each other. So awful."

Yes, it was awful. And as for the odds, I didn't like them at all.

In the back of my mind, Karen whispered, *That's the weird part. She said it was a ghost.*

17

Courtney didn't notice me until I was the next customer in line.

She kept her focus on the customer in front of her, an older Hispanic woman with thick glasses, smiling and chitchatting as she scanned and bagged her items. Courtney had her blonde hair pulled back in a ponytail, now highlighted with streaks of purple, and her baggy blue vest looked recently washed.

I caught myself watching her and looked away.

I glanced around the store, realizing this was the first time I'd been here since the eighth grade. After high school, I had forgotten about my lifetime ban but never bothered to shop here—I lived on the other side of town. I wondered if Gregg still worked here, and if he did, if he would recognize me.

As Courtney finished bagging the last couple of items, she glanced up to take in her next customer. Our eyes met. She paused and frowned briefly before counting out the change.

I glanced behind me. A middle-aged woman with two kids and an overflowing shopping cart was already in the process of emptying her items onto the conveyor belt, giving me a curious glance every couple of seconds—it didn't appear as if I had anything to buy.

The rack of gum in front of me caught my attention, and without thinking I grabbed a yellow pack of Wrigley's Juicy Fruit. I stepped up and placed it next to the scanner.

Courtney had been greeting each customer with an enthusiastic "Hi, how are you?" but with me, her perpetual smile faded, and her voice went flat.

"What are you doing here?"

"I stopped by your apartment to see if you were there. Nobody answered when I knocked."

"Terri won't answer the door for anyone."

"I tried calling your cell. It said it was disconnected."

"I ran out of minutes. Look, my supervisor doesn't like us socializing, especially when it's busy."

Her gaze flicked past me when she said this, toward a large, curly-haired woman who stood to the side, surveying all the open registers.

Turning back to her, I whispered, "Destiny passed away."

Courtney's eyes widened. "What? When?"

"Six months ago."

"How?"

"I'm not sure. The obituary was vague."

Courtney was quiet for a moment, then grabbed the pack of Juicy Fruit and swiped it over the scanner. The quiet beep accompanied the dozen others along the line of registers.

"My shift ends in a half hour. Give me a ride home?"

I nodded.

Courtney punched a key on the register, and suddenly the perpetual smile was back on her face, her voice once again chipper.

"That will be a dollar. Would you like to pay with cash or credit?"

Courtney sat in the passenger seat, squinting down at my cell phone screen. Before I had left my mother's, I'd copied the URL of the obituary, and Courtney pored over it as I steered us out of the parking lot and onto the main highway.

"Jesus Christ," she whispered, shaking her head. "How did you find this?"

"One of my mom's Facebook friends sent her the link. Jennifer Wolff's mother—does that name sound familiar?"

"Was she in our class?"

"One grade below us, apparently."

"Maybe. I remember some Jennifers. Still, Jesus Christ, Destiny too?"

"It might not mean anything. I mean, there might not be any connection between Destiny and Olivia. From the obituary, it says Destiny 'suddenly passed away,' so she could have died in some kind of accident."

"Or suicide."

Courtney didn't say it hopefully, but there was a slight eagerness to her tone, like this would make the most sense after what we'd learned about Olivia.

After our fight last week, it felt strange being in the car with her. Part of me had thought I was never going to see her again. Now I was driving her home from work like we were good friends.

I said, "Yes, but maybe not. Still, when I heard what happened, I thought of our conversation from last week."

Courtney was quiet, staring out her window. It was just past seven o'clock, and the sun was already starting to set, the sky awash with orange and purple.

"You mean Grace?" she said, not looking at me.

"I'm still not ready to buy into the idea that Grace is who Olivia meant when she talked about a ghost. But I figure there's only one way we can know for sure."

Courtney turned her head. "How?"

"Olivia's fiancé."

"Do you think he'll talk to us?"

"I don't know. But first we need to find him."

Courtney gave me a grin.

"What?" I asked.

"I've already found him."

We climbed the stairs to the second floor of building E, the stairwell still dark, the smell of mildew strong.

Courtney had a hop in her step.

"Terri is going to be so surprised that I'm home early. Can't wait to see the look on her face. It usually takes me forty-five minutes, sometimes an hour, on the bus."

She reached into her purse, pulled out her keys. Then she lightly tapped her knuckles twice at the top of the door, twice at the bottom, and once at the middle.

"It's our code," she said when she noticed my confusion. "This way Terri knows it's me. We mix it up every so often so the neighbors don't catch on. Not that I'm worried about my neighbors, but better safe than sorry."

She opened the door. The hallway inside was empty. The TV was on in the living room, its volume low.

Courtney glanced back at me, her brow furrowed, and entered slowly, almost tiptoeing as she advanced. After five paces, she had almost reached the living room and the doorway to the kitchen.

Terri popped out of the kitchen, her hands held up at her sides.

"Boo!"

Courtney leaned down and grabbed her daughter, started tickling her. Terri howled with delight.

I stepped inside, closing the door behind me, and watched the two of them wrestle each other for several seconds before Courtney got winded and stood back up.

"Terri, do you remember Aunt Emily from last week?"

So I was Aunt Emily again.

Terri waved at me. Tonight she had her hair in cute French braids. "Hi."

"I was the one who knocked earlier."

Terri glanced up at her mother and offered a sheepish smile.

"I'm not supposed to answer the door for anyone."

"That's right, you're not," Courtney said. "You're a good girl. Why don't you show Aunt Emily your new picture while I change out of these clothes?"

As Courtney drifted off to the bedroom, Terri motioned me into the living room. Her paper tablet and colored pencils were spread across the floor. She knelt down, grabbed one of the papers, and handed it to me.

Jefferson the Turtle was surrounded by three slightly bigger animals. One was a rabbit. Another a raccoon. The third a possum. The three animals looked menacing. The turtle looked scared.

"Those are some of the students at Jefferson's school," Terri said.

"They look intimidating."

Terri nodded, her eyes fixed on the picture.

"Are they bullies?" I asked.

Terri nodded again, her eyes dipping slightly.

"Do you sometimes feel like that at school? Do some of the kids there bully you?"

Her eyes had dipped all the way to the carpet. She clasped her hands in front of her and shrugged.

"Sometimes."

"You know to tell your teacher if somebody is picking on you, right?"

She nodded again but said nothing.

Before I could continue—the therapist in me having clocked in for an impromptu session—Courtney entered the room. She'd changed out of her uniform into jeans and a T-shirt and carried a Chromebook, already open, its screen lighting her face.

"Terri, are you hungry?"

Smiling again, the girl nodded.

"What are you hungry for?"

Terri took a moment to think about it, staring up at the ceiling.

"Fish sticks and mac and cheese."

"Sounds good. Go start the oven and get everything ready, okay?"

Terri sprang to her feet and headed for the kitchen.

Courtney said to me, "She's not allowed to use the oven or stove if I'm not here. But she knows how to make her own meals. I always offer to cook or at least help, but she says she can handle it on her own."

She hefted the Chromebook, and motioned for us to sit on the couch.

"I give my neighbor twenty bucks a month, and he lets us use his Wi-Fi password. It's a pretty sweet deal. You know how much they charge for internet these days?"

She gave me a quick look, as if of course I knew how much internet cost, and I was again struck by how far Courtney had fallen financially. There was a time when she'd gotten whatever she wanted, without exception. Her parents had bought her a brand-new Jetta on her sixteenth birthday. They'd even managed to get one of those giant bows you see on the car commercials.

Courtney shifted the Chromebook to show me the screen. She'd brought up Olivia's fiancé's Facebook profile.

"How did you find this?"

"It wasn't hard. I think I told you how I like to surf Facebook at night when I can't sleep, right? Well, after the funeral I checked out

Olivia's wall and realized that she still had her relationship status marked as engaged to Philip. Remember what Karen said, how they weren't able to delete her account? All these people were posting on her wall, saying how much they missed her. I felt so bad, I did it too."

Philip's profile picture was still of him and Olivia. It looked like it had been taken during the summer, both of them in short sleeves and shorts, standing in front of the Susquehanna River, City Island behind them. I had to admit they looked happy, Olivia especially. Then I remembered Olivia had jumped into that same river and drowned two weeks ago, and a bolt of sadness shot through me.

"Anyway," Courtney said, "so I was able to find Philip's page, and he had two employers listed. During the week he works landscaping jobs—mowing grass and trimming bushes and trees, looks like—and on the weekends he works at Huey's Bar and Grille. I googled it, and it's on the Cumberland County side of the river, maybe an hour's drive from here."

She glanced at me, and I could see it in her eyes, what she was thinking. I saw it because I was thinking it too.

"What about Terri?" I whispered.

"She'll be fine. She's a smart, tough girl. She can take care of herself."

I didn't like it, but I knew Courtney was right. Terri was very mature for her age. A couple of extra hours alone at home to work on her drawings wouldn't be a problem for her.

Courtney asked, "You don't already have plans with your fiancé, do you?"

"He's working a double shift. He won't be home until much later."

I didn't know this for a fact, but it sounded plausible.

"Then it sounds like you don't have any plans," she said.

I glanced back at the Chromebook's screen. At Philip's profile picture. I remembered him storming into the funeral parlor last week, how his eyes had started to water because he'd just wanted to say goodbye.

"Are we really going to do this? What if he doesn't know anything?"

"Then at least we'll know. We can rule out the idea that maybe it was—"

She shook her head, not wanting to voice the thought. I didn't blame her. It felt weird, thinking that a girl from our past—a ghost—could have somehow involved herself in Olivia's life to the point that Olivia killed herself.

For an instant I pictured it: Olivia climbing up on the rails of the bridge, balancing to stand upright, peeking over the edge. Calculating in her mind the distance between herself and the water. How fast she would fall once she stepped off.

The Olivia I remembered had never struck me as depressed, but oftentimes people do a good job of hiding their depression. They know when to smile. When to laugh. How to say the right things at the right time. Until the day finally comes when the depression becomes too strong and they're tired of fighting it.

Terri entered the living room.

"Mom, the oven's ready."

Courtney smiled at her daughter and said that she'd be right there. When Terri was gone, she glanced at me again and lowered her voice.

"Maybe it won't matter, anyway. He might not be there. Mind if I use your phone again?"

I dug it out of my purse, unlocked the screen, and handed it to her.

The Chromebook still balanced on her lap, Courtney brought up Google and entered "huey's bar and grille." Seconds later she was punching the main number into the phone, placing it to her ear.

"Yes, hi, my name's Mary. I'm coming with some of my friends tonight and was hoping at least one of our favorite bartenders will be working. Oh, let's see, either John or Philip. Uh-huh. Really? That's great. Thanks so much."

She disconnected the call. I grinned at her.

"Mary?"

She shrugged. "I wasn't going to use my real name."

"Who's John?"

"No idea. But you have to figure every bar is gonna have a John working there."

"Did they say Philip is working tonight?"

"Yep." Courtney closed the Chromebook, set it aside, stood up. "Let me get Terri situated with dinner and then we can head out. Speaking of which, would you like some fish sticks?"

18

Huey's Bar & Grille walked the line between dive and almost-dive. It certainly wasn't high end, nor was it the type of neighborhood place where teachers stopped by after school for happy hour or parents wanting a night off from the kids went for an intimate drink.

The parking lot was filled with a mishmash of cars, pickup trucks, and motorcycles. Neon beer signs buzzed in the windows. The interior was separated by a thin glass partition: the dining area on one side, the bar—where people could smoke—on the other.

Courtney and I bypassed the register at the door and headed straight for the bar. The air wasn't thick with smoke, but I knew my hair and clothes would stink of it by the time we left. High-top tables were scattered about, half of them occupied. The bar itself had only a few patrons, mostly older men hunched over glasses of beer.

We climbed onto two stools at the end of the bar, in the corner. The bartender, a tall, fit man with tattoos ribboning his arms, acknowledged us with a quick smile and said he'd be right with us.

Courtney leaned into me, whispered, "I don't have any money."

"Don't worry about it. I'll get you."

We ordered drinks—Courtney a diet soda, me a Miller Lite—and once the bartender drifted away, Courtney promised to pay me back. I told her again not to worry about it, then eyed the soda on the coaster set in front of her.

"You can order something harder."

Courtney took a sip of her soda, shook her head.

"I haven't had alcohol in years." Then, scanning the room, she leaned in close again. "I don't see him."

"I don't either."

"Do you think they were lying to me on the phone?"

That was when the door behind the bar pushed open, and Philip appeared. Like the bartender who'd gotten our drinks, he wore jeans and a black T-shirt with the bar's name on the back. He bumped fists with our bartender, then started checking the coolers to see what beers needed to be stocked.

We were quiet, watching him as he went about his work. He must have noticed us staring; at one point he looked up and flashed us a smile before continuing to stock the coolers.

Courtney took another sip of her drink.

"So what should we do?"

I slowly turned my head to look at her. "I thought you had a plan."

"Why would you think that? This was your idea."

My hand tightened around the bottle, and I glanced around the bar again.

"Well, we can't exactly talk to him like this."

"Why not?"

"He's working."

"But that was the point. He works here. That's why we came."

I wasn't sure what to say. I took a sip of beer, set the bottle back down. Suddenly I regretted this whole idea. It was stupid. What did we hope to accomplish?

"Well?" Courtney asked.

I thought about it for a moment, watching Philip interact with the old men down at the other end of the bar, and then said, "We wait."

We didn't have to wait long. Maybe a half hour later, Philip grabbed a cigarette from a pack on the back of the bar. I thought he was going to give the cigarette to one of the old men, but instead he started for the door, telling our bartender that he'd be back in a minute.

Courtney was already stepping off her stool.

"Pay the tab and meet me around back."

I found Courtney standing with her back to the wall, peeking around the corner. I took a self-conscious glance over my shoulder, scanning the parking lot, but there was nobody around. I stepped up close to Courtney and dropped my voice to a whisper.

"What are you doing?"

She whispered back, "Waiting for you. Look, he's almost done."

Philip stood beside a dumpster, his knee bent, his foot against the wall, staring down at his phone. Courtney was right: his cigarette was almost gone.

I looked at Courtney. Courtney looked at me. I saw the uncertainty in her eyes, the doubt. What the hell were we doing? Part of me wanted to tell her it was time to go. We'd slink back to the car, drive back to Lanton; I'd drop her off at the apartment before driving home.

But then I pictured Olivia lying in her casket, and what Karen told us Olivia had said to her, and I steeled myself as I stepped around the corner.

Philip didn't notice me at first. The soft glow of the phone's screen lit his face. He took what looked like the last drag of his cigarette and crushed it with the heel of his shoe.

That's when he noticed me approaching. It was dark back here, only a few dim lights posted around, most of them directed at the parked cars, but I saw the panic flash in his eyes.

"What do you want?"

It wasn't his question that caught me off guard so much as his tone. Hesitant, almost startled. His eyes shifted from me to Courtney, who was trailing a few steps behind, and then settled back on me.

"What the fuck do you want?"

The smiling, good-natured bartender was gone. Now he looked scared, like a cornered animal, his eyes continuing to dart between the two of us as he took a step toward the door.

"Philip?"

I tried to keep my tone neutral, friendly, but hearing me say his name caused a new kind of panic to flash in his eyes. He looked ready to bolt, which was the last thing I'd expected.

"Philip, we want to ask you some questions. We were friends with Olivia."

The panic in his eyes faded, but only a bit. It was clear he was still scared, though I couldn't imagine why.

"I've never seen either of you before."

"We were at Olivia's funeral last week."

"So?"

"We grew up with Olivia. We were best friends in elementary and middle school. We—"

His new expression cut me off. There was recognition there, an understanding.

"Holy shit," he said. "You're them, aren't you? The Harpies. Olivia told me what you did to that girl."

That girl. Just hearing him say the words caused a cold finger to touch my spine.

"Olivia told you about what happened in middle school?"

"Yeah, she did. Why do you sound surprised?"

Because I didn't tell my fiancé, or anyone besides my therapist, and I never intend to.

"I'm just surprised she would tell you about something that happened so long ago."

He shrugged as if it wasn't a big deal.

"We were engaged. We loved each other. We told each other everything."

"But you cheated on her," Courtney said.

There was more bite in her tone than she probably intended. Philip's eyes hardened.

"How do you know about that?"

"Olivia's sister told us," I said.

His jaw tightened and he shook his head, kicked a small rock toward a bush.

"Karen hates my guts. She thinks I'm the reason Olivia killed herself. And, fuck, I guess it's true. Olivia killed herself because of me. Because of what she thought I did. But I *didn't* do it."

I traded a glance with Courtney, then focused again on Philip.

"We don't think you did either."

The tension in his body seemed to relax, and his eyes softened.

"You . . . don't?"

"That's why we're here. We're trying to figure out the truth."

Philip glanced back at the door again. Stared for a beat, then turned back to us.

"What else did Karen tell you?"

Courtney said, "She told us you got drunk one night with your friends and hooked up with an ex."

He looked away, nodding. "Yeah, that's right."

"And Olivia took you back."

"Yeah, she did. And I promised her I would never do it again."

"So what happened a few weeks ago?" I asked.

He shrugged, started scanning the back lot. "That's the thing. I have no idea."

"Karen said you cheated on Olivia again."

"I guess I did—Olivia sent me the pictures—but I don't remember doing it."

Courtney said, "Were you drunk?"

"No, it's nothing like that. I honestly don't remember it happening at all."

Courtney and I frowned at each other. I asked Philip, "What is that supposed to mean?"

He checked his watch. "Look, I don't have time for this. I need to head back in."

He started to turn away. Courtney and I locked eyes. I didn't know about Courtney, but there was no doubt in my mind that this would be the last time we'd speak to Philip, the last chance we got, so I decided the only way to keep him here was to hit him where it hurt.

"Did you even love Olivia?"

That stopped him cold. He stood frozen, his back to us, and then he slowly turned, his eyes narrowed.

"What the fuck did you say?"

Maybe messing with the guy who'd just lost his fiancée wasn't the best idea. For all I knew, he was the type of guy who wouldn't think twice about hitting a woman. But I stood my ground and held our stare.

"Philip, we were at the funeral. We know you loved her. We saw. All you wanted was to say goodbye one last time."

The memory of this nearly broke him. He pressed his lips together; his eyes started to water. But he didn't cry, didn't even wipe at his tears.

"What do you want from me?"

"We want to know what happened. Who the girl was that sent Olivia those pictures. Did you know her?"

"No."

"Had you ever seen her before?"

"No."

"How did you two meet?"

Philip glanced over his shoulder at the kitchen door, and then turned his attention back to us.

"Okay, look. I don't remember much. Two Saturday nights ago I was working late. There was this girl at the bar—I'd never seen her before—and she kept trying to flirt with me, but that happens a lot, and it's always harmless, you know; it doesn't go anywhere. I usually just smile and get the girls their drinks and try not to screw myself out of a tip. Anyway, the next thing I know, the girl's gone, just disappeared. I didn't think about her again until I got home that night and she was waiting for me."

I glanced at Courtney, and then frowned at Philip.

"Who?"

"The girl from the bar. She was right there when I stepped out of my truck, and then . . . that's all I remember until I woke up in bed late the next day with a massive headache. I was completely naked and my sheets were"—he paused, uncomfortable—"you know, stiff in places."

"Where was Olivia?"

Olivia had been at her place, Philip said. She usually stayed there on nights he worked late. And Philip stressed that he never slept naked. Never. He never turned his phone off, either—in case Olivia needed to get hold of him—but it had been powered off.

When he turned it on, he had three voice mails and a dozen text messages, all from Olivia. The first couple told him to call her. When he didn't respond, she'd gotten pissed and the messages had become more aggressive. Calling him a bastard. Calling him a liar. Saying that he had promised her and that she had believed him and that she was never going to make that mistake again.

"She . . . she had sent me *pictures*. Of me and that girl in bed—*in my bed*—having sex. She said the girl had sent them to her on Facebook. And the pictures—" He shook his head, his hands balled into fists. "It was like she was taking selfies while we were doing it. I mean, what the fuck is that about? Who the fuck does that?"

He stared at us, desperate now, wanting an answer. No—*needing* an answer. The whole thing had no doubt haunted him since it had happened, especially after it had become clear that Olivia had done what she did because of the pictures. Because of what Philip had participated in.

Only we had no answers for him. If anything, now we had even more questions.

"Do you still have the pictures?" I asked.

He jerked like I'd just slapped him.

"The fuck kind of question is that?"

"My friend and I think we might know the girl who did this to you. We think it might be the same girl from middle school. The one that Olivia told you about."

A glimmer of hope sparked in his eyes.

"Seriously? Do you think that's possible?"

He scrambled to pull the phone from his pocket, then paused.

"I tried calling Olivia back, but there was no answer. It wasn't until I called Karen that I found out what happened."

He shook his head, squeezing the phone in his hand.

"I tried to give my side of the story, but Karen and Olivia's parents didn't want to hear it."

I held out my hand, tentative. He tapped the phone's screen a couple of times, swiped, paused.

"Let me find one of the pictures that shows her face."

Courtney asked, "How many did Olivia send?"

"Six. There are a few of the girl going down on me like *I* was taking the pictures, and then a couple with her on top. Here."

He twisted the phone so we could see. He'd zoomed in so that only the girl's face could be seen, and not what she was doing with her mouth. The top of her face, mostly, just above her nose.

It wasn't bright in the room, but it was still bright enough to see her gray eyes. Her pale skin. Her dark hair.

Courtney squeezed my arm. She saw it too. But before she could say anything, I shook my head.

"I'm sorry, Philip. That isn't her."

19

"Why did you lie to him?"

We had just left Huey's Bar & Grille, headed toward the highway that would take us back to Lanton, and Courtney didn't hesitate.

Because that was the question, wasn't it? Why *had* I lied to Philip?

When I didn't answer, Courtney tried again.

"Emily, come on. You had to have recognized her. That was Grace, without a doubt."

I didn't react at first—my focus on the road, my fingers tight around the steering wheel, a steady beat of blood in my ears. Then I glanced at Courtney, who had shifted in her seat to watch me.

"I know it was her."

"Then why did you lie?" Courtney made a face. "Wait. Are you trying to protect her?"

I frowned at the idea. "No. It's just . . . complicated."

"Grace tracked down Olivia. She *followed* Olivia's fiancé home and, what, somehow knocked him out and got him into his apartment where she *raped* him and took pictures of it."

It was strange to hear that Philip had been raped, but if his story was true, then that's what it was. It made sense now why he'd looked scared when we'd first approached him behind the bar; in a way, he was probably suffering from PTSD.

The urgency in Courtney's voice ticked up a notch.

"What are we going to do about this? Maybe we should call the police."

"And tell them what, Courtney? As far as we know, no crime took place."

"Grace roofied Philip and had sex with him!"

"First, we don't know if he was roofied. And even if we did, how would we prove it? There are *pictures* of them having sex. Even if Philip was unconscious during it, I doubt the pictures show that. Otherwise, Olivia might not have reacted the way she did."

Courtney didn't speak for several seconds. Her gaze burned into me.

"You *are* trying to protect Grace, aren't you?"

"No, Courtney, I'm not. Do I feel guilty for what happened in middle school? Yes. Does that excuse any of the stuff she's done since then? Absolutely not. But had we confirmed to Philip that Grace was the one in the picture, what do you think he would have done?"

"I don't know."

"I don't know, either, and in that moment I felt it was best not to bring him into this."

Courtney was quiet. We were on the highway now; I was in the right-hand lane, driving the speed limit. I'd barely had two beers, but I was still so wired after our conversation with Philip that I didn't want to go too fast and attract the attention of a cop.

Courtney cleared her throat, her voice soft.

"We need to find out exactly what happened to Destiny, don't we?"

"Yes."

"We should contact Mackenzie and Elise too."

"Do you have their numbers?"

"No, but I'll shoot Elise another message on Facebook. She responded to my initial message, by the way. I forgot to tell you. It was the day after the funeral. As for Mackenzie?" Courtney's lips twisted. "She blocked me."

I glanced over at her, surprised. "Mackenzie blocked you on Facebook?"

Courtney nodded, slumped in her seat.

"Facebook suggested her because we had some mutual friends, so I sent her a friend request. The privacy settings on her Facebook page must have been set to public, so I was able to look at her profile. She had pictures of her kids—it looks like she has twins, two boys—and her husband. I think she's a stay-at-home mom, though judging by the size of her house, I wouldn't be surprised if they had a housekeeper."

"But you said she blocked you."

"That's right. My friend request was never accepted, and when I went to check out her profile again, I couldn't find it."

"Maybe she deactivated her account."

"Oh no, she blocked me. It's embarrassing, but I have a fake account to keep tabs on certain people I work with. I know you're going to think I'm a gossip queen, but sometimes it's good to know what my coworkers are up to without being friends with them on Facebook. Anyway, I used that account to search for Mackenzie, and she came right up. Hence, the bitch blocked me."

"What about Elise—is she big into Facebook?"

I couldn't quite picture it, but of course it had been years since I'd seen her. She was once my best friend, but I wondered if she'd accept my friend request, or even send me a friend request if she happened to stumble across my profile. I wondered if I would do the same.

"I never see her post anything, but some people are like that, you know? They have an account but they almost never go on, or they do go on but never interact, just lurk. Maybe Elise'll have a way to contact Mackenzie. She may be a bitch, but she deserves to know what's going on."

Courtney tapped her fingers on the door, glanced over at me.

"Have you had any contact with Elise since high school?"

"None. Except, wait, I do remember seeing her once a couple of months ago."

"Where?"

"My therapist's office."

"I thought you said you were a therapist."

"I am. That doesn't mean I can't see my own therapist too."

"So what happened?"

"Nothing. I typically have noon appointments on Fridays, but that day I needed to come in early. I was in the waiting room, paging through a magazine, when Elise came out from the back. I recognized her at once, but I don't think she saw me. She headed straight for the door."

I didn't want to add that I'd found myself frozen in place on my chair. I was so embarrassed for Elise to see me that I had quickly tilted my face down. Even at twenty-eight, I felt like a Harpy again, worried what the girls thought of me, the things they whispered behind my back.

"Do you think you both see the same therapist?"

"No idea. There are two others in the office. There's a chance Elise saw one of them, but five minutes later, my therapist came out to get me."

"No offense, but I think it's weird you work as a therapist and see a therapist."

"I need to talk to somebody about what's going on in my life."

"Does it help?"

"Sometimes." I paused, unsure how much I wanted to disclose, then said, "I've been seeing my current therapist for almost two years. After my dad passed away, I was feeling really down, and I thought it would help to talk to someone."

"Two years sounds like a long time."

"It is. After we worked through the stuff about my dad, I talked to her about Daniel and work and . . . everything. To be honest with you, I don't have that many people in my life to talk to about personal stuff."

"You said current therapist. Did you see one before?"

I nodded. "Yeah, briefly, back in high school."

"When? I don't remember you ever telling me that."

"That's because I didn't tell anybody, not even Ben. I was still feeling guilty about what we'd done to Grace." I paused and looked over at Courtney. "Can I ask you something? Why don't you drink anymore?"

Courtney didn't answer, staring out her window at the dark buildings and fields off the highway. I thought I'd struck a nerve, but then she released a heavy breath and leaned her head back against the headrest.

It was a couple of years ago, she told me, when Jane was still alive and could look after Terri. Courtney had slipped at work and broken her arm. Had it in a cast for a couple of months. The doctor had given her Oxycodone for the pain. It had really helped. But then she'd just kept taking it. Even when the pain wasn't so bad, she'd told the doctor it was still there. He'd kept prescribing, no questions asked.

On weekends, Courtney would still go out to the club. She'd be high as a kite on Oxy, and she would drink and dance, and she would just . . . black out. Oftentimes she couldn't remember what happened next. One time she woke up in a random guy's bed, naked. Another time she'd woken up behind a Wendy's, and her underwear was missing. She knew she had a problem, that she had to stop, but she wasn't going to sign herself into rehab. She had to work. She had to take care of Terri.

So she stopped going out on the weekends. That wasn't so hard. Stopping the drinking and the Oxy was harder. She had to wean herself off. But once she was off, she promised she would never do either ever again. She was coming up on four years sober.

"Congratulations," I said.

Courtney forced a smile, wiped a few stray tears from her eyes.

"Thanks. But I'm leaving something out."

"What's that?"

"You."

I glanced at her again, confused, and she forced another smile.

"I never did thank you for that night you came over to the house. It was right before you left for California. I know Jane called you. I don't remember much, but I remember saying something really stupid about how Terri would be better off if I killed myself, and then you slapped me. You told me I could handle being a mother. That I was stronger than I thought I was. Do you remember that?"

I found myself smiling too. "Yeah, I remember I said that a couple of seconds before you threw up. Fortunately, I got a trash can to you just in time."

Courtney gave a soft laugh. "I was so embarrassed. I wasn't sure what to say the next time I talked to you. But then . . . you never returned my calls. You just fell out of contact."

This hit me harder than I'd expected, because the truth was I didn't have a good reason why I'd stopped talking to Courtney. So what if she had brought up Grace and said I was mostly to blame for what had happened? Courtney had been drunk, and in a way she was right. I just hadn't wanted to accept it at the time.

"I'm sorry about that."

Courtney waved a dismissive hand. "Don't be sorry. Friends drift apart. It happens."

It felt like she was letting me off too easy. Part of me wanted to apologize again, try to explain, but I wasn't sure it would be worth the trouble. Courtney probably didn't even remember what she'd said.

Courtney tapped the door handle again, shifted in her seat.

"Anyway, I never forgot what you said. About how I was stronger than I knew. I mean, I know that's the shit you say to people when they're in crisis, but it really did stick with me. Even when I started taking Oxy, I kept telling myself that I was stronger than I knew because *you* had said it. At the time I don't think I really wanted to stop. It was only one day when I looked at Terri and remembered the awful thing I'd said that I decided to *prove* I was stronger."

I was quiet, not sure what to say. Courtney gave me more credit than I was due. She was the one who'd proved how strong she was. I had nothing to do with it. I was opening my mouth to tell her this when she spoke again.

"So what should we do about Destiny?"

"I'm not sure."

"I can try to find more information. I don't want to toot my own horn, but I've gotten pretty good at digging through Facebook and stuff. You give me a name, I pretty much guarantee I can find that person on social media. Unless they've made their privacy settings so strong that they're only visible to family and friends. I've run into that before. They're there, but you can't see them."

Courtney paused, her face screwed up in thought.

"Actually, Grace might be that way. I tried searching for her after Olivia's funeral, but I can't find her. Nothing even came up on Google. I mean, there are a few Grace Farmers, but not *our* Grace Farmer. Anyway, the article you showed had Destiny living down near Ocean City, Maryland. Maybe her family is still down there."

"Yeah, maybe."

I said the words automatically, thinking about how different life would have been if we'd had social media in middle school. I knew how bad cyberbullying had gotten; half my clients dealt with it on a daily basis. I couldn't begin to imagine the amount of harm we would have done if we'd had a computer screen to hide behind. It almost made me sick, realizing how much worse we might have been under different circumstances.

Courtney said, "I'm not sure I'll be able to go down to Maryland with you if that becomes the plan. I can't leave Terri by herself that long."

She slumped down in her seat again, staring out her window. It sounded like she was speaking more to herself than to me as she said softly, "It would be great to take her, though. She's never seen the ocean before."

I kept my focus on the highway, actually biting my tongue. Part of me didn't want to disclose what Terri had told me earlier tonight—what I felt was her secret, a bond between the two of us—but another part knew that her mother needed to know.

"Courtney?"

"Yeah."

"I think Terri is being bullied at school."

"Yeah."

This caught me off guard, the simple way she said it.

"You know?"

"Of course I know. She's my daughter. She tells me everything. I've already spoken to the school about it, but bullying is a real problem there. They put on a show about how kids aren't supposed to bully each other, but it keeps happening. If I could pull her out, put her in a better school, I'd do it in a heartbeat."

Courtney fell silent, staring out her window again. She shook her head.

"It shouldn't be that surprising for you to hear. You remember how it was in school. There are bullies everywhere."

20

Daniel was dozing on the couch when I got home. The TV was on, playing a rerun of *The Office*, and he didn't stir until I closed the front door. As it clicked shut, he opened his eyes and shifted to sit up on the couch.

"Welcome home. How was your girls' night out?"

"Pretty uneventful."

"Meet any hot guys?"

Daniel smiled when he said it, but there wasn't any smile in his voice. As if he was testing me.

See the tiny bubbles swirling around the couple as the temperature of the water continues to rise.

I didn't say anything, just stood there with my bag in one hand, a candy bar in the other.

Daniel's eyes shifted to the candy bar, and his smile faltered.

"Is that what I think it is?"

"Yep."

"Did you . . . buy that for me?"

Obviously I did. I didn't care for candy bars. Daniel loved them, or at least he loved this particular one.

It was a Hershey's Whatchamacallit. When Daniel had gone to Hershey Park with his foster family when he was thirteen, he'd tasted the candy bar for the first time. And maybe because it was different from any other candy bar he'd ever had or maybe because it had been such a great foster-home experience, Whatchamacallit had become his all-time-favorite candy.

Daniel had shared this story with me after the first month we were together, and I had filed it away in the back of my mind for future reference. In fact, it was a nugget of information I always used come Christmastime to slip a few bars in his stocking—though, come to think of it, it had been at least a year or two since we last exchanged stockings on Christmas.

I set the candy bar on the coffee table without a word, turned to the closet to hang my bag.

Daniel picked up the Whatchamacallit, said, "I haven't had one of these in a while. Thank you."

I didn't bother telling him that when the idea struck me—after I'd dropped off Courtney and was headed home—I stopped first at one gas station to purchase the candy bar, but the place didn't have any, so I'd stopped at another gas station, which also didn't have any, and so it was the third gas station where I'd finally found one, just two miles away from the town house.

Instead, Daniel's comment had gotten under my skin, and the sweet gesture I'd planned—simplistic, yes, but wasn't it always the thought that counted?—was now something I'd begun to regret.

I started for the stairs and only paused when Daniel asked, "Where all did you go?"

Because no other bar names came to mind, I told him the truth.

"Huey's Bar & Grille."

"I don't think I know that one."

"It's not around here. It's up on the West Shore."

"Why'd you go all the way up there?"

"That's where Courtney wanted to go."

"Did you at least have fun?"

"Yeah."

"Good. I can't remember the last time you went out with one of your friends."

I couldn't tell if this was a dig or if he truly meant it. There had been a time when Daniel had encouraged me to socialize more. Usually that was with his friends and coworkers, because it was pretty clear I didn't have many friends of my own. But after I made up one too many excuses not to go out, Daniel had stopped asking.

"I reek of smoke. I need a shower."

Daniel glanced down at the candy bar in his hand, and then quickly stood up from the couch.

"You hungry? I was going to make myself a grilled cheese. I can make you one too."

It was funny, but Daniel made the most amazing grilled cheese sandwiches. He'd told me that in some of his placements growing up, that was all the families fed the kids, and so he'd acquired a taste for perfection. Buttering the slices of bread just right. Setting the stove to the perfect temperature. Adding just the right amount of cheese. Too much, Daniel once said, and the sandwich would be ruined. Too little, and the sandwich would be ruined. It had to be just right.

There had been times, when we'd first started dating, that Daniel had tried to teach me how to make one of these perfect sandwiches. He'd set out the bread and the cheese and the butter on the counter and stood close behind me, gently guiding my hands as I buttered the bread. Then, the two of us side by side at the stove, he'd whisper instructions, telling me when to flip the sandwiches, and he would sometimes nibble at my ear, kiss my neck.

Now, standing at the base of the stairs, I couldn't remember the last time Daniel had offered to make me one.

"Thanks, that sounds great."

He nodded and started toward the kitchen. I climbed the steps but paused halfway up.

"What's your schedule like this weekend?"

"I'm off until Monday. Was thinking about hitting up the Boys & Girls Club either tomorrow or Sunday. Why?"

"Just wondering."

I continued up the stairs, stripping out of my clothes as I went. I threw them in the washer and turned on the shower. As I let the water warm, I hurried into the bedroom and connected my phone to the charger. Courtney and I had stopped at a gas station on the way home, and I'd purchased more minutes for her cell phone. I didn't expect to hear from her tonight, but I wanted to make sure my phone wasn't dead if she tried to call or text.

I didn't stay in the shower long. When I shut off the water and made it back into the bedroom, a text from Courtney was waiting.

Call me.

I dialed quickly, worried something may have happened. The phone rang two times before Courtney answered, her voice a whisper.

"Hey."

"Everything all right?"

"Yeah. Terri is asleep in the next room, so I don't want to talk too loud. Anyway, I found Destiny's wife."

"Her wife?"

"Yeah, it turns out Destiny was gay. Her wife's name is Charlotte. It actually wasn't that much work. They mentioned the vet clinic where Destiny worked in her obituary. I found their Facebook page, which had done a nice post about Destiny, and they tagged her wife, and from her wife's profile I was able to figure out that she—this is the wife now—gives riding lessons at a place called Ridgeway Farm every Saturday. Unless something comes up, she should be there in the afternoon."

I didn't say anything, just sat on the edge of the bed, feeling my wet hair dripping onto my bare shoulders. Thinking about confronting Destiny's widow. A woman who didn't even know us.

"Emily? Do you think you can make it down there? I mean, assuming you think we should still hear what she has to say."

"I absolutely do think we should hear what she has to say. But how about you come with me?"

A soft sigh on her end.

"You know I wish I could, but I'm not going to leave Terri here by herself all that time. It's bad enough I left her alone most of today."

"I know. But what if we brought her with us?"

Five minutes later, I padded down the stairs to the first floor, wearing sweatpants and a T-shirt. I found Daniel in the kitchen, standing over the stove.

"Good timing," he said. "These bad boys are ready to go."

He slid our sandwiches onto two separate plates. Because he knew the way I liked my grilled cheese, Daniel didn't bother asking me if he should cut it. He automatically grabbed a knife and sliced the sandwich diagonally before handing me my plate.

Unsurprisingly, it looked perfect. The bread golden and warmed just right. The melted cheese sticking out just a little, not running all over the place.

Still, I didn't touch it. Daniel, who was chomping away, frowned at me.

"Something wrong with it?"

"No, it looks great."

I took a quick bite but didn't taste much, my thoughts still running, everything a jumbled mess inside my head.

Daniel set his plate on the counter, wiped at his mouth with a napkin.

"Look, I didn't mean to be rude earlier. I just . . . I miss hanging out with you. I think I was jealous that you went out without me. And thank you again for the candy bar. I'd offer to share it, but I already ate the whole thing while you were in the shower."

I smiled at him, thinking that maybe Lisa was wrong, after all, that neither of us was in that metaphorical boiling water, and then something else occurred to me and I asked, "What do you think about going to the beach tomorrow?"

21

Grace Farmer's first day at Benjamin Franklin Middle School was a holiday. Probably the worst holiday a girl could pick to be the new kid in school.

Valentine's Day.

My first-period class was math with Mrs. Galloway. Five minutes after the bell, there was a soft knock at the door. Principal Ackerman stepped inside, a petite girl trailing him. She had her face tilted down, so all you could see was her long dark hair.

"Mrs. Galloway? Got a new fish for you."

Principal Ackerman chuckled at his lame joke, which was the type of thing he was known to do, and somebody in class—probably Bobby Wallbridge—let loose a loud, sarcastic laugh that cut off as soon as Ackerman whipped his head around to see who was making fun of him.

Mrs. Galloway placed her hands together in what I guessed was meant to be pleasant surprise.

"Ah yes. This is Grace Farmer, correct? Hello, Grace. I'm Mrs. Galloway."

Mrs. Galloway held out her hand. At first, the new girl just stood there, staring at the floor. A second or two ticked by with no response, and then Grace Farmer seemed to realize it was her turn to do something. She reached out and gave Mrs. Galloway what appeared to be a limp handshake.

Principal Ackerman kept the forced smile on his face. "Have a good day, Mrs. Galloway. Have a good day, class."

A good majority of the class, just to be silly, responded in unison: "Thank you, Principal Ackerman."

After he left, Mrs. Galloway directed Grace Farmer to an empty desk near the front of the classroom. Grace had a purple backpack that she gently placed on the floor beside the desk as she slid into it.

Mrs. Galloway frowned at the backpack.

"As a general rule, I do not allow backpacks in my classroom—they are meant to stay in your locker—but as this is your first day, I will allow it just this once."

She smiled when she said this, but you could tell she wasn't really being nice. She softly cleared her throat, adjusted her tortoiseshell eyeglasses.

"Now, Grace, if you would be so kind as to come up to the front of the class and introduce yourself . . ."

Mrs. Galloway let it hang there, the smile still on her face. When she gave a direction, a student was expected to comply.

But Grace Farmer didn't. She stayed seated at her desk.

Feeling some power start to shift in the teacher-student dynamic, Mrs. Galloway kept the smile going as she leaned in slightly.

"Grace, dear, all new students introduce themselves to the class. There are no ifs, ands, or buts."

Now everybody was watching the new girl. Waiting to see what she would do—or not do—next.

It didn't look like Grace was going to do anything at first—just keep sitting there, still as a statue—but then she twisted in her seat to stand and let Mrs. Galloway lead her to the front of the room.

She wore jeans, a red top, and sneakers, all of which looked like they had been newly bought from Walmart or T.J. Maxx—her sneakers, in fact, looked exactly like a pair I'd owned last year, and I felt the stirrings of dread in the pit of my stomach at the thought any of the other girls might notice.

She was pretty in a plain sort of way—soft cheekbones, a small nose, her dark hair just touching her shoulders and her bangs just an inch or so above her eyebrows—and it didn't look as if she was wearing any makeup.

I glanced at Elise, sitting three rows away from me. Elise, her expression tense, watched the new girl. We all knew this was going to be painful.

"My . . . my name"—her voice was barely audible, and what was audible trembled—"is Grace . . . Farmer. My mom and I . . . just recently . . . moved here."

We waited, silent, for Grace Farmer to say something else. She didn't. After a moment, she tilted her face down again and made a beeline for her desk. She slid into her seat and sat with her shoulders slouched forward, her back slightly bent, like she was trying to make herself as small as possible.

I glanced again at Elise, then at Olivia, who was sitting two rows away and one row back, but neither seemed interested in Grace Farmer. Elise was writing a note, probably to slip to whatever guy she was flirting with that week, and Olivia looked to be busily copying her math homework off somebody else. Neither of them seemed to see what I'd seen in those few seconds that Grace Farmer stood in front of the class.

The solution to my problem.

Seventeen: that was the number of carnations Mackenzie ended up getting during lunch.

We were all in the cafeteria, sitting at our regular table, when Teddy Fisher and Dash Malone approached. The two of them were on the student council and were among the students tasked with distributing carnations during lunch. Dash gave seven to Elise, five to Courtney, six to Olivia, and five to Destiny.

I got three. One was from Steven Getz, who I knew had a crush on me, and one was from Judah Howard, whom I had gone out with earlier in the year for a week or two. He always tried to shove his tongue down my throat when we were kissing.

The third card was signed simply *E.* I shot a quick glance at Elise, but she was busy shuffling through her own carnations. I figured she had sent me one on the off chance nobody else had, and I wasn't sure whether to feel gratitude or resentment.

"Where's mine?"

Mackenzie didn't ask so much as demand, and that was when Teddy set the bucket of seventeen carnations on the table beside her tray. Most of them were red, but a few were white and pink. Teddy didn't say anything else, and neither did Dash. They both turned and headed back to the corner of the cafeteria.

Elise said, "You're pathetic."

Mackenzie was busy scanning the attached cards. "Excuse me?"

"How many of those did you buy yourself?"

"Bitch, please. I didn't buy myself any."

"Bullshit."

Mackenzie gave Elise the kind of look she typically gave me: bored irritation.

"Don't be mad at me, Elise, just because you only got—how many are there—*seven*?"

The two of them started a back-and-forth that would eventually sputter out and die. My attention drifted. The cafeteria was louder than usual. Several tables away, a few boys were using carnations like whips to hit each other.

I noticed Grace Farmer sitting at a table off in the far corner. It was one of the tables where the nomads sat. Only one other person was there, a girl named Megan Fennelly. Megan was pudgy and often wore hoodies and Doc Martens, even when it was hot outside. She was always reading a book, so it made sense that she would be reading now. Teddy and Dash had yet to drop off any carnations for her; I doubted they would.

As for Grace, she stared down at her tray but didn't seem to be eating. I didn't blame her. Today was hot dogs and baked beans, and both tasted disgusting.

I left my own tray and the carnations at the table and drifted over to Grace. Megan Fennelly glanced up when I approached, but she knew I wasn't there for her and dove back into her book, a beat-up copy of *The Fellowship of the Ring*.

"You're the new girl."

Grace froze, her plastic fork suspended midair. I didn't know how long she'd stay like that, and I didn't want to be like Mackenzie and test it.

"Your name's Grace, right? I'm Emily."

Grace set the plastic fork down on her tray. She tilted her pale face up to me and nodded.

This would be tougher than I'd thought.

"Do you have any brothers or sisters?"

Glancing back down at her tray, she shook her head.

I looked over at Megan Fennelly, who I knew was watching us from the corner of her eye, and I leaned in close to Grace, made my tone as good-natured as I could.

"You said you and your mom moved here recently, right? Where from?"

For a second or two she didn't respond, just kept sitting there staring down at her tray, and I thought maybe I had wasted my time. I couldn't even make friends with the shy new girl. How pathetic was that?

I was about ready to turn and head back to our table when Grace spoke in a quiet voice.

"Up north."

I nodded, not sure what to say to that, and then asked, "Would you like to come sit with me and my friends?"

Incredibly, it took more convincing than I would have imagined. For some reason I really had to sell it, and by that point I *needed* to make it work. I couldn't return to the table empty handed, especially when I caught a few glances from Courtney and Olivia across the cafeteria. They knew something was up, and if they knew, so did Mackenzie.

In the end, finally, I convinced Grace to leave the nomad table and come sit with us.

She followed me slowly, and I had to check over my shoulder several times to make sure she didn't wander away. When we reached the table, I sat and motioned for her to take the open space beside me. That was when all the girls stopped talking to stare.

I knew this scheme of mine might backfire. If it didn't go the way I planned, I might end up being excommunicated sooner than anticipated. So I cleared my throat, and put as much conviction in my voice as I could.

"This is Grace. She's new."

Glowering at me, Mackenzie said, "Bennett, what the fuck are you doing?"

"She's new," I repeated, staring squarely at Mackenzie. "I invited her to sit with us."

"I don't care who the hell she is, she's not sitting with us." Mackenzie sat with her shoulders back, her chin tilted up, and spoke about Grace like she wasn't even there. Which was obviously the point. "Who gave you permission to bring her over here, anyway?"

At that moment I was very close to telling Mackenzie to fuck off. My plan—if you could even call it that—had blown up in my face. I glanced at Grace to see her reaction, but she had her face tilted down, her shoulders slouched, trying to make herself as small as possible.

My hands squeezed into fists under the table. I felt my teeth pressing hard against each other. I glared back at Mackenzie, ready to say something stupid, and then Elise yawned.

"Relax," she said. "I told her it was cool."

Mackenzie whipped her head around. "Without consulting me first?"

"Oops."

Mackenzie didn't like it. She knew Elise was covering for me, and she especially didn't like that. Her drilling stare shifted from Elise and bored into me.

Then her eyes lit up, and she smiled.

"What did you say her name was?"

Again, talking about her like she wasn't even there. I glanced at Grace, expecting her to answer, but of course she didn't.

"Grace," I said.

"Right, Grace. Well, Grace, you're more than welcome to sit with us. First, though"—Mackenzie grabbed the bucket of carnations, held it out over the floor—"pick these up."

And she tilted the bucket, letting the carnations tumble down. All seventeen of them.

Mackenzie didn't take her eyes off me the entire time. Not when the final carnation fell on top of the others. Not when she set the empty bucket on the floor. She just sat there, watching me, waiting to see what the new girl would do next.

For a couple of seconds, Grace didn't do anything. She just sat there beside me, her shoulders slouched. Then, very slowly, she tilted her face to glance at me.

I nodded.

Grace stared for another moment. Then she stood up, circled the table, and crouched down to start collecting the carnations off the floor.

Mackenzie watched her for several seconds before she looked around the table, a new light in her eyes. We all sat, silent, as Grace Farmer picked up each and every carnation, put them in the bucket, and held it out to Mackenzie.

"Very good, Grace. I'm impressed."

After another moment, Mackenzie motioned to the table. When she spoke next, she was again staring straight at me.

"I suppose you can stay. For now."

22

We didn't smell the ocean until we were ten miles away, and even then I wasn't sure if Terri knew what it was. She sat in the back with Courtney, on the driver's side, so that she'd have a good view of the water once the highway veered close enough.

I glanced back at her from where I sat in the passenger seat of Daniel's car.

"Do you smell it?"

The windows were down, and Terri's braids jittered around her head.

"Smell what?" she asked.

"The ocean."

The sky was cloudless, the sun bright. So far there were only houses and sand and tall grass. Terri stared out her window, sniffing the air, and then shook her head at me.

"I don't think so."

She said it almost apologetically, like she was afraid to hurt my feelings.

I smiled at her. "Don't worry. We'll be there soon enough."

Turning back in my seat, I saw Daniel looking at me. I smiled at him, and he smiled back. For once, he seemed sincerely happy. He had his phone on his leg, the Google Maps app open, the blue line headed right down the highway, which was predictably busy on this late Saturday morning.

"How much farther?" I asked.

He glanced at his phone. "Depending on traffic, maybe another ten minutes."

In the back seat, Terri asked, "Mom, do you have any bubblegum?"

Courtney didn't make a show of checking her purse. She already knew the answer and said simply, "No, baby, I don't."

"I don't have bubblegum," I said, "but I do have gum."

I opened my purse and dug around until I found the yellow pack at the bottom. It was still sealed from when I'd purchased it at Walmart. I tore it open and handed a piece back to Terri. She chewed it for a couple of seconds, and then smiled at me.

"It's good," she said. "Thank you."

"You want the rest of the pack for the beach?"

"Yes, please."

She took it from me, and I sat back in my seat and stared out the windshield at the traffic ahead of us. A minute later, I could hear Terri sniffing loudly.

"Aunt Emily?"

Aunt Emily. Hearing her say the name made me smile.

"Yes?"

"I think I do smell it now."

"What does it smell like?"

She took a moment to think.

"Salt?"

Courtney said, "I don't know what you two are talking about. I smell dead fish. Daniel, don't you smell dead fish?"

With that, she leaned over and tickled her daughter, who giggled delightedly. I stole a glance at Daniel, who was watching them in the rearview mirror, a soft smile on his face. When he noticed me watching him, he cleared his throat.

"Almost there."

Unsurprisingly, there were no open parking spots near the boardwalk, and the lots were incredibly expensive. That was okay, since we were just dropping off Daniel and Terri. But Courtney wanted to be with her daughter when she saw the ocean for the first time, so Daniel dropped them off in a no-parking zone and kept the four-ways flashing while we stepped out and met each other at the front of the car.

"Thank you for doing this," I said.

"Of course."

On that other timeline, Daniel would bend his head down to peck me on the lips, maybe even give me a hug.

He didn't do either, so I leaned up on my tiptoes, brushed my lips against his.

This clearly surprised him, and he just stood there for a second, not doing anything. Then he leaned forward to kiss me back, but by then I'd stepped away, was staring past him at the crowd of people across the street.

My sudden gasp, barely audible, made Daniel frown.

"Emily?"

I didn't answer at first, still staring across the busy intersection.

"Emily," Daniel said, a bit more urgently now, and he touched my arm.

I blinked, looked at him, looked back out at the crowd across the street.

He asked, "Are you okay?"

That was when Courtney and Terri appeared at the top of the boardwalk and headed our way, Terri's flip-flops slapping eagerly on the steps.

Daniel gave me another worried look, and then turned to them, smiling.

"So? How was it?"

"Awesome!" Terri shouted.

Courtney gave her daughter a quick hug as Daniel went back to the trunk and pulled out a backpack full of towels and sunscreen, bottles of water and plastic snack bags of Goldfish crackers and pretzels. More than enough to get them through the few hours it would take Courtney and me to drive out to Ridgeway Farm and back.

Daniel stepped close to me and touched my arm again, his expression once more filled with worry.

I forced a smile. "I'm fine. You two have fun."

"Oh, we will." He glanced at Terri. "Ready?"

"Ready!"

Daniel smiled at us, readjusted his aviator sunglasses.

"We'll see you when you get back."

According to Google Maps, Ridgeway Farm was an hour from the beach. I drove, Courtney up front in the passenger seat, our windows still down and the air messing up our hair.

"Daniel seems like a really great guy," Courtney said.

I didn't answer.

"Emily, you okay?"

I blinked, glanced over at her. "What? Yeah, I'm fine."

"Are you sure? You seem . . . kinda off."

What was I supposed to say to that? That for a second, while I'd stood there with Daniel back at the boardwalk, I'd looked across the intersection and thought I'd seen Grace?

It had been for only a second, nothing more, just a woman with a pale face and dark hair standing across the street, staring back at me. But when I'd blinked and looked again, she wasn't there. Like she had never been there in the first place.

"No, I'm fine. Just didn't get much sleep last night."

"You want me to drive?"

"Do you even have a driver's license anymore?"

Courtney grinned at me, and then her expression became all at once solemn.

"Are you sure you're okay?"

"Oh my God," I said. "Yes, I'm fine. Seriously."

But was I? Maybe I was just seeing things. That made the most sense, after all. There was no reason *not* to tell Courtney, but I was worried what she might say, how she might react.

"Anyway, what did you say about Daniel?"

"I said he seems like a really great guy."

"He is."

"And you haven't tied him down yet? Girl, I don't know what you're waiting on. What did you tell him about our trip, anyway?"

"That I had learned about another old friend who passed away a couple months ago. I said we wanted to pay our respects to her wife, but the only way we could both make it was if someone watched your daughter. He seemed to like the idea of getting to hang out on the beach and boardwalk all day."

This was more or less the truth. But it had taken much more convincing than it would have several years ago, when things were better between us. Then, Daniel would have done anything for me without question. Now, he was open to the idea of doing anything for me, but he needed a reason beyond simple love and devotion. As he'd already been planning to volunteer at the Boys & Girls Club, I'd suggested that he could volunteer to help out Courtney's daughter instead.

Courtney slumped down in her seat, and stared out her window.

"I wish we all could have just stayed at the beach. The closer we get, the more I'm dreading this."

"Me too. It's going to be awkward showing up out of nowhere. There's no guarantee she'll talk to us, assuming she's even there."

"Like I told you, I called the farm early this morning and asked if Charlotte would be there today. They said yes, that she would be giving her lessons like she does every Saturday. But that's not what I meant."

I shot a curious glance at her. "What did you mean?"

Still staring out her window, Courtney said, "I'm dreading what she might tell us."

23

Ridgeway Farm wasn't the sprawling acreage I had envisioned. It was just a farm set a quarter mile off the road, with two sets of stables behind a white-brick farmhouse with blue trim and fencing that seemed to run everywhere. A few horses grazed in one of the fields, while in another a woman walked beside a horse with a child on top.

I parked beside the stables closest to this field. The car next to us was an aging Toyota Corolla, a nasty dent in the rear bumper and one of its hubcaps missing.

Unclipping her seat belt, Courtney said, "I always thought people who rode horses were really well off."

"Maybe it's hers."

I tilted my chin toward a middle-aged woman in jeans and a T-shirt standing on the outside of the fence, her arms folded on one of the planks as she watched.

We got out of the car. The sky was a vibrant blue, the air warm and scented with hay and freshly mowed grass.

The woman smiled at us as we approached and offered a soft hello.

We smiled back, watching Charlotte as she slowly walked the horse around a series of orange cones. It was clear that she was beautiful, her skin a deep brown, her long black hair tied in a side-braided ponytail. She wore jeans and cowboy boots and a checkered shirt.

The child on the horse wore jeans and what looked like a large bicycle helmet. He seemed to have trouble paying attention, his focus drifting off; Charlotte needed to redirect him every ten seconds or so. It didn't help that Courtney and I had arrived, adding an extra distraction. At one point, Charlotte glanced over her shoulder, frowned at us, and then shifted her attention back to the boy.

After a couple of minutes, the woman leaning on the fence spoke quietly.

"That's my son. His name is Adam. We've been coming here every Saturday for the past two months. Charlotte's great with him, and he loves horses. Though"—a smile—"he can get distracted quite easily."

I smiled at the woman. "That's wonderful."

"Does your child work with Charlotte?"

Before I could respond, Courtney said, "That's why we're here. I'm thinking about enrolling my daughter."

"Does she have autism too?"

"Yes," I said before Courtney could answer. "She was diagnosed when she was two years old. She's six now, and one of her doctors recommended she come here."

The woman's smile brightened up a notch.

"I think she'll love it. There's a special connection between a child and a horse. At least, that's what I've come to see with Adam. This morning he was having a hard time. He wouldn't do anything I asked him to do, and he kept hitting me, but when I got him in the car and he realized we were coming here, he settled down. He loves riding Jasper."

Jasper, presumably, was the horse.

"The only downside"—the woman's smile faded—"is our insurance doesn't cover equine therapy. So I'm paying out of pocket. But Charlotte is great. She's worked out a payment plan with me."

A silence fell, and the woman turned her attention back to her son. Inside the fence, Charlotte continued to walk Jasper through the cones, redirecting Adam's focus every time he glanced toward his mother or off toward another part of the farm. She continued for the next five minutes before she started to lead the horse toward us. She gave Courtney and me another curious glance before smiling at Adam's mother.

"He did great."

Adam's mother beamed.

"Of course he did," she said. "He and Jasper are best friends."

The boy's focus was back on us as his mother spoke again.

"Adam, you did so great!"

He grinned as Charlotte halted Jasper. She took the reins, tied them to the fence post, said, "Ready, Adam?" He barely reacted, still staring at his mother, who needed to prompt him—"Adam, pay attention to Miss Charlotte"—and only after several of these prompts did he blink and look at Charlotte, and that was when she reached up to start to pull him off.

As soon as Adam realized he was being taken away from Jasper, he started screaming. The horse, to its credit, barely reacted. I wasn't surprised. Animals can be unpredictable, but therapy horses like Jasper were chosen for a reason. Loud noises didn't startle them. Besides, Jasper was probably used to Adam and knew that he wasn't a threat.

"It's okay, it's okay," Charlotte cooed as she placed Adam on the ground. His face was red now, and he started to hit Charlotte, but it was clear he didn't really know how to make a fist. Besides, he was a tiny kid, weighing no more than sixty pounds. Charlotte kept cooing to him—"It's okay, Adam, we do this every time, don't we, we say goodbye to Jasper"—and she deflected his blows easily until he started to tire out.

In the end, Charlotte managed to get Adam settled and walked him over to pet Jasper, which he did happily. Then she directed him toward the gate, where his mother was already waiting to kneel down and squeeze him in a hug.

"You did great, honey!"

Adam's face had started to lighten. He kept glancing at us, the new strangers, and I worried that our presence might trigger him. After all, us being here was not part of the routine. The change might set him off even more.

Charlotte said to Adam's mother, "Same time next week?"

"That would be great. And I get paid next week, so I can bring a check then."

"Sounds fine."

Adam's mother took her son's hand and lifted it up.

"Say goodbye, Adam."

Adam kept staring at Jasper.

"One of these days," his mother said, and the hope in her voice broke my heart.

Charlotte nodded enthusiastically. "Absolutely. You both have a great weekend."

"We'll try." Then, as if remembering they had an audience, Adam's mother pointed at Courtney. "Oh, and she wants to talk to you about getting her daughter started."

As Adam and his mother drove away, Charlotte went back to Jasper and untied the reins from the fence post.

"Did we have an appointment scheduled today? I can't remember one, but it may have slipped my mind."

As we had with Philip, Courtney and I glanced at each other briefly, realizing we didn't have an exact game plan and waiting for the other to speak first.

Charlotte noted the uneasy pause, and her voice became guarded. "What can I help you with?"

I softly cleared my throat, decided to jump right in.

"We actually wanted to talk to you about Destiny."

She shifted seamlessly, pivoting on the heel of her boot so that she was on one side of Jasper and we were on the other. Her light-brown eyes hardened as she stared at us over the horse's back.

"Who the hell are you?"

"We're old classmates of Destiny's. We learned recently that she had passed away and wanted to give you our condolences."

Charlotte's hard eyes shifted back and forth between us.

"That's it?"

"No. We also had some questions."

"What kind of questions?"

"We were wondering how she passed away. It didn't say in her obituary."

Her face remained emotionless, like she was trying to steady her nerves. This wasn't heading in the right direction, and I feared that we would lose our opportunity very soon, so I went for it.

"Did Destiny take her own life?"

It was as if time had stopped. The sound of the wind, the other horses in the adjoining field, and the birds in the trees all went silent.

Charlotte said, "Who are you?"

"My name is Emily Bennett. This is Courtney Sullivan."

Courtney raised a hand to wave, as if that would help the situation, but Charlotte didn't seem to notice. Something was different in her eyes. As if a switch had been flicked on.

"Jesus Christ," she whispered. "Emily and Courtney."

I didn't like the way she said it, as if she already knew us.

"Did Destiny talk about us?"

"Yes. About what you and your friends did to Grace Farmer."

Now it was my turn to steady my nerves.

"You know about Grace?"

Charlotte kept her gaze steady with mine.

"Of course I do. She's the reason Destiny is dead."

24

We waited outside while Charlotte stabled Jasper. When she reappeared, a backpack hanging off her shoulder, she had an electric cigarette laced between her fingers.

"I was a smoker when Destiny first met me. She hated it. Hated how it got into my hair and my clothes, but mostly she hated the taste of kissing me. I knew I couldn't stop cold turkey, so after two years I'm still puffing away on these."

She held up the electric cigarette, a thin silver tube, and stared at it.

"Ever since Destiny died, I've been using them more and more. I've been tempted to go back to the real thing, but I just can't do it. I *want* to, but I won't."

I cleared my throat again, hoping to break her from her daze.

"What happened to Destiny? How is Grace involved?"

Charlotte eyed me, sucking again on the electric cigarette.

"I know, I know. That's why you're here. Part of me wants to tell you, but another part . . . another part wants me to tell you both to fuck off."

She watched us when she said this, probably trying to elicit some type of reaction, but neither Courtney nor I moved. We just stood there, quietly, and waited. As far as we were concerned, she could be as mad as she wanted. She'd lost her wife. She deserved to be angry.

Charlotte sucked on the electric cigarette, shaking her head.

"Maybe I'm not being fair. I know you two aren't responsible for Destiny's death. Destiny, based on the story she told me, was just as complicit in what happened. You were all the popular girls in school, she said. Called yourselves the Harpies, for some stupid reason. To be honest with you, in my school, I hated the popular girls."

"I'm not a fan of the popular girls we had in our school either."

Charlotte gave me a slow smile.

"She liked you, you know. She told me a couple of years back, right around the time we first started dating. We would talk about when we first knew we were gay. For me, I always suspected, but it wasn't until college that I finally accepted it. I'd dated guys all the time, told myself that was what I needed to do, but it never felt right. Destiny was actually my first girlfriend, and then she became my wife. How crazy is that?"

It was clearly a rhetorical question, so neither Courtney nor I answered. Charlotte shook her head, looked out across the farm.

"Anyway, Destiny told me she knew early on. I asked her who her first crush was, and she said it was somebody in middle school. A girl named Emily. Did you ever suspect?"

I remembered that weekend before Christmas at the mall, when Destiny hugged me outside Hot Topic. I remembered, too, how Destiny had always been especially nice to me when Mackenzie and the other girls dismissed my ideas. How she'd always ended up sitting next to me in the cafeteria or when we went to the movies. I'd seen her as a friend, an ally against Mackenzie and nothing more, but, to be fair, I had been so consumed with losing my spot in the group that I hadn't had time to notice much else.

To Charlotte's question, I answered simply and honestly.

"No."

"Not even a little?"

I shook my head. Charlotte smiled again, and shrugged.

"Oh well. I was just curious. It doesn't matter, anyway. I always thought it was cute, Destiny being popular. Once I asked her to show me pictures from middle school. She said she didn't have any, and I believed her, but after she told me what you all had done to Grace, I started to wonder if maybe she just didn't want to look at those pictures again, even if she had them."

"We were young," I said quietly.

Charlotte said, "Not that young. You were eighth graders. Fourteen years old. You chose to be cruel."

"We're not here to defend what happened. We know it was wrong. If we could go back and change things, we would."

Charlotte was quiet. Her eyes shifted from my face to the field and fences and the trees beyond.

"Destiny was the one who introduced me to equine therapy. I'd been riding almost all my life, but I never made the connection—you know, that riding a horse could be therapeutic to kids with special needs. But it's true. When you're riding, you feel a real connection to the horse. You become one. There's a trust there. I took some extra classes, and now here I am, doing my bit to help."

"Charlotte?"

"Yes."

"Are you stalling on purpose?"

"Yes."

I traded a glance with Courtney. I didn't want to push too hard or give Charlotte a chance to clam up. She seemed like she wanted to tell us what had happened to Destiny, but something was holding her back.

"We came a long way to talk," I said. "If you don't want to tell us anything, that's up to you. But we really need to know the truth."

"Why?"

Like with Philip, I didn't want to say too much. She had suffered enough. She didn't need to know that Grace Farmer might have been responsible for somebody else's death. That Grace was still out there, maybe getting ready to terrorize another one of us.

"She was our friend."

Charlotte snorted and shook her head.

"Your *friend*? When was the last time you even spoke to your *friend*? When was the last time you saw her?"

"We don't want to upset you, Charlotte. If you want us to leave, we'll leave."

"How very kind of you." She said it sarcastically, then sighed, biting her lip. "Honestly, it doesn't matter what I want. It matters what Destiny would have wanted. And I think she would have wanted you to know."

I let a moment of silence pass, but only a moment. I needed to keep Charlotte focused and talking. Especially now that she'd given us this opening.

"How did Grace cause Destiny to die?"

"She didn't."

"But I thought you said—"

"Yes, I did say that Destiny is dead because of Grace. But Grace had nothing to do with it."

Destiny had started seeing Grace at different places, Charlotte told us—or somebody she thought was Grace. When they were down at the boardwalk. Another time at the grocery store. Again at the mall. They'd be walking along, holding hands, talking about whatever, and Destiny would stop short. Charlotte would look at her, and Destiny would be staring off into the crowd.

The first couple of times, Destiny shook her head and said it was nothing when Charlotte asked her what was wrong. And it really seemed like it. A couple of days would go by with no problems, and then they'd be out in public and Destiny would see Grace.

Only Charlotte didn't think it *was* Grace. She never saw anyone, though of course she didn't know what Grace looked like. Destiny would grab her arm and point and ask if Charlotte saw her. Every time Charlotte looked, she didn't see anything.

"I mean, I saw people—we were always out in public—but it was never the person Destiny thought. She tried to snap pictures of her one time when we were at the mall, but all the photos were just blurs. Once, Destiny took off into the crowd, chasing after her, but of course she never found her."

Charlotte paused, looking at me now. Her eyes narrowed.

"I'm telling the truth," she said.

I opened my mouth, not sure what to say. This entire time I'd been trying to hide my emotions, trying to act like I, too, hadn't seen Grace—or somebody who looked like Grace—only an hour ago. Charlotte was telling us a story about how Destiny went mad, and it seemed like the first step was seeing Grace in public places, and my entire being wanted to scream.

"I don't think Emily is doubting you," Courtney said.

I nodded quickly, telling myself to stay calm, that I hadn't really seen anything back at the boardwalk, that it was just my imagination.

"That's right. I'm not doubting you at all. It's just this whole thing . . . it's a lot to take in. How many times did Destiny think she saw Grace?"

"Oh, Jesus. I can't remember. Maybe a dozen? And that was over the course of two months. Destiny started having trouble sleeping. She stopped eating too. It wasn't healthy, but she refused to tell me what was wrong. When she took off in the mall, running through the crowd, pushing people aside, I finally told her enough was enough. I demanded she tell me what was going on. That's when she broke down and told me about Grace. And two weeks later . . . she was dead."

"I'm sorry. Can I ask how she died?"

Charlotte's eyes were glassy with tears. She wiped them with the back of her hands.

"She texted me one day that she was tired and was going to go to sleep and that she loved me. I didn't think much of it at the time; I just thought she was going to take a nap. But when I came home, I found her in the garage. She was behind the steering wheel. Her car was still running."

Courtney's hand went to her mouth. "Oh my God."

"Did she leave a note?" I asked.

Charlotte nodded, wiped at her eyes again.

"I guess so."

"What does that mean?"

"If by note you mean some kind of explanation, then no. She didn't explain why she did what she did. Her last text to me didn't make any sense. It was just one word."

"What word?"

"Vesper." Charlotte paused again, frowning at us. "Does that mean anything to either of you?"

We shook our heads.

"Me neither. Doesn't mean anything to Destiny's parents or brother. I googled the word, and it means evening prayer, but that makes even less sense. Neither of us was religious. I've thought maybe it was some kind of autocorrect mix-up, but for the life of me I can't figure out what else she may have been trying to type."

"So she texted you the word *vesper*? That's it?"

"Yes. I was busy at work. It was maybe an hour later when I saw it and texted her a question mark. But there was no response. All this time I've just"—Charlotte's voice cracked—"I've wondered what might have happened if I'd replied sooner. If maybe that might have changed things. That . . . that had I called her, maybe she wouldn't have killed herself. Do you think that might be true? That in some way I could have saved her?"

25

They say power corrupts, but usually they mean people who are high up on the food chain of life.

Police officers. Judges. CEOs. Congressmen. Presidents.

Not fourteen-year-old girls in a middle school in Central Pennsylvania.

Looking back, our close friendship created that power. If you had separated us, whatever power we might have held would have fizzled. Mackenzie was absolutely the brashest, but would she alone have done to Grace what we as a collective had done? Would any of us have done it individually?

In eleventh grade our English teacher, Mr. Huston, had us read *Lord of the Flies*. When the class finished the book, he suggested that the events in the novel wouldn't have happened had girls been the ones stranded on the island. Girls, he reasoned, were more rational and better at teamwork, and events would not have escalated nearly as badly. Would there have been tension? Sure. Power struggles? Absolutely. But in the end, the girls would have let reason overcome their pettiness, and everybody would still have been alive when the naval officer arrived at the island.

Most of the students nodded their heads, acknowledging Mr. Huston's theory. But I knew better, and so did Courtney, who'd been in the same class (and who would find out in another month that she was pregnant). Courtney and I understood how power corrupts, how girls could be just as manipulative and vicious as boys, if not more so. If we'd been trapped on that island in middle school, Grace never would have gotten the chance to attempt suicide, because we would have sniffed out the weakest ones early on, and she would have ended up like Piggy, crushed under a boulder.

◆ ◆ ◆

"I'm going to take a shower," Daniel said the moment we walked into the town house. He dropped his backpack by the door and started up the steps, already pulling his T-shirt up over his head and exposing his freshly tanned back.

I watched him go, wondering if I should follow him. That was something we used to do—take showers together, soaping down our bodies under the running water—but I couldn't remember the last time it had happened. Maybe now was the moment. Daniel could use a nice reward after putting up with Courtney's daughter all day, though in reality, Terri had been great and not an issue at all, at least from what Daniel had said. After we'd dropped them off at Highland Estates, I'd given him a chance to vent his frustrations, but he hadn't said one negative word about the trip.

He was still in the shower when I came up. I lingered outside the bathroom door, biting my lip. Should I ask if he'd like me to join him? On that other timeline, I wouldn't even hesitate—I'd strip off my clothes and step into the shower; Daniel would immediately turn to me, his erection already growing, and pull me close.

We'd shared a nice moment at the beach, hadn't we? I'd kissed him, and he'd leaned in to kiss me back.

Only then I'd pulled away when I spotted Grace standing across the busy intersection. Just a pale face among a large crowd. A pale face staring back at me, just like it had done to Destiny before it broke her and she decided she'd had enough and she—

"No," I whispered, shaking my head as if to clear it. "I didn't see Grace. I didn't see anyone."

I turned away from the bathroom and found my laptop on the bedside table. I flipped open the lid and googled Grace Farmer. Courtney had told me on the drive back from Huey's Bar & Grille last night that she'd tried it with no luck, but I wanted to try it for myself.

Several different people popped up, just like Courtney had said, but true to her word, none appeared to be our Grace Farmer.

Where had Grace come from, anyway? Somewhere upstate, that was all we'd gotten out of her. She hardly ever spoke, let alone about herself. We knew that she'd moved to Lanton with her mother, but we had never been to their apartment.

I thought about the private investigator I'd hired in high school. I remembered his face, his deep voice, the way he exuded authority, but his name escaped me. I used Google to search for private investigators in the area, thinking that might trigger something, but none of the search results seemed right.

I was still sitting on the bed, my legs crossed, when Daniel came out of the bathroom. He had a towel wrapped around his waist and was drying his hair.

He didn't say anything to me. I didn't say anything to him.

I hated this. Hated that this was what had become of our relationship. Once lovers, now roommates. We split the rent and utilities. We never went out to dinner. Never went to the grocery store together. One of us would start a list, and the other would eventually stop by the store and buy whatever was on it. Milk. Bread. Cereal. Yogurt. Tampons.

I remembered what Lisa had said about how Daniel wasn't going to be the one to end our relationship: *He's a good guy, but emotionally he isn't strong enough to stand up for himself.*

My cell phone vibrated on the bedside table. I reached over and saw a text from Courtney.

It was a photograph. Terri hugging the giant stuffed panda bear Daniel had won for her, a goofy smile on her face. Daniel had made a crack about having to play a hundred times to knock down some stupid bottles at the boardwalk stand to win the thing, but he'd laughed when he said it, and you knew he would have played a hundred more times if needed.

The phone vibrated again.

Tell Daniel Terri loves her new bear!

I smiled, opened my mouth to say his name, but when I looked up, Daniel had already dressed in a T-shirt and sweatpants and was heading out of the bedroom.

The phone vibrated with a third text message.

Btw, Elise got back to me. Said she can meet us tomorrow night. Pick me up at 6?

My stomach clenched. I had seen Elise at my therapist's office and had barely been able to breathe. And now I was expected to sit across from her after all this time. I wasn't sure I'd even be able to form words. It had been over a decade since I last spoke to the girl who was once my best friend, my lifeline against Mackenzie.

I typed back a quick yes, and then set the phone aside, closed the laptop. I started for the bathroom, stripping out of my clothes. Daniel had left the fan on, but the air was still thick with steam.

In the shower, I stood motionless, my face tilted down, letting the water beat at the back of my head. My right hand on the knob, increasing the temperature ever so slightly. Waiting to see how much pain I could endure.

26

We'd invited Grace to the mall that weekend, and Mackenzie had talked her into "borrowing" something from one of the stores, speaking in her hushed surreptitious tone while we sat at our typical table in the food court, D.B. and her crew nowhere in sight.

"Don't think of it as *stealing*. None of us *steal*. We have more than enough money, except maybe Bennett, and that's because her family's basically living on food stamps."

She said it like I wasn't there—she didn't even glance my way—and that somehow made it worse. Because I realized that this was how Mackenzie talked about me when I wasn't around. Like any other girl in school who happened to cross her path, and not somebody she'd known since kindergarten.

I opened my mouth, wanting to say something like "Screw you, you bitch," but Elise caught my eye and gave a slight shake of her head, her expression telling me that it wouldn't be worth it.

Mackenzie motioned at Grace's clothes—her stonewashed jeans, bland sneakers and T-shirt—and offered up a disappointed sigh.

"Based on this mess, I'm guessing you don't have much money either. But that's okay. We can make that work. Again, this isn't *stealing*. It's proving that you can do anything and get away with it. You want that, Grace, don't you? You want to be the kind of person who can get away with anything."

Grace tilted her head in a subservient nod. Mackenzie flashed a bright smile, her teeth so white and straight they barely looked real.

"That's my girl," she said. "Now, let's go prove you have what it takes to be a Harpy."

We ended up waiting outside of Macy's. Elise volunteered to accompany Grace into the store, to keep an eye on her to make sure she followed through and didn't attract too much employee attention.

Macy's was on the edge of the mall, and we sat on two of the benches and talked and laughed, acted like nothing was amiss, until ten minutes had passed and Grace and Elise emerged from the store. Grace walked stiffly, her face tilted down, but that was how she always walked.

Elise gave us a slight nod, which told us all we needed to know.

Back in the food court, Grace fumbled the tiny bottle of perfume from her pocket. It was one of those travel-size bottles, not even an ounce of fluid inside, but it didn't matter. She'd followed through. She'd stolen it.

"Dolce & Gabbana," Mackenzie nearly shouted, impressed, and then squirted some of it on the back of her hand. "This doesn't smell too bad. I like it."

She offered her hand to the rest of us, so we could sniff the scent. I was the only one who abstained. This slight didn't go unnoticed, but Mackenzie did a good job of ignoring me as she turned back to Grace.

"You're more than welcome to keep this, Grace—you did borrow it, after all—but mind if I keep it instead?"

Of course Grace told Mackenzie yes, though I wondered what Mackenzie would have done had Grace said anything else. The first sign of independence. Of possible disrespect. The idea thrilled me, and reminded me that I hadn't actually stolen anything myself. Which meant that so far Grace had proved herself as a Harpy, and I hadn't.

That was why, the next day at Walmart with my mother, I'd tried to steal the earrings. To prove to myself that I could. That I was brave enough.

Of course, I got caught, and then I got grounded, which meant I wasn't there for the following two weekends with the girls. Including the second weekend, the one that resulted in Grace Farmer being labeled a slut by almost everybody in school.

Destiny was the one who filled me in. It was early Monday morning, the two of us in the bathroom between classes. Destiny told me they'd all been over at Mackenzie's house, even Grace. Eventually they'd ended up at the Farmhouse.

But it wasn't only the girls. Some boys were at the Farmhouse too. Older boys, freshmen or sophomores, Destiny didn't know which. She said it looked like they'd stepped out of an Abercrombie & Fitch catalog. They were athletic—no doubt all of them were on the same lacrosse or soccer team—had supercute smiles, and wore shorts and bright polo shirts and had gel in their hair.

They were already there when the girls arrived, and they had beer and weed. Mackenzie knew one of them, and she'd gone up and talked to him, laughing in that fake way of hers (and here Destiny rolled her eyes).

Soon Mackenzie beckoned the other girls to join. The boys shared their beer and weed, and Courtney shared the Grey Goose she'd managed to sneak out of her house. After an hour or so, they sat sprawled on the dusty hardwood floor—the Farmhouse had no furniture—all of them quite drunk.

That was when Mackenzie turned to Grace, a mischievous smile on her face.

"You ever kiss a boy, Grace?"

Grace had been hanging in the background, smiling and laughing quietly when needed, though judging by the look in her eyes, Destiny thought she was also drunk. It was hard to tell—Grace looked so guarded—but she tilted her head down at Mackenzie's question and shrugged.

Mackenzie leaned in close to Grace, their bare legs touching.

"Don't be embarrassed," she whispered. "Have you ever kissed a boy?"

Her eyes still lowered, Grace allowed a small nod.

"Oooh," Mackenzie said dramatically, laughing with the others in the circle. Then her smile winked out, and all at once she went serious.

"What about sucked a boy's dick—you ever do that?"

Everybody except Grace burst out laughing. Grace sat silent, her shoulders slouched forward, still not looking at anyone, and allowed another small nod.

"Bullshit," Olivia said.

Mackenzie held up a finger to silence her. "Now, now, be nice."

She grinned once again at Grace, without warmth.

"Tell us, Grace, did you swallow or spit?"

Another burst of laughter from everybody except Grace, who kept staring down at the floor.

Mackenzie leaned in closer, and spoke in a stage whisper.

"Personally, I prefer swallowing. It doesn't taste great, but the boys love it. Don't you, boys?"

As the boys hooted and hollered in agreement, Destiny started to have a bad feeling. She was drunk, yes, and she figured this was just Mackenzie being Mackenzie, but the questions didn't seem right, especially in front of these high school boys.

Once everyone had quieted down, Mackenzie handed the bottle of vodka to Grace.

"This is your first time at the Farmhouse, isn't it? I think you need a tour. Take another drink, and I'll show you the upstairs."

Grace, eyes still lowered, took a hesitant swig from the bottle. Almost immediately Mackenzie was on her feet, reaching out for Grace, and then they were headed toward the stairs, Mackenzie asking for the boy she knew to help them, and that boy jumped right to his feet, and they all three disappeared, heading to the second floor, which was just as empty as the first.

A minute later, Mackenzie came bounding back down the steps. Alone. She rejoined the circle and grabbed the joint. After a couple of minutes, the boy who had been upstairs came back down, and another boy hurried up.

It went on like that for the next half hour or so: another boy would head upstairs when one returned, though Destiny noted that not all the boys went, maybe three or four, the others looking a bit unsettled, their laughter at times uncomfortable.

By then, Destiny told me, she no longer had a strong sense of time. Somehow it was all on the periphery, the action happening beyond her reach.

"I knew it was wrong," she said, a few seconds before the bell rang, signaling the start of third period. "I watched those guys go upstairs, one after another, and I just . . . I did *nothing*."

After a while, the boys had left, several of them with smug smiles on their faces. A few, Destiny said, were fist-bumping each other. One of them handed another joint to Mackenzie, who passed it to Courtney as she stood and motioned for Elise to follow her upstairs.

A minute or two later, they returned with Grace.

Her knees were dirty, as were her shorts and T-shirt. Her hair was mussed up. She wouldn't meet anyone's eyes. She kept her face tilted toward the floor like usual and sank down into her place in the circle.

Reclaiming the new joint, Mackenzie took a hit and then smiled at her.

"You wanted to be popular, Grace? Now you're popular. Those boys are going to remember you forever."

27

My mother's car wasn't in the driveway, so I used my key to let myself in the front door.

"Mom?"

No answer, which was what I'd expect for a Sunday morning. My mother still went to church.

I'd grown up in this house, had lived here off and on during college and grad school, but it didn't feel like home anymore, not after my father's death.

I didn't bother going upstairs. The year after I'd gone to college, my parents had decided to turn my room into a guest room, despite the fact that they rarely hosted friends or family overnight. They'd boxed up all my stuff and stored it in the basement, repainted the walls dark beige, hung new curtains, and replaced my double bed with a queen.

Despite this, I placed one foot on the first step leading to the second floor, my fingers grazing the banister. Maybe stepping inside my room would trigger a lost memory. Help me remember the private investigator's name.

But no—like Charlotte outside that stable yesterday, I was stalling. I left the stairs and walked through the house, toward the door leading down to the basement.

The basement wasn't finished. Furnace, water heater, washer and dryer, and dehumidifier on one end, cardboard boxes and rubber storage totes on the other. Not all of them belonged to me, but a good portion did.

Staring at them, I didn't know where to start. I didn't know whether or not this would be a waste of time. I could have tossed the business card. Or my parents might have found it when they'd cleaned out my room and thrown it away because they thought it was trash.

I could easily get the answer I needed with a simple phone call, but I didn't want to do that. Not unless I had no other choice.

Ben was the one who'd suggested the private investigator. We were seniors, had been dating almost two years by that point, and things were starting to get serious.

I'd known Ben since sixth grade. We'd been friends, but never close. Once, at a skating party in seventh grade, Ben had asked me to skate, so I thought maybe he had a crush on me. The truth was, I sort of had a crush on him, too, but he was husky and recently cursed with a spate of acne on his face, so he wasn't what we girls considered popular, and I had no choice but to say no.

Well, of course I had a choice, but all I could think about was what Mackenzie and Elise would say if I'd agreed to skate with Ben, and that fear quickly helped me make up my mind.

Later, in high school, once I realized it didn't matter whether or not Ben was popular, we started talking again, spending more time together and eventually dating. Ben could be sweet and funny, and he had a childlike eagerness to please me at any turn. He had become tall and fit and had managed to lose his acne. He had dark brown eyes, short brown hair, and dimples in his cheeks.

Once things started to get serious, I'd made the mistake of telling him too much. Letting him in on the thing that had haunted me the past four years. And because he was just a boy—eighteen years old, yes, but still a boy—he didn't know any better. Didn't know his only job was to listen. He wanted to help. To fix things.

His dad was a state trooper, and after I'd told Ben how much I regretted what had happened to Grace, how I wanted to apologize, Ben came up with the idea of a private investigator. I shrugged it off, thinking he might let the whole thing go, but then he'd gone and asked his father for recommendations. His dad offered up the name of a recently retired state trooper who had started his own private investigation firm. The man hadn't set up an office yet, so he met Ben and me at a coffee shop, and I explained that I wanted to track down an old classmate from middle school.

I didn't have much information on Grace other than her name, but the man said he'd see what he could do. Because I would be his first client, and because he'd worked with Ben's father, he gave me a discount. Three hundred dollars up front, to cover expenses. Sure, it was expensive, he said, but with an arrogant smile he told me he was worth it.

Of course, in the end, he wasn't able to track down Grace. He offered to refund my money, but I told him no. He hadn't given me any information, nothing of his work, but he had given me a business card. I remembered it being heavy card stock, the print so thick that when I ran my thumb over the letters, it felt like braille.

Around that time, things started to sour between Ben and me. I stopped seeking him out in the hallways. Didn't always return his phone calls or write him back when he slipped notes in my locker.

It wasn't until years later that I would realize my drawing away had nothing to do with Ben. It was me. I'd lied to myself for years, sealing myself in a glass case and telling myself I wasn't broken, that what had happened was terrible, but it was over and I needed to move on. By confiding in Ben, by telling him how I still held guilt, I had cracked the glass case open. I was afraid of what would happen if it shattered, if the broken me—the true me—was revealed, so I did the only thing that made sense at the time.

I pushed him away and never looked back.

28

Courtney rubbed her thumb over the business card and murmured the name: "Henry Zimmerman." She looked up at me. "Did you try the number?"

I nodded, keeping my attention on the highway, Walmart behind us and the bar where we were meeting Elise ahead. I had found the business card in a pile of old boxes in my mom's basement, right where I'd hoped it would be. The heavy card stock contained a phone number and email address written in thick, embossed lettering.

"The number doesn't work anymore. At least not for Henry Zimmerman. I got the voice mail for an accounting firm."

"Did you google the name?"

"I did. Nothing recent came up. It doesn't look like he's in business anymore."

"Why are you so focused on this guy, anyway? You said he sucked at his job."

"That's the thing—I can't believe he was really that bad. The way Ben made it sound, the guy was a great detective. So, really, it shouldn't have been that hard for him to find Grace. He knew her name, where she'd gone to school. I find it hard to believe he came up with nothing."

Courtney flipped the business card over and over between her fingers.

"Maybe he went out of business because he sucked at his job."

"Maybe."

"But you don't think so."

"It's more like I don't hope so. I was young when I dealt with him, and embarrassed about the whole thing. Honestly, I was relieved when he told me he hadn't had any luck. Part of me was afraid of what might happen *had* he managed to track down Grace. That I'd feel the need to confront her. I mean, that was what I wanted, but at the same time . . . I was scared to face her."

I thought about sitting in that coffee shop with Ben, Henry Zimmerman seated across from us, and how all I wanted to do was leave. Just stand up, apologize for wasting the man's time, and make a quick exit. But I knew that would have disappointed Ben, so I'd stayed.

"And now?" Courtney prompted.

"And now I think it's bullshit he didn't have any luck. Especially when he offered to give me all my money back." I sighed, feeling all at once depleted. "I guess I need to talk to Ben."

"Won't it be awkward?"

"I hope not. You said he married Julia Freeman?"

Julia had been a year younger than us, a star on the cheerleading squad. She reminded me of Mackenzie, or how I imagined Mackenzie would have evolved physically in high school: thin and fit, a nice even tan, her lips slick with gloss, her blonde hair often pulled back in a ponytail, ticktocking back and forth in rhythm to her tight butt as she swaggered through school. She could get any guy she wanted, and often did, but still she always smiled at Ben in the hallway, even when he and I walked to class holding hands.

"That's right," Courtney said. "We're not Facebook friends, but I'm friends with Melissa Hogan. Remember her? She posted some older pictures from Ben and Julia's wedding. That's when I searched for them. I couldn't find Ben, which I guess makes sense, since he's a state trooper just like his dad. But Julia's on there; she keeps it pretty private, but you can see her profile picture, and she's holding a baby."

If I was expected to have some kind of emotional response to hearing that my ex-boyfriend had gotten married and become a dad, none came. For a moment, I wondered if that was normal, if I should feel some kind of resentment.

But I just asked, "Do you think you can get us in contact with Ben?"

Courtney gave me a lopsided grin.

"Of course I can. Who do you think you're talking to?"

As soon as Destiny told me what had happened to Grace, I knew I needed to track down Elise.

Part of me didn't want to believe it was true. That Elise had been party to something so awful. None of us were angels when it came to sexual stuff, but as far as I knew, none of us had ever been in a position where we didn't have a chance to say no.

After the fourth-period bell rang and everybody headed to the cafeteria, I hurried through the throng of students. Elise was walking with Olivia, laughing at something Olivia had said, and for an instant I thought maybe they were making fun of Grace and what they'd let those high schoolers do to her.

I stepped up in front of them, ignoring Olivia completely.

"We need to talk."

With one of her easy smiles, Elise hooked my arm and led me down the hallway. Not even thinking about it, just seeing her best friend and wanting to include her in the group.

"Sure, what do you want to talk about?"

"No."

I said it more forcefully than I had anticipated, jerking my arm out of her loose grip.

"What the hell, Emily?" Olivia said, real outrage in her voice.

I didn't answer her, keeping my focus on Elise.

"I need to talk to you alone. Right now."

Elise frowned at Olivia, then told her to go on ahead. I felt Olivia's eyes on me as she slipped past—burning into me, trying to read my thoughts—but I kept ignoring her. It was nothing personal. I'd have done the same to Courtney or Destiny or Mackenzie. All of them had been at the Farmhouse Saturday night, and if Destiny was to be believed, none of them had done anything to help Grace.

As soon as we were alone, the easy smile slipped off Elise's face.

"What's your problem?"

The second-floor stairwell was only a few yards away. I grabbed Elise's hand and tugged her forward. We pushed through the doors to find two sixth graders making out under the stairs.

"Beat it," Elise said, her tone pure Eighth Grade Queendom, and they hustled out into the hallway. She turned to me, her arms crossed, and did that shrug of hers, giving me a look that simply said, *Well?*

"Grace didn't come to school today."

"Okay, so? She's probably sick."

"I know what happened at the Farmhouse, Elise."

Elise had been standing with her shoulders pushed back and her arms crossed, a posture she and Mackenzie had perfected over the years, one meant to relay their authority. I suspected Mackenzie always knew when she did it, but I thought maybe Elise had started doing it unconsciously. I was right; after what I'd just told her, her shoulders fell, and she released a soft breath.

"Tell me it's not true," I said.

Elise's eyes shifted away, and in that moment I knew. Not that I hadn't believed Destiny, but Destiny had said she was drunk, so there was a chance she hadn't seen things the way they'd really happened. Even though Elise had probably had the same amount of alcohol and weed, I trusted her more.

So when she looked away, it was all the confirmation I needed.

"How could you let them do that to her?"

Elise shrugged again, made a face.

"It's not a big deal."

"I heard the guys were taking turns."

"Nobody got hurt. Me and Mackenzie talked to her afterward. She said she was fine. She *looked* fine. Why didn't she come to school today? I don't know. Maybe she's embarrassed."

"You think?"

I said it more forcefully than I'd intended, and Elise's expression started to close up.

"Don't play all high-and-mighty, Emily. You were the one who invited her into our group."

"Are you *really* going to blame this on me?"

"No. But don't act like things would have been different if you'd been there. What—you would have stopped those guys?"

It hadn't even been an hour since Destiny told me what happened, and I'd been so angry and upset for Grace that the thought hadn't crossed my mind. Now it gave me pause. *Would* I have stopped those guys? Part of me wanted to say yes, of course I would have, but another part knew better.

When it became clear I wasn't going to answer, Elise sighed. She stepped forward, placed her hands on my shoulders, leveled her gaze with mine.

"Look, things got out of hand. I'll admit that. Am I proud of it? No, but it happened, so we need to deal with it."

"How are you going to do that?"

"I don't know. I need to talk to Mackenzie. We'll take care of it."

"Promise?"

Elise nodded, her hazel eyes serious, and held out her pinkie finger.

"Promise."

A simple gesture, one of trust, but part of me wondered whether I was wrong, if she was just as shallow and petty as Mackenzie. Telling me what I wanted to hear. Sneering at me behind my back.

But Elise was my best friend. Had been ever since kindergarten. That had to mean something, right?

I curled my pinkie finger around hers, and Elise smiled again.

"I got this, Emily. Everything's going to be okay."

The bar was one of those local pubs, not even three blocks from the hospital where Daniel and I had met, the kind of place nurses and doctors might stop by after work.

Courtney and I took a table out on the deck and sat beside each other, facing the entrance. My heart pounded in my chest. This was the first time I'd see Elise in a social setting since middle school.

When the waitress approached, Courtney whispered to me, "I only have like five bucks right now."

"I'll get your drinks," I whispered back.

We ordered, and when the waitress left, Courtney said, "I'll pay next time."

Elise arrived one minute before six. I recognized her at once, just as I'd recognized her at my therapist's office. Tall and lithe with short-cropped dark-red hair. Narrow cheekbones. Strong jaw. A pair of thick-framed glasses that gave her a sort of bookish sophistication.

She scanned the bar, walking toward the back, and noticed us out on the deck when Courtney and I waved. Her smile was radiant as she approached, and when she reached us, she leaned down to give us both hugs.

"I love your hair," she said to Courtney, noting the purple highlights. Then, stepping back: "My God, I haven't seen you two in forever. How have you been?"

This close, I noticed the tiny diamond on her nose, and the engagement ring on her finger.

The waitress, spying a new customer, was at our table before either of us had a chance to answer.

Elise noted our beers—Courtney's nonalcoholic—and ordered one for herself. When the waitress left, she said, "I typically drink cosmopolitans, but what the hell. Haven't had a beer in a while."

She looked back and forth between us, studying our faces, and her smile started to fade.

"What's wrong?"

29

Elise barely touched her beer. She sat forward, carefully peeling strips of the label off the bottle. She was quiet for a long time, then glanced up at us with a frown.

"This is some kind of joke, right?"

Courtney and I said nothing. Our beers had also gone untouched. We'd been at the table for a half hour or so. The waitress had passed by several times, eyeing the full bottles, but she hadn't bothered us.

I kept my gaze steady with Elise's.

"All of it's true."

Elise shook her head and shifted her focus back to her beer.

"What you're saying . . . it sounds insane."

"We know."

"I mean, I heard about Olivia passing away. I saw that on Facebook. Part of me wanted to go to the funeral, but with my job, things are crazy and I couldn't get away. I had no idea she'd killed herself."

"The family was keeping it pretty private," Courtney said. "We didn't know any details until the funeral."

Elise looked pale. "And that's when Karen told you Olivia said something about a ghost?"

I nodded. "But Karen didn't know the significance. And even if she did, I don't think she would have put two and two together."

"I can't believe you confronted her boyfriend."

"We didn't have much choice. We needed to know."

"Whether or not it was Grace who'd slept with him," Elise said, her tone flat, like she didn't believe it. But I could see in her face that she was starting to connect the dots. She shook her head. "Look, it's been fourteen years. How can you even be sure it was Grace?"

"Her eyes," I said. "I've never forgotten her eyes."

Courtney leaned forward in her seat.

"Trust me, Elise, we've worked through this already. We asked ourselves if we were seeing things. Like, maybe it was a coincidence that Olivia said that to Karen. Maybe we already had Grace on the brain."

"But then we learned about Destiny," I said.

"And that happened how many months ago?"

"Six."

"But you said Destiny's wife never saw anything. She thought it was all in Destiny's mind."

"Yes," I said, and my voice was calm and collected, because by then I'd determined that I hadn't seen anything down at the boardwalk, not like Destiny. "And maybe if that's all we'd heard, we wouldn't have the worry we have now."

"And what worry is that?"

Courtney said, "That Grace is back for revenge."

It was the first time either of us had voiced the thought to somebody else, and hearing it out loud—here in public, among couples and friends drinking and having a good time—sent a chill racing down my spine.

Elise didn't react at first, her face expressionless, and then she cracked a grin and coughed out a laugh.

"I'm being serious," Courtney said.

Elise shook her head, raised her hand.

"I know, I know, and I'm sorry to laugh. But . . . this wasn't what I was expecting. I thought the two of you just wanted to get together and catch up. I can't remember the last time I saw either of you. Then you throw all of this at me. It's a lot to take in."

An awkward silence fell. To break it, I nodded at the diamond on Elise's finger.

"I see congratulations are in order."

Elise smiled, and glanced down at the ring. "Thanks. His name is James. We're getting married in the fall."

She slipped her phone from her purse, pulled up a picture: Elise and James, their arms around each other as they smiled brightly at the camera.

"This was the night James proposed. He works up in Harrisburg at the Capitol Building." She put her phone away, and nodded at the diamond on my finger. "Congratulations to you too. When's the big day?"

"We haven't picked a date yet."

Elise asked Courtney, "How's your daughter?"

"She's great."

"How old is she now?"

"Almost eleven."

"Wow!"

"I know. She wants to be a writer when she grows up. She's already started working on a picture book."

The waitress appeared to ask if we needed another round. We told her we were fine, and she stalked away.

I asked Elise, "Do you ever think about her?"

Elise shifted her eyes away, and shook her head.

"To be honest, I put all of that stuff behind me a long time ago. We were shitty to Grace, no question about it, but . . . well, maybe I just didn't want to think about it anymore. Call it shame, I guess. I'm ashamed of what we did, but it's behind us, you know?"

"I've been thinking a lot about her recently. Especially what happened to her at the Farmhouse. I mean, I wasn't there that night, but I can't stop thinking about what those boys did."

Elise didn't flinch at the disgust in my voice. She just looked back at me, her expression at first blank before it shifted into confusion.

"I told you, I'm ashamed of what we did, especially that. It makes me sick to my stomach just to think about it. But at least Grace got back at those guys."

I traded a glance with Courtney, then frowned at Elise.

"What are you talking about?"

Elise stared at us for a beat. She looked confused, but then the expression transformed into a small grin.

"Shit, that's right. Mackenzie and I never told any of you. Mackenzie"—she shook her head as she rolled her eyes—"she was so overdramatic with keeping secrets."

Courtney said, "You and Mackenzie never told us what?"

The small grin faded, and suddenly Elise was all business. Despite the loud music pulsing from the speakers around the deck, when she spoke next, her voice was quiet, and Courtney and I had to strain to hear.

"One night about a month after the . . . incident, we found out those guys—those tenth graders—were going to be at the Farmhouse. Mackenzie had been keeping tabs on them. When she heard most of them would be there, Grace and I met at Mackenzie's house."

"What about the rest of us?" I asked. Even after all these years I couldn't help but feel a tinge of envy that I'd been left out.

Elise gave a slight shake of her head.

"We didn't want to involve you."

"Why?"

"Mackenzie's decision. It was basically all her idea. I think she felt the worst out of any of us for what had happened to Grace. Especially since Grace had started acting weirder than usual. She started having that attitude, remember? So Mackenzie had me and Grace over, and we put on dark clothes and sneaked over to the Farmhouse."

I leaned forward in my seat, ignoring all the people around us.

"What happened?"

"You know exactly what happened."

"The Farmhouse burned down."

"Yes."

"The police showed up."

"Yes."

"But those boys . . . they didn't start the fire."

"No."

"*You* did that?"

"Not me. Grace. Like I said, it was Mackenzie's idea. She'd brought along the lighter fluid. You remember Mackenzie—always prepared."

I thought about all of us following Mackenzie down that trail by her parents' cabin, the pink backpack with the ropes and towel inside bouncing on her shoulders.

"But those guys," Courtney said, "nothing ever happened to them."

"Yeah, well, that's what happens when your parents are filthy rich. The country club didn't want to press charges, but the cops still cited some of the guys. If I remember correctly, none of them even got probation. It's disgusting how money can keep you out of jail. That's one of the reasons I work as a public defender for juveniles. I want to make sure the court doesn't screw those kids over just because they don't have any money."

Elise lifted her beer, took a half-hearted sip. Her voice was soft when she said, "I can't believe Olivia and Destiny killed themselves. It doesn't sound real."

"Believe it," I said. "We saw Olivia in the casket. We read Destiny's obituary and met with her widow."

"Have you told Mackenzie yet?"

"We haven't. We were hoping maybe you'd stayed in touch with her."

Elise shook her head. "I haven't seen or spoken to Mackenzie in years. The last time was back in high school, and it didn't go well."

"How so?"

"Did you know her parents got divorced not too long after everything went down with Grace? Their divorcing had nothing to do with what we did, obviously, but I think part of Mackenzie blamed what happened on her parents splitting up. When I tried talking to her at some party senior year, she didn't want anything to do with me. I asked a mutual friend what her problem was, and she told me about the divorce and how Mackenzie had always been sour because of it. It made me think about how she made fun of Olivia's parents divorcing when they didn't even actually get divorced. Do you remember that?"

Courtney and I nodded, and then Courtney said, "I found Mackenzie's address. She lives down in Bryn Mawr. We're going there tomorrow to see her."

Elise looked surprised. "You're just going to show up in the middle of the day at her house?"

"If we have to, yes. But on Facebook, Mackenzie is pretty open about her activity. She checks in almost daily at a yoga studio in town. We're going to try to catch her there."

Courtney didn't add that she'd determined this from her Facebook account that hadn't been blocked by Mackenzie.

Elise nodded, taking this in, and then said to me, "What are you doing these days?"

"I'm a therapist. I've got some unused PTO."

"What about your clients?"

"They should be fine," I said and immediately wanted to kick myself, thinking about Chloe and all the other kids I saw who self-harmed. I kept telling myself that they would be okay, that missing one appointment wasn't going to be detrimental, but still I couldn't shake the guilt.

Elise asked Courtney, "What about you?"

"I work in retail."

There was tension in Courtney's voice, though I didn't think Elise caught it. I knew Courtney felt embarrassed being here with the two of us, Elise a lawyer, me a therapist, and Courtney a cashier at Walmart who had to take the bus every day because she couldn't afford a car. I felt bad for her, and decided to ask Elise another question before she could ask Courtney that dreaded follow-up.

"As a lawyer, do you have any thoughts on this?"

Elise took a moment to think about it, using her fingernail to scrape off the bits of label that hadn't easily peeled away from her beer bottle.

"Assuming I had all the facts I needed, I guess the question would be: What law has been broken? From what you told me, we don't know for sure Grace is actually involved in any of this. Say she did drug Olivia's fiancé and sleep with him—you'd have a hard time proving it in court. I mean, if what he's saying is true, the guy was raped, but I would be shocked if he'd be willing to press charges. It's rare enough for women to press charges against their attackers. It's rarer for men. Right now, I think the best idea would be to try to track down Grace."

"We've tried. I mean, Courtney and I have done Google and Facebook searches. But we're searching for her name from middle school. Maybe she's changed it. I actually hired a private investigator a while back to track her down. He didn't have any luck, but I'm hoping to speak to him again soon."

This raised an eyebrow.

"You hired a private investigator?" Elise asked. She sounded almost incredulous.

"It was back in high school. Senior year. I was still feeling guilty about what happened. I wanted to find Grace and say I was sorry."

Elise shook her head again. She took another sip of her beer, made a face—"Ugh, warm"—and set the bottle aside.

"Look, I'm still not ready to buy into all of this. But I haven't done all the legwork you have. It's hard to believe it's true, but I'm not ready to dismiss it either. I'll be here if you need help. I can't go down to Bryn Mawr tomorrow, but I would like to hear what Mackenzie says. Now, what do you say we finish our beers?"

She lifted her warm beer, and we lifted ours. We clinked the bottles together, and each took a swallow. The waitress noticed and hurried over. Elise already had her Amex out, and handed it to her.

"We're ready to go."

As the waitress moved away, I said to Elise, "Thank you for the drinks."

Elise shrugged.

"It's a couple of beers. No big deal. Anyway"—her eyes lit up, just like they had back in middle school when we'd talked about boys, and I felt a pang in my chest at the wave of nostalgia—"tell me more about this fiancé of yours."

30

Once a rumor starts, you can't kill it. You can deny it, try to spin it, but it will always be there. Even if it's completely false, there will be some who believe it to be true, no matter how much you tell them otherwise.

So it was no surprise that when the rumors about Grace started, they didn't stop.

Over the course of two weeks, I heard bits and pieces from other girls at school, nasty rumors that apparently had originated from those tenth-grade boys.

About how Grace had given them blow jobs.

About how she'd had a hairy pussy.

About how she'd fucked all the boys at least once, a few twice.

About how Grace had been gangbanged by three of the boys, though I'd heard another rumor that it had been six boys in total.

It went on and on. Different variations of the same thing.

Some girls started calling her a slut behind her back.

Some boys started calling her a whore.

I'd heard rumors that some of the high school guys lingered around the middle school at the end of the day, trying to catch a glimpse of the notorious whore, and that some had even asked Grace out or invited her to a party.

Part of me kept wondering if things would have been different if I'd been there. But then another part would wonder whether the same thing might have happened to me if Grace hadn't become a Harpy. If one night Mackenzie would have decided to trade me for a joint.

When these thoughts entered my mind, I was happy that it had been Grace instead, which immediately made my guilt even stronger.

Despite all the rumors and weird looks she got in the hallways, Grace seemed oblivious. Surely she had to have remembered what happened that night, but as far as I knew, she never talked about it, and nobody ever asked her. It was like a secret we all kept, a secret everybody else knew.

After gym one day, Denise Brown and her crew started making fun of Grace. Telling her she better not fuck their boyfriends. Asking if they could see her hairy pussy.

It was at that point Elise told them to shut up. Apparently, there was some bickering, and Elise told the girls to knock it off or *she* would fuck all their boyfriends, and that somehow seemed to do the trick.

When I heard about what happened, I knew I needed to do something. I had no idea what, but I had to talk to Grace.

I managed to catch her alone in the bathroom between classes.

"Are you okay?"

Grace was washing her hands. She didn't answer, just tossed her balled-up paper towel into the trash can as she started for the door.

"Grace"—putting more emphasis into her name than I'd intended, my voice inadvertently echoing off the lime-green tiles—"are you okay?"

She paused, her back still to me. From where I stood, I could see the side of her face in the mirror.

"Do you want to come over to my house this weekend? Just you and me."

Besides Elise, I'd never invited any of the girls over before. I'd been too embarrassed.

"No," Grace said. That was it. Just that one word.

"You don't always have to do what they tell you to do. Especially Mackenzie."

She said nothing. Just kept standing there with her back to me.

"Grace, I'm trying to help you."

She didn't say anything to this, either, and a moment later she pushed open the door and stepped into the hallway.

I watched her go, frozen in place. I'd caught her reflection in the mirror when I told her I was trying to help her.

She'd rolled her eyes.

I didn't know why, but I was stunned. Who was *she* to roll her eyes at me? I'd gone out of my way to invite her to my house, to tell her I was trying to help her, and that was her reaction.

It was then that I decided: I was done feeling sorry for Grace Farmer. Maybe the rumors were true. Maybe she did have a hairy pussy. Maybe she had sucked off all those boys before she fucked them.

I wanted to humiliate Grace. To get back at her for that moment when I'd tried to be a true friend and she'd mocked me. So I decided to come up with a new nickname for her. Something that the rest of the girls would love. Something that would minimize Grace even more in our collective thoughts.

She's so pale and quiet, I said later that day, *she's like a ghost. Grace the Ghost. Don't you love it?*

Of course they did.

31

It took us almost an hour and a half to reach Bryn Mawr, a wealthy suburb just outside of Philadelphia, and it took us another ten minutes before we pulled into the shopping plaza that housed Movement Pilates and Yoga.

Movement had a bright, stylish storefront sandwiched between a coffee shop and a sushi place.

We parked near the corner of the lot so that we would have a good view of anybody coming or going.

I checked the time on the dashboard. A quarter to ten.

"What if she came early and is already inside?"

Courtney was slouched in her seat, scanning the parking lot.

"We can poke our heads inside and see if she's there. But I don't think she came early. I told you, based on her Facebook, she checks in here almost every day around ten o'clock. If she doesn't show for whatever reason, we'll drive by her house and knock on the door."

Both of us sat in silence for the next couple of minutes, the windows down, a nice breeze blowing through.

Courtney said, "Have you ever done yoga or Pilates?"

"I have. Wasn't really my thing. You?"

"Never really appealed to me. Reminded me too much of gymnastics." A distant smile crossed her face. "There was a time in high school

I actually believed I had a shot of someday making the Olympics. Talk about delusional."

"It wasn't delusional."

Courtney smiled at me. "That's nice of you to say."

"I mean it. If you hadn't had Terri—"

I stopped myself, realizing it was an awful thing to say, but Courtney knew what I meant and waved it off.

"You know, it sounds hokey, but I wouldn't have put off having Terri for anything. Not even an Olympic medal."

A shiny black Mercedes SUV pulled into the parking lot. There was only one person inside—a blonde woman wearing sunglasses—and I immediately knew it was Mackenzie.

"She's here."

Both Courtney and I watched as Mackenzie parked five spaces away. She had a cell phone to her ear and was talking animatedly.

For a minute she stayed in the SUV, its engine running, and then she turned off the vehicle and opened her door, and we could hear her voice.

"I don't care. Just come up with something. You need to learn to be a better liar."

She disconnected the call, swearing under her breath, and tossed her sunglasses on the passenger seat before climbing out.

As expected, Mackenzie was decked out in yoga apparel. Black lace-up mesh leggings, mauve open-back support tank top, bright-blue Nike sneakers.

I hadn't seen her since the eighth grade, but she didn't look like she'd changed much. She was taller, yes, but she was still thin and fit and stunningly beautiful—that same artificial beauty she'd possessed in middle school, multiplied by a hundred.

Mackenzie pulled out a rolled-up yoga mat, locked the SUV with her key fob, and started toward the sidewalk. Just like in middle school, she moved with perfect posture, her shoulders back, her chin tilted up, her sleek ponytail swaying with each step.

Courtney and I were out of the car a second later. We wanted to reach her before she entered the yoga studio. When we were only ten yards away, I called out to her.

"Mackenzie!"

She turned to glance back at us. While there was no recognition in her face, something about her body changed. A tension. A slight tremble.

At once she turned back around and kept moving forward, faster now, not quite a jog but not the leisurely pace of seconds earlier.

"Cunt," Courtney muttered, and the next thing I knew both of us were racing forward.

Hearing us, Mackenzie picked up her pace, but she wasn't about to sprint into the yoga studio. People would ask what was wrong. And while Mackenzie had always craved attention, I doubted she was prepared to explain who she was running from and why.

Then we had reached her, just like that, Courtney on one side, me on the other. Mackenzie stopped, her mouth a tight line, her glare the kind that could turn people into stone.

"What do you want?"

"We want to talk," I said.

"Yeah, well, I don't want to talk to you."

Courtney said, "Why are you being such a bitch?"

Mackenzie cracked a smile, but there was no warmth to it.

"Look, we were friends once, but that was a long time ago. I moved on, and my life got a whole hell of a lot better."

Courtney took a step forward. "What the fuck does that mean?"

"It means you were holding me back," Mackenzie said simply, using a French-manicured nail to flick away a strand of hair from her face. "You were all a bad influence on me."

I'm not a violent person by nature, but in that moment, I wanted to slap the shit out of Mackenzie. *She* had been the ringleader. *She* had treated Grace the worst. *She* had come up with the idea of what to do to Grace that weekend at her cabin. Hell, *she* was the one who had made us all cut our hands in that stupid blood oath.

Courtney said, "That is such shit, and you know it."

Mackenzie set her jaw. "What do you want?"

"Olivia passed away," I said.

"I heard."

"Destiny passed away too."

"What does either of those things have to do with me?"

"They both committed suicide. We . . . we think Grace Farmer was somehow involved."

So far Mackenzie had managed to keep her face straight, her posture perfect. But hearing this, she rolled her eyes.

"Are you fucking kidding me? Is this some kind of joke?"

"This is serious, Mackenzie. We're worried Grace may somehow be involved in Olivia's and Destiny's deaths."

"And why should I care?"

Again, that urge to slap her. I took a slow, steady breath.

"Did you not hear anything I just said? Two of our friends from middle school are dead, and there's a chance Grace was involved."

Mackenzie rolled her eyes again, and started to walk past us.

Courtney cut in front of her. "You don't have to believe us. But we wanted you to know, just in case—"

"In case what?" Mackenzie said, a challenge in her tone. "Grace manages to track me down and do whatever it is she did to Olivia and Destiny? You're both pathetic. Especially you, Bennett."

I steeled myself, felt my nails dig into my palms.

"If you'll give us time to explain everything we've learned, maybe then you'll—"

"I'm late for my class."

Mackenzie pushed past us. At the door, she paused to glance back one last time.

"Don't bother me with this bullshit again, or you'll be sorry."

She opened the door and stepped into the studio. We heard the lilt of her voice rising as she greeted everybody inside, like the conversation she'd just had out on the sidewalk hadn't happened. Like Courtney and I didn't even exist.

Courtney's hands balled into fists. She spun away and marched back toward the car. I hurried to keep up with her, wanting to say something to calm her down, but before I could speak, she veered off course.

Right toward the Mercedes.

"Courtney, what are you doing?"

She'd slipped her apartment key out of her pocket. I looked around, scanning the parking lot in case anybody was nearby. I wanted to shout, to tell her to stop, to not do it.

But it was too late.

As Courtney moved past the SUV, head held high so she looked less conspicuous, she dug the key along the rear and front doors on the driver's side, and then kept moving straight toward our car.

She called mildly, "Come on, let's go."

I stood motionless, stunned, and stared at the Mercedes. At the rugged slash scored into the doors.

It looked like a smile.

32

"I still can't believe you keyed her car."

"Why? She deserved it."

I took a sip of my coffee, set the cup back down on the table, and stared hard at Courtney, who sat across from me in the booth.

"You're lucky the alarm didn't go off. Somebody would have called the police, and in an area like that, they'd have shown up in no time. Mackenzie would have been more than happy to press charges on both of us. I could be wrong, but I don't think Terri would want her mom to spend a night in jail."

Courtney issued a disgruntled sigh, wrapped her hand around her own cup of coffee. It was almost five o'clock, and the diner was starting to fill up.

"Still," she said, "it felt good. Totally worth it."

I shook my head and glanced out the window at the parking lot. Traffic zoomed back and forth on the highway. A handful of vehicles were parked out front. So far no sign of Ben.

"Maybe he's not going to show."

"He'll show."

"How do you know?"

"Ben was always a stand-up guy, and now that he's a cop, he'll definitely want to speak to me."

I stared at her. "What did you do?"

"Told him the truth, more or less. That I think I'm in danger but I'm not ready to call the police just yet."

"How did you get in contact with him, anyway? I thought you said he's not on Facebook."

"He's not. But I found someone who works with him and asked him to pass the message along." Courtney's eyes brightened, and she gestured out the window. "I think that's him."

I had to twist in the booth to look. Sure enough, a dark-green Ford Explorer had just parked, and out stepped Ben.

He somehow looked different and the same all at once. A bit heavier around the middle. Fuller face. He had a buzz cut, probably to hide the fact that his hairline was receding. He wasn't in uniform, just jeans and a blue polo shirt, and as he entered the diner and scanned the booths, Courtney raised her hand and waved him over. She tracked him with her eyes, smiling widely, and when he reached us, she slid out of her side and motioned for him to take her empty spot.

That was when Ben turned to greet Courtney's friend. His face froze. He stared, then blinked.

"What the hell is this?"

"Please, Ben"—Courtney gestured again to her empty spot as she slid in beside me—"take a seat and we'll explain."

He looked around the diner, uncertain, and then cautiously lowered himself into his side of the booth.

Courtney reached across and grabbed her cup just as the waitress appeared and asked Ben if he'd like anything to drink. He ordered a cup of decaf, and the waitress nodded and was gone, leaving the three of us stuck in an awkward bubble of silence.

I cleared my throat. "It's been a while."

Ben nodded, and finally looked at me. "It has. You look well."

"Thanks. So do you."

His gaze momentarily shifted down to my coffee cup—no, I realized a second later: to my hand, resting beside my cup, and my engagement ring.

"I see you're getting married."

Had something changed in his voice? I couldn't tell. In high school, we'd sometimes talked about marriage. Well, more Ben than me. He'd always been the one who'd brought it up. The one who'd talked about what kind of house we would build and possible names for our children.

When I didn't answer, he shifted his focus to Courtney.

"You wanted to talk," he said. "You feel like you're in some kind of danger?"

"Yes."

"Somebody is threatening you?"

"Kinda."

His face turned to stone. It looked like Ben might get up to leave, but the waitress appeared with his coffee. He thanked her, watched her go, then glanced at us again.

"I've had a long day. I want to get home to my family. And now I feel like I'm being jerked around."

"Henry Zimmerman," I said.

He frowned at me. "What?"

"Do you remember Henry Zimmerman?"

"Yeah, he worked with my father."

"And when he retired he became a private investigator."

"Right. I introduced you two when you said you wanted to track down Grace Farmer. What about it?"

"Do you know if he's still alive?"

The frown deepened. "What the hell is going on here?"

"I'd like to speak with him, if possible. I found the business card he gave me back in high school, but the number on it doesn't work. I tried googling his name, but he didn't come up."

"Why do you need to speak to him?"

"Because he was supposed to find Grace Farmer, and he never did. Does that make sense to you?"

"Do you think he was lying?"

"He offered to give me back my money."

"Yeah, and you should have taken it. I always wondered why you didn't."

"The truth? Because I was embarrassed. Because I never wanted to go through with hiring him in the first place."

"But you had told me—"

Courtney cut him off.

"I think we're getting off track. It doesn't matter what happened back then. The fact is, we'd like to talk to this Henry Zimmerman if he's still around."

"I understand that. But you still haven't made it clear *why*."

I glanced at Courtney. Courtney glanced at me. I turned my focus back to Ben and took a deep breath.

And told him everything. From start to finish. From hearing of Olivia's death to our encounter with Philip to our meeting with Destiny's widow to our failed trip down to Bryn Mawr to see Mackenzie—though I left out the part about Courtney keying the Mercedes.

"And now we're here with you. Sounds pretty crazy, doesn't it?"

Ben didn't speak for a long time. He hadn't touched his coffee since the waitress had poured it, but now he lifted the cup, took a sip.

"We're not making this up," Courtney said.

Ben shook his head slowly. Didn't say anything.

"You're a cop," I said. "Can you look up Grace in your system or database or whatever it is you guys use?"

"It's not that simple. I could look up her name, but . . ." He paused. "Christ, you *are* being serious, aren't you?"

"Yes."

Ben shook his head again, muttered, "This is insane."

Courtney asked, "What are your thoughts about this as a cop?"

"For starters, I'm not a detective. Something like this, it's beyond me. And from what you've said, a lot of it is circumstantial. Neither of you has actually *seen* Grace. You're trying to connect dots, and there's a chance those dots won't lead to anything."

"We know," I said. "That's why I'd like to speak to Henry Zimmerman. See if he remembers anything. I figure if we can track down Grace's mom, maybe we can find her. Grace might have nothing to do with any of this. But until we know for sure, we're going to keep searching."

Ben's eyes were distant; he stared out the window, watching the traffic on the highway. He opened his mouth, was about to say something, but then shook his head.

I frowned at him. "What?"

"You realize it wasn't just Grace. Back in middle school, you girls were mean to practically everybody. Who's to say Denise Brown or somebody else you bullied isn't the one back for revenge?"

I had to admit the thought had never crossed my mind. I'd been so consumed with the idea that Grace was behind everything, the one pulling the strings, I'd focused only on her and ignored everybody else that we'd made fun of or started rumors about or did whatever we could to make their lives a living hell.

Courtney said, "I actually googled Denise and her crew the other night, just to see what most of them were up to. To make sure"—she paused, shrugged—"none of them had died recently too."

Ben raised an eyebrow. "And?"

"As far as I can tell, only Olivia and Destiny are the ones who've died recently. The ones who've . . . killed themselves."

There was another moment of silence, and then Ben pulled out two dollars, tossed the bills on the table.

"I need to go home."

He started to slide out of the booth and only paused when I spoke again.

"What about Henry Zimmerman?"

"I haven't seen or spoken to him since"—a brief pause—"my wedding. I'll call my dad, see if he knows where Henry is. If he does, I'll let you know."

"Do you want my number?"

He paused again, and grinned.

"Julia would kill me if she knew I was here with you. She's always been jealous. Still is, even after all this time. But I'll risk it and take your number anyway."

33

Jefferson the Turtle had gotten himself in trouble. Not just him, but Lenny the Lemur too. They were both in Principal Porcupine's office, and Principal Porcupine wanted to know who had started the fight out at recess.

"This is really good," I said.

I was sitting on the couch with Terri, who beamed at me. But the smile quickly faded.

"I know it can be better."

"I think it's great. I do have one question, though. I've noticed almost all the names of your characters have some kind of alliteration. Do you know what alliteration means?"

Terri nodded. "Alliteration is when you put words together that start with the same letters."

"Right. So you have Lenny the Lemur. And Carol the Cat. And Doug the Dog."

"Okay," Terri said cautiously, like she wasn't sure where I was going with this.

"Well"—I tapped the title character with my fingernail—"Jefferson the Turtle is the only one that doesn't start with the same letter."

"Oh."

"I think Jefferson is a great name. I'm just surprised you didn't name him Tommy or Tony or something else that starts with *T*."

Terri shrugged again, and looked away. On the other side of the couch, Courtney laughed.

"Look at her blushing!"

"Mom," Terri said quietly.

I looked back and forth between them. "What?"

Courtney asked her daughter, "Do you want to tell Aunt Emily, or should I?"

"Mom."

Courtney grinned at me. "There's a boy in Terri's class named Jefferson."

"Oh."

I put special emphasis on the word, and Terri's nose wrinkled as she bunched up her face.

"I'm going to my room."

She grabbed the page out of my hands and marched off down the hallway. We heard her door close. Not slam, but there was a message in her closing the door that made us both laugh.

"Should I apologize?"

Courtney made a face. "She's fine. Only embarrassed. She got so angry when I figured out she has a crush on this boy. Jefferson. That's what the kids in his class call him. Not Jeff, but Jefferson."

The pizza Courtney and I had picked up on our way back to Highland Estates was still on the coffee table. I leaned forward, flipped open the lid, saw there were three slices of pepperoni left. I flipped the lid shut again.

"You still hungry?" Courtney asked. "Have another slice."

"I better not. I haven't been to the gym the last couple days."

"Good Lord, I haven't been to the gym in years." She opened the lid, grabbed the biggest slice, and winked at me as she took a bite. "Talk about amazing metabolism, huh?"

I grinned and picked up my phone, glanced at the screen. Almost eight o'clock.

"Text from Daniel?" Courtney asked.

"No, just checking the time. I should head home soon."

Courtney smiled and nodded slowly. "I get it."

She thought I wanted to head home to be with Daniel, but that wasn't the case. Well, that wasn't entirely the case. I certainly enjoyed being with him, despite the fact that much of our time was shared in silence, but that wasn't why I needed to leave.

"Oh, I meant to ask," Courtney said. "How is your mom doing?"

"She's good. I think she's dating somebody. I ran into her as I was leaving the house yesterday morning. She'd just gotten home, and she was dressed up a little too nice, even for church. Had her makeup done and everything. I'd jokingly asked if she'd been out on a date, and she got so flustered. In fact, she got nearly as embarrassed as Terri."

From down the hallway, Terri's faint voice called through the door. "I was not embarrassed!"

Courtney called back, "Yes, you were! And brush your teeth. It's bedtime."

The door opened, and Terri peeked around the corner.

"Do I have to?"

Courtney just stared at her.

Terri waited a beat, then shrugged, said, "Worth a try," and headed to the bathroom.

Courtney said to me, "Just wait until you and Daniel have kids."

I forced a smile. I thought about telling Courtney the truth. About how things hadn't been great with Daniel for a while now. How I'd tried to do something sweet for him just the other day, like when things were good between us, and how it hadn't made much of a difference.

But despite everything Courtney and I had been through recently, I just couldn't open up to her like that.

Soon Terri reappeared, flashing her teeth.

"Did you floss too?" Courtney asked.

Terri nodded.

"Let me see."

She hurried over and opened her mouth wide. Courtney peered inside, then leaned forward and kissed her on the forehead.

"Looks good, kiddo. You head to bed now."

"Can I read for a little?"

"Just a little. It's getting late. And say good night to Aunt Emily."

"Good night, Aunt Emily."

Terri started for the bedroom but paused, turned back around.

"I decided I'm going to change his name."

Courtney frowned. "Who?"

"Jefferson."

"Okay. So what's his new name?"

"Danny."

Courtney rolled the name around on her tongue.

"Danny. Wait—is that short for Daniel? Like Aunt Emily's Daniel? Terri, do you have a crush on *Daniel*?"

Terri's nose wrinkled. "No!"

Courtney started to sing, "Terri and Daniel, sitting in a tree."

Terri hurried away. "I'm going to bed!"

This time, we didn't hold back. The sound of her door closing was muffled by our laughter.

34

Mackenzie's street was lined with ritzy, overlarge houses. All different shapes and sizes, each one a hodgepodge of sloped roofs and irregular windows, like the architects who built them were drunk when they began to sketch the layout.

Almost ten o'clock at night, the street was quiet and idyllic, all the lawns perfectly manicured. I was sure no home in this neighborhood cost less than a cool million.

I passed by Mackenzie's house—a mansion, really; tan stucco and brick siding, three-car garage—before making a U-turn at the end of the street. The driveway was empty, but I parked a few houses down anyway. Kept the engine running but turned off the headlights.

I thought about Mackenzie's threat to us earlier that morning, after we'd tried talking to her about Grace.

Don't bother me with this bullshit again, or you'll be sorry.

It wasn't just a threat, I knew. It was a promise. And that was before Courtney had vandalized her car.

Still, I couldn't let petty grievances get in the way. Two people were dead—two people who were once close friends, fellow Harpies—and there was a chance any one of us might be next. And despite how much I loathed Mackenzie in middle school, she deserved another chance to hear what Courtney and I had discovered, and if she still refused to believe, then so be it.

Staring at the house, I took a deep breath.

This was going to be harder than I'd thought. Which was why I hadn't bothered telling Courtney my plan. She would have talked me out of it. Convinced me that it was all a waste of time.

Regardless, I was here now. All I needed to do was park in the driveway, walk up to the front door, and knock.

And hope Mackenzie didn't immediately call the police.

But before I could put the car in gear—before I could flip the headlights back on—one of the three garage doors opened, bright light from inside suffusing the dark driveway.

The same black Mercedes SUV that Courtney had keyed glided out.

Even in the dark, I could see that Mackenzie was behind the wheel. Nobody else appeared to be inside.

She didn't glance my way as she reached the end of the driveway and took a left out onto the street.

I waited a beat, watching her receding taillights, and then I put the car in gear.

I caught up with Mackenzie in no time. But still I tried to maintain a decent-size buffer between our two vehicles, despite the fact that it was the middle of the night and we were practically the only two moving through the neighborhood.

Mackenzie barely paused at a stop sign before zooming out onto the highway.

I had to wait for traffic before making the same turn, and then I had to punch the gas to make sure I didn't lose sight of the SUV.

It was there, maybe one hundred yards away, and thanks to traffic lights, I soon caught up.

At one red light, Mackenzie was the first car, I was the third, and I was at an angle where I caught her trying to see me in her side mirror.

Or at least that was how it appeared. And then the light turned green, and the Mercedes bolted into the intersection, though instead of speeding forward she made a sudden turn and looped back in the opposite direction, the scar along the driver's side of the SUV prominent in the bright glow of the street lamps.

I could see her glancing my way, only briefly, and before I knew it, I jerked the wheel and maneuvered an awkward three-point turn, a car in the oncoming lane screeching to a halt and blaring its horn.

Now Mackenzie was going even faster than before, swerving around cars, and I did my best to keep up—the speedometer going from fifty to sixty to seventy—unsure what was happening but not wanting to let the SUV out of my sight.

After another mile, Mackenzie made a sudden turn—up a one-way street.

But I didn't spot the sign until after I'd slammed on my brakes and twisted the wheel to make the same turn. I almost rammed straight into a car that was approaching down the street, a car that Mackenzie had nearly clipped.

I could see her just up ahead, the Mercedes's taillights flashing as it made another sudden turn onto a side street.

The car I'd almost hit beeped repeatedly. The couple inside—a younger couple, probably out on a date—were shouting at me and making rude gestures.

I ignored them and squeezed past, sped up to the side street, but the roadway was dark and deserted.

Mackenzie was gone.

In the middle console, my cell phone vibrated.

I glanced down, startled. I didn't recognize the number. At first, I thought maybe it was Mackenzie, calling to ask me what the fuck I thought I was doing following her, but then I remembered there was no way Mackenzie had my number.

I didn't realize I was shaking until I picked up the phone, placed it to my ear.

"Hello?"

It was Ben.

"Sorry to call so late, but I just got off the phone with Henry Zimmerman. He said he remembered you."

I didn't answer at first, still trying to process what had just happened with Mackenzie, and when Ben spoke next, he sounded worried.

"Emily, are you there?"

"Yes, I'm here. Will he talk to me?"

"He will. In fact, he wants to meet face-to-face. You made it sound urgent, so I asked if he was free tomorrow and he said he was."

"Do you have his address?"

"Well, here's the thing. I don't feel comfortable with you meeting him by yourself."

I had turned the car around, was headed back down the one-way street to the main highway.

"I'm a grown woman, Ben."

"I know that. And it's not about you. It's this whole situation . . . the whole thing is fucked up, and, quite honestly, I'm not entirely sure why Henry Zimmerman is so adamant about meeting with you in person. That's why I'd like to be there."

I didn't say anything, sitting now at the stop sign, watching the late-evening traffic on the highway pass back and forth.

"Emily?"

"Whatever. How soon can I see him?"

"Well, I work second shift tomorrow, so the morning would be best. I can meet you at the diner, and you can follow me to Henry's from there. Say, nine o'clock?"

"That works. I'll meet you there." I paused a beat, and added, "Thank you, Ben. I appreciate it."

There was a brief silence, and then he said, "I'll see you tomorrow morning," and hung up.

I sat there for another minute, not sure what to do next. Then light filled up the interior as a pickup truck came down the street behind me, and when I didn't immediately pull out onto the highway, it flashed its high beams.

I waved an apology, lifted my foot off the brake, and headed home.

35

Mackenzie's parents owned a cabin at Silver Lake Park. Since the third grade, it had been a tradition on Memorial Day weekend that Mackenzie's parents would take us girls up to the cabin. There wasn't much to do except swim in the lake or walk the trails, but they gave us our space, and we always looked forward to the trip.

That year, Mackenzie and Elise had decided to invite Grace. I wasn't sure why. It wasn't like she was a real Harpy. And by that point I'd come to detest her, just like the rest of the girls.

Grace's mother dropped her off at Mackenzie's house that Saturday morning, which surprised us all, as up until then none of us had actually seen Mrs. Farmer. Usually Grace just showed up at the mall, or at Mackenzie's or Elise's house. Mackenzie's mom had spoken to her once on the phone, but that was it. Mackenzie said her mom thought Mrs. Farmer sounded like a dumb hick, but none of us really believed Mackenzie's mom would say such a thing.

Now we finally had a chance to catch a glimpse of the elusive Mrs. Farmer. She drove an ugly red hatchback. She never got out of the car, which she'd stopped at the end of the long driveway. At that distance, all we could make out was a woman with frizzy hair. Grace had climbed out of the car, carrying her purple backpack, and started up the driveway toward Mackenzie's house as her mother drove away.

Mackenzie waited until she reached us—all of us standing beside Mr. Harper's SUV, decked out in short shorts and tank tops and flip-flops—before she overdramatically sighed.

"About time. My parents wanted to leave five minutes ago."

It really hadn't been a big deal. As far as I could tell, Mackenzie's parents weren't in any rush. But my dislike for Grace trumped everything else, so I sniggered along with the rest of the girls while Mackenzie ran inside to tell her parents we were ready to go.

A minute later, Mr. and Mrs. Harper exited the house, Mackenzie following a step behind, a bright-pink backpack hanging off her shoulder.

Mr. Harper clapped his hands together.

"All set?"

The SUV was crowded, especially with all our bags, but we managed to squeeze in. I ended up between Destiny and Grace. The drive would be at least an hour, and I was stuck next to a girl I couldn't stand.

That should have been my first clue that the trip wasn't going to go well.

As Mr. Harper started the SUV, Mrs. Harper turned in her seat to glance back at us. Her sharp cheekbones twitched as she grinned.

"You girls ready to have some fun?"

36

Henry Zimmerman's wife, Martha, brought us coffee. She was a small, stoop-shouldered woman with a poof of white hair and the warmest smile I'd ever seen.

Ben and I, on the couch in the sunroom, thanked her and set our cups down on the glass coffee table.

Henry Zimmerman sat in an easy chair across from us. He was in his late sixties now, his skin wrinkled and dotted with age spots, but the stern expression he'd had when I first met him was still there.

"Is there anything else I can get for you?" Martha asked.

"No, dear, thank you," Henry said, and there was a gentleness in his tone that betrayed his stern expression. When his wife left, he said, "The coffee smells good, doesn't it? I miss drinking it some days."

I asked, "You don't drink coffee anymore?"

"It's difficult when you can't keep your hand still." He raised his quaking right hand, held it up for a moment, then let it drop back down on his lap. "The shakes come and go, but lately they've been around much longer than usual."

"I'm sorry," Ben said. "Is it Parkinson's?"

"Yes. I haven't told most people. So I'd appreciate it if you kept it between us."

There was a brief, uneasy silence. Outside, in the backyard, a squirrel chased another across the grass and disappeared in the bushes.

Ben glanced at me before clearing his throat.

"So the reason we're here."

Henry waved his quaking hand.

"Yes, I know. It's been over ten years since I last saw you both together. An entire decade later, you show up at my home out of the blue. I assume whatever the reason, it must be important."

I could feel Ben glancing my way, but I held my gaze steady with Henry Zimmerman's and said, "I came across an old eighth-grade yearbook the other day. It made me think of Grace Farmer, and I remembered hiring you to track her down."

This was a lie, of course, but the old man didn't need to know that. I had already told Ben we weren't going to be one hundred percent truthful about the events leading up to this meeting. It would raise too many questions.

Henry Zimmerman's face remained expressionless.

"And?"

"And to be truthful, at the time I don't think I really wanted you to find her. So when you told me you hadn't had any luck, I felt some relief and went on with my life."

"What's changed now?"

"Now that I'm older and a bit wiser, and a bit more inclined to see her again, part of me feels like you lied to me."

I'm not sure what I expected the old man to do, but his expression didn't change. Not at first. He stared back at me, his dark eyes flat, and then little by little the sternness cracked like a shale of ice, and he smiled at Ben.

"Shame you didn't end up with this one. She turned out to be a smart cookie."

"Why did you lie?" I asked.

Like that, the smile faded, and Henry shifted his gaze out at the backyard.

"I never wanted to retire. Sounds crazy, doesn't it? Most cops like the job well enough, but after they put in their twenty, they're ready to get out with their pension. For me . . . being a trooper was the only thing I'd ever known. It was my first job, and I figured it would be my last. But I was at the age where I didn't have a choice. They were basically forcing me out. That's why I decided to become a private investigator."

He smirked, and shook his head.

"Do you know what the job entailed? Following cheating husbands. Tracking them on their lunch breaks. Most of the time they weren't doing anything wrong. The wives were just suspicious. Other times, well, yes, they were cheating, and I had to be the one to tell those wives."

He paused. When he spoke next, his voice had softened.

"To be honest with you, I think I cursed myself with that very first case. I didn't handle it right. I lied to you, and because of that, all the following cases were tainted. I didn't work as a private investigator very long. I've regretted what I'd done; I even thought about contacting Ben, asking him to put me in touch with you, but I never did. I grew up in a generation of stubborn men, and I think part of me will forever be stubborn, no matter how much I'd like to change."

I inched forward on the couch. "Why are you telling me this now?"

His eyes met mine again.

"You found me. You tracked me down. I feel it's only right you finally hear the truth."

He shifted his jaw back and forth, then said simply, "I found your friend. It wasn't difficult. I looked into some records—she and her mother had moved back to where they'd lived previously. Do you know where that was?"

"Somewhere in northern Pennsylvania."

The old man nodded and shifted in his chair to get more comfortable.

"Bradford County, in a town just over the county border. What we call Appalachian Country. Where the coal crackers live." He smirked. "I suppose that's a derogatory term, but it's apt. They're wired differently up there. Live by a different set of rules. They work hard and they drink hard and they live hard. A lifetime down in those mines will change a person. You don't want to mess with them if you can help it."

He paused again, staring once more out at the backyard, and told us that when he'd found the address for Grace and her mother, something in his gut told him he should check it out first. Having worked as a trooper for thirty years, he knew it was always best to trust his gut. So he'd decided to drive up there.

The moment he'd turned onto their road, he had a strange sense of dread.

"At the time, I was a man in my late fifties. I'd been a cop. And I immediately knew this wasn't any place for an eighteen-year-old girl. Because it wasn't like I had a number for you to call your friend. All I had was an address. Either you would send a letter, or you would get in your car and drive all the way up there. And that feeling in my gut told me neither would be a good idea. That's why I said I hadn't had any luck."

"It wasn't your place to make that decision," I said, and it took everything I had to keep my voice steady and calm.

"Oh, I know. I knew it at the time, too, but it felt like the right thing to do. You don't understand the feeling I got when I saw that trailer home. Only one at the end of the road. Set off on a hill. I didn't even see anybody outside; there were some broken-down cars, rusted appliances, but . . ." He trailed off, then murmured, "A young girl like yourself didn't belong there."

"Good thing I'm not a young girl anymore."

The old man nodded. "This is true."

"Do you remember the address?"

"Not exactly, and I shredded those old files years ago. But I remember the name of the road. As a boy who grew up in an Episcopalian family, the name had a peculiar meaning to me, and I've never forgotten it."

"What?"

Henry Zimmerman looked nervous now, his gaze skipping to different parts of the room just so he wouldn't have to look at me.

"Keep in mind, young lady, it's been over ten years. There's no guarantee your friend still lives there. Or that her family does. For all we know, the trailer may be gone."

I inched forward again on the couch, to the point where I was literally sitting on the edge of my seat. When I spoke, I tried to hide the eagerness in my voice.

"What's the name of the road?"

He stared straight back at me.

"Vesper."

37

"Promise me you won't go up there."

Ben said it the moment we left the house, as we were heading down the brick walkway toward our cars parked in the driveway. The morning sky was clear, and a light breeze rustled the trees along the road.

I walked one step ahead of him and said over my shoulder, "That's cute. You're still trying to look out for me."

"I'm serious, Emily. That man was a good cop. I never worked with him, but my dad did, and he trusts his judgment. If Henry says it might not be safe for you, I wouldn't call his bluff."

I was parked behind Ben in the driveway. He followed me to my car, waiting for me to answer.

I didn't.

"Emily."

I looked at him. "I'm a big girl now, Ben. I can handle myself."

"Henry's right about that area. It's dangerous. Everybody up there has a gun, and they won't think twice about shooting you if you step on their property without permission. Their motto is shoot first, hide the body later."

I rolled my eyes, fishing the car keys from my purse.

"Give me a break."

"Listen, I know you want to go, and I'm not saying you shouldn't. But at least wait for me to come with you."

"My knight in shining armor. I'm not sure your wife would want to hear that."

He didn't look amused.

"I'm off this weekend," he said. "I can drive up with you then."

"This weekend? That's four days away. I'm not waiting that long."

"Emily—"

"You know about Olivia and Destiny. Maybe Grace had something to do with what happened to them. Maybe she didn't. But I can't wait that long to find out."

As I lifted the handle to open my door, Ben moved forward, using his leg to hold it in place. I turned to him, surprised, and for an instant I saw anger in his face.

In that moment I realized he was no longer Ben Evans. He was State Trooper Evans. And what do you do when an officer of the law asks you a question? You tell him whatever it is he wants to hear.

"Fine. I'll wait until this weekend. Now, do you mind? I have to get to work."

This time, Courtney noticed me the moment I got in line. I didn't have anything on me, so I grabbed another pack of Juicy Fruit, and when it was my turn in line, I handed it over.

"Did you find everything okay?" Courtney said brightly.

I whispered, "How late do you work?"

Her voice, too, lowered to a whisper: "Four."

"I just met with Henry Zimmerman. He told me where Grace's family lives, or at the very least lived. You're never going to guess the name of the road."

Her green eyes grew intense, her voice still a whisper.

"What?"

"Vesper."

The intensity in her eyes went off like a bomb.

"You're joking."

"It's up in Bradford County, about a three-hour drive from here. I plan on going tonight. And I got Daniel to agree to babysit Terri."

"Seriously?"

I nodded, and Courtney beamed.

"Perfect," she said. "Terri will love it."

"I called Elise. She's going to see if she can leave work early to come with us."

Courtney's bright smile faded. "You spoke to Elise before you spoke to me?"

She said it in a wounded tone, like I was playing favorites.

"I tried calling you first. The phone went straight to voice mail."

"My phone's been acting up. I think the battery's shot."

The woman behind me had finished placing the final item in her shopping cart on the belt and cleared her throat to get our attention.

I smiled at her.

"Beautiful day, isn't it?"

She scowled back at me.

Courtney, grinning, scanned the yellow pack of gum, said brightly, "That will be a dollar. Would you like to pay with cash or credit?"

Terri was ecstatic, just as Courtney had predicted. She sat in the back of my car, bouncing with the beat of the music on the radio, some of her drawings on her lap. When I pulled into my typical parking spot, Terri asked which town house was mine. I pointed, and she jumped out of the car and raced for the door.

Courtney laughed. "The girl has it bad for your fiancé."

I told her to wait and stepped out of the car as Daniel opened the town house door. He acted shocked to see Terri standing there, though of course he knew she was coming.

"What are *you* doing here?"

Terri giggled. "I'm hanging out with you!"

"Are you sure?" Daniel said, still playing dumb, which elicited another giggle from Terri.

I approached the door. "Hopefully we'll be back before midnight."

Daniel nodded but said nothing. I asked Terri, "Do you like grilled cheese sandwiches?"

"Of course."

"Ask Daniel to make you one. He makes the best grilled cheese sandwiches in the whole world."

A skeptical gleam entered her eyes.

"The whole *world*?"

I nodded once, my expression all too serious.

"The whole world."

Daniel waved to Courtney, and then he and Terri went inside. Once I'd returned to the car, Courtney asked, "Now what?"

"Now we pick up Elise. She said she'd meet us at the diner."

"And then?"

I placed the car in reverse.

"And then we go see Grace."

38

If you look on a map, the route from Lanton to Bradford County twists and turns like a snake heading north up the state.

I was using the GPS app on my phone, just like Daniel had when we'd driven down to the beach, so my focus was mostly on listening to the robotic voice's occasional reminders and not on reading the signs posted along the highway.

But Elise, sitting in the back, noticed.

"It's in another mile," she said quietly.

I glanced at her in the rearview mirror. "What is?"

"Didn't you see the sign we just passed?"

Courtney, in the passenger seat beside me, said quietly, "I saw it."

"Saw what?" I asked, but then just as quickly I gave the highway and the passing trees another look, and my stomach tightened.

"Oh," I said.

A few seconds later, a large sign announcing **DON'T MISS SILVER LAKE PARK YOU'RE ALMOST THERE** loomed on the right.

Then, several seconds after that, we zoomed past the exit.

In the back, Elise said, "I forgot this was the way Mackenzie's parents always brought us. Then again, I think maybe I wanted to forget."

I nodded, knowing exactly what she meant. Fourteen years ago, Silver Lake Park had hosted a handful of cabins spread around the massive lake. I imagined there were even more cabins now.

"I lied to you both the other night at the bar," Elise said.

I glanced at her again in the rearview mirror. "What do you mean?"

"I still think about Grace. I have nightmares about that night. Which is crazy, right? We weren't the ones being bullied. But sometimes in the nightmares I'm standing in Grace's place, and . . ."

"And what?"

She turned her face so she was staring straight back at me.

"You know."

Yes, I did know. We all did. We'd lived it. We'd *caused* it.

Our yearly trips to the cabin had always been fun, though on that Memorial Day weekend a shadow had fallen over everything. Grace had been acting weirder than usual, hardly speaking, and she hadn't been her normal compliant self. We were careful around Mackenzie's parents, just as we were always careful around adults, to not treat her too badly. The angry looks, the taunts, the disrespect—that was only for us.

I remembered the cabin had four bedrooms and a large living area. The living area was where we'd slept. Mackenzie's parents had air mattresses stored away. We typically spent the night whispering to each other about boys, trying to one-up each other's stories of sexual daring, but it had been too awkward with Grace. That first night we'd all had a sense that she shouldn't be there. That her mere presence would ruin the weekend. But we couldn't leave for another two days, which meant that we were stuck with her.

Maybe that was why, the next morning, while Grace was in the shower—Mackenzie's mother allowed us five minutes each, using the kitchen timer and calling out a one-minute warning—Mackenzie told us we needed to do something about her.

"Like what?" Olivia had asked.

Mackenzie had never looked more serious than she had in that moment, not even several days later when she gathered us in her bedroom and showed us the paring knife.

"Put her in her place."

Before Mackenzie could say anything else, the water stopped; the shower curtain slid back, and we all scattered in different directions, as if we'd been caught standing over the dead body of a person we'd just murdered.

The rest of the day, Mackenzie's words kept running through our minds, but we were never alone to discuss it further. Not when we strolled around the entire lake, throwing bits of stale bread at the ducks that followed us in the water. Not when we loaded into the SUV so Mackenzie's parents could drive us to a local restaurant for dinner. Occasionally we managed to steal time, but by the evening there still wasn't a solid plan in place. At least not one that I was aware of.

Maybe the others hadn't known either. Maybe none of us had known how bad it would be until we started out into the woods.

Now, fourteen years later, Elise issued a heavy sigh.

"It could have been so much worse, you know? At work I represent kids who get arrested for really awful stuff, and many times it's not like they even planned it. That night . . . what if she'd been unconscious when we went back in the morning? What if she'd been dead?"

She let the thought hang in the air.

"I'd like to think we would have done the right thing—gone straight to Mackenzie's parents, had them call an ambulance—but then I think hard about that moment, and how we all were back then, and I . . . I have to wonder, would we have tried to hide what happened? Like, would we have tried to bury her body somewhere, or come up with a story to tell our parents so that we didn't get into too much trouble?"

Elise stared out her window, shook her head again.

"I know it sounds ridiculous, but some of these kids I work with end up in the wrong place at the wrong time, and when they're there, they make the worst decisions. All of our lives would have been ruined, and for what? We were just stupid girls."

Elise fell silent, still staring out her window, and I glanced at Courtney, who looked back at me. It was clear Courtney had nothing to say, so I felt the need to fill the silence.

"We were stupid girls," I said. "But we're not anymore."

Elise once again met my eyes in the rearview mirror. She stared for a moment before wiping absently at her cheek.

"I hope you're right."

39

Dixon Township sat just over the border into Bradford County. At almost eight o'clock, the sun was nearing the horizon as we crossed.

We passed some houses, a Citgo station, a beer-and-soda outlet, and a Dollar General. After driving several miles down the rural highway, passing more houses, the countryside became more rugged.

I passed Vesper Road without realizing it. The signal on my phone dropped out momentarily, so for about a minute we were without GPS, and I had to turn around in one of the driveways a quarter mile away. I drove back, going slowly now, craning my neck to spot the sign.

It looked more like a hidden driveway than a road. I made the turn and drove for another quarter mile before seeing the first home: a trailer, sitting off in a field, both the American and Confederate flags hanging from the front porch.

Three hundred yards farther ahead was another trailer home. This one had two pickup trucks and an SUV parked out front. A swing set that looked like it had seen better days sat in a cluster of tall grass.

We kept going. Henry Zimmerman had said the Farmers were at the very end of the road. Which started to curve as the sun dipped below the trees. The car's headlights illuminated our way. It wasn't much farther. The road did indeed end. And sitting at the end was another trailer home.

This one was bigger than the previous two. It sat up on a slight hill. A pickup truck was parked outside, and another car sat in the yard, with weeds growing around it. The car didn't have any tires, and the rims had rusted.

It took me a moment to recognize Grace's mom's ugly red hatchback.

I pulled over to the side and stared through the windshield at the trailer before realizing that the headlights were still on. I quickly flipped them off, and shut off the engine too. Then the three of us just sat there in the sudden silence.

Elise whispered, "I don't think I want to go in there."

Courtney spoke just as quietly. "I have to agree with that."

Without a word, I slid the key from the ignition and stepped out of the car.

The sound of our doors shutting shattered the stillness. This far from the highway, there was no sound of traffic.

Up on the hill, the door to the trailer banged open. A woman's raspy voice called out, "Help you with something?"

I traded nervous glances with Courtney and Elise, and started toward the trailer. Best to have this conversation without yelling. But I got only a couple of paces before the woman called out again.

"That's far enough. I don't know you three. I suggest you get back in your car and leave."

I paused, not sure what to do. With the light behind her, I couldn't make out any of the woman's features. I thought maybe she had frizzy hair, but couldn't tell for sure.

Courtney and Elise hadn't moved.

"We're looking for Grace Farmer," I said.

It was a risk using her name. Despite the relic that was the red hatchback, there was no guarantee anybody who had known Grace fourteen years ago lived here now.

The woman said, "What do you want with Grace?"

Adrenaline flooded my veins.

"Is she here?"

"No."

"Do you know where we could find her?"

Even though I couldn't see her face, I could tell the woman was studying me.

"Who are you?"

"I'm a friend of Grace's. From back in middle school."

The woman asked, "What middle school?"

"Benjamin Franklin."

"Benjamin Franklin." She repeated the name slowly, as if getting a taste for the words. "You're from all the way down in Lanton, aren't you?"

"Yes."

"And you came all the way up here. Why?"

That threw me for a second.

"We were hoping to speak to Grace," I said lamely.

"Uh-huh. I got that much. I ain't stupid."

"If Grace isn't here, can you tell us how we can get in touch with her?"

The woman didn't answer. Another figure appeared in the doorway, a child, scampering up and clinging to her leg. She turned and directed the child to move out of the doorway, and then she looked back at me.

"Like I said, Grace ain't here. But let me see what I can do. I don't normally invite strangers into my home, but since you're friends of Grace's, why don't you come in and have a seat while you wait?"

It was clear by their expressions that the last thing Courtney and Elise wanted to do was go inside. But I didn't want to be rude. Not to this person who obviously knew Grace and was most likely a family member.

I turned back to the woman, and forced a smile.

"We'd be happy to."

40

The inside of the trailer was cramped and cluttered. There were two children, the boy we'd seen, who looked to be about three, and an older child, a girl, maybe nine years old with purple glasses and her brown hair in pigtails, her tiny feet clad in pink Crocs.

The girl sat on the floor and used a glass coffee table to work on what looked to be her math homework, while the boy sat in front of the TV, which was playing *SpongeBob SquarePants*.

A couch and love seat took up much of the living area, and it was the couch that the woman cleared of a small clutter of toys and magazines that she simply dumped on the floor beside the love seat. Then she grabbed a cell phone from the coffee table and settled back down on the love seat, her thumbs punching the screen, and when she noticed us still standing, she gestured at the couch.

"Go ahead, make yourself comfortable."

I glanced back at Courtney and Elise, both of whom still looked nervous, and then sat on the end of the couch closer to the love seat. After a moment, they sat down as well.

The girl, holding a pencil poised over a worksheet, gave us only a cursory glance before diving back into her homework.

Unlike the girl, the little boy's attention was fixed on us. His dirty-blond hair was neatly combed, the only incongruity a cowlick sticking up near his crown. The skin around his mouth was ringed red, like either he licked his lips constantly or he'd been drinking red Kool-Aid most of the day. He stared, his mouth slightly open, as if he had never seen visitors before.

The woman stared at the cell phone for a moment before she nodded and leaned forward and placed it back on the coffee table.

"She'll be here shortly."

The same burst of adrenaline I'd felt outside shot through me again.

"Grace?"

The woman didn't answer. She was probably in her fifties, but her face looked ten years older, drawn and weathered. Her raspy voice was clearly the result of decades of smoking; a pack of cigarettes and an ashtray sat on the coffee table, along with several used scratch-off lottery tickets.

"These are my grandkids," she said. "That's Vanessa, who's the brightest girl you're ever gonna meet, and that's Matthew, who sure does love his cartoons. My daughter, Jackie, works second shift, so I watch 'em most nights. I'm Sheila, by the way."

"You're Grace's mother?"

The woman smiled, flashing her nicotine-stained teeth, and shook her head.

"No, no. Her aunt. Her mother was the one I was just texting. She should be here soon."

"What about Grace?"

"What about her?"

"We came to see her."

"Yeah, I get that part. But I still don't see why. If you went to school with her in Lanton, that was, what, over ten years ago. Why show up now all of a sudden?"

I didn't answer, and neither did Courtney or Elise.

Sheila reached down, grabbed the pack of Newports off the coffee table, lit one with a cheap plastic lighter. She took a long drag, watching us.

On the TV, SpongeBob and Patrick were driving Squidward crazy.

"My husband's a truck driver," Sheila said, blowing smoke from the side of her mouth. "He's supposed to be gone most of the night. So when I saw the headlights outside, for some reason I thought maybe it was him. Sometimes he calls beforehand, sometimes he doesn't. Cell reception ain't the best out here. Have to say, I wasn't expecting to find the three of you. As you can probably guess, we don't get many people coming down this dead-end road."

I said nothing, unsure what to say. Courtney and Elise must have felt the same way. We were clustered on the couch, each of us sitting on the edge, our shoulders squeezed together, because the whole place looked dirty, and we didn't know what kind of creepy-crawlies might be hiding under the cushions.

"Any of you want a drink?" Before we could answer, Sheila tapped the girl on the arm. "Vanessa, be helpful and get these girls some water."

"Thank you," I said quickly, "but we're okay right now."

Sheila eyed me. "You sure? It ain't no trouble."

"Really, thank you, but we're good."

Sheila glanced at Courtney and Elise. "I don't think I heard either of you say a word yet. She speak for you?"

Courtney said, "No, but I'm not thirsty, thank you."

"Me neither," Elise said. "But thank you."

"All those thank-yous. Such polite girls. Your parents must've raised you right, didn't they?"

Despite the sound of the cartoon, we heard a vehicle pulling up outside. Headlights splashed the windows before winking out.

"That'll be Bethanne," Sheila said, standing up from the love seat.

I leaned forward. "Grace's mother?"

Sheila nodded, biting her lip now, watching the door. She glanced at the TV, stared for a moment before walking over and turning it off.

The boy, Matthew, cried, "No!"

"It's too loud," Sheila said. "You both go in my bedroom and watch while your aunt Bethanne talks to these girls."

"But I wanna watch it *here*!"

Sheila took a drag off her cigarette, placed her hand on her hip.

"I don't give one good goddamn what you want, mister, and you should know that by now. Vanessa, take your brother into the bedroom. You can finish your homework in there, and he can watch his cartoon on the TV."

Silently, the girl gathered her worksheet and pencil and stood up and grabbed her brother's hand. The boy clearly didn't want to comply, his face turning red, but then he stomped his foot and let his sister guide him away.

Sheila shouted, "And shut the door!"

The door in the back snapped shut just as the front door opened and Grace's mother stepped inside.

41

"Bethanne, these are the girls I was telling you about. Their names—well, come to think of it, I never learned their names."

Sitting back down on the love seat, Sheila smashed her cigarette out in the already cluttered ashtray, grabbed another, and lit it. A cloud of smoke hung above her head like a halo.

"Like I texted you, they came the whole way from Lanton looking for Grace. They said they went to middle school with her."

The woman, Bethanne, hadn't moved since stepping foot inside the trailer. She looked to be about Sheila's age, though her face wasn't nearly as worn. There was a hint of Grace in her thin face, mostly in the eyes. Her dark hair wasn't frizzy like it had been that day at Mackenzie's house—tonight it was down, almost touching her shoulders—but she was clearly Grace's mother.

She wore faded jeans, white sneakers, and a T-shirt with BLACK DOG TAVERN stenciled in white lettering on the front—her work uniform, I realized after a second. She stood there, silent, assessing us.

Uneasiness flashed through me. I wasn't sure I could go through with this. We had no right to be here. No right to step back into this woman's life and start trouble. She didn't need to deal with the girls who had once terrorized her daughter.

The silence was heavy and uncomfortable; the only sound was the TV in the bedroom. Something told me Grace's mother was not going to be the first to speak, so I stood and held out my hand.

"My name's Emily Bennett. This is Courtney Sullivan and Elise Martin. We went to Benjamin Franklin Middle School with your daughter."

Bethanne Farmer stared at my hand. It was clear she had no intention of shaking it. I dropped it to my side, and then, feeling awkward, sat back down on the couch.

Sheila snorted quietly from her place on the love seat. She shook her head, tapped ash into the tray on the coffee table.

Another moment of awkward silence, and then Bethanne Farmer cleared her throat.

"Why are you here?"

Her voice was low and tremulous, not raspy like her sister's. Her dark eyes shifted between the three of us but settled on me, as I had apparently made myself the spokesperson.

"We came to see Grace."

"I get that"—her gaze bouncing between us—"but *why*? It's been fourteen years since you would have last seen Grace. Why now did the three of you decide to get in your car and drive all the way up here on a Tuesday night?"

Because we think your daughter is out for revenge. We think she has already caused the deaths of two of our friends, and we're afraid there will be more deaths very soon.

"We were thinking about her recently," I said. "We know . . . what happened to her in middle school was terrible, and we've always felt bad about it."

The woman stared at me. "So you came here to apologize?"

"Yes."

"After fourteen years, you decided one night to drive all the way up here to apologize for how you treated my daughter?"

Grace's mother looked at the three of us, then at Sheila, before shaking her head. She moved for the first time, keeping her back to the TV.

"I'm not sure I'd want you to see Grace."

We said nothing.

Bethanne Farmer started to pace back and forth in the small area, keeping her back to the TV.

"I never did get to meet any of you when we lived in Lanton. Grace didn't want me to embarrass her. She never came out and said as much, but I wasn't stupid."

She tilted her chin at her sister.

"The people here in Dixon Township—we're born here, we live here, and we die here. And fact is, there ain't much here to begin with. There used to be good jobs, but most of them closed with the mines. Grace being my only child, I wanted the world for her. Her daddy did too. And then . . ."

She squeezed her eyes shut, shook her head.

"And then he died at work. I won't bore you with the details, but the mine was at fault, and after a lotta back-and-forth between the lawyers, I ended up with enough money to buy ourselves an actual house. But I wanted what was best for my daughter, so we packed our bags and left. We didn't even know where we were gonna end up—we just got in the car and started driving. Too bad for Grace, we ended up in Lanton. And she ended up at your school."

Her fingers were flexing in and out of fists now, I noticed. My stomach twisted as she continued.

"We got an apartment. Everybody said it was supposed to be a good area. A good school. It seemed like the best place to start over. Grace . . . she had a good heart. She meant well. And the only thing in the world she wanted was to be liked."

She paused, and stared hard at us.

"Grace was so excited that first day of school. Came home and told me all about how she had made friends. And not just any friends, she said, these girls were *popular*. I have to admit, something about it didn't feel right. But I had lived my entire life in Dixon Township, and now I was in a new town, and I thought, well, maybe things are different down here. Maybe kids are nicer to each other. But it turns out kids are the same no matter where you go."

Bethanne Farmer kept pacing, almost frantically, looking all over the trailer except at us.

"Those first couple weeks, Grace was so happy. But then . . . something started to change. It was little at first, but I was her mother, and I noticed everything. She put up with some bullying, didn't she? I didn't know at the time, but later she told me all about it. How in front of other people you were so nice to her, included her in everything, but when it was just her and the rest of you, you treated her like shit. Eventually it got to be too much. Especially after you let those high school boys have their way with her."

Courtney's hand found my leg, squeezed tight. I glanced over and saw that she had her eyes shut. Tears ran down her cheeks.

"Sure, go ahead and cry about it now," Grace's mother said. "But you were laughing about it at the time, weren't you?"

I shook my head. "No, we—"

"No? So you *didn't* treat my daughter like shit when you were alone with her? So you *didn't* tell her she was worthless and that she should do the world a favor and kill herself?"

I took a deep breath, attempted to steady my nerves.

"We're sorry for what we—"

Grace's mother cut me off again.

"You're sorry, huh? What exactly are you sorry about? You probably laughed when you first heard Grace tried to kill herself."

Courtney's hand was still squeezing my leg, tighter now, as more tears fled down her face.

I grabbed her hand, pulled it free, and stood.

"I think we should leave."

That was when Grace's mother made it clear why she hadn't shown us her back. Silent, she reached behind her and brought out a silver-plated revolver.

"Do you?" she said. "Is that what you think?"

I stared at the revolver, stunned, blood thrumming in my ears.

"People know we came here."

Bethanne Farmer shrugged. "So?"

"If anything happens to us, this will be the first place they'll look."

Another shrug.

"Again, so?"

I didn't say anything. I couldn't think of anything to say.

Courtney's entire body shook, her voice a halting whisper.

"Please, I have a daughter."

Grace's mother barked out a guttural laugh.

"*Do* you? Well, then I guess we have a lot in common, don't we? Or wait—has your daughter been fucked by a bunch of high school boys? Called a slut by the whole school? Been treated like dirt by the girls who are supposed to be her friends?"

Courtney started crying.

"Boo-fucking-hoo," Bethanne Farmer said. "Do you really think I give a shit if you have a daughter? Do you think I give a good goddamn?"

I said nothing. Neither did Elise, still sitting on the couch, her purse in her lap; she was a bit more composed than Courtney but still looked terrified.

Sheila shook her head again, tsking at us like we were naughty children.

"I told y'all to get back in your car and leave. Course, I didn't know who y'all were. I thought you were lost or something. When you told me"—she issued a low whistle—"well, I knew exactly what Bethanne would have in mind for you. My sister, she used to be the nice one, the even-tempered one. But fourteen years ago, she started to change. Became angry. In the past year, she's become even angrier. Like one of those volcanoes about ready to erupt. She even talked about what she'd do if she ever met up with one of you. Didn't you, Bethanne?"

Grace's mother said nothing. The gun stayed at her side, her finger tapping the trigger guard.

Sheila snorted. "Yeah, she told me she'd make sure you paid for what you'd done to Grace. Can't say I blame her. When some kids were bullying Jackie back in high school, I went and shot out their tires. That's how we do things around here."

"So, what," I said, "you're going to *kill* us?"

Courtney nearly cried out when I asked the question.

Grace's mother said, "Not sure yet. Maybe I'll kill you, maybe I won't. Guess it depends on how much more you piss me off."

"What do you want from us, then—money?"

Bethanne's face went red, her jaw tightened, and her voice shook with anger.

"*Money?* You think *money* can save you from what you did to my daughter?"

Courtney's body kept shaking, tears all over her face.

"We're *sorry*! We're sorry for what we did!"

Bethanne Farmer mimicked it back at her.

"We're sorry, we're sorry, we're sorry. Yeah, you better be fucking sorry."

"That's why we came here," I said. "We wanted to find Grace, to apologize."

"After fourteen years you just one day decided you wanted to apologize to my daughter?"

"Yes."

Bethanne's jaw tightened again as she shook her head.

"I don't buy your bullshit. You probably came because you wanted to see what kind of shithole Grace lived in. Didn't you?"

I said nothing.

"Didn't you?"

The gun jerked in Bethanne Farmer's hand. Suddenly the barrel was pointed straight at my face.

I said, as calmly as I could, "My husband is a state trooper."

"You think I care? Hell, if he's a cop, he'll know the law is on our side. The three of you trespassed on our property. We told you to leave. You refused. We threatened to call the police, and you just laughed, said your husband was a cop, so you were above the law. That's when things took a violent turn. You became combative. We had no choice but to defend ourselves."

As she spoke, I pictured it in my mind. The events this woman would explain to the police. Somehow it would be convincing. Somehow they would get away with it.

Ben's words echoed in my head: *Their motto is shoot first, hide the body later.*

Grace's mother's voice ticked down an octave.

"Or maybe we'll take you out into the woods, just like you did my daughter. Leave you there for a couple days. We'll get rid of your car. Your husband comes looking for you, we'll either say yeah, we saw you and sent you on your way, or we'll tell him we don't know what he's talking about. What do you think about that?"

The barrel of the revolver was still aimed at my face. Grace's mother stood less than ten feet away. At that distance there was no doubt in my mind she wouldn't miss if she squeezed the trigger.

"Nana?"

The soft voice split the silence like a gunshot. I even jumped, startled, and looked past the gun at Bethanne Farmer's face. Her eyes had shifted away from me, toward the right. I followed her gaze and saw the boy standing beside the couch, right next to Elise.

His eyes were wide. His red-ringed mouth hung open. The cowlick on his crown now drooped like a dead flower.

For a moment, nobody moved.

I noticed, then, that Elise had her hand in her purse. She must have been slowly moving it there the entire time. From this angle, I could see she was now gripping the handle of a small handgun.

In an instant I imagined the worst. Either Bethanne or Sheila spotting the gun. Bethanne firing her revolver. Elise, if she wasn't hit, drawing her gun and returning fire. Courtney jumping to her feet, screaming, and getting caught in the cross fire. The boy, too, being struck down by a stray bullet. Complete and utter chaos.

"Don't," I said firmly, and while the word was meant for Elise, it was at Bethanne Farmer I now directed my focus. "Don't do this."

Sheila whispered, "Matthew, go back into the bedroom. *Now.*"

The boy didn't move. He was frozen with fear. His eyes still wide, staring at the gun in his aunt's hand.

Sheila stood there shaking. It was clear she wanted to bolt forward, grab the boy, usher him to the back of the trailer, but she wouldn't dare move, not with her sister's gun between her and her grandson.

"Listen to me," I said with as much authority as I could manage, my eyes still on Bethanne. "I'm a therapist. I actually became a therapist because of Grace. Because of what we did to her. Trauma affects children in many different ways. Some manage to get past it, but others don't. Some live with that trauma the rest of their lives."

I was rambling now, I realized, but I couldn't stop, knowing that as long as I kept talking, it meant we were still alive.

"Matthew," Sheila cried out, still frozen on the other side of the living area, "go now!"

I ignored the woman, kept my focus on Bethanne.

"The reason I'm bringing this up is because I don't want anybody else in your family to be traumatized. Maybe the boy's used to seeing guns, I don't know, but I do know that if something happens to us now, he's never going to forget it. He'll remember it the rest of his life. Maybe eventually he'll manage to move past it, but there's never any—"

I closed my eyes when I heard the bedroom door open and the girl scramble out into the living area. She wasn't being at all stealthy like her brother, her pink Crocs pounding across the carpeted floor. She had no doubt heard her grandmother shouting and become curious, wanting to see what all the fuss was about.

The girl's footsteps stopped suddenly, and she released a soft gasp.

I opened my eyes, glanced over to see the girl standing behind her brother, her face frozen, her eyes wide, and then I turned my attention back to Bethanne Farmer.

"Don't do anything to us with them both here. Make sure they don't see it. Make sure they don't even *hear* it. In fact . . . make sure my friends aren't here either."

Something changed in Bethanne's eyes. At first slight confusion, then after a second she seemed to understand what I was saying just as I realized what I had just said.

"You can do whatever you want to me," I said quietly. "You can take me into the woods, leave me there for days. You can kill me. Whatever. Just . . . don't let the children see. And let my friends go."

Another beat of silence. The only sound Sheila's raspy breathing, ragged and anxious.

Then Grace's mother lowered the revolver, bit by bit, until it was back at her side.

Sheila took that as her cue. She rushed forward, fell to her knees, wrapped both the boy and the girl in a tight embrace.

I glanced over at Courtney, who was still crying, and Elise, who had taken her hand out of her purse, and then I glanced back at Bethanne, whose face and eyes had hardened again.

"Get the fuck out of here before I change my mind," she said.

Elise rose to her feet at once. Courtney, still crying, didn't look like she was able to move on her own, so Elise and I helped her up and moved her toward the door.

I should have remained silent, thankful that we were able to make an escape, but I couldn't help myself.

"What about Grace?"

Bethanne Farmer stared at me. Her finger tapped the trigger guard again, but she didn't raise the gun.

"You just missed her by about a year." Her voice was low and tremulous again, her jaw tight. "That's when she decided enough was enough."

Elise had started to open the door but paused. We all looked at the woman now, silent.

Grace's mother nodded, her face grim.

"That's right. My daughter finally managed to kill herself. And it's all your goddamned fault."

Seven days she'd been at Riverside Psychiatric Hospital—seven long days with kids and staff she didn't know, the food tasting like cardboard, every door and window locked so that nobody could escape—and finally her mother had come to see her.

Grace couldn't blame her for not coming sooner. Riverside was near Pittsburgh, almost a four-hour drive, and to be fair, her mother had called the unit every evening, though Grace had agreed to speak to her only three of those times, and even then she hadn't said much.

Still, when Miss McGuire brought Grace into the family room—the tight dank space smelling of must and desperation—and she saw her mother sitting at the table, it was like seeing her for the first time in years, when in reality it had been only a week. The last time she'd seen her was in the ER, after her mother had found her in the bathtub, the warm water diluted by her blood.

Now her mother sprang to her feet and hurried across the room, her face squeezed tight, tears already filling her eyes. She meant to pull her into an embrace, but as soon as her mother touched her, Grace jerked away.

Her mother stopped short, her eyes widening.

"Grace?" she said, and her voice was so timid, so unlike her mother's that it didn't even sound real. "Honey, what's wrong?"

Miss McGuire, her assigned therapist on the unit, barely thirty years old, short curly brown hair and kind eyes, offered up her professional smile and gestured at the table.

"Please, Mrs. Farmer, why don't you take a seat."

Her mother stood, stunned, staring at Grace like she didn't recognize her.

"Honey?"

She reached out again, intent on making physical contact, but Grace shrank back against the wall, pushing herself into it, as if pushing hard enough might somehow defy the laws of physics and allow her to pass through the wall as if it were only smoke.

"Mrs. Farmer"—Miss McGuire's tone all patience—"please have a seat."

Finally, her mother relented, dropping her shoulders, giving Grace one last look before returning to the table.

"What's wrong with her?" she whispered, like Grace would somehow not hear her.

Miss McGuire softly cleared her throat.

"As we discussed on the phone, your daughter has continued to struggle. She displays textbook PTSD, which makes sense after what we've managed to learn, about what those boys did to her and how badly she was treated by her friends."

"Friends," her mother snapped. "Those girls are not Grace's friends." She paused, cleared her throat. "Did you . . . did you say she attacked a girl the other day?"

"Attacked might be too strong a word. But yes—a girl on the unit was conversing with some other girls and started to laugh, and we believe Grace thought the girl was laughing at her. Grace lunged at the girl in question, started screaming and slapping at her. Staff was nearby and managed to intervene almost immediately, so the girl didn't sustain any serious injuries."

"My God," her mother whispered. And then she started to cry, a soft sobbing Grace hadn't heard since last year, when her father died.

Miss McGuire handed her a tissue, and Grace's mother blew her nose and wiped at her eyes.

"The first couple of days Grace was here," Miss McGuire said, "she refused to participate in therapy. But recently she's started to open up. That's how she told us about what her friends—I'm sorry, the girls—did to her, as well as those boys. Speaking of which . . ."

The therapist let it hang there, and Grace's mother dabbed at her eyes again as she nodded and finished the thought.

"You think I should press charges."

"It's not my decision, of course, but there should be consequences for what those boys did."

Grace's mother shifted uneasily in her seat.

"Yeah, well, I'm not sure what would happen. From what I heard, those boys barely got a slap on the wrist for burning down that god-awful place. Besides, I wanna put it all behind us. I imagine Grace does too. If we press charges, she'll have to go to court and tell everybody what happened . . ."

Her mother let the thought trail off and glanced over at Grace again.

"No," she said, "I don't want that for Grace. She's suffered enough. Grace, honey, please come over here. Please look at me!"

Grace didn't move. Just kept standing in the corner, her forehead against the wall.

Miss McGuire said, "Let me give you some time alone. I was hoping we could have a family therapy session, but maybe that won't work out today. How many days did you say you were going to stay up here?"

"As many as I need to. I broke the lease on our apartment. All our things are in the car. As soon as Grace is allowed to leave here, we're going straight back to Dixon Township."

Miss McGuire rose from her seat and crossed over to the corner. She lingered just beside Grace, stepping close to her, and said softly, "Grace, dear, your mother wants to talk to you. Will you talk to your mother?"

Grace nodded her head against the wall.

"Can you go sit with your mother at the table? She came a long distance to see you."

Grace nodded again.

But after Miss McGuire left them, Grace still didn't move. She stayed in the corner, eyes closed, forehead pressed against the fading paint.

After a few moments, she peeled herself off the wall. She lowered herself into the seat Miss McGuire had vacated, her hands in her lap, and stared at the table. Her mother didn't speak, just let the silence play out.

Grace cleared her throat. Still not looking up at her mother, she asked, "Are you gonna sue them?"

She heard the frown in her mother's voice.

"Who?"

"Those girls and their parents. Isn't that what you told Aunt Sheila on the phone?"

Her mother was quiet for so long that Grace wasn't sure she'd heard her. She lifted her eyes and saw her mother's pained expression. She was staring down at Grace's arm, at the bandage that covered her left wrist. When she realized Grace was watching her, she looked away, shaking her head.

"Baby, I wish I could—I wish I could sue 'em all—but we don't have the money for that. Those girls' parents are rich, and they can afford good lawyers. Same with those awful boys."

Another silence fell. Her mother looked like she was on the verge of sobbing again, and Grace realized she didn't want her to feel worse than she already did.

"I think . . . I'm starting to feel a little better."

Her mother stared at her, a burst of hope flaring in her eyes.

"Really?"

Grace nodded. "I just . . . I didn't know what else to do."

Her mother's bottom lip started to tremble, and Grace, fearing her mother might cry again, hesitantly reached out her hand.

Her mother took it, squeezed it tight.

Grace said, "Are we really moving back to Dixon Township?"

Her mother nodded adamantly, squeezing her hand again.

"That's right, baby. We're done with Lanton. We're gonna put all that nastiness behind us. You're never gonna have to see those awful girls ever again."

PART III:

Sticks and Stones

42

"How did she die?"

"Apparently in a fire."

"Grace's mom told you that?"

"No, she didn't want anything more to do with us. And because we were worried she might change her mind, we got out of there real quick."

We were in my car, Lisa and me, parked in one of the spaces outside Lisa's office. It was early morning, a half hour before they officially opened, but Lisa had agreed to meet me privately to discuss what had happened.

As a professional courtesy, she'd given me her cell phone number, but I had never bothered to use it until late last night. At first she'd said no to the early meeting—it's unethical for a therapist to meet her client outside the office—but she must have sensed the desperation in my voice, the urgency, because she'd eventually agreed.

And so here we were, the sky overcast and spitting down rain, the windshield wipers off, the world outside a strange blur.

"So how did you find out?"

"Courtney looked it up on her phone on the drive back. She found a local news article from a little over a year ago. The article didn't give a name—there was a sentence about how the family wanted to keep the identity private—but it confirmed a young woman Grace's age had died in a meth-lab explosion. Those places are apt to blow up all the time, I guess, but police noted that they suspected it may have been done on purpose."

I paused, shook my head again.

"No wonder that woman was so angry. I guess part of me thought that after all this time she would have gotten over what happened to Grace in middle school. I never imagined she would . . ."

I trailed off, and Lisa filled in the rest.

"Try to kill you and your friends?"

I didn't answer right away, thinking about it.

"I guess part of me refused to believe she would really kill us. That she was just, I don't know, trying to intimidate us."

"Is that why you stood up to her?"

"I don't know. Courtney asked me later how I'd been so calm. I told her it was because I'd spent that time working as a crisis worker at the ER."

"Are you sure that's it?"

"What do you mean?"

"I brought this up last week. How you've always felt guilty for what you and your friends did to Grace. And how part of you has always felt you deserved some kind of punishment."

I turned in my seat to look at Lisa.

"You mean like letting that crazy woman kill us?"

"I'm not saying it was a rational part of you. But maybe a part felt that whatever the woman did would have been justified. After all, you more or less offered to sacrifice yourself to save your friends."

"The only reason I went up there was to try to find Grace."

"I understand that," Lisa said. "But instead you found her mother, who wanted to kill you or punish you in some way. I'm surprised you didn't call the police the second you got back in your car."

"We didn't want to make a big deal out of it."

"She pulled a *gun* on you, Emily."

Yes, and Elise almost pulled a gun of her own—a gun that I purposely failed to mention to Lisa—but that was beside the point.

When it became clear I wasn't going to respond, Lisa said, "So if you didn't call the police, then what did you do—just went home?"

I nodded. I told Lisa that we had driven back to Lanton mostly in silence. That we'd all been shaken by the events of the night and what we'd learned. That Grace was dead; that she'd been dead for just over a year.

Lisa said, "And so your theory that Grace somehow managed to track down Olivia and Destiny before they died . . . what did you and your friends ultimately decide?"

"I'm not sure. I got the sense Elise was the most annoyed. After all, she had come along based on what Courtney and I told her. She hadn't seen the picture on Olivia's fiancé's phone. Or met with Destiny's widow."

"About that picture . . ."

But Lisa didn't say the rest, prompting me to continue in that direction.

"Yeah, I know. I've been thinking about that. How Courtney and I both thought it was Grace. I mean, it's been fourteen years. Grace wouldn't look the same anymore, right? And it's not like Courtney and I knew her for very long. I don't even have any pictures of her. I thought I recognized her eyes, but I guess I was wrong."

"What are you thinking now?"

I slumped in my seat, dropped my head back on the headrest.

"I don't know. That maybe all of this was coincidental from the start. Hearing about Olivia killing herself, Karen saying that Olivia told her it was a ghost—right then I was already thinking about Grace. When Courtney and I saw the photo . . . I don't know, I guess we both expected it to be Grace—hoped it would be, in a way—so that's who we saw."

"But that doesn't explain what Destiny's widow told you."

"No, it doesn't," I said, and did everything I could to keep my voice steady, thinking again about being down at the boardwalk and glimpsing a pale face across the street, who I had at first thought was Grace but now knew was just my imagination. "That's the weird part. Charlotte said Destiny was driven to suicide after supposedly seeing Grace wherever she turned, and the last thing she texted was the word *vesper*, like Vesper Road, where Grace grew up. It seems like more than a coincidence, doesn't it?"

Lisa said nothing. She just sat there, a pained smile on her face, looking first at me and then away.

"What are your thoughts?" I asked.

Lisa grabbed her Starbucks coffee from the cup holder, took a sip.

"I'm not sure what my thoughts are," she said after a while. "I don't want to discount any of what you told me, but it doesn't add up. Especially now that you know Grace died over a year ago."

I covered my face with my hands, did everything I could not to scream out my frustrations.

"I could barely sleep last night. And when I did fall asleep, I had that same nightmare where I'm in school and a girl is standing at the end of the hallway and her wrists keep bleeding. Only this time . . . this time it was different."

"How so?"

"This time I managed to walk past the girl and see her face."

"Who was it?" When I didn't answer, Lisa studied my eyes, and said, "It was you."

I nodded and looked away. For some reason I felt embarrassed. Like I should have known the girl with the bleeding wrists was me this entire time. Even though I had never cut my own wrists. Even though I had never even contemplated suicide.

Lisa took another sip of coffee and glanced out the window as a car pulled up beside us. It wasn't the only one. A few other cars had parked in the last couple of minutes. The office was almost ready to open.

"I need to go," Lisa said, "but I do want to see you sometime this week. Clearly you've been going through a lot."

I nearly let out a desperate laugh.

"You could say that. I called in sick Monday and Tuesday, and I don't have a doctor's excuse. I didn't even bother trying to get one. I've been avoiding my boss's calls. I'll probably get written up, and you know what? I deserve it. I feel foolish, really, because I canceled all those appointments for what's turned out to be nothing. God, can you imagine if something happened to one of my clients? Like, what if one of them went to the ER because of a crisis? Maybe had they seen me earlier in the day—been able to process what was bothering them—it wouldn't have happened."

Lisa gathered her purse in her lap. She had her umbrella on the floor between her legs.

"I'm sure your clients are fine. And I wouldn't say it turned out to be nothing."

"What do you mean?"

"You know what happened to Grace. That should at least put away the doubt in your mind."

"I guess so. But to be honest with you, that's only made things worse."

It was clear Lisa was ready to leave—her hand on the door handle—but she paused to glance back at me.

"How so?"

"Because if it wasn't Grace who was somehow involved in what happened to Olivia and Destiny, then it had to be somebody else, right? If it's not Grace or somebody else, then the third option is something I'm not yet prepared to accept."

This made Lisa frown. "What's the third option?"

"That I'm losing my mind."

43

The lobby of Safe Haven Behavioral Health was empty when I walked through the entrance. This was typical, as clients weren't scheduled for the first hour. Gave the staff time to prepare.

Claire was already at her desk, staring at her computer screen. She glanced up at me briefly, did a sort of double take, and then leaned forward to slide the glass partition open.

"Good morning. Are you feeling any better?"

"A bit."

Claire didn't need to know that I hadn't been sick. Nor did she need to know that I'd gotten very little sleep last night and was still shaken after my talk with Lisa. I'd hoped the meeting would help calm me down, but in a way it had made things worse. After talking about what had happened—actually saying the words out loud—it had begun to hit me once again just how crazy everything had gotten.

I was headed for the door leading back to the offices when Claire spoke again.

"Wanda needs to see you."

The office manager. Great.

"Where is she?"

"Conference room A."

As if to reiterate, Claire gestured to the other closed door in the corner of the lobby.

"She's in there now?"

"Yes," Claire said, and her voice had taken on a cautionary tone, as if she was unsure just what to tell me. "They are waiting for you inside."

They. I didn't like the sound of that.

I paused again, eyed the door to conference room A and the door I'd just walked through. I could leave. Hurry through the rain to my car, start the engine, drive God knows where.

But no. I knew what this was about, my calling in sick for two straight days, and I needed to face the consequences. Up until now, I'd been a stellar employee—never written up, never late. This behavior must have raised a red flag.

I placed my hand on the doorknob. Started to turn it, but decided to knock first.

A voice spoke from inside.

"Come in."

I opened the door. Saw who *they* were. Wanda, yes, but also Janice, the head of HR, and a man I'd never seen before in a gray suit and red tie. They sat at the long table, all on the same side. A chair was set up across from them, already pulled out and waiting.

Wanda didn't even fake a smile.

"Please shut the door," she said.

I didn't move. Something felt off. Janice wouldn't be here just because I'd called in sick two days in a row, would she? And who was the man in the suit?

Wanda spoke again.

"Have a seat, Emily."

No warmth to her voice. Hardly any inflection. It was like the woman I'd known for the past three years was a complete stranger.

"May I ask what this is about?" I said, stepping in and pulling the door shut behind me.

Now it was Janice who spoke.

"Sit down," she said. Her voice was cold.

I thought about turning around. Opening the door. Fleeing whatever the hell was going on here. It would be so easy.

It would be cowardly too. I crossed over to the chair and sat down.

The table was bare except for a single manila folder in front of Janice. She had both hands spread on top of it, her stubby fingers dotted with rings.

"Do you like working here, Emily?" Janice asked.

I glanced first at the man and then at Wanda before focusing my attention back on Janice.

"What is this about?"

"You've only been here three years, but you've established yourself as one of our best therapists."

Based on the current tableau and their stern expressions, I hadn't been expecting a compliment.

"Um, thank you."

"Are you happy working here?"

I frowned. "Of course I am. What are you talking about? Who is this man, anyway?"

"This"—Janice gestured to him as she spoke—"is Chad Perkins from legal."

"And why is Chad Perkins from legal here? All of this because I called in sick the past two days?"

Janice paused a beat.

"No," she said. Then: "Well, in a way, yes."

I looked to Wanda for clarification, but she just sat there, her lips pursed, staring back at me.

I said to Janice, "I don't understand what's going on here."

Janice issued a soft sigh. She went to open the folder but paused, said, "Emily, you are aware of the company's zero tolerance policy regarding social media and the potential violation of HIPAA, yes?"

"Of course. What does that have to do with anything?"

Janice gave me a curious look, as if she wasn't sure I was being serious, and then opened the folder. I wasn't sure what I had expected, but it didn't look so bad. Only a few papers with text on them.

Janice took the first page, turned it around so it was facing me, and pushed it across the table.

"Would you care to explain this?"

I glanced down at the paper. A screenshot. My name was there, as was the date—Monday—and the time—7:45 p.m.

> *There's something I need to get off my chest. The kids I work with are the worst. Most of them are entitled brats, and the others are stupid retards. There's this one kid, his name is Andrew, and he has autism. He says that at night he sees spiders crawling on the wall. Obviously there are no spiders, but that doesn't matter because he's a fucking retard. God, I wish these kids would do the world a favor and kill themselves.*

I read the paragraph twice—my body going even tenser the second time—and glanced up. Opened my mouth, shut it. Wet my lips. My entire body trembled, and when I spoke next, my voice was hoarse.

"What the hell is this?"

All three of them watched me with no expression.

Janice said, "Isn't Andrew Williams one of your clients?"

"Yes, but I never—"

I stopped myself as the realization hit me, like ice injected into my veins. All at once the room went cold. I stared back down at the paragraph in front of me, then glanced up at the open folder. At the other papers stacked there.

"What else do you have?"

This seemed to confuse Janice. She frowned at me, then frowned at Wanda and Chad Perkins before she cleared her throat.

"Five other status updates, each naming a different client."

"Which clients?"

Again, Janice looked confused, but she quickly managed to compose herself.

"Does it matter? Each status update makes some harsh or vulgar statement about the client. My goodness, Emily, they are *children*."

I wet my lips again. Wanted to speak but wasn't sure what to say.

Janice said, "The updates started Monday and went into Tuesday. Wanda told me that when she saw them, she tried calling you to find out what was going through your mind, but there was never any answer. And so it was surprising to Wanda when you texted her last night, saying that you would be at work today."

Wanda kept staring at me like I was a stranger. Or worse—diseased. Which made sense. Based on these status updates, the person she thought I was had turned out to be a lie. The only problem was: I hadn't written them.

"Where did you find these?"

Now it was Janice who gave me an irritated look.

"Come on, Emily. Don't do this."

"I'm serious. I didn't write these."

"Then who did?"

"I don't know. But it wasn't me."

Wanda finally chimed in, her brow furrowed as she glowered back at me.

"You know very well those status updates are from Facebook."

"I don't have a Facebook account."

It took everything I had not to scream it at them. I dropped my hands below the table because I realized they were shaking.

Wanda rolled her eyes, turned to Janice and Chad Perkins.

"Can we get this over with?"

I said it again, this time with more emphasis: "I don't have a Facebook account."

Pure contempt flashed in Wanda's eyes.

"Stop it, Emily. You're Facebook friends with nearly everybody in the office, including me."

I was shaking my head now, opening my mouth to speak, to say something, *anything*, that could refute what was happening. But of course there was nothing to say. I'd never created a Facebook account, but that didn't matter. As far as Wanda and Janice and Chad Perkins were concerned—not to mention everybody else in the office—*I* was the one who had been interacting with them all this time. Liking their status updates. Commenting on their photos. And then, two days ago, snapping and doing the one thing that would make me a pariah to my colleagues and lead to my immediate termination from Safe Haven Behavioral Health.

I could try to defend myself, explain how the person who had written those status updates was not really me, but that would make me look even crazier than I already did. So I sat up straighter in my seat, pushed back my shoulders, and addressed Janice.

"Can I at least clean out my desk?"

"Your desk has already been emptied. By now Claire should have the box ready. I hope you enjoyed working as a therapist, Emily, because I'm not sure you're going to find work in this field ever again."

44

Relief flooded me the instant I saw Daniel's car outside the town house.

I'd called Courtney several times, had even texted her, but there was no answer. I'd considered stopping by Walmart but didn't want to get her in trouble. I'd even considered contacting Elise, but after last night I was probably the last person she wanted to hear from, and besides, I worried she wouldn't believe what happened. I'd considered contacting my mother, but she would have a thousand questions that would only add to my stress, so I hurried home, realizing that right now my only support was Daniel.

I parked beside him and shut off the engine, grabbed the box of my things off the passenger seat, and sprinted to the front door.

Inside, I released a heavy breath. I wasn't sure how I would tell Daniel what had happened. All he knew was that my old friend Olivia had died, and I suddenly had a friend I hadn't spoken about before, a friend whose daughter he'd babysat.

"Emily?"

Daniel's voice, coming from the second floor.

His footsteps were at the top of the stairs, and I turned to look up at him—but paused once I saw Daniel's suitcase sitting upright on the carpet near the TV.

Daniel started down the steps, and from my vantage point, all I saw were his sneakers. Then his jeans and T-shirt and finally the confused expression on his face.

"I thought you went to work."

I still had the box cradled in my left arm. I set it on the table by the door, pointed at the suitcase.

"Why is this here?"

He looked nervous. Almost embarrassed. He came the rest of the way down the stairs and started toward me, but stopped. He opened his mouth, but closed it again. Looked away from me.

"Are you moving out?"

See the couple in the boiling water, bubbles swirling around them.

Daniel looked back at me, his expression pained, and I knew it was true.

"Emily"—his voice just above a whisper—"this shouldn't be surprising."

See the man, scalded and broken, trying to pull himself out of the water.

I shook my head. "This is the last fucking thing I need right now."

"What do you want me to say, Emily? Things haven't been right between us for a long time."

I thought about what Lisa had said last week, about how Daniel wouldn't be the one to break up with me.

"So, what," I said, my voice tremulous, "you decided to pack your things and move out before I got home from work? Were you even going to tell me? Or just send me a text after the fact?"

"No, of course not. I planned to be here when you got home. I would never do this"—Daniel shook his head, looking even more pained, as if he couldn't find the right words to explain the situation—"by text or whatever. You don't deserve that."

"I don't deserve that?" I almost laughed out loud.

He gave me a new look, studying my face.

"Are you okay?"

"What does it matter to you?"

"Emily, don't."

"Don't tell me what to do, Daniel. You're walking out on me."

"I'm not *walking out* on you. I'm giving you space. I'm giving *us* space. At this point, I don't know what else to do."

"What a gentleman."

Ignoring the dig, he said, "I'm going to stay at Zack's for a while. I figure you'll need time to either move back to your mom's or find your own place. Let's say a week."

It struck me that I didn't even know who Zack was. A friend of Daniel's, obviously, but I couldn't picture his face or how Daniel knew him or whether I'd even met him before.

"A week," I echoed.

"Please, Emily, don't make this harder than it has to be."

Now I did laugh out loud, an almost hysterical cackle.

Daniel said, "I know you may not want to believe this, but I've never stopped loving you. I'm just . . . no longer *in love* with you. And I'm pretty sure you feel the same way."

"Don't tell me how I feel."

"Emily."

"No, fuck you. You can't do this to me today."

Daniel offered up a half-hearted shrug.

"If not today, then when? The fact is, this has been a long time coming, and we both know it. We just . . . want different things. I don't know about you, Emily, but I'm tired of wasting my life."

Part of me knew he was right, but another part wanted to throw something. Slam a door. Scream out loud. Tell him I'd never really loved him in the first place. Hurt him because I didn't know what else to do, not with everything else that had suddenly been piled on my shoulders.

"What the hell is that supposed to mean?"

"Children, for one. When we met, you made it clear you never wanted kids. I made it clear that I did. And I thought, well, maybe you'd eventually change your mind. Which, I will admit, was completely unfair on my part. What's even more unfair is I thought maybe I could change your mind someday, make you see that you *do* want kids. I guess I was delusional. But what makes me even more delusional is thinking that after all this time—after you kept putting off the wedding date—you actually wanted to marry me in the first place."

The trembling I'd felt on the drive home had almost dissipated. Now I felt nothing. Numb. Hollow. Daniel's words were reaching my ears, being processed by my brain, but none of it resulted in the appropriate emotion.

"For the longest time I ignored it, but the space between us has gotten bigger and bigger. I kept thinking that one day things would change. One day you'd wake up and decide you at least wanted to get married."

My jaw was set, but still I needed to ask.

"So what changed?"

"Terri," he said. "Hanging out with her . . . I remembered how much I want to be a dad. And if that's going to happen, I can't keep waiting for you to be the one to end things."

"Is there somebody else?"

The question caught him by surprise. He blinked at me.

"What?"

"Somebody else. You know, a slut you've been fucking behind my back."

He kept his gaze steady with mine.

"No," he said, "I haven't been sleeping with anyone behind your back."

I didn't believe him. I thought of the fake Facebook account, the other Emily floating around out there in the ether. About Philip standing behind Huey's Bar & Grille with his phone, showing us the picture of the girl who looked like Grace. The one who had set up the entire thing to get back at Olivia. To drive her crazy.

I took a step forward, trembling now, my jaw tight.

"Who is it?"

Confusion shadowed his face.

"Who is what?"

"Do you have a picture?"

"I told you, there isn't anyone."

"Let me see her picture."

"Emily."

"Let me see her picture!"

Daniel just stared at me. Concern had overtaken his confusion. He studied my face again, and then looked past me at the cardboard box I'd set on the table by the door.

"Why are you home so early?"

When I didn't answer—standing only feet away from him, still trembling—Daniel took a step toward me.

"Emily," he said, his voice soft, measured. "Are you all right? Maybe you should sit down."

I blinked and looked at Daniel. At the suitcase on the floor. Back at Daniel.

And then I did something that surprised even myself. Without a word I turned, opened the door, and walked out into the rain.

45

The state police cruiser appeared at the back lot of the self-serve car wash and slowly drove toward me, its headlights on despite the fact that it wasn't yet noon. The sky was thick with dark clouds, and the rain was still coming down hard.

The cruiser eased to a stop, and Ben motioned me to get in. I stepped out into the rain and slid into the passenger seat. It was tight, due to the laptop set up on the center console, the bulky radio issuing quiet chatter between officers and dispatch.

"Thanks for coming," I said.

Ben nodded, looking concerned. "Are you going to tell me what's wrong?"

After I'd left Daniel's—I wouldn't let myself think of the town house as home anymore—I called Courtney again, but there was no answer.

I still wasn't ready to call Elise. Losing my job and fiancé within an hour was embarrassing enough, but the worst-case scenario was that she'd dismiss me, not believe it when I told her about the fake Facebook account. So I'd called Ben, and once he heard the desperation in my voice, he'd agreed to meet me. Since he was still on shift, he said it would be best to meet somewhere he could drive to easily. Because of the rain, the car-wash bays weren't being used, and the back lot was deserted, giving us privacy.

"I should have listened to you," I said, staring out at the rain sluicing down the windshield, at the wipers slowly swiping back and forth.

"What do you mean?"

"About waiting for this weekend so you could go with me up to Dixon Township."

"You went already? What happened?"

I told him about last night, how Courtney and Elise and I drove all the way to the end of Vesper Road. About Grace's mom pulling a gun on us. About talking her into letting us go and what we learned from the news article Courtney had found online.

"Jesus Christ," Ben said. "And you didn't call the police?"

"No. We just wanted to get out of there. Besides, we got the answer we'd come for."

"That Grace is dead."

"Yes."

"I'm sorry."

"About what?"

"Just everything. All this time, you've thought Grace was still alive."

He shook his head like he wanted to say more, but didn't.

"Ben, Destiny's last text message to her wife was *vesper*. Grace lived at the end of Vesper Road."

"Yes, and I can't explain that, but obviously it wasn't Grace."

Ben didn't look like he wanted to argue. He just sat there, watching me, and there was a tenderness in his eyes I hadn't seen for a long time, a tenderness that filled the hole in my heart Daniel had just left.

But no—I was feeling stressed and vulnerable, and I needed to focus. Needed to keep things in perspective.

"Even if you're right, something else happened this morning."

I told him about my meeting with Wanda and Janice and Chad Perkins from legal and the Facebook status updates they'd shown me.

Again, Ben said, "Jesus Christ. And you have no idea who might have written them?"

"No. But whoever did clearly knew I'd get fired. And they've been planning this for a while; from what I can tell, the account wasn't new. I think whoever's behind this is trying to mess with my head, just like they messed with Destiny and Olivia. I think"—I paused, swallowed—"I think they're trying to push me to the point where I'll kill myself."

"Come on, Emily. Do you know how crazy that sounds?"

"Destiny and Olivia are dead, Ben. They killed themselves, or at least their deaths were made to look like suicides."

"Okay, now you're just sounding crazy."

"I am *not* crazy!" My voice echoed inside the car. "But I . . . I do feel like I'm losing my mind."

Ben just stared, clearly unsure what to say.

"And then"—I shook my head—"I come home and Daniel's leaving me."

Ben cocked his head as if he hadn't heard me right.

"He had his suitcase already packed," I said.

Ben's eyes shifted to the diamond on my finger.

"But your ring—"

"I know. I'll have to give it back to him. I didn't even think about it until I got in the car, and by that point I didn't want to go back inside."

Ben said nothing at first, only watched me. The tenderness in his eyes had started to fade.

He asked, "Why are you here?"

"What do you mean? I called you because—"

"No, I mean, why are you back in my life? I never thought I would see you again. To be honest with you, Emily, you broke my fucking heart."

I said nothing. Wasn't sure how to respond.

Ben looked away, stared at the steering wheel, slowly shook his head.

"Julia was only supposed to be a rebound. I never intended on staying with her. Never intended on *marrying* her. Christ, never intended on having children with her. But this is my life now. This is what you fucking made me."

"What are you talking about?"

Still staring at the steering wheel: "I hate it that I never got over you. I kept telling myself that I'd been stupid. That I'd been too nice. Too naive. Too ready to do whatever you asked of me. And then Courtney contacts me and I show up and you're there and I just . . . I knew I should have said no, should have said fuck it and left, but I just couldn't do that. Goddamn it."

The rain kept beating at the windshield; the wipers kept swiping back and forth.

"There are times I'm with Julia and I wonder what it would be like if she were you." He paused a beat. "I'm wondering now what it would be like."

His voice had gone low, and when he looked at me, there was a hunger in his eyes I'd never seen before.

He started to lean in.

I leaned away and said, "What the hell are you doing?"

That look of hunger vanished at once, replaced first by confusion, then anger.

"You fucking tease," he said, his face filling with color. "Why do you keep messing with my head?"

"What are you talking about?"

He turned away, staring at the steering wheel again. His nostrils flared.

"Get the fuck out of my car."

Without a word, I opened the door and stepped out into the rain.

Immediately the engine roared and the cruiser sped away, tires squealing as it made a hard turn around the end of the car wash and out of sight.

46

The overhead fluorescents felt too bright, too consuming. Their starkness gave me a headache. I kept my head down as I walked the line of registers at the front of the store, searching the faces of the cashiers.

None of them were Courtney.

Maybe she was on break. Or in the bathroom. Did she always run a register? Maybe she was working back in the stockroom.

I started toward customer service, but there was already a line five deep, and besides, I didn't want to get Courtney in trouble. For whatever reason, she'd made it sound like she was already on thin ice at work, and I didn't want to do something to crack that ice.

I picked a checkout lane where a pleasant-looking older woman was working the register and grabbed a pack of Juicy Fruit. When it was my turn, I placed the gum on the belt. The cashier smiled at me as she ran it over the scanner.

"Still raining?" she asked.

I nodded, looking past her at the other cashiers down the line, and said in a soft voice, "Is Courtney here today?"

The cashier's smile faltered. "That depends. You a friend of hers?"

"Yes."

"What's her daughter's name?"

"Terri."

"What's her son's name?"

"She doesn't have a son."

The cashier studied my face, then hit a key on her register and set the gum aside.

"Courtney left. Two women showed up and spoke to her—not too long ago—and Courtney got real upset and left with them. No idea who they were. But Vivian sure is pissed. She's always had it out for Courtney. Wouldn't be surprised if Vivian tries to use this against her somehow, get her fired."

I didn't bother asking who Vivian was. I just murmured, "Thank you."

"You try calling her?"

"I did."

"Well, I'd try again. Maybe she's too upset to answer the phone. Now, that will be a dollar even. Cash or credit?"

I climbed the stairs to the second-floor landing, which was as dark and dank as the first time I'd visited. I raised my fist to knock on the door, then leaned forward and put my ear close to the frame.

Silence.

I knocked on the door. Waited a moment, then knocked again.

No answer.

I pulled out my phone and dialed Courtney's number, but it went straight to voice mail. This time, I left a message.

"I'm standing outside your door right now. I stopped by Walmart earlier, and someone told me you'd left. I'm really starting to worry. Call me."

I started back toward the stairs, but then inspiration struck. I returned to the door. When I knocked, I used that three-part knock I'd watched Courtney do when she wanted to let Terri know she was outside. Top, bottom, middle.

I waited for something—the sound of feet shuffling on the carpet, a hushed voice inside—but still there was silence. I considered speaking, yelling, screaming, but I wasn't sure what to say.

Before I left, I tried the doorknob, just in case. It didn't turn. Of course it didn't turn. Nobody was home. Courtney and Terri were . . . well, where were they?

"The school," I whispered.

Yes, that was it. I would check Terri's school next.

I headed back down the stairs, more purposefully now. In my mind I was already picturing the scenario—speaking first to the office staff and then asking to see the principal—so when I stepped outside into the rain, glanced across the parking lot, and saw someone on the other side, I didn't think twice about it, focusing instead on running toward my car.

It took an extra second or two before it all registered. I paused and looked up again.

The person was still there. Wearing a yellow rain slicker. The hood was down, so nothing obscured her long dark hair and pale skin.

She was staring straight at me.

Smiling.

Grace.

I raced through the parking lot. Weaving between the cars. Keeping my eyes on Grace. I knew the moment I looked away—the moment I blinked—she would disappear.

She didn't move. She just stood there, smiling at me.

When I was halfway across the parking lot, she reached behind her, flicked on her yellow hood, and ran in the opposite direction, down the narrow alley between the two apartment buildings.

"Grace, stop!"

I shouted it as I started sprinting, the rain battering my face, soaking me. I could see her farther ahead, at the end of the alley.

She disappeared around the corner.

"Grace!"

I kept running. Faster now. Wet hair stuck to my face. My purse bounced at my side.

I reached the end of the alley. Grace had turned left, and that's where I turned too.

And stopped.

I stood there, frozen, and scanned the back of the apartment complex.

Two dumpsters sat against the wall a few yards away. A scattering of trees stood off on the hill behind the complex.

Nobody was there.

I shook my head, started murmuring, "No, no, no, no," looking left and right again, looking out at the trees.

She had been here, right? *Right?*

A sound joined the noise of the rain, a soft tinkling of a glass bottle tipping over by the dumpsters.

I spun toward it, my body going tense.

"Grace?"

No answer.

Of course there's no answer, I thought. *Grace is* dead.

But still I started forward, one slow, unsteady step after another. I approached at an angle, veering toward the trees.

"Grace?" I said again, and part of me felt ridiculous speaking her name like this, walking cautiously behind the apartment building as the rain kept pouring and soaking me while another part was certain that I'd *seen* Grace, that she was right this moment crouched between those dumpsters.

When I was only a few more feet away, movement shot out. It was dark and low to the ground, and I realized at once it was a cat, sprinting past me into the trees.

I watched after it, the cat's tail flicking once as it disappeared, and I wanted to laugh out loud because if I was laughing, then I wouldn't cry.

Suddenly, I had the feeling that somebody was behind me. That Grace had in fact been between the dumpsters this entire time and was now silently walking up behind me, a knife in her hand.

I spun around, raising a fist . . . but of course there was nobody there.

I spotted the bottle the cat had tipped over, an empty green Yuengling. A few other bottles were still standing tall, hidden by a drenched cardboard box, probably left behind by teenagers in the apartment complex who'd sneaked it from their parents' fridge.

By that time I was completely soaked. I started back the way I'd come, down the alleyway.

Despite myself, I kept glancing back over my shoulder as I went.

47

The waitress brought my tuna melt and chips and set the plate down in front of me with a warm smile. In her other hand was a coffee urn, which she used to refill our cups before asking Elise if she'd decided on anything to eat.

"I'm fine right now, thank you."

The waitress smiled again and drifted away toward another table. Elise took a sip of her coffee, watching me over the brim of the cup.

"You should eat something."

I shook my head and pushed the plate away. "I'm not hungry. I just feel bad taking up a table."

Elise looked around the diner. "It's not like there's a rush right now."

She was right. It was just after three thirty, and only half the tables were occupied. Outside, the rain had slowed to a drizzle, but dark clouds still crowded the sky.

Elise took another sip of coffee, studying my face. She wore the same sympathetic expression my mother often did when she was worried about me.

I said, "I'm *not* crazy."

"I didn't say you were."

"I *saw* her, Elise. I swear to God."

"I believe you. I mean, I believe you *thought* you saw her. But you've been going through a lot, Emily. You must be exhausted. After all, when I came here, I found you asleep in your car. Which is completely understandable. All this stress you've been dealing with, especially after last night . . ."

She let it hang there, so I decided to change the subject, especially as I didn't want to mention also seeing Grace down at the boardwalk.

"What about you?"

She frowned. "What do you mean?"

"I can see in your face that something bad happened. Now spill."

Elise took another sip of her coffee, shifted her gaze out the window at the highway. Didn't say anything for a full minute. Then, softly clearing her throat, she spoke.

She told me about how she hadn't heard from her fiancé that morning, which was strange, because they usually texted each other in the mornings. She'd texted him but hadn't received any response. Today was a court day, and she had checked her phone between every docket, but still James hadn't texted. Elise admitted that she'd received my text asking her to meet, but she'd ignored it, still irritated from last night. It wasn't until court broke for lunch and she'd gone to her favorite deli that James had called.

"I was standing in line with everybody, and I just . . . It sounds weird, but this strange relief washed over me, and I was so excited, like I was a silly eighth grader again. But he didn't even say hello."

"What did he say?"

She pursed her lips, staring down at her coffee. Shifted her eyes up to meet mine, and I had never seen her so vulnerable before, so pained.

"He called me a bitch. Called me a whore. Called me a slut. All these awful things, he just shouted them at me at once. I didn't know what to do. I almost started crying right there in front of everybody, so I left the line and headed straight for the restrooms. I found one that was empty, and I locked the door and just stood there and listened as he kept shouting."

"What was he shouting?"

"Basically that if I hadn't wanted to marry him, I could have just told him and not brought his parents into it."

I pulled a napkin from the dispenser on the table, handed it to her so she could dab the tears forming in her eyes.

"Bring his parents into what?"

There was this guy Elise had dated before James, a guy named Travis whom she had spent a weekend with in Las Vegas. They'd had a good time there, staying at The Venetian, and their last night in the city they'd gotten drunk and Travis had talked her into letting him film them while they were having sex.

Part of Elise knew it was stupid; another part had liked the idea, but just to be safe, she'd told him he could only take pictures with her phone, and when he agreed, she'd posed for him in several different positions. Then they'd started getting intimate, and he'd filmed all of it, the pictures and video going to the cloud, and as far as Elise knew they were still there—she'd never bothered to delete them, even after she and Travis broke up—and *somehow* somebody had gained access and sent them to James's parents.

"My God," I whispered.

Elise took off her glasses to wipe the fatigue from her eyes.

"After he hung up on me, I stayed in the bathroom for a few minutes trying to get myself together, and then I left. Didn't even bother returning to court—didn't even call anybody to let them know I wasn't coming back. I went to my apartment to lie down, but that was when I remembered your text and replied that I'd meet you here."

"Do you think once James has a chance to cool down, he'll listen to your side of things?"

"I don't know. I hope so. Even if I do explain it, though, he's going to want to know why I never deleted those photos of Travis and me. To be honest, I don't have a good reason. It's not like I ever looked at them. I have hundreds of photos that I never look at."

"Who besides you would have access?"

"Nobody. I'm the only one."

"Then how—"

"I have no idea." Elise rubbed her hands up and down her arms like she couldn't get warm. "But it's terrifying."

I took a sip of my coffee, not sure what more to say, and then glanced at Elise's bag on the booth beside her.

"Can I ask you a personal question?"

The corners of her mouth lifted in a half-hearted smile.

"Of course, Emily. You can ask me whatever you'd like."

"Do you carry your gun with you everywhere you go?"

Her hand instinctively touched the bag, and the half-hearted smile collapsed.

"How do you know about that?"

"I saw you reaching for it last night."

Elise looked away, embarrassed, and shook her head. When she spoke next, her voice was barely a whisper.

"I thought she was going to kill us. I . . . I didn't think I'd have any other choice."

"But do you carry it with you everywhere?"

"Everywhere I can. Obviously I can't take it into the courthouse, so I lock it in the glove box."

"How long have you been carrying it?"

"Almost two years."

"May I ask what happened?"

She looked away again.

"You don't have to tell me if you don't want to."

"No, it's not that. It's just . . . Look, it's pretty simple. I was raped. I was working late one night, and I left the office by myself. A guy came out of nowhere in the parking garage. I had no way to protect myself.

If I'd had the gun—" Her voice dropped off, and she shrugged. "Maybe it would have changed things. Maybe not. Anyway, I've carried it with me ever since."

For an instant, I remembered the hunger in Ben's eyes in the police cruiser.

"Last night was scary for sure. I'm glad you didn't need to use the gun. And . . . I'm sorry Courtney and I dragged you into this."

I said this last part just as quietly, and immediately a mix of worry and guilt flashed through me.

"Courtney's okay, Emily. She has to be okay. After all, she's a Harpy, isn't she?"

I wanted to smile but couldn't. I opened my mouth, then shut it, took another sip of coffee.

Elise frowned. "What?"

"Nothing. Just . . . there was a moment this morning, after I ran into that alleyway, when I wondered if Courtney was somehow behind all this. She knows the ins and outs of Facebook, right? I figured setting up a fake account to get me fired would be nothing to her. But that's just crazy."

Now it was Elise's turn to take a sip of coffee.

"What?" I said. "You don't think it's crazy?"

Elise set the cup down, shrugged again.

"I don't know. A lot of insane stuff has happened recently. Has happened *today*. As for Courtney . . . part of me wonders just how honest she's been with you from the start."

"What do you mean?"

"Do you remember when we met for drinks, and you mentioned what happened at the Farmhouse?"

"What about it?"

Elise gave me that expression again, the worried one perfected by my mother.

"Emily, you *were* there that night. At the Farmhouse. With the rest of us when those boys—"

"No," I said quickly, feeling my body stiffen. "That's not true. I was grounded."

"Destiny was the one who wasn't there that night. Her parents made her go on some trip that weekend. But you . . . you were there with us."

I said nothing. I couldn't speak. I felt gutted. Was it true? Had I been there that night and just forced myself to forget? It was certainly possible. When people go through trauma, sometimes they'll bury those memories or push those memories onto somebody else. It's called dissociation. I'd had clients who'd suffered the same thing.

I pictured that Monday morning in the bathroom between classes when Destiny told me what had happened over the weekend at the Farmhouse, but maybe that wasn't true—maybe it had been me telling Destiny, saying how I knew what happened was wrong but there was nothing I could do about it. Maybe it had been Destiny who'd sought out Elise later in the hallway. Staring past Olivia and saying that she needed to speak to Elise right that second. And then, in the stairwell, Destiny had confronted Elise about what had happened to Grace while I'd stood right there beside them.

Maybe my memories were so vivid because I had been there for all of it.

"Maybe Courtney didn't remember it either," Elise said. "Or maybe she missed you saying it. But it had just struck me as weird that she didn't mention anything. Then again, I didn't say anything about it either, so I'm not much better. You were already so upset, and I didn't want to make it worse."

"I was really there that night?"

She nodded. "I'm sorry. I wish it hadn't happened either."

Now looking shaken herself, Elise took another sip of her coffee, then pulled her suit sleeve up to glance at her watch.

"Maybe you should try Courtney again," she said.

Feeling hollow, I nodded and grabbed my phone. I dialed Courtney, but it again went straight to voice mail.

"Nothing."

Elise offered up a worried nod. "Maybe we should stop by Highland Estates after this."

"I think we should."

"Where do you plan on staying tonight?"

"I'm not sure. I guess the town house. I don't think I could face my mother right now."

Elise took another sip of her coffee. The diamond on her finger glinted in the diner's light. I loosened my own ring, turned it back and forth on my finger.

"Are you going to keep it?" Elise asked.

"No."

"I'm pretty sure there are legal grounds to keep it."

"It's not that. As far as I'm concerned, this was the symbol of a promise between the two of us. I broke that promise."

"What are you talking about? He's the one who broke up with you."

Still staring down at the diamond, I shook my head.

"Daniel said he didn't think I wanted to marry him. It's true. I did, once, very much. Don't get me wrong, I did love him—*do* love him—but I haven't been fair to him."

"How so?"

"Children. I've never wanted them. Or no—that's not true. I . . . I'm worried about how they'll turn out. I guess some women worry their kids might be born with some kind of disfigurement or health problem, but for me it's always been something else. No matter whether it's a boy or a girl, they're going to end up in school with other kids. And they're either going to be bullied or become the bullies. After what we did to Grace, that's always bothered me, you know? I worry that kids would bully my child the way we bullied Grace. Or worse, that my child would turn out to be the bully."

My voice got so quiet I could hardly hear it. "Like me."

"Those aren't the only two options."

"What do you mean?"

"Some kids aren't either."

I stared down at my cup, and smiled.

Elise said, "What's so funny?"

"Nothing. Just . . . I've never told anybody that before. Not even my therapist."

I remembered then that Elise and I shared the same therapist, or at least saw therapists in the same office. I thought about mentioning it but figured that might embarrass her.

"Sorry if I'm making you feel uncomfortable," I said.

"No, not at all. I'm glad you feel okay telling me this stuff." A smile briefly lit her face. "It's just like when we were kids growing up and sharing secrets."

Her turn to look away. She cleared her throat and added, "To be honest, after middle school, I didn't think I would ever talk to you again. Not just you, but any of the girls. My dad was pissed. I'm surprised he didn't pull me out of school the way Mackenzie's parents did."

Elise stared down at her palm, no doubt remembering the day Mackenzie had gathered us all in her bedroom.

"You opened up to me," she said quietly, "so I think it's only fair I should do the same."

There was something about the way she was staring back at me, the regret in her eyes, that made me nervous. Suddenly I didn't think I wanted to hear this.

"What do you mean?"

"Remember when I told you how Mackenzie and I helped Grace burn down the Farmhouse to get those boys in trouble? After that happened, Grace started acting . . . weirder than usual. Do you remember that? Mackenzie and I confronted her about it one day, and that was when she tried to blackmail us."

This certainly wasn't what I'd expected to hear.

"She tried to *blackmail* you?"

"Well, not in so many words. But she said something like, well, our parents wouldn't want the truth to get out, and Grace and her mom could use some extra money, so it was pretty clear what she was trying to do. And Mackenzie, I mean, you know how fired up she could get. She was *pissed*. That's why she decided to invite Grace to the cabin that weekend. She told me she had it all planned out, how she was going to make sure Grace understood her place."

Elise shook her head, now staring down at her coffee, and I thought about how she'd stared out the car window last night after she'd told us how she was still haunted by what we'd done, and how we were lucky things hadn't gotten even more out of control.

The waitress returned and asked if we needed a refill. She noticed my untouched plate, and frowned.

"Everything okay with the sandwich, hon?"

It took me a moment to respond, still stunned by Elise's impromptu confession. What had seemed so spontaneous at the time had actually been meticulously planned out by Mackenzie. We girls had been puppets, to be used any which way Mackenzie wanted.

Elise tapped me with her foot under the table, and I forced a smile at the waitress.

"It's fine," I said. "Could we get the check, please?"

"Sure thing. Do you want a box for that?"

"No, thanks. You can take it."

The waitress looked pained, but she took the plate without a word.

"Let's make a plan," Elise said. "First, let's take my car. You still look too shaken to drive yourself. And second, if Courtney's not home when we get there, we call the police."

"And tell them what, exactly? It's not like Courtney's a child. Don't adults have to be missing for more than twenty-four hours before you can make a missing person report?"

"Courtney's not a child, but her daughter certainly is. You never did call the school, did you?"

I shook my head, wishing I'd followed through with that initial plan.

"After running into the alleyway, I completely forgot."

"This would be a whole lot easier if Ben hadn't turned out to be such a creep. He might have sway, get somebody to put out an APB for Courtney or something." Elise shook her head, and color came up in her cheeks. "Such a fucking asshole."

The waitress reappeared, the check in hand. She sensed the sudden tension and looked back and forth between us cautiously. But then Elise flashed her a bright smile.

"Sorry, we were talking about her ex-boyfriend."

The waitress offered up her warm smile as she set the check on the tabletop.

"Ex-boyfriends are the worst, aren't they? You both have a great evening. Try to stay dry. And dear"—her gaze now on me—"I took the tuna melt off the bill."

"You didn't have to do that."

"It's no problem at all," she said. "Have a great night."

As the waitress left, I grabbed the check and turned it over. Only the two coffees were listed. Barely three dollars.

Elise plucked the check from my hand, glanced at it, then from her wallet pulled out a twenty-dollar bill. She set it and the check on the table, placed the saltshaker on top, grabbed her bag, and started to slide out of the booth.

"Let's go find Courtney and her kid."

48

It was still drizzling when we arrived at Highland Estates. I was staring out the window, running through everything that had happened in the past twenty-four hours, when Elise parked the car and spoke in a quiet voice.

"Oh, Jesus."

That was when I looked over and saw the two police cars parked near the entrance to building E. Their light bars were off, but still I felt a churning start in the pit of my stomach.

Elise reached in the back seat for her umbrella but paused when she saw the expression on my face.

"Relax, Emily. They might not even be here for—"

I didn't hear the rest. I jumped out of the car and raced through the drizzle toward the entrance, pushed through the door, and hurried up the dark stairs.

When I reached the second floor, two police officers were standing in the hallway just outside an open door.

Apartment 3.

Courtney's door.

I rushed forward, but when it was clear my intention was to enter the apartment, both officers turned to block my path.

"Ma'am," one of them said calmly, "I need you to stop right there."

"What happened?" I stared past them, refusing to meet their eyes. Afraid I'd be able to read the truth there. *"What happened?"*

That was when a man in a tired suit stepped out through the open door.

"Who's this?"

Before either officer could respond, I said, "My name is Emily Bennett. I'm a friend of the woman who lives in that apartment."

The man nodded slowly, staring at me, and then motioned at the two officers.

"Might as well let her in."

The officers stepped aside. I moved past them, my legs suddenly weak, that churning in my stomach threatening to shoot up bile.

"I'm Detective Hernandez," the man said. "Please, come inside and have a seat."

I wasn't sure what to make of the situation. The man seemed to know me for some reason. I stepped past him and took three steps inside but then suddenly stopped as I took in who all was there.

Two women I'd never seen stood off to the side, another officer stood in the corner, and Courtney sat on the couch, still wearing her baggy Walmart vest, her eyes red and a ball of tissues clutched in her hand.

Elise hadn't been too far behind. She stepped up beside me, looked inside the apartment, and asked the only question that mattered.

"Where's Terri?"

49

Detective Hernandez looked to be in his late forties, his hair buzzed short, his gray goatee trim. He invited Elise and me to sit on the couch with Courtney in the middle; once we were situated, he opened his notepad and cleared his throat.

"So to begin—"

Courtney cut him off, no longer able to contain herself.

"They think I did something to Terri! That I *hurt* her!"

The detective said, "Ms. Sullivan, if you could—"

"Terri left for school just like she does every morning, and then I went to work, and then *they* showed up."

She pointed a shaking finger at the two women standing in the corner of the room.

"I'm sorry," Elise said, her gaze on the women. "Who are you again?"

Detective Hernandez cleared his throat, louder than was probably intended, as he tried to regain control of the situation.

"These two ladies are Mrs. Parker and Ms. Henry from Child Protective Services. They'd received a tip that Ms. Sullivan had been abusing her daughter—"

"Which is bullshit!" Courtney shouted.

The detective raised his hand, silently asking for her to wait, and when she quieted down—sitting so close to me I could feel her trembling—he spoke again.

"As I wanted to note, it's an allegation that Ms. Sullivan denies. Ms. Sullivan accompanied Mrs. Parker and Ms. Henry to her daughter's school, where they were informed that Terri Sullivan had not arrived that morning. A text alert was apparently sent out to Ms. Sullivan's phone alerting her of Terri's absence, but Ms. Sullivan has since confirmed to us that her phone isn't working."

He cleared his throat again, much softer this time, and lightly touched his goatee.

"Mrs. Parker and Ms. Henry escorted Ms. Sullivan to this address to ascertain if Terri was at this location. Mrs. Parker and Ms. Henry then contacted our department to report Terri missing. Officers responded and took Ms. Sullivan's statement and a recent photo of Terri, which is now being circulated to every officer in the county. We also have several officers canvassing the area."

"Why not put out an Amber Alert?" I asked.

"Quite simple. Amber Alerts are for abductions. We have no proof that Ms. Sullivan's daughter was abducted. In fact . . . Well, we have to consider the possibility that Terri simply ran away."

Courtney continued to tremble beside me. I couldn't even begin to imagine what she was feeling. Detective Hernandez hadn't said much, but no doubt the police suspected she'd done something to Terri. When something terrible happens to a wife or husband, the spouse is immediately a suspect. The same is true for when something terrible happens to a child: the parent becomes a suspect.

Elise asked, "When was the call to CPS made?"

Mrs. Parker was short, with curly hair and a demeanor that instantly put you at ease; Ms. Henry was tall, with short-cropped hair and a severe don't-take-any-shit expression.

Mrs. Parker said, "This morning, around nine o'clock."

"Do you know who made the call?"

Ms. Henry said, "We can't divulge that information."

"I'm not asking you to give me a name," Elise said. "I'm simply asking if you know who made the call."

The women didn't answer, letting an uneasy glance drift between them.

"It was an anonymous tip, wasn't it?" When the women didn't reply, Elise asked the detective, "Don't you find that a bit odd?"

Detective Hernandez cleared his throat again.

"I'm actually not here about Ms. Sullivan's daughter. Now, don't get me wrong, I certainly hope we find her—and again, every officer in the county has her picture and is on the lookout, not to mention we have officers canvassing the area—but I'm here for an entirely different purpose. Since I arrived not too long ago, I haven't had much of a chance to talk to Ms. Sullivan, but it's just as well you two are here, because I believe you may be able to answer a few questions."

"Such as?" Elise said.

"Does the name Mackenzie Dawson mean anything to you?" He watched us for a beat. "That's her married name. You probably knew her as Mackenzie Harper. And before you ask, the reason I'm here is because it appears she's gone missing. You see, earlier today we received a call from Bryn Mawr regarding Mrs. Dawson. Nobody thought anything would come of it, but when Ms. Sullivan's name came across the wire, I figured I would do my due diligence and come out to meet with her."

He paused, and focused on me.

"Then you happened to show up, Ms. Bennett, which is rather fortuitous, as you were the second name on my list."

The tiny apartment felt especially cramped with the detective and police officers and CPS caseworkers standing around, watching us. Still trembling, Courtney inched forward on the couch, pointed again at the two women.

"Do they need to be here for this?"

"Not if you don't want them to."

Courtney said she would rather they leave, and the detective nodded and asked the caseworkers if they needed anything else. Mrs. Parker did all the talking, asking that they be contacted as soon as there was word about Terri. She left her card with Detective Hernandez, and placed another on the kitchen table.

When the two women had left, Detective Hernandez nodded again.

"Well, then, let me get right to it: When was the last time any of you saw Mrs. Dawson?"

I didn't know about Courtney, but I suspected the detective already knew the answer, so I decided to be truthful—or at least half-truthful, as I wasn't quite ready to talk about my second trip down to Bryn Mawr and how Mackenzie had driven so erratically.

"Courtney and I saw her this past Monday."

This news didn't seem to surprise him.

"Where did you see her?"

"In the parking lot outside a yoga studio."

"That's a peculiar place to run into somebody. How did you end up meeting her there?"

I hesitated. "We checked her Facebook and determined that she often checked in at the studio every morning."

"Okay," the detective said, jotting a quick note in his notepad. "And why did you drive all the way down to Bryn Mawr to talk to Mrs. Dawson?"

I opened my mouth, but before I could answer, Courtney said, "An old friend of ours passed away recently. Someone we knew from middle school. We wanted to make sure Mackenzie knew."

"You mentioned Facebook," Detective Hernandez said. "Why not just send her a Facebook message?"

"Emily isn't on Facebook, and Mackenzie blocked me."

I was surprised Courtney was being so forthcoming, especially as the truth didn't make her look good, but maybe that was because she was scared to lie to the detective—and because she was already terrified about Terri being missing.

"Mrs. Dawson blocked you on Facebook," Detective Hernandez said thoughtfully, touching his goatee again. "But I thought you determined on Facebook she checked in at the yoga studio every morning."

Courtney tilted her face down and nodded. "I checked her page with one of my fake accounts."

"One of your fake accounts," the detective said, his voice flat. "Okay. I'm going to assume your conversation didn't go well."

"It certainly could have gone better."

"May I ask what was discussed?"

"Basically, Mackenzie didn't really care that our friend had died. It pissed me off."

"I see," he said. "And so were you the one who vandalized Mrs. Dawson's Mercedes?"

Before Courtney could answer, Elise leaned forward on the couch and touched her arm.

"You don't have to answer that."

Detective Hernandez gave Elise an annoyed smile.

"I'm sorry, and who are you again?"

"Elise Martin." She fixed him with a steady gaze. "I'm a public defender."

The detective grinned. "You must be Judge Martin's daughter. Well, then I better be on my best behavior. Ms. Martin, you aren't here in any official capacity, are you?"

"I'm not. These are my friends. I went to school with Mackenzie too."

"Did you see her this past Monday?"

"I haven't seen Mackenzie in years. And I'm sorry to hear that she's reportedly gone missing, but the person I'm more concerned about right now is Courtney's daughter."

"The truth is, I am, too, and as I already told you, we have Ms. Sullivan's daughter's picture circulating with all the officers in the area. Believe me when I say they're taking this very seriously, and we're going to do whatever it takes to find her."

He paused, paging through his notepad.

"Again, earlier today, we received a call from Bryn Mawr alerting us that Mrs. Mackenzie Dawson had gone missing sometime last night. She left the house and never returned, and after several hours, her husband called the police. Apparently Mr. Dawson has some pull with the local authorities, so when one of the detectives asked him if his wife had gotten into any recent arguments or altercations, he noted that somebody had vandalized her Mercedes SUV. A black GLS 450, to be exact. Mr. Dawson said that when he asked his wife about it, she said she thought it was probably the two women who'd accosted her outside her yoga studio, women she had known back in middle school. From what I'm told, Mr. Dawson wanted to press charges, but they had no proof that either of you had in fact vandalized the vehicle. During that conversation, Mrs. Dawson mentioned your names and how you were from Lanton, which Mr. Dawson later told the detective, who called up here asking if we knew of either of you. Of course, we said that we didn't, and nobody thought anything would come of it until your name came over the wire earlier this afternoon, Ms. Sullivan, which I guess all leads me to my final question before I get out of your hair: Where were the two of you last evening?"

It struck me that Detective Hernandez was very good at his job. For a second or two, I'd thought he was rambling, but then he'd hit us with that final question, almost out of nowhere, a move no doubt designed to gauge our reaction.

"Last night we went up to Bradford County," I said.

The detective frowned, clearly not expecting this answer.

"Who is we?"

"Emily and Courtney," Elise said. "I stayed to keep an eye on Terri."

"So you were with Terri last night?"

"Yes."

"How was she?"

"I'm sorry?"

"Did her behavior seem strange to you?"

"No, it did not."

Detective Hernandez nodded, chewing this over.

"Okay," he said to me, "so you and Ms. Sullivan went up to Bradford County on a Tuesday evening. Mind sharing why?"

"We went to visit with another friend from middle school."

"To tell this friend about your friend who had passed away?"

"Yes."

"That's quite a drive just to deliver some bad news."

"We hadn't seen this friend in a long time. We had an address but not a phone number."

"I see. And how did this friend take the news?"

"She didn't. It turned out she wasn't even there. The entire trip was a bust."

Detective Hernandez glanced at his notepad again, slowly shook his head.

"I'll be honest with you, ladies, that isn't a great alibi. Before, I thought I was wasting my time, but now—"

"We stopped for gas," Courtney blurted.

The detective raised an eyebrow. "Say that again?"

"On the drive back. We stopped for gas at a truck stop off the highway. There'd be cameras that would have seen us, right?"

The detective nodded. "There certainly should be. Which truck stop was this?"

Courtney glanced at me, and shrugged. "I can't remember the name. It was the first truck stop after we left Bradford County."

Detective Hernandez's dark eyes fixed on me.

"You were driving?"

"I was."

"Did you use a credit card for the gas?"

I shook my head. "Cash."

The detective pursed his lips. Clearly a cash transaction made it much more difficult to trace.

He asked, "Around what time did this occur?"

Courtney said, "About ten o'clock, I think."

The detective's eyes shifted to Elise.

"And you were with Ms. Sullivan's daughter until they came back?"

"Yes."

Detective Hernandez was quiet for several seconds, tapping his pen against the notepad.

"Okay, I think I have everything I need right now. I'll have one of my men call the truck stop to try to verify your story. Is there anything else you ladies would like to tell me?"

Somebody is out there terrorizing us. Somebody who managed to force Olivia Campbell and Destiny Marshall to kill themselves, and who no doubt abducted Terri and right now has her God knows where.

I glanced over at Courtney and Elise, and then shook my head.

"No, there isn't."

Detective Hernandez nodded, like he had expected no less. He regarded Courtney once again.

"We're going to do everything we can to find your daughter, Ms. Sullivan."

Courtney thanked him. She stood, a bit unsteady on her feet, and led him and the other officers to the door.

I gave Detective Hernandez my number and told him I would stay with Courtney until they called. The detective gave me his card.

As soon as the door was closed, Courtney broke down in tears, her legs going weak, and I grabbed her as Elise ran over to help me walk her back to the couch.

50

Once she had calmed down—sitting on the couch again, another ball of tissues clutched in her fist—Courtney looked up at us, her bottom lip quivering.

"Whoever is behind all of this, they took Terri, didn't they? I should have told the detective that, but I wasn't sure what to say. That a—a—a *dead* girl has my daughter?"

Elise and I traded a glance, and then we both told her about our mornings, and when we were done, the three of us just sat in silence.

When Courtney spoke next—her red eyes focused on me—her voice trembled even more.

"Someone . . . created a fake Facebook account pretending to be you?"

"Yes. Which doesn't make sense—didn't you say you'd searched for me with no luck?"

"Whoever made the account probably blocked all your family and friends, anybody who would tip you off that the account existed. They must have tweaked the privacy settings so that only your coworkers could see you."

"Jesus Christ."

"And then later"—she paused, swallowed—"you saw Grace outside?"

I threw a hesitant glance at Elise, and then shook my head.

"It wasn't Grace. Just somebody who looked like her."

"And you," Courtney said quietly, turning to Elise, "those pictures were sent to your fiancé's parents . . ."

Elise looked away, nodding and wiping at her eyes.

"And then there's Mackenzie," Courtney said. "I can't stand the bitch, but I don't like the idea of whoever's doing this getting to her too."

Elise cleared her throat.

"We should call Detective Hernandez and tell him the truth. Tell him everything that's been going on. We never stopped at any gas station. We just sent him on a wild-goose chase, and when he realizes we lied to him, he's going to be pissed—and it's going to make us look even worse."

I said to Courtney, "Why did you tell him we stopped at a gas station?"

She shrugged helplessly. "I don't know. I panicked."

I looked at Elise. "I was surprised you'd lied to him too."

"At the time, it made the most sense. Especially since I don't think we want to drag Daniel into this whole mess?"

She had a point, but I said nothing. Neither did Courtney.

"It might not change anything," Elise said, "but at least it will put all our cards on the table. It'll be better for us if we're up front now, rather than wait until Detective Hernandez figures it out."

I nodded, knowing she was right. Courtney was staring down at the carpet, but she nodded slightly to show she was in agreement too. I stood and walked over to retrieve my phone from my bag.

"How did this all start, anyway?" Elise asked.

The question gave me pause.

"What do you mean?"

"Part of my job as a lawyer is to tell stories. When I'm in front of the judge, I'm there to defend my client, and I want to make sure the judge understands everything that was going on at the time. So if my client stole a car and went joyriding, I don't want to focus just on that. I want to talk about what happened before. The reason my client did what he did."

There was a light in her eyes, as if talking about work was helping her focus.

"Maybe he was being abused at home. Maybe he had an argument with his girlfriend. Sometimes it helps, sometimes it doesn't, but either way, it's good to know a starting point. When I met you at the bar, you told me about Olivia and Destiny, but I just realized it wasn't clear *how* you two found out about Olivia in the first place."

"Emily's mom reached out to me on Facebook," Courtney said, her voice soft. "She was the one who told me about Olivia."

Elise glanced at me. "Do you know how your mom found out?"

"She said somebody on Facebook sent her a link."

"Do you remember who?"

I thought about it for a moment. The name escaped me at first, but then I said, "Norris. Beth Norris. My mom said her daughter Leslie graduated with us."

Elise made a face. "Leslie Norris? Doesn't ring a bell."

"Even so, what does it matter?"

"It matters because . . ." She bit her lip. "Didn't you also say your mom told you about Destiny?"

"Yes. But that was—" I paused again, trying to remember the name. I snapped my fingers once it came. "Anne Wolff. Jennifer Wolff's mother."

"Who's Jennifer Wolff?"

"She was in the grade under us, according to my mom."

Sitting on the couch, still staring down at the carpet in her daze, Courtney whispered something.

I frowned at her. "What was that?"

Courtney blinked and looked up at me. Seeing her from this angle was staggering: her bony arms, her pale face, her hollow eyes. Hopelessness personified.

She said, "What was her first name again?"

"Leslie."

"No, not her. Her mom."

"Beth."

"And Jennifer's mom's first name?"

"Anne."

Courtney stared back at me, her eyes hollow and intense. It took another moment before I got it.

"Holy shit," I whispered.

Elise said, "What are you two talking about?"

Courtney turned on the couch to look at her. "Beth Norris and Anne Wolff. Beth . . . Anne. Grace's mom's name."

"Are you sure?"

"Positive."

Elise made a slow frown, not ready to buy it.

"Could be just a coincidence."

I shook my head. I no longer believed in coincidences. Whoever was behind this had set up a fake Facebook account and friended all my coworkers with the intention of eventually getting me fired. Who was to say the same person hadn't created accounts to get close to my mother and feed her information? News of Olivia and Destiny coming from one person might have been suspicious, but coming from two separate people?

"Whoever's doing this has been planning it out for a long time. They left us a clue with Destiny. Maybe this is a clue too."

Elise looked even more dubious. "A *clue*? Come on, Emily, listen to yourself."

"The last text message Destiny sent her wife was *vesper*, and Grace lived on Vesper Road. That's no coincidence."

Elise took off her glasses so she could massage the bridge of her nose.

"Fine," she said. "Assuming those Facebook accounts are fake, what do you want to do about it?"

"Confirm that the accounts are in fact fake before we contact Detective Hernandez. At least that way it'll give him a starting point." I glanced at Courtney. "Think you might be able to use your Facebook magic to figure it out?"

She shrugged her bony shoulders, staring down at the carpet again.

"Maybe. But I would have to access your mom's account to know for sure. Do you think she'd let us?"

She would, yes, though she'd have a million questions. Which was fine—I'd answer two million questions if it meant getting Terri back safely.

I grabbed my bag, dug out my phone, and called the house.

No answer.

I called Mom's cell. Still nothing. Which didn't make sense. It was a Wednesday evening, almost eight o'clock. Mom didn't like driving at night if she could help it. She should be home.

"She's not answering."

There was the slightest tremor in my voice. A seedling of dread had begun to sprout deep in my heart.

Elise heard it and understood. She pushed to her feet, her car key already in hand.

"Where does she live?"

51

On the outside, the house I'd grown up in looked perfectly normal. The lights were on in the living room, the porch light was shining brightly, and my mother's car was parked in the driveway. By all accounts, she should have been home, but a minute ago—while Elise was taking a sharp turn down the street—I'd called the house again with no answer.

Elise barely had the car parked in the driveway before I flung open my door and jumped out. Already I was imagining the worst. My mother lying dead on her mattress, an empty pill bottle beside her. Or in the bathtub, the water thick with blood from her wrists. In any scenario—and there were many, that seedling of dread having blossomed into a cactus whose spines had begun to prick my insides—my mother would never have taken her own life. She would have been forced to do it by the person who was behind this. Told that if she didn't choose to die, then a little girl would die in her place.

I inserted the key into the lock as Elise and Courtney hurried up the walkway behind me. I hesitated, praying that everything was okay, that we would find my mother in the living room asleep in her chair with the TV on.

I glanced over my shoulder at the silent street and silent houses—feeling like I was being watched—and opened the door.

The living room was empty. The TV was dark and quiet.

"Mom?"

My voice echoed through the empty house. Because the house *was* empty—as somebody who had grown up within its walls, I knew it for a fact. If my mother were here, if anybody were here, I would feel it.

Still, I tried again, this time louder.

"Mom!"

Nothing.

I hurried forward, racing through the dining room and the kitchen before I circled back to the foyer.

Elise and Courtney hadn't moved. They just watched me, unsure what to do. I looked at them, then glanced up the stairs. The cactus of fear had grown so large it was about ready to burst through my chest.

Without a word, I hurried up the steps. Turned to the right, toward the only room that mattered.

The master bedroom door was closed.

I opened it, reached inside, flicked on the lights.

The room was empty. The bed neatly made.

I closed the door, hurried over to the bathroom. Also empty.

Elise called up the stairs.

"Emily?"

I checked my old bedroom, plus the room that had once been my father's study. Nothing. The only place I hadn't yet checked was the basement.

I was halfway down the stairs to the foyer when I felt my phone vibrating in my pocket. I pulled it out, saw it was my mother calling, and quickly answered.

"Mom?"

"My goodness, Emily, is everything all right? I just saw I had several calls from you."

I reached the bottom of the steps and stared at the girls, stunned, as I answered.

"I'm at the house. Where are you?"

A pause.

"Why are you at the house?"

"Mom, where are you?"

"I'm . . . with a friend."

"What friend? It's after eight o'clock on a Wednesday. Where could you possibly—" I paused. "Wait. Are you with a gentleman friend?"

Mom cleared her throat in that disapproving manner of hers. She probably thought I was teasing her. When she spoke next, her voice had gone curt.

"I left my phone in my purse during dinner. Now, what is it that you need?"

"I . . . forget."

"You forget?"

"There was something I wanted to ask you, but now I forget. Look, Mom, I'm in the middle of something. I have to go. Love you. Bye."

I disconnected the call before she could say anything else, and let out a heavy sigh of relief. I wanted to laugh out loud at the absurdity of what had just happened—me thinking my mother was dead when she was simply out on a date—but then I saw the despair in Courtney's eyes and felt my stomach twist again.

"Help me find my mom's laptop."

52

The laptop was in the living room, on the coffee table, beside a Nora Roberts paperback. With Elise and Courtney flanking me, I set it up on the island counter in the kitchen, the same place my mother had broken the news of Olivia and Destiny.

It didn't need a password. My mother never locked any of her devices, despite my telling her numerous times that she should. I opened the browser, clicked on her bookmarks. Facebook was the first one. Within a second, we were in her account.

A message briefly popped up.

GRACE FARMER HAS SENT YOU A FRIEND REQUEST.

Elise whispered, "Holy shit."

Grace's picture was there too. Not a recent one, but what she had looked like back in eighth grade. Pale skin. Dark hair. Gray eyes.

I clicked ACCEPT. Grace's name was added to the list on the sidebar of current online users. A green circle was beside her name.

The laptop chimed as a message box popped up on the screen.

hello emily

Courtney, standing to my left, gasped and clutched my arm. My fingers were suspended above the keyboard, frozen.

The laptop chimed again.

hello elise

hello courtney

Courtney squeezed my arm.

your daughter says hi

Courtney let out a strangled yelp, and Elise stepped over to hold her steady.

haha actually she cant say anything not with tape over her mouth

"Screw this," I said, and quickly typed out a response.

What do you want?

i want you to suffer for what you did

We know you aren't Grace. We know Grace is dead.

if you know everything then i guess we have nothing to discuss

I waited for more, but nothing else came. I typed again.

What have you done with Terri?

For several seconds there was no response. I glanced back at Elise, who was holding Courtney as she continued to sob. Then the laptop chimed.

she is safe 4 now

Where is she?

before i tell you i want you to know im sorry you lost your job

im sorry elise lost her fiancé

Another long pause, and then the laptop chimed again.

haha jk you all deserve to be miserable

Who is this?

dont ask stupid questions

What do you want?

would you like to see what terri looks like tied up in the trunk of a car

Before I could respond, a picture came through. Terri in her school khakis and forest-green polo shirt, twisted up in a cramped space. Her legs bound. Her hands tied behind her back. Duct tape over her mouth. A blindfold over her eyes.

As soon as Courtney saw the picture, she started sobbing again, this time with much more force, and Elise had to hold her tight so that she didn't fall to the floor.

The laptop chimed with another incoming message.

should a daughter pay for the sins of her mother

I wasn't sure how to respond, so I glanced back at Elise. She stared at the screen.

I typed, *No.*

are you sure

What do you want?

do you want to save her life

Yes.

then do as i say and you will have the chance

the 1st thing is no police

if you contact them or anyone i will know and terri will die

do you understand

Yes. Where is she?

sticks & stones

I stared at the chat screen, my fingers still suspended over the keyboard, not sure what to type next. In the end it didn't matter; the green dot by Grace's name disappeared.

Elise said, "What was that last part?"

"Sticks and stones."

She frowned at me. "What does that—"

But then she cut herself off, all at once seeming to remember. Even in her distressed state, Courtney did too. Her sobs became a guttural wail.

After fourteen years, those three words still meant something to each of us. Those three words had haunted my dreams. Now it looked like we had no choice but to confront the nightmare again.

I nodded for Elise to shut down the laptop. Then I stepped forward and held Courtney tight, felt her body jerking with each sob.

"It's okay," I whispered to her. "Terri's okay. We'll save her. Do you hear me? We'll save her."

53

At night, Silver Lake Park looked just as it had fourteen years ago.

We drove slowly through the entrance and then on the gravel road leading around the lake and stopped in front of the familiar drive closed off by a chain.

We peered down the drive and saw that the cabin was dark and empty.

Elise said, "Maybe this isn't it."

She sat up front, behind the steering wheel. I had opted to stay with Courtney in the back, her hand clasping mine for much of the ride.

I stared out the window, down the dark drive.

"This is it."

Elise eyed me in the rearview mirror.

"How do you know?"

"It has to be."

We inched down the road, going maybe five miles per hour. The lake dark and peaceful to our right. The trees tall and menacing to our left.

Elise pulled off to the side on a strip of grass. It was nearly eleven o'clock, and while the rain had stopped, the sky was still overcast. A few cabins were occupied around Silver Lake Park—lights inside each twinkled between the trees—but nothing came from the cabin that had once been owned by Mackenzie's parents.

Elise opened her bag on the passenger seat, slipped out her gun. She glanced back at me, then focused on Courtney.

"Maybe you should stay here."

Courtney's voice trembled as she whispered: "No. I'm coming too." Then, her eyes going wide: "Since when do you have a gun?"

Elise didn't answer her question. She said, "Just don't do anything rash."

I reached for the door handle.

"She'll be fine. Now come on. Let's stop wasting time."

Elise had given me a flashlight from her glove box—a small steel-gray Maglite—but I didn't use it as we stepped over the chain and continued toward the cabin. By that point our eyes had started to adjust, and while we couldn't make out much, we could tell where we were going.

The smell of the damp trees triggered my memory. All of us stuffed in the back of Mackenzie's parents' SUV. Mackenzie and Courtney and Olivia; Destiny and Elise and me. And Grace, always quiet, always forcing a smile, always wondering if she truly belonged.

She hadn't, of course, but we had fooled her. We'd made her feel welcome, had betrayed her trust, had broken her.

"Hey."

Courtney's voice was barely a whisper, but it was enough to draw me out of my thoughts. I blinked, realized I'd slowed my pace and was just standing on the drive, the Maglite in my hand. If it came to it, I could use it as a weapon, but it was nothing compared to the firepower Elise held.

Elise, now several paces ahead, continued down the drive. She'd had a pair of ballet flats in the trunk and wore those instead of her heels.

I nodded at Courtney and started forward again. Soon we were walking side by side, following Elise. The cabin was dark, but it was the trees around us that I watched. Anybody could be behind them.

We came to the cabin.

Elise went to place her foot on the first step, but I grabbed her arm. When she turned her head to look at me, I motioned for us to check around the back.

We walked even slower. Making sure our footsteps made as little noise as possible. Like Elise, I worried that Courtney might do something rash, but if Terri was here, Courtney had to be the first thing she saw. The first person she hugged.

No car was parked behind the cabin, but that didn't mean one hadn't been there recently. I clicked on the Maglite. I heard Courtney inhale sharply, but I ignored her as I swept the beam across the ground. There didn't appear to be any recent tire impressions.

Elise gestured at the cabin, and I nodded. Keeping the flashlight on, we circled the cabin, checking the front and back doors. Both locked. We peeked through the windows, the Maglite's beam darting from top to bottom. There was furniture inside, covered with white sheets to protect it from dust, but no Terri.

Courtney tried to suppress another bout of sobs, and steeled herself as she looked at us, her voice an unsteady whisper.

"If she's not here, where the hell could she be?"

I looked at her, and even in the dark she saw the answer on my face. Courtney shook her head.

"It has to be at least a half mile away."

I turned and shined the flashlight beam at the narrow path behind the cabin. The same narrow path we'd taken fourteen years ago. We had been foolish girls when we'd first gone down that path, reckless and irresponsible. But when we'd returned, there was no more denying what we had become.

Monsters.

54

Mackenzie's mother hadn't wanted us out after dark, especially up in the mountains, for fear we would be abducted by lowlifes in pickup trucks. Mackenzie's father had chuckled at this, saying anybody stupid enough to mess with seven teenage girls would be lucky to make it out alive. Clearly, Mrs. Harper didn't like the idea of us going, but she'd relented when Mackenzie begged her to let us walk around the lake.

But we didn't. Instead of heading up the drive toward the gravel roadway, we started back down the narrow path leading into the woods. We'd walked that path on our previous visits but hadn't ventured down it that weekend. That night, we followed Mackenzie, the light from our three plastic flashlights slicing through the dark.

We walked quietly, none of us speaking, yet somehow Grace was still the quietest. She didn't once ask where we were going. Didn't ask why Mackenzie was the only one wearing a backpack or what was in it. She just went along with everything, which for some reason annoyed me even more.

How stupid was she? Didn't she realize she wasn't welcome? That we only kept her around to make fun of her and make her do the shit we didn't want to do?

We walked in silence, but insects made noise all around us. At one point I thought I heard an owl hoot, but didn't want to break the silence to ask if anybody else had heard it too.

After maybe fifteen minutes, we came to a small clearing. The path branched off in two directions. One seemed to head back toward the lake; another headed deeper into the woods. A large tree stood on the border between the two paths. When Mackenzie's flashlight swiped past it, the beam caught at least a dozen initials engraved in the bark.

Mackenzie turned back around to make the simple proclamation. "This is the place."

She let the backpack fall to the ground and pulled out one coil of rope, then another. It looked like the kind of rope my mom used to hang laundry in the summer.

She tossed one to Elise, another to Olivia, and told Grace to stand against the tree.

Grace didn't move.

Mackenzie said, "You want to be a *Harpy*, don't you? You want to be our *friend*? Then this is part of the initiation. Stand. Against. The fucking. Tree."

Grace still didn't move, and I wondered what might happen next. If maybe Mackenzie and Elise and the others would grab her and force her to follow Mackenzie's command.

But then she stepped forward, moved past Mackenzie, and turned to place her back against the tree.

"Good girl," Mackenzie said.

Each coil of rope was more than long enough to do the job. We tied it first around the bottom portion of Grace's body, then around the upper portion. We made sure each rope was tight enough that she could barely move.

Grace didn't speak at all while we did this, just stood there quietly. We finished, and I looked at the other girls, guessing that now we would head back up the path to the cabin.

That was when Mackenzie shined her flashlight at Grace's pale face.

"Now for the second part. Do you know what the second part is, Grace?"

Grace, her expression blank, said nothing.

"Now we tell you exactly what we think of you."

Elise and Olivia seemed to know exactly what to do, because after Mackenzie's turn—"You're a waste of space, and your mother should have aborted you"—Elise stepped up to speak her part. Then Olivia. And Courtney. And Destiny. And me.

By that point, mob mentality had taken over. It would be another three years before I'd sit in Mr. Huston's classroom and listen to him lecture about *Lord of the Flies*. But as the class discussed the book, I'd think about what we'd done to Grace. Not just the night we'd taken her down the trail and tied her to the tree, but all the times we'd isolated ourselves, like we'd created our own island where we were free to do whatever terrible thing we pleased. No adults. No peers. Just ourselves, and those we wanted to hurt.

I'd had no intentions of openly hurting Grace's feelings, but in that moment the rush overtook me, and I came up with my own hurtful insults. After me, I thought it was over, but then Mackenzie started again, followed by Elise, and down the line it went.

The entire time Grace stood there, strapped to the tree, her eyes closed, absorbing our insults like a sponge. Not just her ears but her entire body—soaking in every hateful word.

During the second round of insults—"Your vagina probably smells like day-old tuna"; "You and your mom are so ugly your dad probably killed himself just to get away"—Grace started whispering something. At first it was impossible to know what she was saying, as her lips barely moved, but as the third round started, her voice began to grow in pitch.

"Sticks and stones may break my bones but words will never hurt me."

We spat at her. Laughed at her. Told her we hated her. That she was worthless.

"Sticks and stones may break my bones but words will never hurt me."

We told her the world would be better off without her. That nobody in school liked her. That nobody in the world liked her. That she was better off dead.

"Sticks and stones may break my bones but words will never hurt me."

The more awful the things we said, the louder her whispering became. Her eyes were still closed as she repeated the rhyme, but the louder she got, the louder we got in response.

Until Grace started doing something new.

She started banging her head against the tree.

It was slow at first, just a slight rocking, but then she started hitting the back of her head harder and harder; she kept going with the rhyme, nearly shouting it.

"Sticks and stones may break my bones but words will never hurt me!"

We looked at each other, and nervously scanned the dark woods. How far were the other cabins? Would somebody hear us?

"Fuck this," Mackenzie said, and pulled a towel from the backpack. She and Elise approached Grace and tied it around her head so that it was in her mouth.

Even then, Grace kept trying to speak, nearly screaming now. She didn't stop banging her head against the tree either.

Destiny said, "Shit."

Courtney asked, "What should we do?"

I said, "Let's untie her."

Olivia said, "No way. Not while she's acting like a psycho."

We stood there, watching her, and soon the muffled cries began to lessen, and the banging stopped. Grace didn't open her eyes, but tears managed to squeeze through her closed lids and run down her pale cheeks.

Again, I whispered, "We should untie her."

Mackenzie picked up the backpack off the ground and shouldered it.

"Let's head back."

The cruel indifference in her voice shocked me, and even though I'd come to loathe Grace, I knew we couldn't just leave her there.

"We should at least check the back of her head."

"She's fine."

Mackenzie said it like she said most things—full of authority—but Grace wasn't fine. We'd find out in the early morning, once we returned to untie her, that the hair on the back of her head was dry with blood. Even the bark would be spotted with it.

"Let's go."

Mackenzie didn't wait for a response. She started up the path. Elise followed a second later. Then Olivia. Then Courtney. Then Destiny.

I was the last one. I didn't have a flashlight, but I stared at Grace tied to the tree. Even in the dark, I could see that her eyes were open. She was watching me. Pleading with me to untie her. To not leave her there, alone in the dark.

Destiny whispered, "Emily, come on!"

I turned away and hurried to keep up with my friends.

Now we walked without the use of a flashlight. I had the Maglite but didn't want to use it, not yet.

Elise walked slightly ahead of us down the narrow path. She still had the gun out, held low at her side. We'd been walking for almost fifteen minutes already—Elise leading the way, Courtney behind her and me behind Courtney—the woods around us quiet except for the sound of water falling from branches and leaves.

Elise stopped suddenly, and it wasn't until I stepped up next to Courtney that I saw the reason why.

Ahead, through the trees, shined firelight.

As we advanced, our pace starting to increase, we saw that two tiki torches had been set up on either side of the tree we'd tied Grace to nearly fifteen years ago.

Now Terri was tied to that same tree.

55

As they had with Grace Farmer, two ropes kept Terri in place. Her face was tilted down, and she was motionless; for a second I thought she was dead. But she started to stir when she heard us approaching. Her face came up, but there was a blindfold over her eyes and duct tape over her mouth.

Courtney started running, shouting her daughter's name. She pushed past Elise, nearly knocking her over, and sprinted into the clearing.

Elise shot me a look, but I ignored her and started running too.

Courtney had already reached Terri and taken the blindfold from her eyes. She was telling her that everything was okay. That she was safe now. I was smiling, feeling tears of happiness sting my eyes, and then I realized this was a trap and stopped short.

Whoever had abducted Terri—no doubt the same twisted architect behind Olivia and Destiny killing themselves—had tied Terri to the tree for a reason, and that reason was to bring the three of us here.

The silence of the woods deepened. I clicked on the Maglite and shined the beam around the clearing, into the dark trees, searching for whoever was watching us. Somebody with a rifle or knife or ax, whatever weapon he or she would use to finish this.

The Maglite's beam struck Elise in the face, and I saw the same worry there, the anticipation that something terrible was about to happen.

She stood motionless, the gun held at her side, and watched me.

We stared at each other, waiting for whatever was going to happen next, and then Courtney shouted, "Help me untie her!"

Her voice snapped us into action. I hurried over to the tree. The blindfold lay in the mud where Courtney had flung it. Tears were visible in Terri's eyes, and Courtney was working to peel the duct tape off her daughter's mouth.

I circled to the back of the tree to examine the knots.

Elise stepped up beside me, the gun still at her side.

I said, "You don't happen to have a knife hidden away, do you?"

She shook her head. She looked around the dark woods one last time, and tucked the gun into the back of her pants.

"Those knots look too tight."

"You're right. Grab one of the torches."

It took a minute for the flame to burn the first rope enough to snap it apart, then another minute to burn the second rope, but finally Terri lurched away from the tree into her mother's arms.

Courtney was on her knees, sobbing as she held her daughter tight. Terri was crying, too, her entire body shaking, as she squeezed hold of her mother.

I watched them, wanting to hug Terri myself, and then I remembered Detective Hernandez's card in my pocket. I was going to pull it out, dial the number and tell the detective that we'd found Terri, but before I could, Courtney gasped.

"Oh my God, what happened to your head?"

She had been hugging Terri tight, running her hands all over her body, and I realized that she had instinctively been searching for bumps or bruises. And she'd found one. Right on the side of Terri's head. I shined the Maglite on what looked to be a nasty goose egg.

Terri flinched when Courtney touched it, and Courtney held her tight again, telling her that everything was okay now.

"We need to call the police," I said.

Courtney shook her head. "We need to get her to a hospital."

"The police will want to see what happened here."

"Then they can meet us at the hospital afterward. I don't want Terri to be here one second longer than she needs to be."

I couldn't argue with that. Lanton General was a good forty-five minutes away. Daniel would most likely be working, and it might be good for Terri to see him. The more familiar faces, the better.

"We can take her to Lanton General. Daniel should be there."

Courtney seemed to understand my line of thinking, because she smiled at her daughter.

"How about that, Terri? Would you like to see Daniel?"

Terri nodded silently, holding tight to her mother.

Elise stood off to the side, the gun still in the waistband of her pants. She crouched down to get on eye level with Terri.

"Do you know who did this to you?"

Terri didn't answer, still holding tight to her mother.

Elise's tone ticked up a notch.

"Did you hear their voices?"

"Stop it," Courtney said. "We'll worry about that later."

Elise glanced at me, and I saw the frustration in her face, probably the same frustration I felt. The person who'd been chatting with us on Facebook—who had used an old photo of Grace Farmer—had planned all this out. They had abducted Terri and tied her to this tree and lit those torches knowing we would come running.

And then . . . what? What was the endgame?

56

Terri couldn't tell us much about what had happened as we sped down the highway. She remembered leaving the apartment and hurrying through the parking lot in the rain toward the bus stop; remembered somebody stepping out from between two cars and putting a dark cloth bag over her head. She'd been picked up and thrown into the trunk of a car. Her wrists had been yanked back and bound behind her back. She'd shouted and she'd kicked, but nobody had heard her, or if they had, nobody had come to save her.

The car had driven for a while and then stopped; the trunk opened, but she couldn't see who was there. Maybe one person, maybe two. Probably two; she thought there'd been an extra hand holding her in place when she'd been thrown in the trunk. But the bag was still over her head, the fabric thick and scratchy, and the bottom lifted just enough so that duct tape could be pressed over her mouth.

The person had a deep voice and told her if she did not do everything she was told, her mother would die.

Petrified, Terri had nodded, ready to do whatever was asked of her. Which wasn't much. She'd spent what felt like several hours in the trunk; then it opened again, and she'd been ordered to close her eyes. A blindfold was tied around her head. There was silence, and somehow she'd known the person was taking pictures of her, pictures that would be sent to her mother, and the thought had made her want to cry, but before she could, she'd been pulled out of the trunk and marched down a muddy path and tied to that tree.

"I was so scared, Mom. I thought I'd never—"

Her voice broke. Courtney leaned down, kissed her forehead, squeezed her tight again.

I'd texted Daniel to tell him we were taking Terri to the ER, hoping that he was on duty. Daniel had responded first by asking what was wrong, and when I told him nothing beyond a nasty bump on Terri's head, he'd confirmed that he was working and would do all he could to help. And that was how we'd left it, just that, and for the first time I didn't imagine what we might have said to each other on that alternate timeline, because I knew there were no other timelines except this one, and on this one Daniel and I were no longer together and would never be together again.

Elise whispered to me, "Call the detective now?"

I leaned back in my seat and stared out the windshield at the highway. I tried to keep my voice calm when I answered.

"When we get there."

In the back seat, Terri started sobbing again. When Courtney tried to comfort her, reminding her that she was safe now, Terri choked out that it was gone.

"What's gone, baby?"

"My b-b-book. It was in my b-b-backpack. It's *g-g-gone*."

Elise pulled up to the ER entrance twenty minutes later. I stepped out of the car to help Courtney and Terri. I'd left my door open, and when Elise asked me to close it so she could go park, I told her I would be right back.

Just before we reached the entrance, I touched Courtney's arm to stop her.

"I need to ask you a question, and I don't want you to think too hard about it. Just answer, okay?"

She frowned at me, clearly confused. But when she nodded, I asked my question, and after she'd answered it, I told her and Terri to head inside.

As I watched them walk through the sliding glass entrance doors, I sent Daniel a quick text letting him know we were here. Then I tapped the screen a few more times, dropped the phone into my pocket, and headed back to Elise's idling car.

I slid into the passenger seat and sat staring at the dash.

Elise asked, "Are you going to call the detective now?"

I blinked, and shook my head.

"Not yet."

"Why not?"

"I guess I need some clarification first."

"About what?"

"About who helped you, and why."

Her brow furrowed slightly, and she did a good job looking confused.

"Who helped me do what?"

"Abduct Terri."

57

Elise kept her brow furrowed, that look of confusion still spread across her face, and for the first time I realized just how good she was at those expressions. Even back in middle school, she could shoot me a look across the classroom or down the hallway that spoke volumes.

Of course, back in middle school I'd thought I knew her well, but she'd been playing me even then.

Finally, she said, "What the hell are you talking about?"

I wanted to be wrong. Wanted it more than anything in the world. But the longer I stared at her, the longer I searched her face, the more I realized that there was no other explanation.

"Is it Mackenzie?"

The confusion transformed into exasperation.

"Is *what* Mackenzie?"

"The one who's working with you. Who helped you abduct Terri today, and who helped you drive Olivia and Destiny to the point that they killed themselves."

That was how they were back in middle school, Elise and Mackenzie; they worked as a team. They had helped Grace burn down the Farmhouse to get those tenth graders in trouble, but later, when Grace tried to blackmail them, Mackenzie came up with the idea of inviting Grace to the cabin and tying her to that tree.

At least, according to Elise. *She* had been the one to tell me that. She'd told me a lot of things recently.

"I went down to Bryn Mawr late Monday night. My plan was to give Mackenzie a second chance, try to explain everything that was going on. But I caught her right as she was leaving the house, so I followed her, and once she realized somebody was following her, Mackenzie did everything she could to get away. I thought maybe she thought she was being stalked, but if that was the case, she would have told her husband, and according to Detective Hernandez, Mackenzie only told him about somebody keying the Mercedes."

"If you were so worried about Mackenzie being stalked, why didn't you say anything to the detective?"

"Because it's no coincidence Mackenzie went missing last night, is it? This way she had a lot of freedom to move around behind the scenes. And then when this was all over, she would just . . . show back up again? Return to her family with some silly excuse? At the very least, she could have mentioned herself on the Facebook chat. That's what really tipped me off."

Elise shook her head sadly and glanced at the rearview mirror, making sure no other cars had come up behind us.

"You're tired, Emily. All this stress has really started messing with your head. I'm just as confused about everything that's happened as you. Why don't you and I go inside and—"

I cut her off.

"Voices."

She frowned again. "What was that?"

"You said voices. Back in the clearing. You asked Terri if she had heard their voices. Not voice, but voices."

Elise was giving me a new look now, a mixture of pity and concern, the same look she'd given me back at the diner when I told her I'd seen Grace, and I realized how I must have sounded. Like I'd gone completely mad. Accusing her of kidnapping and murder. But despite all that, I pushed on.

"Back in the clearing, you looked confused, like you expected something to happen while we were out there. I thought the same thing. Somebody got us out there for a reason, and then . . . nothing."

"Emily, I'm starting to worry about you. Maybe a doctor should examine you too. You've been under a great deal of stress."

"Highland Estates."

Another frown.

"What?"

"Back at the diner, you said we should stop by Highland Estates to see if Courtney was there."

"Of course I said that. That's where Courtney and her daughter live."

"But how did you know that?"

"Courtney told me."

I shook my head, stared straight back into Elise's eyes.

"No, she didn't. She's embarrassed about where she lives. She told me because we were close in high school, but she never would have told you."

"That's ridiculous."

"I just asked her. I asked her if she'd ever told you where she and Terri lived. She said no."

"Courtney's been under a great deal of stress too. She isn't thinking clearly."

Headlights appeared behind us as a car pulled into the patient drop-off area. Elise moved the gearshift into drive. Every door automatically locked, and I jumped at the sound.

The car started rolling forward, and for the first time I eyed Elise's bag on the center console. Her gun was inside.

"Okay," she said, "so let's say in theory you're right, and I was behind Terri's abduction. I guess the main question would be: Why?"

A parking garage was situated beside the hospital, and Elise made the turn into the entrance.

"After all, in theory, if I did abduct Terri, then that means I would have been behind your firing today, and—what—my fiancé breaking up with me?"

Every parking spot on the first level was full, so Elise continued up to the second level. Blood thrummed in my ears, and my breathing had slowed, the car all at once feeling too cramped.

"Let's say in theory that's all true too—that, I don't know, maybe I don't even *have* a fiancé, that I just bought myself an engagement ring and only wore it when I was around you and Courtney, that I had my picture taken with some random guy so I could show him off as my fiancé, and that everything I told you about my day this morning was complete bullshit . . . That would be pretty crazy, right?"

There were a few open spaces on the second level, but Elise kept going toward the third.

"And let's say earlier this year, I traveled down to Maryland every weekend and dressed as Grace Farmer and stalked Destiny and her wife to try to drive Destiny crazy. I would have had to wear a wig, of course, because my hair isn't dark like Grace's. Or maybe it was Mackenzie who dressed up as Grace. Is that what you're thinking?"

The garage's ceiling was low and the lights dim, making it hard to see her face.

"In theory, maybe after a while we got bored terrorizing Destiny and decided to surprise her one day when she was leaving for work. Maybe we held a gun on her and forced her to turn on the car in the garage while Mackenzie and I wore gas masks. And then, after she was dead, we sent that text to Destiny's wife because, I don't know, we thought it would be funny?"

We were heading to the fourth level, the car going no more than five miles per hour, the engine a gentle purr.

"Then, months later, let's say, we decided to start messing around with Olivia, and one of us dressed up again as Grace to sleep with Olivia's fiancé and took pictures and sent those pictures to Olivia. Maybe added a note that if she wasn't such a Double Stuf her fiancé wouldn't keep cheating on her. That's a pretty fucked-up thing for people like Mackenzie and me to do, don't you think? I mean, in theory."

Only a handful of cars on the fourth level, but Elise drove on toward the fifth, the top of the garage opening up, the sky a deep, dark expanse above us.

"In theory, maybe Mackenzie and I had planned for Olivia to take her life a different way—an overdose, say—but then later that night we saw the perfect opportunity to force her over the bridge into the river. Before that, though, Olivia unwittingly did us a favor and happened to call her sister and used the nickname we gave Grace—the same nickname, I should add, that you came up with."

Elise coasted to the farthest open spot and eased the car to a stop.

"But if Mackenzie and I *were* involved in what happened to Destiny and Olivia and Terri and all the rest—in theory, of course—that would lead us back to the original question. *Why* would we do something like that? *Why* would we take such a risk?"

She shifted in her seat to look at me for the first time since she'd started talking, and there was something different about her hazel eyes, a coldness I'd never seen before.

I said, "Once a Harpy, always a Harpy. There is no why. That's what you and Mackenzie always said when we were in middle school, right? Why steal from all those stores? Why start those rumors about D.B. and her friends? No reason at all. Just to do it. Just to see how far you can take things and get away with it."

The light from the dashboard glinted off Elise's glasses, and I wondered if she even needed glasses, or if they were simply part of her facade.

She stared back at me for a long moment, and then the corners of her mouth lifted in a small smile.

"Could it be that simple? In theory, of course. Everything we're talking about is in theory. But could everything that's happened with Destiny and Olivia and Terri have no rhyme or reason other than that simple truth: I'm bored with my life?"

When I said nothing, Elise smiled again.

"Or, who knows, maybe one morning I happened to look at myself in the mirror and realized just how miserable my life was. Almost thirty, a well-paying job, looks that could get any guy I want—all of that should have made me happy, right? Should have given me some . . . fulfillment. But no, maybe I realized I was miserable, and the simple truth was there was nothing I could do about it. That is, until one day I received an email from an old friend."

"Mackenzie," I whispered.

Elise continued without skipping a beat, like she hadn't even heard me.

"Maybe this old friend was miserable too. Like me, maybe she had a great life—a successful husband, two wonderful kids—but she felt trapped. Every day waking up to the same boring thing: get the kids ready for school, perform mindless chores around the house, smile when her husband told his lame jokes. This friend, she didn't tell me this by email, of course—maybe that first email contained only a link to one of those encrypted messaging apps, the kind that deletes your messages after a day—and after some back-and-forth she came up with a great idea: why not check in on our old friends, see what they were up to with their lives, whether or not any of them were miserable like us."

Still smiling, Elise slowly shook her head.

"Maybe Destiny was the first one we checked in on. Saw that she was happily married, working in a profession that she loved. She was happy, truly happy. Just like Olivia, who had gained a lot of weight over the years, but maybe that didn't bother her anymore—maybe she had built up some self-esteem—and she seemed to be happy with her job too. Plus, she had a fiancé that she was head over heels in love with despite the fact the guy couldn't keep his dick in his pants. And then there was Courtney, who maybe didn't have the best job, was struggling financially, but she had a daughter that she absolutely adored, and you could tell that even though she sometimes struggled to pay rent every month, she was happy with her life."

The smile faded from her face, and her eyes became thoughtful.

"And then maybe there was little Emily Bennett. Working as a therapist, which she seemed to enjoy. Had herself a good-looking fiancé, just like Olivia, only unlike Olivia, Emily's fiancé kept his dick in his pants. Little Emily Bennett, who on the outside appeared to have a perfect life, and yet . . . looking at her, you could tell she didn't have anybody in her life outside her mother and fiancé. That she didn't have any close friends at all. That, in many ways, she used her therapist as a friend, somebody to talk to, to confide in. Which, let's admit, is pretty pathetic, but I guess that's what happens when somebody isn't happy. Keep in mind, this is all hypothetical, but even so, Emily, tell me why that would be? Why couldn't a young woman like yourself find happiness?"

I said nothing. Not because I had nothing to say—now I had plenty—but I didn't want to give her the satisfaction.

The smile reappeared.

"So say all of that happened. Say that, in theory, this friend and I decided it wasn't fair that we were the only ones miserable with our lives. Because, like you said, once a Harpy, always a Harpy. So pretend we decided to have some fun of our own and spent months, maybe a year, working on how to make it happen. Sure sounds like a lot of planning went into everything, and today . . . Well, it all seemed a bit rushed, don't you think?"

"Rushed because we finally learned the truth."

"And what truth would that be?"

"Grace Farmer is dead."

"Ah yes. I guess that makes sense. In theory, of course."

Up here on the top level, with the cars empty and dark, it felt like we were alone in the world.

"We were supposed to die in that clearing tonight, weren't we?"

"Who is *we*?"

"Courtney and her daughter and me. You . . . you were expecting Mackenzie to be there. But she didn't show, and that messed everything up."

Elise smiled again, and somehow the smile was even colder than the look in her eyes.

"Such a fascinating theory, Emily. Very scandalous. And say it were all true, what would happen next? You'd call Detective Hernandez, I guess, and then . . ."

She let it hang there, cocking her head to the side, waiting to see what I would say, and when I didn't say anything, she grinned.

"Sure sounds crazy when you say it out loud, doesn't it?"

I glanced down at the bag on the middle console. Thought again about the gun. Wondered if I was quick enough to grab it away from Elise.

"I have another theory," Elise said.

Her left hand dipped between the seat and the door and came back up with the gun. She set it on her lap, with the barrel pointed at me.

"In this theory, you've never been happy with your life. Things have always been difficult for some reason. Probably because you bullied a girl when you were in middle school, and it got to the point that the girl tried to kill herself. But what can you do? You were a kid at the time. A dumb, reckless, irresponsible kid. Still, it's always haunted you, and after hearing about the deaths of two old friends, you start thinking about that girl a lot more, becoming almost obsessive. It gets to the point that you have a mental breakdown. You post some things you shouldn't have on Facebook, things that get you fired from your job. Then your good-looking fiancé breaks up with you. Your friend's daughter goes missing, and yes, she's found, so it's a happy ending there, but still all of it becomes too much for you that you just . . . Well, you just can't take it anymore."

I wet my lips, and found my voice.

"You can't force me to kill myself."

"Do you honestly think so?"

"I'll tell the police everything."

"I'm sure the police would find it very entertaining. The question, of course, is what evidence would you have that I was involved?"

I wondered if anybody would hear the gunshot if she pulled the trigger.

"There's the Facebook chat with Grace Farmer. A picture of Terri bound in the trunk of a car."

For the first time Elise laughed, a soft, steady chuckle.

"You're right; the police would be quite interested in seeing that. Unfortunately, that chat exchange doesn't exist anymore."

My first impulse was to frown, to tell her that she was wrong, but then I understood.

"You shut down my mom's laptop before we left."

"Yes."

"You deleted the chat."

"Yes."

"But my mom's still friends with the fake Grace Farmer."

"You'd think so, wouldn't you? But that's the problem with social media these days. You can make somebody disappear with a click of a button."

"Data like that doesn't just disappear. It can be recovered."

"True. But even if you did recover it, what exactly would it prove? Somebody abducted Terri. Somebody chatted with you on Facebook. But that somebody was obviously not me. I was standing right there beside you the entire time."

"I wasn't at the Farmhouse that night, was I?"

"Maybe you were, maybe you weren't. Does it really matter at this point?"

When I didn't answer, Elise smiled again.

"I know who you are, Emily. I've known ever since kindergarten when I saw you standing by yourself at recess. I knew you were weak then, just like I know you're weak now. And you know what? That's okay. The world needs weak people. They can't all be strong like me. There needs to be a balance. And so you may think you're tough, that you're smart, that you can somehow fight this, but we both know you're scared. And that's okay. Sometimes you need to be scared."

I looked again at the gun, then shook my head at Elise.

"What happened to you?"

"I grew up. Just like you did."

I glanced down at the scar on my palm, whispered, "We're nothing alike."

"You're right. Sometimes girls like us leave the meanness of our youth behind." Something lit up in her eyes, a brief fire. "But not me. I *loved* it."

She paused, and smiled again.

"In theory, of course."

Her hand moved just slightly, enough to motion with the gun.

"Show me your phone."

My hand instinctively touched my left-hand pocket.

"Why?"

Elise said nothing, just stared back at me. Feeling like the car's interior had somehow grown even tighter, I reached into my pocket and slid out the phone.

"Show me the home screen," she said.

I just stared back at her. Elise shifted the gun so the barrel was pointed at my face.

"Don't make me ask you again."

I tilted the phone, enough to wake it from sleep. The time and date and generic wallpaper was what usually lit up on the screen. Now it was the voice-memo app, actively recording our conversation.

"I take it back," Elise said. She sounded almost impressed. "You're not completely scared. Of course, now I'm going to need you to delete that."

The barrel of the gun was still aimed straight at my face, motionless in Elise's steady hand.

I tapped the screen to stop the recording, tapped it again to delete. Seemingly satisfied, Elise shifted her wrist again, this time motioning with the gun at my door.

"Good girl," she said. "Now get the fuck out of my car."

I reached for the door handle but paused.

"And then what?"

"You tell me, Emily. Remember, you've never been happy with your life. You lost your job today. Your fiancé. You're deeply depressed. You can't take it anymore, so maybe you decide to . . ."

She glanced at the ledge of the parking garage, glanced back at me.

"End the pain."

"I'm not killing myself."

"I know. Such a pity. But the simple truth is, I can't force you to do anything right now. We're at a hospital, after all. There are cameras everywhere. Had I driven away with you, and your body was later found, they'd see you getting into my car, and I'd be a prime suspect. And I haven't managed to get by all this time by being stupid. In theory, of course."

"You and Mackenzie aren't going to get away with this."

"Get away with what? Again, assuming what all I told you is true, what evidence is there that Mackenzie or myself was involved in anything?"

I didn't answer. I knew she was right. And it pissed me off. But there was nothing I could do about it, so I opened my door.

"Oh, and Emily? You might want to keep this conversation between the two of us. Because Terri got lucky tonight, but she might not be so lucky next time. Or, who knows, maybe your mother might accidentally slip down the stairs one day and break her neck. That would be quite a shame, wouldn't it?"

"Did you ever tell me anything that wasn't a lie?"

The question seemed to catch her off guard. A beat, and then she grinned.

"Of course. Both of our names start with the same letter."

I stepped out of the car and shut the door. Stood back and watched as Elise backed out of the parking spot and drove away, down toward the fourth level, the car's taillights flaring red as she turned the corner and disappeared from view.

58

I tilted the phone again to wake it from sleep. I knew which number I needed—I'd called it earlier today, after all—and now I typed out a text message and sent it and then hit the number to dial. It rang three times before voice mail picked up. I didn't leave a voice mail, just called the number again.

By that point I'd run across the parking level and pushed through the door to the stairwell, the phone to my ear, listening to the voice mail pick up again. The fourth time I tried calling, he finally answered. His voice was a harsh whisper, and I pictured him in the bathroom just off the bedroom where his wife slept.

"What the fuck do you want?"

I paused to catch my breath. "I texted you a license plate number. I need you to find out who owns the car and where they live."

Ben said, "Why would I do anything for you?"

I started down the steps again, feeling the need to crush the phone in my hand.

"Because if you don't, then I'm going to tell your wife you tried to kiss me earlier today."

A derisive snort on his end.

"She won't believe you."

"Won't she? You said it yourself; she's always been jealous of me, even after all this time."

I pictured him gritting his teeth, his face going red. If it wasn't the middle of the night, he probably would have picked something up and chucked it against the wall.

Even at a whisper, his voice oozed contempt.

"Give me a half hour."

"You have fifteen minutes."

I disconnected before he could say anything else, hit the ground floor, and pushed through the door.

A couple of yards from the ER's entrance, a woman sat on a bench, hunched forward, smoking a cigarette. I saw her out of the corner of my eye, the way you see most people, but as I ran past, something about her caught my attention, caused me to stop and turn back around.

"Mrs. Kitterman?"

The cigarette was almost gone, just another puff or two before it hit the butt. Chloe's mother held it laced between her fingers and glanced up at me cautiously, like she wasn't sure who I was. She didn't look like herself, at least not the self she so meticulously put together before she left the house to take her daughter to therapy. She wore jeans and a T-shirt and sneakers, and it didn't look like she had on any makeup.

She stared at me for a while before recognition filled her face, and then she said, "I heard you got fired."

I glanced toward the ER's entrance doors, wondering if Terri had been seen yet.

"Is Chloe okay?"

Mrs. Kitterman took a drag on the cigarette as she eyed me.

"Safe Haven called to cancel Chloe's appointment for later this week. They said you were no longer employed there, that they could schedule her with another therapist. I asked what happened, and they wouldn't tell me, but I could read between the lines."

"What happened to Chloe?"

The woman scoffed. "What do you think? She went and cut herself again. I don't know what's wrong with that girl, but she needs to get her shit together."

Kind of hard for a gentle girl like Chloe to get her shit together when her mother had this kind of attitude. Now that I was no longer employed by Safe Haven, I was free to tell Mrs. Kitterman what I thought of her.

But that wouldn't benefit anyone. Especially Chloe.

"Is she okay?"

Mrs. Kitterman rolled her eyes.

"Of course she is. She only does this for attention. She's going back to another inpatient facility. I've already signed the paperwork. The crisis worker is calling around, trying to find a bed."

"Would you mind if I speak to her?"

She flicked the cigarette away, into a puddle off the sidewalk, and rummaged in her bag to find another.

"Now why should I let you do anything pertaining to my daughter? You're no longer her therapist."

"Because Chloe and I were developing a rapport. She seemed to feel comfortable talking to me."

Mrs. Kitterman lit the new cigarette and stared down at the glowing tip. I could see the drawn lines at the sides of her mouth. She took a drag and nodded.

"Go ahead, try to talk to her. Maybe she'll say something to you. I don't remember the last time she spoke one full sentence to me. I don't understand that girl at all."

I found Courtney and Terri in the waiting room. In the harsh glow of the overhead lights, their muddy clothes stood out like fresh blood.

Courtney had her arm around Terri, who appeared to be sleeping. A TV was on in the corner, playing CNN, though its volume was muted.

Courtney whispered, "I thought maybe you'd left."

I glanced around the waiting room to make sure nobody was sitting nearby. A half dozen other people sat sprawled in chairs, some wearing surgical masks even though flu season was over.

"Was just having a conversation with Elise."

"Where is she?"

"She had to head home."

"Why'd you ask me earlier if I'd ever told her where we lived?"

I hesitated. Wasn't sure what to say. Knew that the last thing I wanted to do right now was to get into it with Courtney. Her hands were already so full taking care of Terri that I couldn't imagine what extra stress would come from learning that Elise and Mackenzie had been behind all this, though I knew at some point I would have no choice but to tell her.

Terri stirred beside her mother. I crouched down in front of her and touched her knee.

"Hey, kiddo. How are you feeling?"

She shrugged.

I asked, "Did Daniel come out and see you?"

Courtney nodded and hugged Terri closer.

"He was out here for maybe a minute. He said they're really busy tonight, but he's going to try to make sure he's Terri's nurse. Did you call Detective Hernandez yet?"

I told her no and turned my focus again to Terri.

"A policeman is going to come here soon to talk to you. Tell him everything that happened, okay?"

Terri nodded, her eyes nervous. She would need a new pair of glasses. I wondered how much that would cost. How much a new backpack would cost. How many times she would need to see a therapist to process what had happened to her.

I started to stand back up, but paused, touched her knee again.

"I'm sorry your book was stolen. But just because the pages are gone, it doesn't mean the story is. The story is still in your head, right?"

Terri nodded again.

"See—the book is always going to be with you. And when you write it down again, I want to read it. Deal?"

It was a weak attempt, but still Terri managed to smile.

"Deal," she whispered.

I texted Daniel again, and it took five minutes before he was able to poke his head out from the back. He scanned the waiting room and lowered his voice.

"What the hell happened tonight? Why are Terri and Courtney covered in mud?"

I slipped the engagement ring off my finger, held it out.

He looked past me at the people in the waiting room, whispered, "We don't have to do this here."

"I know. Let's call it a trade."

"A trade for what?"

"Your car keys. I need to borrow your car."

Daniel took the ring, held it in his palm for a beat, and then slipped it into his pocket.

"The keys are back in my locker. I need to check on somebody first, and then I'll bring them out."

"Does the name Chloe Kitterman sound familiar?"

"The last name does, yeah. She's not one of my patients. I think she's back in seclusion."

That was a blocked-off section of the ER, the place people were put when they were a danger to themselves or others. Only four rooms, the walls padded, just beds and sometimes a chair.

"She was a patient of mine at Safe Haven. I saw her mom outside, and she said I could see her. Can you let me back?"

"That depends. Are you going to tell me what happened to Terri?"

"Not right now, but eventually."

Daniel didn't look like he wanted to let me back at first—it wasn't really following protocol—but then he stepped aside and held the door open.

"I'll bring you the keys in a couple of minutes. I'm parked out in the employee lot."

The door to the seclusion area was locked. Luckily, one of the nurses recognized me from my days as a crisis worker. She knew I was engaged to Daniel, and she smiled when she saw me and asked how I'd been.

"I was hoping to see Chloe Kitterman," I said, smiling brightly back at her. "I spoke to her mom outside, and she said it would be okay. I've worked with Chloe as her therapist."

At the mention of Chloe's mother, the nurse made a face, which made me think Mrs. Kitterman had been extra difficult when she'd arrived. Then the nurse directed me to one of the rooms and told me to let her know when I was ready to leave.

Chloe wore blue scrubs and lay on the low plastic bed in a fetal position. A chair was just inside the door, and as I slowly sat down, I said her name.

No response.

"It's Miss Emily."

Still nothing.

From this vantage point, I could see only her back. The lights were brighter here, and I realized her long red hair was gone. It looked like she'd dyed it black.

"Chloe, are you awake?"

Again, nothing.

I could stand and walk over to her, kneel down beside the bed, and try to speak to her that way. But in the little time I'd had to get to know Chloe, I had gotten the sense that that approach wouldn't work. You had to wait her out. Let her feel comfortable enough to open up.

In my pocket, my phone vibrated twice: a text message. I pulled it out and saw an address. Immediately tapped it to open the maps application. It looked to be a cul-de-sac in a neighborhood maybe twenty minutes away. Not an apartment like Elise had said she lived in, but a house.

My phone vibrated again.

Never contact me again.

And again.

Bitch.

I shook my head and slipped the phone back into my pocket. Now that I had the address, all I needed were Daniel's keys.

On the bed, the papery fabric of the scrubs shifted. Chloe turned over and sat up. She kept her face tilted down, but I could see her hair better now. Not only had she dyed it black, she'd cut it, and from the looks of it, she'd done it herself. I pictured her standing in the bathroom at home, glaring at her reflection in the mirror as she used scissors to chop off fistfuls of hair.

Her left wrist was scarred from old cuts, but her right wrist wore a fresh bandage.

She sat there, silent, refusing to meet my eyes.

I wasn't sure what to say, so I said nothing. Giving Chloe the chance to speak first.

Finally, she did, her voice soft.

"Why are you here?"

"I like to hang out in the ER on weeknights."

No reaction. Not even the hint of a smile.

"My mom said I can't see you anymore. That you got fired because you were bad at your job."

"What happened, Chloe?"

Her shoulders slouched forward, Chloe shook slightly as she tried to hold in the tears. Not even a full month had passed since she was last at an inpatient facility. I knew she was depressed, but I had hoped her depression wasn't this bad. I'd seen it with many of my patients, and it was like being caught in an undertow. The more you fought, the stronger it became, making it nearly impossible to break the surface. And so, time and again, you used up all your strength, gave up, and let the undertow drag you down.

"Why did you cut yourself?"

She didn't respond, still staring down at her lap. Eventually she shrugged. Said nothing for nearly a minute.

Then, bit by bit, she lifted her face. Pained desperation and hopelessness in her eyes.

When she spoke next, her quivering voice was barely a whisper.

"Why are they so mean?"

There was a good chance I would never see this girl again. And because of that, I didn't want to lie to her. Didn't want to tell her something just for the sake of saying it. I wanted to be honest with her, as honest as I could be, though I wasn't sure how much it would help in the end.

I glanced down at my hand, at the hairline scar running across my palm, and told her the truth.

"I don't know."

59

The knife didn't look too scary. It was short and thin. Mackenzie had fetched it from the kitchen, a simple paring knife, meant to cut fruit and vegetables. The blade designed to pierce apples and peaches and carrots.

Not flesh.

Courtney said, "What are you *doing* with that?"

Mackenzie hefted the knife in her hand, her pink-painted fingernails chewed down to the quick.

"I told you. We all need to promise not to say anything."

"Yeah," Olivia said, her voice tense, "we all agree on that. But why the knife?"

"It's called a blood oath. I saw it in a movie. It means that we make a promise with our blood. It can never be broken."

We were in Mackenzie's bedroom, the six of us. Boy-band posters dotted the pastel walls. The scent of deodorant and despair hung thick in the air. Mackenzie's parents were somewhere downstairs. We kept our voices hushed so that they couldn't hear us.

Courtney shook her head, her cheeks already going pale.

"But we don't need to *cut* ourselves. That's crazy."

Mackenzie's delicate fingers squeezed the knife's wooden handle.

"We *do* need to cut ourselves. It's the only way. Do you know how much trouble we could get in if our parents found out what we did?"

Destiny said, "She just *tried* to kill herself. She didn't actually *die*."

Mackenzie's blue eyes pulsed with intensity.

"Do you think that matters? This might go on our records. This could ruin our *lives*."

Olivia folded her arms over her chest.

"You're being overdramatic. She might not even say anything."

Mackenzie shook her head, solemnly, and shifted the knife in her hand to run the blade across her palm.

For an instant, nothing happened. We stared, frozen, mosquitoes stuck in amber. Then, all at once, Mackenzie's palm began to weep a thin line of blood.

We gasped.

Mackenzie looked down at the blood on her palm, then held up the knife, her frantic gaze skipping around the room at each of us.

"Who's next?"

I didn't wait to see who was next. Every bedroom in Mackenzie's large house had its own bathroom, and I rushed into hers, dropped to my knees in front of the toilet, and began to dry heave.

I heard the girls whispering out in the bedroom, and then the quiet click as the door opened and closed. I knew it was Elise even before she knelt down beside me, placed her steady hand on my back.

"Are you okay?"

I leaned back, wiping the saliva from my chin. I shook my head.

"I can't . . . I can't do this."

"It'll be all right, Emily."

"She tried to kill herself."

"Emily, it'll be all right. Trust me."

"How do you know?"

Elise offered up her easy smile. "I just do."

"I'm not cutting myself. Mackenzie is nuts."

The easy smile faded from her face.

I said, "You can't be serious."

"Once a Harpy, always a Harpy."

"Are you crazy? This isn't a game, Elise. Grace tried to *kill* herself."

Elise reached out, placed both hands on my shoulders. Leveled her gaze with mine.

"You're right, Emily. This isn't a game. This is real life. And you know what? Mackenzie is right. This could ruin ours. We need to stick together."

I shook my head again, looking past her at the closed bathroom door.

"I'm not going to do it. Not for her."

"Then do it for me. Forget Mackenzie even suggested it. Just think about it as a promise between us. That we're never going to lie to each other. That we're always going to be there for one another. That we'll be friends forever."

Was Elise being sincere? In that moment I believed she was because I couldn't believe anything else. I was a terrified fourteen-year-old girl who felt like she didn't have anybody else in the world to protect her.

"Promise?"

Elise grinned, held up her pinkie finger, and waited until I'd curled my pinkie around hers.

"Promise."

60

Put a group of prepubescent boys on an island by themselves, unsupervised, and anarchy follows. They will attack each other. They will kill each other. Chaos will reign.

Put a group of prepubescent girls on an island by themselves, unsupervised, and they'll manage to keep calm. They may argue from time to time, but in the end they'll keep order and make sure nobody dies.

Mr. Huston may have had an interesting theory, but that's all it was, a theory. Despite being married, despite having a daughter of his own, he didn't truly understand the opposite sex. He didn't know just how ruthless we could be. How conniving. How feral.

No matter how many might be in our group, we'll always sniff out the weakest. We may never do anything about it—may leave the weakest alone—but we will always know who will be first to go down if need be.

That was another thing Mr. Huston never understood.

We girls—girls who will eventually become women—will do whatever it takes to survive.

Even if it means destroying everybody else.

◆ ◆ ◆

At nearly two o'clock in the morning, the cul-de-sac was quiet. It must have been trash night, as oversize cans and recycling bins were stationed at the mouth of each driveway. Every house had put out their trash except one.

Elise's house, or at least the house whose address Ben had sent me, had its walkway light burning bright. The windows were dark, but that didn't mean she wasn't home. Maybe she was already in bed, soundly asleep.

I flicked off the headlights as I pulled into the driveway. Turned off the car. The windows were down, and I tried to hear past the tick of the cooling engine to the rest of the neighborhood.

Silence.

Detective Hernandez would have made it to the hospital by now. Hopefully Terri had been taken back to a room and seen by a doctor. The detective and a few of his cops would listen closely as Courtney told them what had happened, what had led up to Terri's abduction. The detective would wonder where I was—I'd called him as I weaved through the employee lot toward Daniel's car—and Courtney would tell him I'd gone to find Elise.

That was all I had told her. I still wasn't sure what I would say to Courtney when the time came. Right now, I still didn't have any evidence. That was why I was here—to get some kind of irrefutable proof that Elise and Mackenzie were involved, that they were behind everything, that what Elise had said to me wasn't just a theory born of a malicious mind.

I pulled out my phone and dialed 911. But I didn't press the green "Send" button. Not yet. I had to make sure Elise was here—and Mackenzie, if I were so lucky. If they were, I would slip the phone back into my pocket, just as I'd done before I'd gotten into Elise's car. Only this time, everything would be recorded on 911's end. No way for Elise or Mackenzie to force me to delete our conversation this time.

A second or two after I'd rung the doorbell, I began to wonder if maybe this was the wrong house. I had no doubt Ben had given me the address associated with the license plate, but what if Elise had stolen the car, or swapped out the plate with another? Maybe she'd changed her identity at the DMV. For all I knew, I could have just woken an innocent family. Maybe they had a newborn baby that would start crying at any moment. Or a dog that would start barking.

I held my breath and listened, but the street behind me remained dark and quiet. So did the house. Not even a light came on behind the drawn shades.

I went to ring the doorbell again, but paused. Elise had had her chance. If she were going to answer the door, she'd have done it by now.

I gripped the door handle, expecting it to be locked. The door moved without protest, and I stepped into the foyer.

"Elise?"

No answer.

I closed the door behind me, flicked all the light switches on the panel beside the frame. The foyer light came on, as did the lights in the living room and dining room.

The dining room contained a bare wooden table with four chairs.

The living room had a couch and chair and TV and coffee table.

The walls, I realized, were bare. Not one framed photograph or painting.

Everything looked preternaturally spotless, like somebody lived here but cleaned up after themselves every second of every day.

"Hello?"

Still no answer.

I headed deeper into the house, flicking the light switches as I went. The kitchen was as bare as the other rooms. Nothing on the tiny table beside the patio door. Nothing on the refrigerator. Nothing on the counters except Elise's cell phone and a yellow legal pad.

A pen lay on top of the pad. A simple message had been written across half of the page.

Once a Harpy, always a Harpy.

A chill streaked through my body, from head to toe. This was our motto, the thing that connected us all. It was also what I'd told Elise tonight. The way to explain why she'd done all these terrible things.

There is no why, I'd said.

I turned and noticed two doors. One looked to be for the pantry. The other was partly ajar and looked to lead down into the basement.

The door squeaked slightly when it opened. I flicked the switch just inside the door, and a dim light bulb came on near the bottom of the steps.

Don't go down there.

The thought kept racing through my head. Just leave. Turn out the lights; get the hell out of the house. Go back to the hospital and tell Detective Hernandez everything. He'd be angry with me, and he deserved to be, but at least Terri was safe. That was all that mattered. The rest of this didn't mean a thing.

But I knew that wasn't true, and that's why I started down the steps.

I took my time, taking each step carefully, tilting my head to try to see what was or was not in the basement.

The first thing I saw was the tipped-over wooden chair.

Then her feet.

Then her legs.

When I reached the last step, I paused a beat to close my eyes and take a breath, and then I turned and looked at her.

The rope was stronger than the kind we'd used to tie Grace to the tree. One end was tied around a thick metal pipe that spanned the ceiling. The other was squeezing her throat.

She wore the same pantsuit she'd had on earlier tonight. Even the ballet flats. Her feet were maybe six inches from the floor.

I stared at her, remembering how confident she'd been as she'd slowly driven us through the parking garage, the smile she'd given me when she'd placed the gun on her lap, and then I finally hit the green "Send" button on my phone.

"Nine-one-one, what's your emergency?"

I gave my name and the address and said that I'd found Elise Martin hanging in the basement.

There was a pause on the dispatcher's end.

"Is she still breathing, ma'am?"

I opened my mouth, but before I could say anything, I heard a noise coming from the corner, from a small room probably meant to be the laundry room. From where I'd been standing, I hadn't noticed it.

The dispatcher said, "Ma'am, are you there?"

I heard the noise again, what sounded like distant moaning.

I wet my lips, and managed to answer in a soft voice.

"I'm here."

The dispatcher said, "I've notified the police and am sending an ambulance. Is the person still breathing?"

I glanced at Elise as I walked past her toward the door. Her head was tilted down, and her eyes were closed. I almost felt compelled to pick up the chair and set it upright but left it where it was. The phone was still against my ear as I reached out with my right hand to open the door.

The dispatcher said, "Ma'am?"

At first I didn't recognize her.

I stepped to the side so the light could shine in.

She was sitting on the ground in her underwear, in what looked to be a fresh puddle of urine. Her body was covered with bruises. Her hair was just as dark as I remembered it, though it was dirty and greasy and stuck to her forehead with sweat. Duct tape covered her mouth, much like it had Terri's earlier tonight, but what kept her in place was the pair of handcuffs securing her wrists to a pipe.

She squinted up at me, cowering like a beaten animal.

The dispatcher said, "Ma'am, I need you to answer me."

I wet my lips again, and this time my voice was a hoarse whisper.

"She's here too."

"Who?"

"Grace Farmer."

Ashlee had talked about leaving Dixon Township since high school—a typical refrain she'd started in eleventh grade, how she was gonna leave this shithole and go to New York City or Los Angeles—but it had been almost ten years since they'd graduated, and she was still there. Working odd jobs, stocking shelves down at the Dollar General; sweeping up popcorn and trash at the movie theater. Serving drinks at the Black Dog Tavern. And, just in the past couple of months, stripping at a club a few towns away, a place called Cleopatra's, the name making the place sound much classier than it really was.

Grace had never been to Cleopatra's—she'd never been to any strip club—but she could imagine what it was like. Could see the large dark room lit by flashing lights, smell the smoke and beer and cheap perfume. Ashlee hadn't told Grace about the strip club at first—she hadn't told anybody, apparently—but it was there she'd met a guy who claimed to be a "producer" who could put her in "films."

Ashlee knew what he really meant, but that didn't bother her. She knew she was hot, and she liked having sex and she liked making money, so why not start using what the good Lord gave her?

That's why they were all here tonight at the Black Dog, maybe a dozen of them in total. To celebrate Ashlee's last night in town. Well, okay, maybe not her last *night in town—she might not leave for another day or two—but it was Saturday night, the best night for everybody to get together, and so she decided, fuck it, we'll have the party now.*

Only Grace knew where Ashlee was truly headed. Ashlee had told her a few days ago because she'd been bursting to tell somebody, and Ashlee had always considered Grace one of her best friends. Grace herself wouldn't say she had many to choose from, and she probably wouldn't have called Ashlee a good friend, but she was always there when Ashlee called or texted to complain about one guy or another or needed a ride to the clinic for STD testing or, once, an abortion. Grace had been there because there was no place else for her to be, and it was because of their connection—at least in Ashlee's mind—that Ashlee had told Grace where she was going and what she was going to do.

To her family and friends, Ashlee had said she was driving out to Los Angeles to find an apartment and start auditioning for commercials and parts in TV shows and movies.

To Grace, however, Ashlee had told the truth: how her "producer"—who had already taken pictures of her naked, as well as a few videos of her in various sex acts that were promptly uploaded to multiple porn sites—was putting her up in a place just off the Strip in Las Vegas to get her acquainted with the business out there. The money, Ashlee told Grace, was good. If Ashlee was lucky, it could be great.

And then she had squinted at Grace, as if seeing her for the first time, and said, "You could probably do pretty good out there, too, if you wanted. Some guys are really into the plain-Jane look."

Grace, taking it as a compliment because she knew that was how Ashlee meant it, had merely smiled and said she wasn't interested. Sure, she'd love to get out of Dixon Township, but it had to be for the right reason.

The last time she'd left was for those brief months in Lanton, and it was because of what had happened there that her mom worried so much, even now that Grace was twenty-seven. Always wanting to know where she was going. Who she was hanging out with. What she was planning to do on the weekend.

Her mom meant well, but the constant nagging got on Grace's nerves. Of course, her mom didn't know that, half the time, Grace wasn't telling her the truth. Like her current boyfriend, Jesse—even that label was suspect, because they didn't date so much as hook up, and Grace knew for a fact that Jesse was also fucking Ashlee behind her back—who made most of his money cooking meth in a trailer overlooking the river. Sometimes Grace helped him when she was bored.

Anyway, tonight was Ashlee's last night in town, and they had all come to the Black Dog. Grace's mom was working, of course—she worked most nights in her jeans and black T-shirt, running drinks and food from one table to another—and her mom had managed to switch with another server so that she had their table, which Grace guessed was because her mom knew Ashlee, too, and wanted to be part of her last night.

So there was Grace and there was Jesse and there was Ashlee and a bunch of other friends—Mary and Alexis and Floyd and Jeremy—and they were having a great time, sitting around one big table, the music loud and people shouting to be heard, smoke thick in the air, beer bottles clinking against one another, and shot glasses being thrown back and slammed down on tabletops. Jesse had his arm around Grace, and she was snuggled into him, feeling buzzed, her hand absently stroking the inside of his thigh under the table, and her mom came and went with drinks and food, and Grace sorta felt bad for her because she knew her mom was gonna get screwed over on the tip—all her friends were broke—but in a way that was her mom's fault because she'd switched with that other server for their table, and, besides, Grace was laughing along with her friends, everybody there for Ashlee, who they had known since they were kids, Ashlee who wanted to become the world's most famous porn star but refused to let anybody besides Grace know about the pictures and videos online, though Grace figured pretty soon the secret would get out—one would have to assume some of these guys, if not most, watched porn, and they would eventually stumble across her videos.

The night was getting late, and the music was getting louder, and at one point Grace told Jesse she needed to use the bathroom, and so she stumbled up from her chair and started toward the bathrooms in the corner, noticing her mom off on the other side of the room keeping an eye on her—her mom never forgetting that day she had to break down the bathroom door because Grace hadn't answered her—and then she was in the women's room, the place smelling heavily of bleach, and by the time she came out of the stall, somebody else had come in and was standing by the sink, dressed in tight jeans and cowboy boots and a checkered shirt, her red hair tied back in a ponytail and laced through the gray Phillies baseball cap pulled low on her head, and despite all the years that had passed, she was still recognizable as she turned and smiled at Grace.

"Remember me?" Elise Martin asked.

PART IV:

Discharge

"You saw Grace Farmer yesterday?"

"Yes."

"How did it go?"

Silence.

"Emily," Lisa said, shifting in her mesh ergonomic chair to better gauge my reaction, "how did it go?"

◆ ◆ ◆

Winfield State Hospital was located an hour and a half north of Lanton. It sat on the side of a mountain in the middle of nowhere. The closest town was ten miles away. Tall white ash trees stretched out in all directions.

This was a place to ship the sick and mentally ill when their families could no longer take care of them. The front parking lot was small, only a half dozen spaces. The patients at Winfield didn't get many visitors.

The police had offered to give me a ride, but I preferred to drive myself. Mostly because I didn't want to be stuck in a car for three hours with somebody I barely knew. I still got the sense that the police were ticked off at me for not telling them the truth early on. Had I called Detective Hernandez immediately, maybe Elise Martin would still be alive and behind bars . . . though they weren't clear on what crimes she would have been charged with since, as far as they could determine, Destiny's and Olivia's deaths were in fact suicides.

Elise *had* lied to the detective when she said she'd stayed with Terri while Courtney and I drove up to Bradford County—and by extension, since we hadn't disputed this, the rest of us had lied, too, not to mention we'd never stopped at any gas station on the way back—and while we'd gotten a stern lecture, in the end Courtney and I weren't charged with anything.

I was ten minutes early, but several people were already waiting for me inside the hospital. Detective Ervin with the Pennsylvania State Police, two state attorneys, Gloria O'Grady from Judge Dyer's office, and Frank Atkins, the smarmy lawyer who had volunteered to take Grace's case pro bono because he thought it would help him make a name for himself.

Once I stepped through the door, Frank Atkins started shaking his head and pacing back and forth, his arms crossed.

"I can't believe this is actually happening."

The state attorneys ignored him, as did Gloria O'Grady and Detective Ervin. That didn't stop the lawyer from continuing to pace and mumble under his breath.

"This is bullshit, and you all know it."

One of the state attorneys said, almost by rote, "You can make a complaint to Judge Dyer's office."

"You're goddamned right I will. Fact is"—his gaze shifting to Gloria O'Grady—"I already did."

The lobby didn't have any windows. There was only one door. Two benches sat against the brick wall, as did a cluster of small gray lockers. I eyed the lockers, my phone and keys in hand, knowing that I would need to turn them in.

The door opened, and an older man with glasses and a balding head stepped out. He gazed around the lobby at each person before his eyes fell on me.

"Ms. Bennett?"

I nodded.

"I'm Dr. Preston. Thank you for coming today."

I nodded again but said nothing.

Dr. Preston once more took in the group.

"Well, I'm happy you all decided to come for our little experiment. Especially you, Mr. Atkins. I know you do not agree with what we are about to do."

"You're goddamned right I don't. This is a violation of my client's constitutional rights."

Dr. Preston smiled like he was debating with a seven-year-old.

"Yes, well, Judge Dyer does not see it that way. He grants that your client may be mentally ill at this time, but that is why she is here, to become mentally well again. Thus far, we have not had much luck—Grace refuses to speak to anybody, even her mother—so my team and I thought she might speak to Ms. Bennett. After all, Ms. Bennett was the one who saved her."

Saved was a bit of an overstatement. I was simply in the right place at the right time. Besides, I didn't buy the theory that Elise had been keeping Grace chained in the basement, periodically beating her. I'd explained that to the police—how I'd seen Grace the previous day in the parking lot outside Courtney's apartment, and how clearly somebody had been working with Elise and how that person hadn't been Mackenzie, not based on what we now knew—but the police didn't want to hear my theories. They were still angry with Courtney and me for not telling the truth after Terri had been abducted. And for not calling the police as soon as we found Terri. They'd gone out to the clearing in the woods, but to our bewilderment, there was no evidence of torches or rope.

Frank Atkins could have taught a master class in faux outrage. His long face colored crimson, his jaw tightened, and he thrust a trembling finger in my direction.

"*She's* the one responsible for my client's condition. She and her friends from middle school. My client is the *victim* here. Besides"—another finger thrust—"*she* thinks my client was working with Elise Martin. Which is ludicrous! Elise Martin *tortured* my client. That's why my client tried to kill herself."

Dr. Preston kept the smile on his face.

"Be that as it may, Judge Dyer has signed off on a court order. Yes, Mr. Atkins, as you mentioned, Grace is on suicide watch. As the others know, Ms. Bennett"—his eyes met mine, and his gaze was sympathetic—"Grace made a noose out of her bedsheet and tried to hang herself two nights ago. She has been on one-on-one supervision ever since. With this in mind, Mr. Atkins, as discussed, you will be able to monitor what happens along with the other lawyers here, as well as Mrs. O'Grady and Detective Ervin. My staff will be right outside the room in case anything happens, but, quite honestly, we don't think anything will."

He paused, clasping his hands together.

"For the most part, Grace has been a compliant patient. She does not speak, but she will respond to certain things. Food, for instance. She will not tell us what she wants, but if we provide her a choice of meal options, she will always pick the same thing. She likes red Jell-O. She likes lemonade. She likes tuna fish sandwiches. She likes chewing the same brand of gum. I could go on, but that is not why you have come all this way."

He directed his smile at me.

"Now, Ms. Bennett, if you would be so kind as to leave your things in one of those lockers?"

◆ ◆ ◆

Lisa quietly cleared her throat, and shifted again in her chair.

"Can you clarify something for me?"

"I can try."

"If Grace didn't die in that meth-lab explosion, whose body was it?"

"A girl named Ashlee. She went to high school with Grace in Dixon Township. They were friends, apparently."

"How could she disappear and nobody notice?"

"She was supposed to go out to California. To Hollywood, to be an actress, from what I'm told. Things were never good between her and her parents, so when she didn't contact them, they assumed she'd cut ties. Before she left, I guess Elise and Grace managed to . . . stop her. The medical examiner confessed to the police that Elise paid him twenty thousand dollars to identify the remains as Grace's."

"So Grace was clearly complicit in some of what happened."

"The police think so. That's why there are pending charges. They may have tried to charge Mackenzie, too, but . . ." The words were still hard to say, to process. "They found her in her SUV two days later. Apparently she'd overdosed on amphetamines and alcohol."

"Do the police suspect foul play?"

"From what I'm told, no. The SUV was locked, and there were no unusual prints inside or out. Her phone had the same encrypted messaging app on it that Elise's phone did. As far as I know, the police haven't been able to recover any of the messages, but it certainly shows a connection."

"Why do you think Elise told you as much as she did? The way you made it sound, she confessed to you without really confessing."

"My guess is her narcissism. She wanted to brag. Wanted to show me just how smart she was. I don't think she could help it, not after I'd called her out like I did."

"Going back to Mackenzie, do the police know why she left the house that night?"

"Apparently she went out a lot when her husband was working late. She'd have the housekeeper stay for a few extra hours so she could meet up with various lovers. The housekeeper apparently had no idea what was really going on. She just thought Mackenzie was meeting up with friends."

Which explained why Mackenzie had tried to lose me that night when I'd gone back down to see her. It had nothing to do with Elise—she was probably heading out to see one of her lovers and noticed me following and thought I was either a private investigator a suspicious wife or girlfriend had hired, or was a wife or girlfriend myself, set to do my own investigating. It was doubtful Mackenzie had recognized me at all, only noticed that I was a female, and so she panicked.

"Various lovers?" Lisa asked, somewhat shocked, and I nodded.

"I managed to piece it together from the little Detective Hernandez told me, as well as what was in the news and what Courtney managed to find on Facebook. When the police went through her phone, they found out she'd been having an affair with at least three men. One actually worked with Mackenzie's husband. There might be others, but I stopped paying attention."

"Wow," Lisa said. "Okay, sorry for interrupting. What happened next?"

I walked through a metal detector and followed the doctor down a long corridor. I was taken to a small room with a single wooden table and two wooden chairs. Dr. Preston indicated the camera in the corner of the ceiling and reiterated that they would be monitoring everything.

"Are you ready?"

I gave a small nod, and he offered a warm smile.

"No reason to be nervous. I can't say Grace will be happy to see you, but to be honest, that's the point. Maybe this meeting will help jar something loose, get her to open up. If anything does happen, my staff will be right outside the door. Any questions?"

I told him there weren't, and Dr. Preston smiled again, motioned me to take a seat.

"Grace will be in shortly."

He left, and I sat with my back to the window so that I faced the door.

Maybe two minutes passed before it opened again.

Grace wore blue sweatpants and a white T-shirt, socks, and slippers. Her black hair had been cut short. She stepped inside and looked at me, but there was no reaction.

Dr. Preston entered the room behind her. He pulled out the chair.

"Grace, why don't you have a seat?"

Grace didn't move at first, her gaze fixed on me. Then she slowly drifted forward and lowered herself onto the chair.

"Perfect," Dr. Preston said. "Now, I will be just outside if you need anything. Okay, Grace?"

Grace didn't answer. Just kept watching me.

Dr. Preston waited maybe ten seconds before he gave me a quick nod of encouragement and let himself out of the room.

When the door closed, there was complete silence. For a moment, I felt like I couldn't breathe, and then I glanced at the camera in the corner, thought about all the people watching us, and let out a slow breath.

I looked at Grace. She was still watching me. Her pale face emotionless. Her dark eyes blank. I knew what Dr. Preston wanted from me—to be nice to Grace, to try to get her to open up—but I couldn't do it.

"I know you're faking."

Grace didn't answer. Didn't even blink.

"I saw you that morning outside Courtney's. I thought maybe I was seeing things, but it was really you."

No answer.

"And you were at the boardwalk that day, weren't you? You'd followed us down there and made sure I saw you in the crowd."

Still nothing.

"'Once a Harpy, always a Harpy.' It made for a creepy suicide note, like there was some hidden meaning, but it was bullshit, wasn't it? Elise didn't write that. You did."

Silence.

"Was it your idea to add all those clues? To send friend requests to my mom from fake accounts so that you could eventually feed her information? Beth Norris and Anne Wolff, both whom I've since confirmed don't exist, but when you put their first names together, you get your mother's name. How about Destiny's wife—whose idea was it to text her the word *vesper*?"

More silence.

"For the longest time I felt sorry for you. All I ever wanted was to apologize. But now . . . now I don't even know what more to say."

Little by little, her lips started to tremble. At first I thought she was on the verge of tears.

Then I realized she was trying to speak.

I glanced again at the camera. From that angle, the corner of the ceiling, they wouldn't be able to see her lips.

I leaned forward. "What are you saying?"

Her voice was just below a whisper. I wished the table wasn't between us. I thought about standing up, moving closer, but I knew I should stay seated.

"Grace, what are you trying to say?"

Another second ticked by, and her lips kept trembling. The tone of her voice picked up a bit. Enough for me to understand.

"Sticks and stones may break my bones but words will never hurt me."

"Grace, knock it off."

Louder.

"Sticks and stones may break my bones but words will never hurt me."

"You're not fooling any—"

Even louder.

"Sticks and stones may break my bones but words will never hurt me!"

She started screaming it, and before I knew what had happened, she'd launched herself over the table. My chair tipped back and we fell to the ground, Grace on top of me, screaming the same thing over and over—"Sticks and stones may break my bones"—and I tried to push her off but she was too strong, holding me down, and that was when the door flew open and the staff rushed in.

They grabbed Grace's arms to pull her off—Grace's mouth so close that spittle hit my face—and then she was off me, kicking out at the staff, and even more people appeared and grabbed her legs while someone rushed forward to help me up.

Seconds later I was in the corridor, breathing heavily, Dr. Preston asking if I was all right. Before I could respond, another door opened and Frank Atkins stormed out, his angry voice booming through the corridor.

"I knew this would be a mistake. I goddamned knew it! *You*"—he thrust his finger at me—"you fucking set her off. *You* did that."

He stalked toward the exit. The two state attorneys followed him, as did Gloria O'Grady, who already had her phone to her ear. Detective Ervin lingered, his expression sympathetic, while Dr. Preston stood there, motionless, looking shell-shocked.

"That did not go as anticipated," he said quietly. "Then again, that reaction is more than anything we have managed to get out of Grace since she arrived. Are you sure you're all right, Ms. Bennett? Would you like to use the restroom to clean your face?"

I wiped the spit off my cheeks, and shook my head.

"I want to leave."

"Completely understandable. Let me walk you out."

◆ ◆ ◆

Lisa noted my pause and tilted her head to the side, watching me.

"And then?"

"And then I left. Drove straight home to my mother's. Had some tea."

"What do you think is going to happen next?"

"I have no idea. The police believe Grace was involved, but that her involvement was minimal, and of course it stopped once Grace became Elise's"—I made a face, trying to come up with the right word—"hostage."

Lisa glanced at the clock on the wall, and offered me a somber smile.

"I'm sorry."

"You've already said that."

"And I'm sure I'll say it again."

"There was no way you could have known."

"Still. I feel just as violated as you probably do. I feel violated for my other patients."

It turned out Elise had seen Lisa, but only three times. Her first appointment was probably to survey the room, try to figure out a good hiding spot for the bug she'd placed on her second or third visit. Lisa thought it was the second, because she remembered walking Elise out, and Elise saying she'd left her cell phone in the office and backtracking before Lisa could stop her. It would have only taken a couple of seconds, and once the bug was there, secured behind the artisanal clock, Elise was set.

She heard everything. Every time I told Lisa about my strained relationship with Daniel. Every time I told her about my patients. There was confidentiality in Lisa's office—one therapist speaking to another. I'd never hesitated in mentioning my clients' names. Those, of course, were in the Facebook posts that got me fired.

Lisa set her notepad on the desk.

"How are you settling into your new office?"

"So far so good. Thank you again for putting in a good word."

After everything came out—how Elise Martin had been behind what happened to Courtney and me; how she might have been behind what happened to Olivia and Destiny, too—I was offered my job back at Safe Haven. It had been tempting, as I badly missed my patients, but I felt it would be too uncomfortable. I needed a fresh start.

Lisa spoke to her bosses, who were happy to hire me, though I had asked that they allow me to accept patients on medical assistance. Management hadn't liked the idea at first—it would cause more legwork on the billing side of things—but in the end they relented, though they made it clear that my salary would not be as much as previously discussed. I was fine with that.

Management also said I would need to stop seeing Lisa, which made sense, as we would now be colleagues. Besides, I knew it was long overdue. So today was the last time I was seeing Lisa as my therapist. In many ways, this was our discharge meeting.

"Our time together is almost over," Lisa said, "so can I ask you one more thing?"

"Sure."

"Are Daniel and Courtney still—"

"Yes."

"And you're okay with it?"

"Daniel's a good guy. He deserves to be happy. So does Courtney. And so does Terri."

"Do you still see Courtney and Terri?"

Of course. It had been only a few months since the night Terri had been abducted. I still saw them, and I still spoke to Courtney on occasion, though I did wonder how long our friendship would last with Daniel in the picture. From what I could tell, he and Courtney weren't officially dating, but Daniel was spending a lot of time with her and

Terri. Maybe nothing would come of it. Or maybe it would be something real. In the end, it didn't matter to me.

I decided to ignore Lisa's question and pushed myself up from the couch.

"I have a new patient coming in soon. I want to look over his file one more time before he and his mom arrive."

Lisa stared at me, studying my face.

"Yes?" I said.

"Is that all that happened up at Winfield? Is there anything else you want to discuss?"

I smiled, and headed for the door.

"Nothing comes to mind. If anything does, I'll let you know."

I was lying, of course.

But I wasn't about to tell Lisa what else had happened at Winfield. I wasn't about to tell anyone, not even Courtney. She was already obsessing over Terri, thinking about all the ways she could have done things differently. I'd pointed out that, in the end, we'd gotten Terri back, and that was all that mattered. There was definitely going to be emotional scarring, and it would take time for Terri to get past it, but she was a strong girl, and I knew she would be fine in the end.

As for me? I knew something nobody else did.

After my visit with Grace, as I returned to the lobby with Dr. Preston, I reached into my pocket for the locker key. It was the only thing they'd allowed me to take into the room.

As I pulled it out, I felt something else in my pocket. A piece of paper. A white gum wrapper, the word Wrigley's on one side in red, scrawled black ink on the other.

I glanced at it for just an instant, stuffed it back in my pocket, and addressed Dr. Preston as I opened the locker and retrieved my keys and phone.

"Did Grace know I was coming today?"

"Yes. We debated whether or not she should be informed, and ultimately decided that she should."

I closed the locker door. "You mentioned Grace likes chewing gum."

The statement clearly took Dr. Preston by surprise. "I did mention that, yes. May I ask why you bring it up now?"

"Just curious. What kind of gum?"

He stared at me, uncertain, and then said, "Juicy Fruit."

I told Dr. Preston I'd changed my mind and would like to wash my face, after all. He directed me to a small restroom off the lobby. The tight space was stuffy. Just a toilet and sink; the light in the ceiling buzzed, and the toilet had a water ring inside it.

The second I shut the door, I reached back into my pocket and pulled out the gum wrapper. I turned it over and looked at the inked side.

The print was small but legible. Just one line.

I guess we know the answer now, don't we?

I read it twice before shaking my head. I had no idea what it meant. The answer to what? This was something I could show the police, though I knew in the end it wouldn't mean anything. There was no proof Grace had written it. And if I could somehow prove she had, what then? It was just a question. A question I didn't even understand.

But it confirmed my suspicion. Grace was playing the police. What happened after I'd seen Elise that night—how she'd ended up hanging from a noose in her basement, with Grace chained up in the adjoining room—was beyond me. I didn't think I'd ever find out.

I thought about Grace. How she'd been so quiet in middle school. Always doing whatever we said. Never questioning. Never complaining.

How many times had I gone to Walmart and grabbed a pack of Juicy Fruit gum at Courtney's register? Had Grace been watching me each time?

In middle school, we'd thought Grace was the weakest. The easiest to manipulate. And all that time, we were wrong. If we'd been stranded on an island with her, Grace would have picked us off one by one. She would have been the last one standing.

I read the note one last time—*I guess we know the answer now, don't we?*—and then I dropped the note in the toilet and flushed it.

I thought about this again as I walked down the hallway to my office. I'd been there for only a week. It didn't feel like my own yet. I kept thinking about my old patients, especially Chloe. I wondered what had become of her. If she'd managed to stop cutting. If she'd managed to deal with what was troubling her on her own.

At my desk, I pulled up the file of my new patient. Name: Peter Dunbar. Age: eight. The reason he'd been referred to me: physically and sexually abused by his father, who was currently awaiting trial. His mother was the one bringing Peter to the intake today. I would want to talk to her too. Make sure she saw her own therapist. If Peter had been abused, there was a good chance she had been abused as well.

I shut the file, sat back in my chair, and closed my eyes.

Some days I wonder why I do this work. Every day I meet children who are dealing with severe mental health problems. I talk them through their depression and anxiety. Try to help them see that life is worth living, that there is still good out there in the world, even if it's just a glimmer.

Elise called me weak, at least compared to her, and I guess that's true. The world is filled with weak and strong people. I may not be as strong as Elise was, or as strong as Grace is, but that's okay. I just want to be strong enough to help these kids, the ones caught in that undertow. It's my job to make sure they don't give up. I want to be there; I want to be strong enough to reach down and grab their hands. To let them know that they're not alone. That there is more to life than the pain they're feeling. That no matter how low they get, there is always something for them to look forward to. Something nobody else can take away.

Hope.

Elise had called thirteen times, all in the past ten minutes, and it was on her fourteenth try, as the garage door opened, that Grace finally answered.

"Hello, Elise."

A pause—Elise no doubt surprised she'd finally gotten an answer—and then her voice dropped to an angry growl.

"Where the fuck were you?"

"I was there."

Another pause.

"No, you weren't."

"I was. I was in the woods. Watching to see what you would do."

Elise issued a frustrated scream.

"Emily fucking Bennett figured it out. I wanted to shoot her in her fucking face so bad, but she confronted me at the hospital. There were cameras everywhere. Where the fuck were you?*"*

"I decided not to go through with our plan while I was tying that poor girl up to the tree. I remembered what it felt like when you and the others tied me up. How helpless I felt. How alone."

Grace paused a beat.

"Then again, maybe I'm not being totally honest. For a while now, I knew I wasn't going to go through with our plan. At least when it pertained to the girl. Seriously, Elise, why else would I demand we make her wear a blindfold if the plan was to kill her?"

Elise paused again. She had entered the house and was pacing the living room.

"What the fuck are you talking about? Where are *you?"*

"It doesn't matter where I am. I'm far away. We've had our fun, Elise, but it's time for things to come to an end."

"Fuck you. If it wasn't for me, you'd still be stuck in that shitty-ass town."

"Oh, you want me to say thank you, is that it? You want me to show my gratitude? Let me tell you a story, Elise. When I first came to Lanton, I was a shy, quiet girl who had just lost her father. All I wanted was to be accepted. To have friends. I never thought I'd be invited into the popular crowd. I should have known better—that somebody like me could never be cool—but I thought maybe you girls were different. That, despite you treating me so badly at first, maybe you were really kind. Maybe you liked me. Then you took me to the Farmhouse that night. You got me drunk and high, and you let those boys . . ."

Grace's already quiet voice ticked down a notch.

"Not one of you apologized to me afterward. Sometimes I wonder if that would have made a difference. If someone would have just taken me aside and said sorry. But nobody did. And I realized the only way to survive as a Harpy—to survive in the real world, in general—was to become worse than all of you. Oh, I still acted all quiet and shy, but it was an act. I wanted to see how far you would take things."

Another pause, and when Grace spoke next, there was a smile in her voice.

"Especially you, Elise. You were the nastiest of them all. Everybody thought Mackenzie was the one in charge—even her—but I knew what you were doing the entire time."

Elise had stopped pacing. She stood very still in the living room.

"Did you do something to Mackenzie?"

"What do you think?"

Silence.

Grace said, "She was also supposed to be out in the woods tonight, wasn't she? Only she would show up after we'd killed Emily and Courtney and Courtney's daughter. She would sneak up with a knife while you distracted me and cut my throat. That was your plan, wasn't it?"

Elise's sudden inhalation was barely audible.

"That's right, Elise. I knew all about your plan. Every single thing you and Mackenzie have chatted about from the beginning. I especially thought it was cute how you tried to warn Mackenzie that Emily and Courtney were planning to confront her. Such a thoughtful friend you are."

"No . . ."

"Yes. Come on, Elise. Did you really think Mackenzie gave a shit about you anymore? You may have been smarter than her, but she was always more popular, and part of you always looked up to her. I knew emailing you pretending to be her was a risk, but you swallowed it whole."

"How . . . No, there's no way—"

"You were suspicious at first, what with Mackenzie just contacting you out of the blue after all these years. But I knew enough about the two of you that I answered all your questions perfectly, didn't I? Made you think the person you'd been messaging all this time was really your old friend, when in reality Mackenzie probably hadn't thought of you in over a decade. In many ways, Elise, it was rather pathetic of you. Over a year of your life, just chatting away secretly on that app, believing this ridiculous idea that Mackenzie could never get away long enough to meet up for lunch. Not even a simple phone call. You'd ask, I'd shoot it down, and you'd go on your way, believing everything I told you because you wanted to believe, didn't you?"

"Is she alive?"

"Again, what do you think? Mackenzie was the main reason I decided to start this so long ago. My main targets were always you and Mackenzie. The other girls, well, they were just collateral damage. I was curious to see how far you would take things, and you managed to take them pretty far, didn't you? I still love how you jumped at the idea of driving up to Dixon Township to try to convince me to help you. Of course, I didn't buy into the

plan right away. I needed some convincing. And you did your damnedest to convince me. And then you were so happy with yourself when you told your old best friend just what a great job you did. Like you wanted a fucking pat on the head."

Elise was silent.

"If you must know, the past several months I've been making visits down to Bryn Mawr. I knew the time would come when I'd need to make my move. And that time was last night, when you and Emily and Courtney went up and had your run-in with my mother."

Grace waited a beat, but still Elise was silent.

"Anyway, I went down to Bryn Mawr and followed Mackenzie when she left the house—she left almost every night to hook up with some guy—and I managed to get into the SUV. When she saw me, she screamed. I don't know if she screamed because she recognized me or because I was holding a gun. Either way, she did what I told her to do. I'd expected more of a fight, but I guess all her toughness—even back in middle school—was just for show. When the police find her, it'll look like she overdosed on uppers and booze. They'll also find the same encrypted messaging app you've been using all this time on her phone. It's doubtful they'll be able to access it, and even if they did, the messages would be gone, but it'll still be a connection between the two of you. Such a shame, really. I'm sure her family and all the men she was fucking will miss her. Before she died, though, I told her the same thing I'm going to tell you."

More silence.

"People treat you differently when they think you're weak. When they think you don't understand—when they think you're too stupid to get what's going on—they show you who they truly are."

Still Elise said nothing.

"You see it now, don't you?"

Elise whispered, "Impossible."

"You wanted to play games. Dropping your little clues. I told you it was reckless. Especially the text message to Destiny's wife. Turns out Emily

and Courtney were smarter than you thought. They found out I was dead way too fast, and so you decided to rush things. Honestly, Elise, the only time you're the smartest person in the room is when I'm not in the room with you."

Elise started pacing again, moving from the living room to the dining room to the kitchen and then back.

"What the fuck are you talking *about?"*

"Do you seriously think I tried to kill myself back in middle school? I only did that to try to fuck you girls over. And it did, didn't it?"

Elise spoke between clenched teeth.

"Where are you?"

"You're never going to see me again, Elise. Especially not once they lock you away in prison."

Elise went still and silent.

"Come on, Elise. I've been compiling evidence from the start. After I eliminated you and Mackenzie, my plan was to disappear. And make it known that you were the one behind all the deaths."

Elise made no reply.

"The police should be at your place any minute now. I called and left them an anonymous tip. Told them where to find the evidence."

Elise's voice dropped to barely a whisper.

"You're lying."

"They're going to find what I put down in the basement. It's damning. They'll probably sentence you to life in prison."

All at once, Elise was in motion. Scrambling through the house toward the door in the kitchen. Flinging it open and flicking the light switch. She cursed when she realized the bulb had blown, but that didn't slow her; she tore down the steps anyway, using the screen of her phone as a flashlight.

She figured she'd be able to find whatever Grace had hidden. That she could dispose of it before the police arrived.

Her mind must have been so focused that by the time she realized Grace had stepped up behind her and slipped the noose around her neck, it was already too late.

After it was done—after Elise had stopped struggling and her body hung suspended, slowly drifting in a circle—Grace used the wooden chair to step up and retighten the light bulb.

She took a moment to watch Elise's dead body sway, and as she did, she worked out the math in her head—the distance the chair would have been kicked over once Elise had stepped off it—placed the chair in the appropriate spot, and headed up the stairs to the kitchen, taking Elise's phone with her.

She went through the call log and deleted all the calls Elise had made to her. They'd show up on Elise's statement, and there was a good chance the police would subpoena them, but that was okay. All they would find was the number for a disposable phone. A cheap plastic thing that Grace slipped into a paper bag and took out to the garage, where Elise kept her tools. Grace took down the hammer and used it on the paper bag, smashing the phone into tiny pieces, and then she replaced the hammer on the wall and left through the back door and carefully crossed to the end of the lawn and slipped out between the trees.

It was trash night—an added bonus—and she deposited her gloves and the paper bag in a trash can across the street. Tomorrow morning the garage truck would rumble through the neighborhood, and any evidence of the phone would be taken away.

She figured she wouldn't be found for at least two days. By then the trash would be long gone, making it impossible for the police to try to sort the neighbors' garbage, even if they decided to take things that far.

Grace had always known she wouldn't be able to disappear. Especially not after this morning, after Emily had seen her outside Courtney's apartment (another one of Elise's stupid ideas, just like making her drive all the way down to Ocean City so she could make her brief appearance at the boardwalk, though Grace had liked the idea of messing with Emily's head).

And there was always the chance that the medical examiner up in Dixon Township would confess. Then the world—well, okay, the state—would be looking for Grace Farmer.

The only way to end this was to dip back into a familiar well. She would become a victim.

For the past two weeks, Grace had been beating herself. On her stomach, her back, her chest, her legs. All the places that Elise would never see.

Earlier that night—after the four of them had left the clearing—Grace had slipped out of the woods to retrieve the torches and rope and duct tape and blindfold. On the drive back to Lanton, she'd stopped off at different locations to dispose of them, as well as some of the items she'd had at Elise's. Her few clothes, her pillow and blanket, her soaps and deodorant.

She'd kept some of her clothes. She'd already put them in a trash bag in the basement.

When she returned to the house, she opened the kitchen drawer, took out the yellow legal pad, and left it on the counter for whoever eventually got worried enough by Elise's absence to stop by the house.

Once a Harpy, always a Harpy, *the note read. Grace had been practicing Elise's handwriting. She had it down pretty good, but still it had taken four tries before she was happy, and that was what she left on the counter. The others she'd ripped up and flushed down the toilet.*

Before she headed back down the basement stairs, she stopped by the bathroom just off the hallway. She stripped out of her clothes and turned on the light—making sure to use the back of her finger to flick on the switch; she'd been very conscious of her fingerprints the last two weeks—and stared at herself in the mirror.

She'd worn the same bra and panties for three days straight. They still didn't look as dirty as she would have liked. That would be okay—her time down in the basement should do the trick. She figured someone would contact Elise's parents. They'd probably be the ones to enter the house. (They most likely had a spare key, given to them by Elise for emergencies, but Grace had unlocked both the front and back doors just in case.) By then Elise would start to smell, and the smell would lead them down to the basement, where they'd find their daughter—and Grace.

In the basement, she stood on the cold cement floor and waited for her eyes to adjust to the darkness. She barely thought about Elise, hanging from the noose a couple of feet away.

When she was ready, she made her way to the door in the corner. There was already a pair of handcuffs inside, as well as a strip of duct tape—from the same roll they'd used to cover Terri's mouth earlier in the day.

Grace stuffed her clothes in the trash bag, tied it shut, and tossed it to the other side of the laundry room. She placed the duct tape over her mouth, pressed down to make sure it was tight, lowered herself onto the floor, and raised her arms, managing to secure both wrists with the handcuffs. She'd needed to use the bathroom for several hours, and now, sitting alone in the cramped, dark space, she relieved herself. The warm urine soaked her panties and ran down her leg to pool on the floor.

She thought about what Elise had liked to say, how it was all about a narrative. Telling a good story, making the judge and jury understand the starting point.

Grace knew all about that. She'd played the victim before. She knew what would be expected of her moving forward. How she'd make sure to never look anybody in the eye. To flinch when somebody closed a door or got too close.

All she needed to do was wait. A day or two or three. Maybe four days. Maybe a week. She could go that long. The more time passed, the more convincing her state of mind would be. The dirtier her body would get. The more compassion the first responders would show her.

So it didn't make any sense when she heard the doorbell. It had only been what, five or ten minutes?

Something was wrong. This wasn't part of the plan.

Whoever it was, they didn't leave. Grace could hear the front door opening, and then a voice calling out.

"Elise?"

A long bit of silence.

"Hello?"

Emily Bennett. What the hell was she doing here?

Grace heard Emily walking around upstairs. She heard the basement door open, and the buzz of the light bulb as it flickered to life. Emily descended the stairs, slowly at first, and then quicker when she saw Elise's body. She started speaking, her voice low and indistinct, and Grace realized she had called 911.

Soon the police would be here. They would find Elise. And they would search the house. Which meant Grace might as well get the show on the road.

With the duct tape over her mouth, she screamed as loud as she could. Obviously, she didn't make much noise, but that was okay. It was enough for Emily to hear her.

Just as she'd done back in that clearing fourteen years ago, tied to the tree with all the initials carved into it, Grace screamed again. Then, she'd done it to wear out her voice, to show that she had truly been panicked and scared. It was all part of the show. Just as it was part of the show now.

As she heard Emily's footsteps approaching, Grace thought how appropriate it was that Emily Bennett would be the one to find her. Because every time Grace thought of Emily, she remembered her first day at Benjamin Franklin Middle School, and how Emily had approached her in the cafeteria, smiling, acting like she wanted to be her friend. How Emily had encouraged Grace to come sit with the popular girls, and how Grace had been reluctant at first, already thinking it was too good to be true, and then Emily had said the thing that would always stick with Grace, the thing that made her smile even now with the duct tape over her mouth.

Fourteen-year-old Emily Bennett, a girl who had never truly felt like she belonged, glancing briefly back at where her friends were sitting before leaning in with a grin to make her final pitch:

"What's the worst that could happen?"

ACKNOWLEDGMENTS

I wish to thank my agent, Tess Callero, and my editor, Alicia Clancy, as well as the entire team at Lake Union. John Cashman, Joseph D'Agnese, Christina Marra, and Adam Perry read various drafts of the novel, and their input was invaluable. Special thanks to Genevieve Gagne-Hawes and Abigail Barce, who opened my eyes to the bigger picture of the story and helped steer me in the right direction. Douglas Clegg and Matt Schwartz are always there to give me advice and support. And, finally, my wife, Holly, is my north star; without her, I'd be lost.

About the Author

Avery Bishop is the pseudonym for a *USA Today* bestselling author of more than a dozen novels.